Jennifer's Journey

Journey through Abuse

First in "The Journey" Series

Susan DeBeeson

PRESS

Authorship of poems

"Friend" Susan DeBeeson
"Alone" Susan DeBeeson
"Baby" (Michael 3 weeks old) Susan DeBeeson
"Take a Helping of All" by Claudia O. Herbinaux
"Sometimes" Yvonne McIsaac
"Rainstorm" Susan DeBeeson
"Angry" Yvonne McIsaac
"My Precious Child" Yvonne McIsaac
"Sometimes" ('The Rest of It') Yvonne McIsaac (edited)

Songs

"Search Me, O God" - Public Domain-James E. Orr, 1936.
"More Precious Than Silver" - Lynn DeShazo, Copyright © 1982 by Integrity's Hosanna! Music.

Cover photo: Max DeBeeson

www.xulonpress.com

Table of Contents

Acknowledgments

My daughters, Yvonne McIsaac and Rebekah Hiltz have been an ongoing encouragement, and have upheld me in prayer, as have my friends, including Marg Bos, Shirley Hamm, Pat Klassen and Dorothy Brotherton. Some have read Jennifer's Journey and given valuable suggestions. A police officer, who was greatly disturbed by abuse, shared his thoughts with me. His concerned attitude became my model for Brent Sullivan. My dear lifetime girlfriend, Esther Miller, proofread diligently, resulting in an excellent list of 'oops'. Thank-you so much, each one of you.

I particularly honor and thank my husband, Max. He has given unfaltering support through years of writing this book. Only at one point did he ask, "Have you considered writing a short story?" I said I didn't have one of those in me. (Who knows?) Later he took on the editing of the book. He was a sounding board, with wise suggestions and provoking questions. His admonition, "Oh, you can't cut *that* part!", was right, as we dealt with the obvious need to shorten. He was "on", every time! I give him my admiration and love.

Above all others, the Lord himself was the one who kept me at it, who gave me ability and desire. I had to tell this story, after decades of learning of human heartaches. God loves the weak – that is all of us before we come to know Him. But especially the abused and "powerless", who cannot help themselves. They will find, when they come, that God's power is sufficient, and His love beyond our words to describe.

Dedication
Claudia Havens Herbinaux
b. October 30, 1913 d. July 5, 2009

I especially acknowledge the strong influence of my mother, Claudia Olivia (Havens) Herbinaux, and dedicate this book to her, and to each of the "Jennifers" in our lives. Mother read to me, wrote poetry, took me on nature walks for the joy of it, and prayed for me. And, in adulthood, we fought. Though her life had been tough, and some of Jennifer's experiences were also Mother's, she finally found peace in giving over those experiences to the Lord in complete trust. Most of her life, she had carried undealt-with baggage, which caused her great difficulty in relationships. Thankfully, in the last several years she let go of unhealthy methods of protecting herself, and experienced the happiness of feeling loved. Thank-you, dear Mother. Enjoy the Lord's ultimate peace!

Prologue

Jenny entered her hotel room and flipped on the light. The clock read 10:30. Later than she had planned. She shouldn't have talked so long with Tyler, but he had been a gentleman. Now she needed a good sleep. A TV blared in a room down the hall. *Wouldn't you know. Sounds like it's in here, full volume. Must be the guy down the hall who gets 'high' on something. If I get in bed and read, I'll get sleepy, or it might get quiet.*

The room was overheated tonight. It was freeze or fry. After she put on a short, thin nightgown, she threw back the covers on the bed. A knock came at the door. Strange. She went over and opened the door a little, holding it secure with her foot.

"Hello?" she asked. Pushing hard, someone forced the door. Her heart pounded as Lennard's face... *Impossible. Lennard? He abandoned me – took off.* "Hello..." she repeated weakly. Fury in his eyes, he pushed into the room and locked the door. He had been angry with her – hit her. But she'd never seen this depth of hatred, hatred that was controlling him. The slap jerked her head sideways, but she took it, standing. He strode to the window, looked down at the cement four stories below, and turned. Jaw muscles tight, fists clenched, he moved back toward her menacingly. His detached stare terrified her most.

He hit her hard in the jaw. Stunned, she fell against the wall, her head swimming. As she struggled for balance, she wondered, *How much can I take? It will be the worst ever... I have no escape... I'll be beaten... to death.*

She was fixed on his eyes, like a deer, helpless in car headlights. She couldn't take her eyes off of his – dead staring eyes – detached from reality.

He is crazy... I am going to die... Michael, my son, what will...

* * *

Jennifer's Journey... what brought this book into being? The haunting question, "Who will tell Jane Doe's story?" The phone jangled. A woman identified herself as a board member of a women's shelter program in Seattle's downtown.

"We need to get a true story written for a newspaper article, and you were recommended. A woman, I'll call her Jane Doe for now, has come through our shelter program. She is willing to tell her story. I hope you will consider doing a feature article for the Seattle Times. It would be a great help in launching a fund-raising campaign, and even more important, in educating the public about the abuse of women."

I contemplated the difficulties. I wondered about the woman... is she willing, or resistant, to opening up? I had listened to other women tell their stories. Their images rose up before me – eyes full of pain, beauty shrouded in fear. I saw the scars on their skin, and the evidence of poorly-mended bones. I remembered their emotional losses most of all. Some women threw up walls – walls against everyone. Some avoided all emotional connection, since any person might become invasive. Even a person who would be truly helpful was shut out. A woman isolated herself from manipulative relationships, and even normal sensitivity was frozen. For others, the sense of personal boundaries was destroyed. Wide open, they shared everything. Then regret set in, and they shut down.

The caller asked me a second time. Would I write for the newspaper? In a flash, I said yes! Allowing my heart to lead me, the decision was made. I took down Jane Doe's phone number. Little did I know that a feature article would become a book.

I rang Jane Doe. Answering in a soft voice, she said, "I'm so sorry. The timing is, well... I'm going on a trip. I'll return on the twentieth and would be glad to meet you and talk then." We left it that she would call me when she came back.

Time passed. Too much time. Then I got a call from the woman who had asked for the article. "I have very bad news. It's about Jane Doe, the woman who was ready to talk…" She paused.

Sensing her difficulty, I said, "Yes, I remember," and waited for her to go on.

"She was murdered last night. The police are searching for her estranged boyfriend as the main suspect. There was a peace bond on him, but…"

My heart sank, my stomach went sick. The woman continued, saying there was evidence of contact. A note pad by the phone indicated that she communicated more than once with the boyfriend. He had arranged a meeting. He apparently extracted her whereabouts from her – in spite of the fact that a safe, secret place to live had been arranged. Now she was dead. My mind filled with confusing thoughts; she was dead, and all because of a little phone chatting and misplaced trust. How could her life be over? Anguish for this woman and all her lost potential came over me. My heart went out to the staff and volunteers working at the shelter who had known her. They cared about Jane Doe and had hoped she would have a healthy future, a safe future. Now they were mourning.

I realized I was still holding the phone when the woman spoke, thanking me for my willingness. When I asked if I might tell this story, she said no. The police work might be hindered. We would have to wait for another woman's story. She told me she would phone if anything developed. What follows is Jennifer's own story, and that of all the lives she touched. It developed into Jennifer's journey.
Signed,
A women's shelter volunteer

PART ONE
CITY LIFE – COUNTRY LIFE

Late April – Early May

CHAPTER ONE

Seattle, Washington

Jennifer Brown hurried out the restaurant door and down the street just as the Seattle Metro bus pulled into traffic. *There goes my six-ten bus home,* she thought. She slowed to a walk, feeling drained. Waitressing for tired shift workers and hungry shoppers took a lot out of a woman. Today the Deli Diner had been a madhouse. Friday, of course. Morning customers had crammed the counter seats and tables, in a hurry to eat *now* and get on with their business or pleasure. The late afternoon crowd were hungrier and even more demanding. Everyone had run out of steam, just like she had. Though it wasn't even May, the first of the tourists had arrived in Seattle. They were in a hurry to get out to their 'toys' and go cavorting in the "great Pacific Northwest".

Jenny suddenly felt bad. *An attitude, that's what I have. It isn't the customer's fault I'm stuck in an exhausting job, day in, day out.* She thought of Michael, her ten year-old son. *We like to have fun, too; just like the customers. While I stand here, waiting for the bus, I can turn the page and leave work behind. Anyway, the people who come in the restaurant simply want an inexpensive, home-cooked meal or a sandwich. I am the means of them getting that pleasure. I like that feeling.* Some customers were pleasant regulars. Through Jennifer's mind went images of people she had waited on that day – a dear elderly man who gave a generous tip for coffee, a working grandma who had struggled with chemo, but was in remission. Many had even become friends of sorts. She looked forward to these regulars. Chatting with them made her happy; she cheered up the lonely ones. Then there was the impossible-to-please type. She had started the day with a grump, immersed in his newspaper. On his empty breakfast plate lay a sucked-on cigar stub. She scooped it into the garbage on her cart. He came alive like a mad gorilla. 'What are you doing? You idiot!' She stood there, anger rising up in her, and yet feeling like a child.

A child... *hurry up, bus.* Always in the back of her mind was her son. Today she had left the apartment at eight a.m. as Michael left for school. Now the daylight was fading. Hopefully he was safe at home for the last two and a half hours. A split shift was bad news. Today she had worked the breakfast rush, then been off duty. When she came back it never let up through lunch, coffee time, and early dinners. She heaved a sigh. It was over.

Jennifer shivered. A cold wind was blowing off the waters of Puget Sound. There was no shelter at this bus stop. Her muscles ached. A strong urge to stretch her whole body, even in public, came over her. Self-conscious, she settled for scrunching up her shoulders and arching her back. She didn't want to draw attention. She rubbed her neck, then ran her fingers through her straight auburn hair. Red highlights shot through as the sun's last shaft of light beamed under a cloud.

I'm glad I washed it this morning. Ah, a hot shower would feel good right now, like a massage all down my back. Yes, home! Home and Michael. Too bad that step-dad Lennard had abdicated any significant role in the boy's life.

Jen's mind went to the outdoor fun she and Michael enjoyed. He loved the beach. Golden Gardens was their favorite. Even in cold weather they took every chance to walk there, beach-combing, watching the seagulls hassle for food. On hot days they braved the cold salt water for a refreshing swim.

The bus came. She hurried up the steps, dropped in her change, and looked around for a seat. One was empty near the front, beside a woman. When she settled into it, her feet almost said "Thank you" out loud. It felt so good to sit down. The older woman next to her turned and smiled. Though Jenny didn't have the energy for small talk, she gave her a nod. The smile, wreathed in white hair, was friendly. A truly warm kind of smile that came from inside. It lit up the woman's clear blue eyes. Jen hated her changeable blue-green eyes.

"Tired after a hard day at work?" the woman asked.

Jenny nodded emphatically with a little "Um-hmm."

"I work at the hospital laundry. It's a steamy job. Still, I'm glad to have the weather get warmer. This spring has been so cold."

Jenny couldn't help responding to the woman's lilting Scandinavian accent, the drawn-out emphasis on first syllables. *Her voice is pleasant,* Jen thought. *More important, she's pleasant; normal. I can risk a little talk.* "I work at the Deli Diner. It's a restaurant that has meals and take-out sandwiches. I waitress."

"Oh, hard on the feet! Bet you are glad to sit down!" Her eyes twinkled. "I have a little energy left. Today I had a short shift. I live closer in to downtown. Just going out to my daughter's now."

Jen nodded. She liked the woman's open manner. Straightforward people were okay. Just not pushy ones. She ran from that kind.

"I *am* tired," Jen said. "Mostly I'll be glad to get home to my boy. I'm overdue. The next-door neighbor is handy for an emergency, but it's lonely for him."

"That's difficult." A look of concern came over her softly wrinkled face. "You must be glad he is in school most of the day. Oh, my name is Cora."

"I'm Jenny. Yes, I am glad Michael's fine for now." She said it slowly. "While school is in session." Almost to herself she added, "He is ten, and very responsible." *What will I do when school ends in a few weeks? He can't be alone all day in summer.* That thought had troubled her for weeks. Lennard troubled her, too, but he had been gone so much in recent months…he seemed to keep himself busy. Her mind again wandered to summer and all the things she would like to do with Michael. She'd buy a pass to Woodland Park Zoo; surprise him. At the beach they'd walk and breathe in the invigorating smell of wet seaweed. Michael would catch sight of little children building sand castles and moats. He would crouch among them, helping them dig and pat. He might try to distract a cranky toddler who was swinging a stick at the other kids' castles. He'd get the little one settled down, and show him how to build his own castle, gently taking his hand and patting here and there. Jen pictured Michael, stripping down to his swim trunks and running into the icy-cold water. In minutes he'd run out again, grab a towel and rub himself to get warm. Their favorite together activity was walking. Michael would pick up shells and tell her their names. He would say that they were common, or rare.

"You know, Yenny, I have been sitting here tinking..." The lady broke into Jenny's thoughts, but then her voice trailed off.

Jenny suppressed a smile at how Cora turned the J into a Y.

"You say that your son is ten?"

"Yes."

"I have a daughter, Mary, who has had to leave her job because she can't stand on her feet for hours. She has begun taking care of two children, nine years old and six. When school is out she will watch the children all day, Monday through Friday. She is well paid for these two, as the parents have very good jobs. She would like one more child for them to play with. She lives farther along this bus route and I'm going to her place now. Do you want me to ask her if she would take care of your boy? Of course you would want to meet her. You don't even know me – but it just seems more than a coincidence that we met. You can talk to her yourself about the cost, but money isn't a concern. It's a compatible child she is hoping to find."

"Oh," Jenny let out a little gasp. *Strangers? She had never even laid eyes on the daughter. Michael would be with the woman all day long, come summer. Still, she should meet her. Check it out. But then, how would she get out of the entanglement if she didn't want it?*

"I don't know, ah... " Jenny paused, glancing into the lady's eyes. "I don't know her..." She felt so dumb. The lady had just said that.

"It is good that you are concerned. I would be. I just thought it might be a temporary answer, at least." She paused, then said, "Well, maybe we will meet on the bus again." A gentle smile warmed her face. "If you want, I can give you my name and phone number, and my daughter's, too, in case you decide you want to get in touch."

Jenny nodded. "Yes, that's good. Then I would have the information… " *I sound so obvious. So basic. So stupid.*

"My daughter's name is Mary." She started writing on a slip of paper.

The woman seemed so straightforward, so genuine…still… Jenny said, "I have to get off soon." *If I used want ads for childcare I wouldn't know the people either. Michael and I can meet the daughter. He is old enough to say if he gets good vibes from someone. I can't afford the cost of regular childcare. It would certainly help to have some consideration on the price… Michael is no trouble.* She watched the lady writing. She looked at the soft, plain face – this woman was just herself – no airs, no deceit, or so it seemed. She took the paper with the phone numbers. "I would like to meet your daughter," Jenny said, and startled herself with her decisive tone. "I have to be on the job again at eight in the morning. Michael and I can ride the bus out to her house… but when would be a good time?"

"Mary will be driving me to work tomorrow morning and doing some shopping. She could come into the restaurant during your coffee break or lunch hour so that you can meet, at least."

"That would work," Jenny said. "My break is at ten, and Michael will be there. He reads in the lunchroom at the Diner until time to go to the museum program for children. I would like him to meet, ah… Mary, did you say?" Jenny glanced out the window. Her stop was next, and she pulled the bell cord. "My phone number is 783-0687." Cora jotted it down, and nodded when asked if she knew the Diner's location. Jenny continued, "Tomorrow at the Deli Diner is good for me, but if your daughter needs to make a change of plans, maybe she could phone me this evening. My name is Jenny. I guess I said that." She stood. "Thanks; I'm glad we talked." *I think I feel good about this. I shouldn't doubt my own judgment, I guess. My sanity is not that far in question.*

"I'm glad, too!" Cora's warm smile gave some assurance to Jen.

"Maybe this will work out for you and Michael. Goodbye now. Nice to meet you."

"Bye," she responded, surprised that the lady had remembered Michael's name. She swung down the steps, turned, and waved.

Jenny made her way down the street, completely occupied with a jumble of questions, and picturing Michael, patiently waiting for her to walk through the door. At least he was old enough at ten to deal with the practical – get into the fridge and cupboard and tide himself over with a snack. But the loneliness was a more important issue.

She pulled open the outer door of the apartment building, and ran right into someone – a fellow resident. Unfortunately he was the "too-friendly man". She muttered an apology, then hurried on. It was better not to start a conversation with him. She went to the stairs, not the elevator. The elevator stunk. Climbing the stairs, tired as she was, gave her the unwinding that she needed. No pressure, just climb the stairs and gather her thoughts. Entering the hall that smelled of old carpet, she knocked twice on her own door with a special rat-a-tat-tat signal and called Michael's name. A lock clicked, the door opened, and he was giving her a big bear hug.

"Good to see you, Mom. I love you." He hugged her again. His brown eyes shone warmly.

"So, I bet you have been wondering when your 'wayward mom' would come home!"

"No. I wasn't. It's Friday. I know it's busy. I watched, and saw you coming from the window. How was work?"

"Busy!" She laughed. "I had to run to fill coffees, take orders, deliver food...*but* that nice Mr. Swanson gave me a five dollar tip on his ten dollar meal!"

"Wow! Is that the old man I met? The one you say is like a father?"

Jen laughed. "It is, but don't call him old. He might be sixty or sixty-five. And, yes, he seems to feel fatherly toward us. He said to tell my boy hello, so, 'hello!'"

"I'm glad he was nice to you. And anyway, I don't mind the time, 'cause in the morning we'll have 'Our Time'!" Michael was smiling happily at her, brown eyes glowing. They were kind eyes –

a window into his nature. Yet, even though he was tender-hearted, he seemed able to cope with the circumstances of life – able beyond his years.

"School was ordinary..." he said, off-handedly. "Except for..." his voice became excited. "Wait till you see!" He dug in his backpack, then held out a paper.

"Wow! A one-hundred on your spelling! That is great!"

"Yeah!" he said, looking pleased. "I'm glad we studied the list a jillion times last night. Thanks." Jenny walked over to the fridge door and put up the paper with a magnet.

"All I have for homework is to correct some math problems for Monday – and I did that – and read a chapter in my socials book. That's it! Do you think we could go to a park on Sunday? You're off work! Please? Huh?" Michael put his hands together in supplication, and raised his dark eyebrows.

Jenny tousled his dark brown hair and hugged him again. "Sure, we'll go somewhere on Sunday. I have some news; good news for the summer, I hope. I met a woman on the bus whose daughter cares for two children. We can meet the daughter; see what she is like. Maybe it will be a place you could stay this summer when I'm at work. She will come to the restaurant in the morning."

"Oh. I hope she's nice. How old are the other kids?"

"Six and nine."

"Are they boys? Is there a place to play?"

"I don't know that. I don't know much. A boy and a girl, I think. We didn't have long to talk on the bus. I wonder, too, but for now we can only wait and see. Anyway, let's eat that leftover chicken from last night."

"Yeah, that was good!" Michael was a big fan of her cooking. When she had time to do it, that is. While the chicken warmed, she had the cast iron frying pan heating with olive oil and margarine. She cut cold boiled potatoes onto a plate, ready to slide into the pan to brown. Michael jabbered on about the two new kids he would meet as he tore up Romaine lettuce for the salad. Together they added a few colorful slices of veggies to finish it. The cost of produce was coming down. That would help her stretch the grocery money.

Money, she thought. Len had said that groceries were for her to figure out. He wasn't around half the time. Even if he were, she didn't expect him to buy any. She used a pancake turner to scrape up a couple of pieces of potato and peek under them. Ah, they were a nice golden brown. She wondered what this Mary thought was a good diet. She wondered what *Mary* was like. Was there a place to play? Wouldn't that be wonderful. But too much to ask, probably. It was worry enough, just to think of what the household was like. Was there a man in the picture? What was he like? She opened the whole-grain bread and put some on the table, thinking how she had splurged to get it.

"Michael, is everything on the table we will need?"

"Yeah, it's set." His words sounded dreamy. Sitting on the floor, he was totally engrossed in his old pocket video game.

"Time to eat." She set the food on. No response. "Time to eat." Still no response. She shook him by the shoulder.

"*Time* to *EAT*". She sounded firmer than she meant to – angry. "Come on," she added a little softer.

"Oh", he moaned, as he slowly got up. "I had over 7,000 points!"

"Well, I am sure you will live to ride again."

"Oh, Mom, not ride! I was shooting aliens! The cowboys are in my book." He hung his arms over his chair and pretended that he could do a headstand on the seat. "Mom, what did you say the kids' names were?"

"I don't know. The grandmother – the woman I met – was Cora. Her daughter was Mary. I don't know about the kids. I didn't write that down. I only have the ladies' names and phone numbers. We'll find out soon enough. Hurry up and sit down at the table while the food's hot."

"Mommm!" he pleadingly dragged out the word, lingering behind his chair. "Can you look in your purse and check for the kids' names?"

"NO." She yanked on his arm to lower him. "Now sit DOWN and EAT." Michael looked hurt and surprised. *Kids!* she thought. *You never know how to deal with them. I wish I had more patience. They don't listen, then they get their feelings hurt.* She hated sounding mean, being mean. She sighed. "I'm sorry. I'm tired. Try to think about dinner for now."

Jen's mind mulled over the conversation on the bus with Cora. *Names in my purse – I don't know much more myself than a couple of names and phone numbers on a piece of scratch paper. I was dumb not to ask more questions. Where does the daughter live – in a crack-house in a drug infested neighborhood? Well, I can extract us from the connection, I guess – I hope. I've let my imagination go. Gotten a picture of a house with a nice yard, everything ideal. What will this daughter be like? What stupid mess have I gotten myself into? Or gotten both of us into, and that's worse.*

Jennifer picked up the ringing phone. Len's harsh voice said, "Do you have dinner ready?"

"Ahh, yes."

"Wha'dya mean, ahhh? Do ya or don'tcha?"

"I do. We are just sitting down, but there is plenty for you. Were you coming home?"

"Well, I had *planned* on it. I *do live* there. Ya know, I doubt it's worth the gas. Or the trouble. I'll grab something here. That useless car is still running terrible. And I have this Buick to finish and get sold. I don't know when I'll be home. Just make sure there is some good food in the fridge." Click.

She hung up the phone and wondered what that was all about. Len normally didn't call to tell her he'd be home. She looked at the chicken and decided to take a small piece so there would be left-overs for him. Michael had grabbed a book. He was reading and eating with automatic movements, engrossed in his story. She pondered the call for a few minutes as she ate. Then Michael shoved aside the book, ready to talk. They finished eating dinner, each sharing thoughts about the day's events.

The evening passed. They watched a favorite TV program and a documentary video from the library on northern mammals. Michael looked over the new spelling list, saying the words and spelling them aloud to get them imprinted correctly in his mind. Then they settled on the couch and took turns reading aloud from "Treasure Island". Michael stopped reading in mid-sentence.

"I want a parrot," he said longingly.

Jenny laughed. "Do you know how much bird poop piles up in a cage? Especially from a bird that big! Somebody has to clean it.

Better to leave the wild creatures outside where they love to be!" He sank back and opened the book again, thumbing through to find the next picture.

Jenny was thankful for Michael's love of reading, and wasn't sure if it held first place, or was second to his love of being outdoors. He didn't waste time whining about what to do. Life was an adventure, even in his imagination. Last summer he actually had been able to run through the pastures and woods of a real farm. He had gone with a friend to visit the granddad's farm for three days. He still talked about it at Christmas.

Michael was reading Treasure Island out loud again. She brought her mind around to the story as Michael finished the chapter. He stretched his slim body. *He's so thin. Wonder when he will put on some weight.* He was studying the picture that began the next chapter. A desperate little group huddled together. Doctor Livesey's face held a kindly expression. One arm wrapped protectively, in a fatherly way, around Jim Hawkins, who pressed against him. He held a single-shot blunderbuss in the other. The frightened group waited, wondering when Long John Silver and his pirates would attack. It would be in their most vulnerable moment. Would any of them come out alive?

Michael had been caught up in their dilemma, but he also had become immersed in the whole tropical island experience. His imagination had moved to a larger scene than he had never before considered. "I wish I could have been there," Michael said. "Just think, jungle to explore, all the parrots you could ever want, flying free – a whole island. There'd be trees to climb and freshwater streams for floating my own handmade boats, watching them go down, down to the sea. Think of it, Mom! You can swim in warm ocean water that has big waves! You could make a raft!" He put the book into the simple unpainted bookcase and hurried off to get ready for bed, calling back, "I'm in an exciting part of my cowboy book! I bet I can stay awake for an hour!"

"You'd better not!" Jenny shot back. "The idea is not to make a marathon of it."

He was allowed to read on his own until he was sleepy.

"There's no school tomorrow, Mom!"

"Oh. True. We should get going early, though, if we want some time at the park before I'm due at work."

"Yeah," he said through toothpaste foam. He bounced back into the room. "It's just that I could finish it tonight." He hugged her.

"I'm being maneuvered with hugs! I'll take that kind of bribe." She gave him a resounding kiss, a real smack on the cheek, and a squeeze. "Goodnight Michael." He quickly kissed his mother.

"Goodnight, Mom." Without giving her a moment to say more, he flew to his room, eager to gallop across the prairie with the other cowboys.

"Good dreams," she said, more to herself and the empty room. She wandered into her bedroom. The wedding picture on the dresser caught her eye. Memories. It had been taken in the park, four years ago, on a lovely early summer day. Len looked so attractive. She remembered feeling protected with a strong man standing beside her. In the background she saw the table where they signed the certificate. When she signed she had seen that his legal name was Lennard, and asked why it was spelled that way instead of Leonard. Mistake. Angrily, he had said because his mother was stupid and didn't know the right way.

Jenny looked again at the picture of the 'wedding couple' – she looked so happy. She contemplated that point in time when she "took the plunge" with Len. She had decided to "do it right". Michael would have a dad, or at least someone to care for him like a dad. That was four years ago. *Well, only in your dreams. So much for life being like a fairy tale – "And they lived happily ever after."*

* * *

In a south Seattle garage Len turned the key and started the 1952 Buick. He nodded his head and grinned. "Hank, listen to that engine purr!" Suddenly jumping out, he grabbed the skinny man, twisting the front of his shirt into a wad in his fist. "You better get that pretty upholstery work finished NOW."

Stiffening, Hank nodded, the shirt collar tightening about his throat. "Yes, Boss," he squeaked.

"I want it DONE. You hear?"

The skinny man again nodded his head vigorously, his eyes wide open. There was the sound of ripping cloth as Len twisted harder. He shoved and let go of Hank, who stumbled into a work bench.

"Yea," Len smiled, "I'll turn a fast buck on this wreck. I've made it sound like new!"

The skinny man nodded and, with a hesitant smile, said, "That sure looks nice, that red velvet and black leather, don't it?"

"Yea, yea, it's okay. But if I hadn't made it run, your pretty work would be going to the scrap yard. You can be glad you took up with me. Let's have another drink. Celebrate – celebrate you getting done tomorrow. TOMORROW – HEAR ME?"

Len came home that night in a bad mood. She heard the outer door open just as she was drifting off to sleep. *So... she thought. He's here... I can imagine just why he is bothering to come home... 'Come home' seems like an ironic description. Home could mean anything – it can mean such pleasant things to some people.* Len didn't talk with her when he came into the room. He landed on the bed beside her and grasped her shoulder, announcing, "I'm here to take advantage of my husband status." She cringed inside. Their relationship had become routine – no, it hadn't *become*; it had always been mechanical. Len not only demanded what he wanted for himself, but more recently he humiliated and hurt her.

She said, "I didn't think you were coming home."

"Yea, well, big surprise. I live here, too – remember?" She thought, *I tried at first to make things homey, so he would want to be at home. There's that word again. I remember asking him if the house felt 'homey'. He laughed. "Homey?" he said. His lips curled in a sneer. "You want to make things homey, huh? That's a joke. You never had a home – how would you know? You had a brothel! What your mother had was a house of ill repute. Some home!" It was only partly true,* she thought. *Only toward the end.* Len got perverse pleasure from flinging that in her face.

CHAPTER TWO

A small acreage near Granite Falls, WA.

On that Friday afternoon, an hour northeast of Seattle, Sylvia Ford trotted down the steps of her sort-of remodeled country home, a two-story farm house. She glanced with satisfaction at the tub of periwinkle-blue pansies, and then hopped into their nine-year old car. Smiling at how Larry kept it running (it was as reliable as their newer lease car), she backed down the long driveway. Stopping at the mailbox that was surrounded by her roadside garden, she jumped out and grabbed the mail. She stooped to notice tiny sweet alyssum seedlings sprouting out of the dirt. They were volunteers from the abundance of seed dropped by last summer's flowers. The green leaves of the daffodils and narcissus waved in the breeze, though their blossoms were withered. *Ah,* she thought, *how I love their fresh fragrance and the way they brighten the pensive blue grape hyacinths around them.* It was a wonder to watch every season change slowly into the one following. After winter, she was impatient for spring with its sense of awakening and new life. She thought how she and Larry had fled the city fifteen years ago. With their young children they began life on their small non-working farm. The two older ones were in elementary school and Nadine was eager to start kindergarten. Now they were in the 'empty-nest' category. In recent years Sylvia enjoyed work in a hardware and variety store in the small town of Granite Falls, nearby. Larry's work required traveling anyhow, so living "in the sticks" was not a handicap. They had, through much hard work, developed the property into a home and grounds that they could be proud of. The rural setting, far removed from the urban hustle, was compatible with their goals. A realtor recently told them their place had more than tripled in value, but they were not lured into selling.

Sylvia fanned through the pieces of mail. None from Issa, or, more properly, Isabel, her world-traveling daughter. *Oh, well,* she thought, *accept it. We'll hear from her when she is ready to write.* Now it was onward to shop for the groceries for tonight's stir-fry: chicken breasts she would slice up, adding water chestnuts, purple onions, bok choi, celery, and bright orange, yellow and green bell peppers. She could picture a nice platter filled with these colors tumbled together. Larry would scoop it over heaped-up rice, and enjoy.

Sylvie, as her friends called her, relished a day off work at Granite Falls Hardware – more accurately a general store. As she drove, she thought how today the garden had gotten a spring-cleaning; she had gathered the dead vegetation for the compost heap. She could mark that off the "to do" list. She slowed the car for a sharp curve, then saw two local kids on horses. They moved over into single file. Safely around them, she picked up speed. She would never trade where they lived for city life, even though they definitely lived "in the country", and it took more time to get to shopping. Larry and she had never farmed their ten acres, but their children's development and happiness had been their goal. Larry was a good father. Sylvia thought back on preschool years with Mark when Larry had been too firm, but he had relaxed and come to enjoy his own boy rather than being distant as at first. They'd seen three beautiful 'crops' come to harvest on this little farm. Well, two of their three children were leading normal, fulfilling lives. Surely Issa would "find herself"; then she might become more settled. Sylvia could picture them involved in their childhood activities. She saw the kids playing on the swing that hung from the biggest fir tree in the front yard. Or they secreted themselves under a sheet laid over an old card table that hid behind a screen of shrubs. It was especially the hideaway of Issa and Nadine and their dollies. A tree-house was attempted.

Soon Mark had his head under the hood of a car with Larry, learning everything he could about 'fixin'. Issa left her dolls for a horse that received constant grooming, until he gleamed a beautiful red-brown in the sunlight. Nadine showed early that her special interest was books. Every day she would 'curl up with Mom' to read, or read by herself. Being the last one meant Sylvie had held onto the special times, treasuring countless walks through the pasture and the woods. She thought, *Now, thankfully, the walks are continuing, even into the present. Hopefully she will make it to Granite Falls to spend a day between the end of university and starting a summer job.* Sylvia realized that during her musings she had arrived at the grocery store.

Walking along the produce display, Sylvia stopped and picked up a large, plump red pepper. Looking at the cost per pound, she put it back and picked up a small one. She sensed that someone was standing, waiting, beside her. "Good afternoon, Neighbor! A long time since I've seen you."

"Why, Bertha! I haven't seen you for two months!"

"Ya, I have been away visiting my older sister." Sylvia enjoyed her Swedish accent. "She vas in the hospital and doing awful poorly. Finally she got out, but needed someone at home with her. So I yust extended my visit."

"Oh, I hope she is much better now."

"Fortunately, ya, she is a little better. I have come back to change things around here at home. She vill be coming to stay vith me for a couple months."

"Oh." Sylvia didn't know what to say. This was *that* sister.

"Ya, I know vhat you are thinking. She is the negative, cranky person in the family. But vhen they need you, they need you!"

"Well, I hope it works out," Sylvia said hesitantly. She had met this sister.

"Say, did you know that the Miller place vas having some work done on it? I hear that the new Mystery Landlord from the city is planning to rent it out. I didn't think that it could be made livable. The last time I vas in it, the floorboards were rotting through, not yust on the front porch, but also by the back kitchen door. I guess anything can be fixed vith enough effort. That is so near to you, are you seeing the activity?"

29

"Well, yes, I did hear noise, and wonder what was up. When I drive by, I can only catch a glimpse from the road with all the brush grown up. I can't see from our yard through the trees. Like you said, I thought it might be demolition."

"I vonder who vill live there…?"

"Yes," Sylvia nodded. "New neighbors… Interesting." *My new neighbors.*

Home again and the groceries put away, Sylvia sliced the chicken and stirred together her own marinade – a combination of low-salt soy sauce, Italian dressing, lemon juice, cayenne pepper and generous spoonfuls of black bean sauce. As she worked she glanced over at the calendar and thought how Mother's Day was two weeks away. Her three children with their busy lives came to mind one by one. She guessed that none of them would be there to celebrate with her. Nadine would have job interviews Saturday and Monday, and that would shorten her weekend. Of course Isabel, or rather Issa as she insisted on being called, was in Britain, or by now, somewhere in Europe. Her most recent home had been Edinburgh in late winter. She had written saying that she was enjoying a job in live theater, working mostly behind the scenes. But time had passed since they heard that, and she could be anywhere. Mark and his wife Marie would come if they could, but it was unlikely. Mark had worked most weekends this spring, but he hoped to change that soon. Nice to be responsible, following his dad's example, but constant work seemed a little too responsible. He really didn't want long hours, since it cut short his time with Marie and their darling Emalie, seventeen months old. *What a sweetheart she is,* Sylvia thought. *Always smiling, always ready to give a hug – this grandmother thing is the reward for parenting! Time together will happen as they are able,* she told herself.

Sylvia looked up, and saw the cross-stitched motto by the calendar. It declared "Friends are Friends Forever". Last Mother's Day Lisa, her dear friend, had made it, and surprised her with a visit from Seattle. She came to cheer up Sylvia after Issa had left in a snit over an offense, and taken off for Europe. Sylvia thought on that time. *It's hard to have your child try her wings and leave home, even though it needs to happen – I accept that. But to have Issa leave the way she did, throwing up this heartbreaking wall of indifference, even coldness, between us…* Lisa, bless her, had filled the silence Issa left behind. Surely the rift would heal. At least Issa was writing occasionally.

Though Lisa and Pete had moved from the area a couple years before, the friendship was strong. At first, both of them had come out for a visit, but they were busy. Lisa continued to be in touch. Her ability to comfort a year ago had stemmed from having been through a painful experience with her own daughter, Lorene. The age-factor with Lorene made it frightening, since she was a young teen. But fear became deeper when a long period passed and they heard nothing. Suddenly Lorene phoned. It was wonderful to know she was alive, but it had put a heavier burden on her parents. She yelled at them, reiterating all their failures, heaping guilt. After recovering from the shock, and thinking it through, Lisa realized more had happened to Lorene in the past than they knew.

Sylvia looked at the old letter from Issa on the bulletin board and hoped she would continue to keep in touch. At least she was older and more capable. Sylvia couldn't imagine Lisa's nightmare of having a young daughter estranged. But Lisa had never made a comparison – nothing smacking of "my owie is bigger than your owie". She truly had cared about Sylvia's pain over Issa's departure. She phoned. She came out and they went to Everett together. Lisa filled the day with the lively bustle of the mall, walking about, looking over "the goods". Then they would sit and talk in a charming coffee shop. Sylvia had many memories, not only of the support in that difficulty, but of the good times over the years. Lisa was a treasure.

Just then Sylvia saw the car out the kitchen window as Larry drove up and parked. She gave the dish of chicken slices a stir and set it in the fridge.

Larry was already coming in the door. "Hello! How is my glad-it's-Friday wife?" He enfolded her in his arms.

"I'm glad it's Friday!" she laughed. They hugged and kissed as Sylvia marveled over being more in love with her husband as the years passed.

"I want to go out and cut the lawn while it's dry. It has really taken off growing with the last rain. Do I have time?"

"Sure. Wasn't it beautiful today? I sure enjoyed being outside. There is time for mowing if you're only doing the yard around the house. You'll be good and hungry. We're having stir-fried chicken over rice."

He 'mm-ed', and said, "Yup, the quickie job." He headed to the bedroom. He came back out wearing his good pants, but buttoning an old shirt, and talking to himself. "I guess I left my grassy lawn-mowing pants in the shed." Going out of the porch, he let the screen door slam shut. He had just re-hung it, after taking down the winter storm door.

The mower revved up. Sylvia peeked out the kitchen window to see Larry and thought of the pleasant time they would have later, in front of the fireplace. She went into the living room with newspaper, wadded it up, and placed it in the grate. Then she went out on the porch to a large wood box, and got an arm-full of firewood, and a hand-full of kindling. In the living room she dropped the wood in the brass holder, and arranged thin cedar kindling sticks on the paper so the air would pass through. Hearing the background noise of the lawnmower, she thought of the evening. *Larry will appreciate relaxing and cuddling in front of the fire after dinner. We'll have a chance to talk about the week. I'll brew some decaf or make herb tea. We can just sit and do nothing together.*

Back in the kitchen, the last of the sunlight gave a glow to the room. She glanced up at a framed cross-stitch of flowers and words, hung by the back door. It was also from Lisa and said "Whatever things are true, noble, just, pure, lovely, whatever things are of good report...think on these things. Phil. 4:8". It was in the same color scheme as the wall, where she had papered the top half. Though her garden flowers were only beginning to bloom, the flowers on the wallpaper were always there to cheer her. "Brush-strokes" of yellow, apricot, and peach suggested petals done in watercolors. They were mingled with a few leaves on a muted white background. The lower half of the wall was very subtle sponge painting. Now *that* had been serendipity! It not only covered a white 'problem wall' that was always smudged, but it was pretty! *She* had done it! Not careless 'splat-splat' sponge painting, either. She'd had to redo the first part.

It took a while to get the hang of the new technique. After putting a lot of effort into it, she finished with pleasing results. The colors she had chosen, laying samples on the wallpaper, softly mirrored the wallpaper colors, so that its pattern remained the focal point.

After the paint and paper were done, she and Larry discussed finishing ideas. They settled on a grooved horizontal board in a narrow width, halfway up the wall, called a chair rail. Larry put it in. It had added that final touch to finish off the room. Old-fashioned, it went with the old house.

Well, it was time to quit daydreaming. The rice was started. She picked up the newspaper Larry had brought, and a paper on the counter underneath it fluttered to the floor. It was notes she had taken down when attending three weeks of messages at a nearby church. Lisa had encouraged her to attend. A new pastor had recently come, and after seeing the invitation in the newspaper, she decided to go. She had enjoyed the series of studies being offered in the book of John, concerning events around the first Easter. She hadn't felt as ill at ease as she expected. Church was a foreign venue. She'd had no church to call her own as an adult. She'd gone with Lisa, but her church was too far away. Larry and she had gone in Seattle, when the kids were little.

As she set the table, she recalled how clear these messages at Easter were. Thought-provoking, too. The new pastor was sincere. He spoke as a person who was confident of the Bible himself.

The sound of the lawnmower stopped, and the peaceful quiet of the country returned. She took out a heavy pan and put it on to preheat. Lifting the bowl of marinating chicken out of the fridge, she set it on the counter, returning for the bowl of cut-up veggies. *Better go check with Larry to see when he'll come in.* She headed out the door, grabbing her jacket off a hook on the porch.

The sunset light was fading. She called out, "Hey there, hard-workin' man!" Larry was standing by the shed with a satisfied, "mission accomplished" expression on his face. "Time to come in and let me baby you!" She looked around the yard as she came, and exclaimed, "What a neat job!" He flipped out the shed light and turned to her for a hug. She cuddled against him. "Say, you're cold!" She felt his ears.

"As soon as that sun drops, it cools off fast. Not summer yet."

"I have a surprise for you!"

"I bet you made a fire!"

"Oh, you!" She gave him a bold kiss. "Not *really* true though," she teased, "it's not lit yet! You are too good a guesser." She made a pretend pouting face, rolling her eyes, and then said, "Let's go eat then, so we can sit by the fire."

CHAPTER THREE

Seattle

In the middle of the night Jen woke up and couldn't get back to sleep. Lying in bed, she replayed the conversation on the bus. What had she done? If this woman, Cora, and her daughter weren't the nice people she hoped, or that they seemed to be, then she was in trouble. They had her phone number and might keep calling and being overly friendly, even after she said no. Len would be furious when his peace of mind was disturbed. She could picture anger twisting his face.

Funny. She didn't know why the thought of *"peace"* of mind came to her. Len, for sure, didn't have any peace of mind. No peace at all. She wondered, *What is it, inside him, that's coming out when he gets so angry? That booklet Maggie gave me tells about that kind of thing – all the stuff a person has buried inside from the past, affecting them now. He can't take being irritated by other people interfering, for sure.* Her thoughts returned to Cora and her daughter, Mary. *Well, what can I do now? I will just have to meet the woman in the morning and see what she's like – and hope I can trust myself to know.*

Then there was the money. The mother said it would be reasonable. What did that mean? Her wages, even with extra hours, barely covered the rent, food, and part of the bills. Those bills had to be paid. Len was able to casually put them off forever. She had to do it. She hated getting threatening phone calls – threats from businesses, threats from banks, threats from collection agencies. Len didn't keep her up to date. She didn't know when these bills were overdue, especially the ones for car parts or the high-quality upholstery material for car interiors. Len also had to pay wages for the upholsterer and the man who did body work. Some of the cars were classics. He wanted to try antiques. When done right – and Len *was* a good mechanic – they sold for a fat price.

Where did that money go? It didn't seem to do much good. Just disappeared – either went into buying another 'discovery', or who knew? She saw little of it. She lay there, watching the clock. Finally she drifted off to sleep. She dreamed she was holding a thick note pad. A long line of strangers approached her, making application to do childcare. One by one she interviewed them, and scribbled her assessments.

Jen woke up and saw the clock. Three-thirty. She lay there for a while, wide awake. Then she slipped quietly out of bed and went into the living room. Several small photo albums were where she'd put them on the bookcase. Settling herself in her favorite worn blue velveteen chair, she stacked them in her lap, picked up the first album, and just held it.

Ten years ago, standing before a rack in a drug store, the baby blue mini-album had caught her eye. She had picked it out for her own baby. She had just developed her first roll of film of newborn Michael.

Jen tucked deeper into the chair, opened the album and looked at the first picture; he was a few hours old. This little bit of humanity – so helpless... *so alone. He was without a dad and I was all alone.* She remembered how she had held him to her for the first time, kissed and nuzzled his soft cheek, stared at the tiny hands and face. Then it happened. She had heard about this mother thing that 'hit' you. Heard about it before Michael was born, and had laughed. Maybe it didn't happen for everybody, but when she held this baby, her own baby, a deep love filled her being. She knew this little bundle was a miracle, and she was filled with wonder. Wonder, and the deepest love she had ever known. As a seven-year old big sister, she had tried her best to care for her little brother and sister. She had felt a bond to them, and she cared. They were 'hers'... but... But this was different. She didn't know quite how.

Jen turned the pages and knew by heart each comment written on the back. Picture by picture she had captured subtle or sometimes obvious facts and changes – *"See how his forearm isn't any longer than my index finger"! "See how his forearm has grown in one week!" "A silly gas-grin." "A one-sided smile – he seems to be sharing a pleasant dream he is having." "A sweet, peaceful smile at four weeks."* What a surprise her feelings had been. Thankfully, she had bought film and set aside money for developing it. She hadn't expected a newborn baby to be so interesting, so entertaining, even. Looking back, she remembered... *My days were enriched, my mood was lifted by his presence in the apartment. No! – by his presence in my life. I don't know where I would be now without him.* Ten years ago she was pregnant and utterly alone. Ten years ago she had failed. Nineteen years old and suddenly no future. And the worst part, no one cared. Filled with doubt, wondering, 'What do I do now? How will I make a living and raise a child, too?' But I remember thinking, *'If life is so dark now, it cannot get worse. There has to be something brighter, something better, waiting ahead for me.* She made up her mind to "hang in" for the duration. When she felt the baby kicking, she knew it was the right decision. She got through the pregnancy by herself, and through the humiliation at the doctor's office and labor classes – no husband appearing, not even his name to put on the office form for emergency contact – certainly not *that* name, 'the father who wanted out'.

After Michael was born a complete turnaround came. The thrill of motherhood was partly responsible. Even in times of weariness, she knew her outlook had been changed. But, after a very dark period, another reason to have hope arrived. Aunt Sally came back into her life. *What a wonderful woman!*

Before Aunt Sally, the fresh joy of a newborn had worn off. The darling gas grins were no longer precious. He had colic. She was exhausted by the constant, demanding cry of this tiny creature piercing her ears night after night. Standing by his little bed, exhausted, she couldn't believe how frustrated she felt – frustrated enough to want to shake him. Jennifer's energy was totally depleted.

Even the days were confusing. She read the baby book. She hoped he'd outgrow this 'colic'. She held and comforted him, telling herself it must be gas pains. Finally, the doctor had an answer. Take him off the cow's milk supplement she used in addition to nursing. He was allergic to it. It worked.

Throughout the bad days, Jennifer had wondered at herself – how she could be angry at this tiny mite. But she was. Turning it over in her mind, she decided she was angry at herself for her awful feelings, fearing she might do something terrible. She also feared depression, knowing a first-time mother could get overwhelmed to the point of despair. She didn't dare "do depression", though people surely didn't intentionally go there. During school days, she had watched teenage girls flaunting pregnancy like a new hairstyle. She walked proudly, hand in hand with an acne-faced boyfriend, and declared "I'm going to be a mother!" Jennifer had already taken over full care of her sister and brother, and thought, *"You are oblivious to what lies ahead. What a shock for you to find that your baby is not a teddy bear, to cuddle and play with. You hadn't bargained for an interruption to your plans, your life. You should have thought this through.* She had watched as the newness wore off. Nobody was around to admire the real-life dolly. The girl had no support, emotionally or otherwise. She had felt sorry for the baby. Funny though, she had to admit, one girl had been a good mother. She got very serious about it. Jen's own introduction to childcare had come much earlier – at age seven. Though it was wrong, and she would never do it to a girl of seven going on eight, she knew she'd gotten a real education caring for her preschool brother and sister. It was discouraging. Her mother worked. How badly Jen had missed her dad. As that time came vividly to mind, she again felt the bewildering emotions, the awful loneliness, being left to 'mother' her siblings. Looking back, she knew that *she* needed the care of a mother. *Why, Mom, did you leave me alone? It's not fair that you expected me to do your job. I was worried. And I never did it good enough – always, always when you came home, there was something not good enough.*

Later her mother brought boyfriends home with her. At first they would just come for a few hours. Then one would stay there all the time. She couldn't talk to her mother. *My own mother, but I couldn't talk to her. I guess she was caught up in her own troubles, finding work, short of money.* At night the drinking and the yelling got bad. Jen would be laying awake in the back room, sharing a bed with her brother and sister. If the yelling got too loud she would pull the blankets over their heads so they wouldn't wake up and cry. One boyfriend was nice. He put food in the fridge. He was kind, and he even talked to her and her brother and sister like he cared. She like the apples and oranges he brought, and there was even meat. She especially liked the milk. Jen shook her head. *Mother...she wasn't happy even then. Well,* she thought, *I got through it all. A tough part of life. It passed, thank God – though I doubt there is one.*

The little albums on Jenny's lap started to slide, pulling her back from her childhood memories. She looked down at a baby picture of Michael. With him, she succeeded. Though she was exhausted, she had met his needs, determined that she wouldn't be defeated – for his sake.

Aunt Sally came. What a change she brought! Jen got some rest. She began to see the world through Michael's baby eyes. Everything was new to him. She found delight in giving him stimulating surroundings. She got women's magazines from the library discards, cut out bright-colored ads, and hung them at his eye-level. She had read that color was important to development. She played music on the radio. She and Aunt Sally sang to him. His smiles and his wiggles of pleasure thrilled her. He responded! She had to go back to work, but she worked nights. Then she could be with him in the daytime as much as possible.

Aunt Sally, Sarah Carlson really, was still working out. Even so, she cared enough to help Jen and baby Michael. Her children were grown. She came some distance and slept there every night to be with Michael. When Jen came home at dawn she crawled in bed, exhausted, and got a couple hours sleep. Then the cheerful voice of Aunt Sally would filter through her dreams, saying "Fresh coffee for Jenny!" The warm memory returned like a video. *Aunt Sally set down the pretty china cup and saucer she gave me as a new mother gift. The aroma of the coffee was delightful, or was it the fragrance of love? It gave me a reason to extract myself from under the covers. I was, I* am, *tremendously thankful for this good woman.*

I also remember trying not to show how tired I was, trying to give the impression I was fully "on hand" for my baby so Aunt Sally could go to work.

Jen began looking through the next few pictures, and smiled at each one. Michael was cuddled in Aunt Sally's arms, or he was sitting, propped up in a high chair with Aunt Sally's hand steadying him, or dozing off on a blanket. What a help that marvelous woman had been. How she missed having her near now. Sally had moved to live near her grandchildren. Too bad that Aunt Sally and she weren't keeping in touch much now. Jen got cards and notes a few times a year. She guessed she badly dropped the ball. It was her fault. She was so slow to answer a letter, or sometimes never did.

Jenny turned the page and saw a picture of Michael and herself, taken 'face on', and she had circles under her eyes. *Sleep,* she thought. *That is what I need right now!* She got up and laid the albums on the bookcase for another time. Len would be sound asleep. She could slip into bed without bothering him. She wondered if he would explain what his plans for the next few days were. He had mentioned a trip with a car he had for sale, but when or where – who knew.

CHAPTER FOUR

Granite Falls, Washington

The early light of Saturday dawned. The house was quiet. Sylvia entered the living room and went to the large front window and the pastoral scene she loved. Looking out on the expanse of nature, contemplating its bigness, its beauty, was the best way to start a day. She gazed across the yard, the road, and then the pasture and woods to the west. Three stately fir trees towered over the front lawn, freshly cut by Larry last night. He had stopped at the tall grass strip near the road. The uncut "rough" was boggy and wet during spring rains, even though there was a ditch along the county road. Scattered across the mowed lawn were rhododendron bushes, sheltered under the trees. Some were large and compact, and others were pruned for an open, Oriental look. All were covered with swelling buds. Near the house a large, rectangular flower bed held pink and purple tulips bobbing in the breeze. A small dogwood tree with the promise of soft pink blossoms stood before the house, ready for viewing by admirers.

Sylvia looked at the clock. She had to go to work at nine. The sun would be up soon, and the day ready to start. *But I will take a walk! Just a quick one, a treat, before I get to the 'practical'.* Larry was tired and would sleep until the alarm. He didn't plan to eat at home. He was meeting a man for morning coffee and some breakfast. Grabbing a windbreaker from a hook as she went through the closed-in back porch, she opened the outside door and stopped.

It was cold. She stepped back in, hung up the light jacket and got on a heavy, woolen one. As she stepped out onto the deck she looked up. There were very few clouds – would be nice most of the day.

She stopped and breathed in the smell of the fresh-cut grass. Turning to the right, she went down the steps, veered across the driveway and took the path on the far side of the garage. The first shafts of sunlight came through trees and lit the pasture. She closed the wooden gate, thinking of winter. She had gotten up in the dark, longing for daylight, going to the kitchen's south-facing window to peek, when she was straightening the house before work. Now the hours of daylight were increasing rapidly.

She walked out into the pasture and just stood there a moment. The April sun came spilling onto her face. The dew-laden grass suddenly shimmered with light. She soaked in the sun, and, though its rays were not yet warm, there was a promise. Two months till the longest day. But her goal wasn't to sunbathe; she started for the creek on the old cow-path. The lovely sound of water rushing over rocks came to her. Spring rains had filled the stream – an ever changing, life-giving force. Jogging closer, she was surprised at the noise coming up out of the canyon. She was eager to see how much water there was, overflowing the usual channel. Quickly she worked her way down the steep creek bank, through wet ferns, catching glimpses of the creek.

Sylvia jumped and slid over a moss-covered rock, then straightened up. There it was. She couldn't see much to the left, upstream. She drank in the sight in front of her as the stream raced away in the direction of the river it would join. On the near bank the water had flooded up over the grass. It bulged over boulders that were normally dry. The old cedar log, her summertime seat, was now submerged, water rippling noisily around the upstream end of it. At the water's edge to the right, a recently fallen tree was laying, a pointer indicating how the creek should flow around the bend and out of sight. Sylvia looked across the swollen waters to the higher bank, sloping sharply off a large hill. Normally that bank was undercut, hanging out over the water. Now the high water covered it, and grass was drawn along in the rushing stream. Above the water, the cloven prints of deer were left in the damp earth where they had walked along the stream. She could picture the deer standing quietly, and she stood as quiet as they, capturing the whole creek canyon scene for her mind's-eye to replay later.

Looking at her watch she realized, *Now I must go back. It would be lovely to stay longer. I'll return and cross on the log bridge. I love that walk up the mountainside to the artesian spring. But for now I'll be content. It won't be long till there's time.* Higher up the mountain was a meadow that was her favorite retreat. Peacefulness held sway. The quiet pool held the freshest water, swelling out of the mountain from a hidden artesian well. Leaves reflected in the surface and around the pool were undisturbed woodlands. Humans didn't come and bring their loud noise. She could collect her thoughts there. For now, though, she could only promise she'd return next week. Western Washington weather was often rainy or gray, so she hoped there'd be sunshine when she did. Turning toward home, she worked her way up the slope from the creek, pulling on strong clumps of grass and brush.

Sylvia jogged energetically along the pasture path to get warm. She pictured being out in the flower beds. The winter trash needed to be cleaned away. Only some of the flower beds were prepared. It was time to sow the rest of the seeds. Then she would have to wait to put the heat-loving annuals into the soil when it warmed. After today, Granite Falls Hardware would only need her part time. She was eager to have the free hours. She could go into Everett, and even meet Nadine instead of waiting for her to get time on a weekend to come out. And Marie, her daughter-in-law in Seattle, was glad to have her come to visit with her and precious Emalie anytime. She'd go more often – even braving the traffic. She could baby sit and give Marie a daytime break. She didn't want to stay after that, and disturb the little time Mark and Marie had together, especially since he was putting in long hours. Besides the traffic was awful once rush hour began.

Sylvie entered the yard and looked over at the untended north side yard where it ran out of sight, bordering a neglected pasture. That strip had never received much attention. It was rough and would need lots of work. She thought, *the big picture is that I'll have free time! Time, just to call my own. Well, I have made the most of this morning's sunshine. What a good start on the day!*

Hanging her jacket on the hook and coming in the kitchen door she heard the digital alarm. Ugly sound. It went silent. Good. Larry had turned it off. He was up. He would meet a fellow from Surrey, British Columbia, at The Coffee Corner. Sylvia's own family had come from British Columbia, the most western Canadian province, almost forty years ago. She started the coffee maker that she had set up for a short pot for her alone, put down the toaster, and walked into the living room.

Inhaling the pleasant, lingering smell of wood smoke took her back to last night. Larry and she had sat in front of the glowing fire and simply enjoyed each other's closeness. They cuddled on the couch, well aware that, after Monday, they would be apart for several days. He was leaving on business. They had talked quietly, the warm glow of the fire filling the room. Looking into the flames had a dreamy effect on them both. Looking for pictures and figures in the flames, they shared with each other what they were seeing. Larry liked to point out pockets of unusual color, like green, which appeared briefly. *Ah, I smell the coffee!* Sylvia thought as it interrupted her reverie. Just as she came into the kitchen, Larry entered from the hall.

"I'm off. See you...whenever. I won't make it back before you go to work." He gave her a quick squeeze and a kiss. "Think I'll go help Mr. Sigurdsen this afternoon. His limp is getting worse. That hip will need attention. He won't say he's hurting, or he needs help, though. Anyway, I won't be home till dinnertime."

"Sure. See you then." She touched his cheek fondly. "I love you."

"Love you, too."

Sylvia enjoyed the drive to Granite Falls, with the lushness of springtime greens along the country road and birdsong in the air. After she started with the dusting at the store, waiting for customers, she realized something was missing. *There isn't the sense of attachment here any more,* she thought. *Oh, well. Why would there be? I'll not be having a part in making this place run smoothly any more. Won't be long now.*

She stepped outside. The town was as charming as ever. Begun in the 1800's as a gold-mining base and a logging community, it had experienced a slump, before revitalization began. Just then, Bertha came along and brought Sylvie to the present.

"I guess you need a customer, right?"

"I do. Want to be one?"

"Ya," she replied in her heavy Swedish accent. She was a favorite with Sylvie. "You have everything here. I vill browse first." They entered the cool store.

"I think I'll turn the heat up a little more. It's not going to get hot outside today."

"No, not today," Bertha said. She was busy checking her list.

"Need any help?"

"No," she absentmindedly answered, in the midst of comparisons.

Few others came in during the day, and it dragged on. Sylvia finished up and locked the door, wishing there had been more customers.

At home Sylvia thought, *I want to call Lisa! It's overdue.* She picked up the phone and punched in Lisa's number.

"Lisa! Just had to hear your voice! It's Sylvie. I have to start dinner, but I wanted to connect! I haven't heard from you! It's been too long."

"Hey, it's good to hear from you! I am sorry I haven't kept in touch lately. I'm sure you've wondered if I dropped off the edge of the earth with no answer to the messages you left."

"I did. Has there been anything wrong? I wondered when I always got the answer machine."

"Nothing wrong with me, but I've had a sick neighbor who needed rides to the doctor and to get groceries; then my mother was down bad with the flu. So I stayed with her a lot of the time. Pete came out there to eat. She's better now. Actually, there has been more going on, but I want to wait on that. How have you and the family been?"

"Oh, okay. Nadine is working hard in school. We got an air letter in late February from Issa and things are about the same. I appreciate all your encouragement, telling me that she's a survivor." *At least*

I hope she is, Sylvia thought. "Mark, Marie and Emalie are fine. They'll be out for Mother's Day, and Nadine is coming, too. Emalie is growing and starting to talk. I'm enjoying this grandma-time more than ever. Easier than parenting. I remember being stressed, worrying about the kids. I enjoy when Marie has an appointment, that I can help by watching Emalie. It's especially nice when I can be with Marie and her together. Larry's fine. Comes and goes. More work travel now."

"Sounds like all is well on the home front."

"I have some good news for me! I'll soon be finished working at the hardware store. I'll taper down from full time. They've hired a new girl. I'll only do a shift when they need someone to fill in. Otherwise I'll be my own boss! How about that?"

"Hey! Sounds good to me! I miss the visits we had. I enjoy our times together so much."

"Me, too. It was so easy when you lived out here. Even though we were both busy, it seems we managed somehow to take a walk, go to town together, or just have a coffee."

"So you're officially retiring, are you?"

"Well, I guess I am. I could go back to the medical office, you know!" Lisa responded with a laugh, knowing very well that Sylvie had tired of phones ringing off the hook years ago. "The hardware store has been pleasant, keeping in touch with people in the community, meeting new arrivals – until now, that is. I was running out of energy. Larry and I have been talking about this for a while – that I'd cut my hours down to zero by summer. I'm really glad I'll be staying home. I found it hard to cope between his schedule and mine. Now when he comes off a road trip I'll be able to spoil him, cook his favorite food, and be free to go places with him. He is getting into all the springtime yard upkeep, now. He hasn't tired of the outdoor work yet, and probably never will."

"I guess that's good, though. What else is happening for you? Did you try that church you mentioned?"

"I did. I attended three weeks in a row during Easter time. It's that one on the road to Snohomish. They got a new pastor. I haven't been back, though. I guess I hadn't told you that I also attended their weekday women's group a few times when I had the right day off.

It was relaxed. I enjoyed that. But, like I told you when we went to yours, I enjoyed going to church as a child with the neighbor, but it's hard to start back when you're older and everyone is unfamiliar."

"Yes, I realize it is. I'm glad you enjoyed it when you went."

"How about Pete, his health? You were thinking he hadn't really let go of the pain over Lorene and that he might be getting an ulcer."

"The doctor checked him. Life is funny. Here I'm in lay-counseling and the doctor said Pete needs a counselor; said that he could be headed for an ulcer. Pete explained how Lorene wants, repeatedly, to tell us what dreadful parents we were, now that she is back communicating with us, that is. Even though we've apologized, and know there were quite a few things we messed up on when she was younger, she wouldn't let it go. There were things we did right, too."

"Oh, for sure. I remember when she was quite little. She gave a very clear impression that she was a happy child. When puberty hit – earlier than usual – it seemed like there was a total change."

"There was. During last winter we went a little deeper with her into that time period. There is still stuff coming out, but I'll tell you more when we get together. Anyway, Pete gave the doctor some of the 'gory details' of how Lorene talks to us. When the doctor heard the whole story he had Pete go talk to a professional counselor. He's finished now. It really helped."

"I'm so glad. He didn't seem his usual good-natured self."

"Ha, I'll tell him you said that!"

"Don't you dare! Most of the time he is good-natured. I'm sure it was hard for you to see him feeling down."

"Yes. And one good thing about the counseling was that it fit right in with the Marriage Encounter principles Pete already knew. Instead of burying it, now he talks to me when he gets to thinking about Lorene and what she's been through, and what she's said to us. Talking helps settles down the 'committee in his head'."

"So things are pretty good now?"

"No. The last episode Lorene put us through was especially bad since it hit Yolanda so hard."

"I didn't know Yolanda was drawn into it."

"Yes, she was, unfortunately. But I had better save that long story for when I see you face to face."

"Oh, okay. I can't imagine how difficult that would be. Well, yes, a little, I can. If Issa had kept on reading the riot act to us and had made Nadine's life miserable, I don't know what I'd do. I can imagine that there'd be lots of lost sleep. But you are doing so well with Yolanda! That must help a little to encourage you."

"Yes, it really does. It helps a lot. And as far as the problems go with Lorene, now that I've had time to think, I know I have to 'let go and let God'. Pete and I take turns reminding each other of that, and it helps us keep on top of our feelings. We remember we can't "fix" Lorene. And we can't set a time. Yolanda is coming along in her emotional growth. Ah, there is so much I wish I'd known to guide Lorene, to watch over her. We thought, when we yielded to her pressure to have more freedom, that she was safe. But she wasn't. I have to let go of that now, however. I know she has had counseling and all the help we could give. I have to accept the fact that this is now. God is there to help Lorene deal with her anger when she lets Him. And only then. We'll just leave it there. I have good things to share with you about Yolanda. But you need to get to dinner prep and we need to talk face to face! I'm glad to find out you'll have more time to do something you like! Let's not wait till you're off work, though. I have a four-day work week now, but the day off is not fixed. How soon do you want to get together?"

"As soon as possible – in the next couple weeks if we can get the same day off. They're usually accommodating at the Hardware. I can't get Tuesday; it's the day I work for sure. I'll change to suit yours. So you still don't mind driving out here?"

"You know me. I love coming out there. And you'd rather not drive as far in as our place. What day is the ladies' Bible study? I wish I could come then, and meet some of the women."

"It has been on Tuesday, the one day I have to be at work. Too bad. I liked them. Another thing I liked was the handout. At the end of the two pages there were questions designed to provoke thought later, at home. We didn't discuss them in class – just for mulling over."

"Sounds good. Wish I still lived there. We could talk about it, and talk, and talk! And I'd better quit! Let you get cookin'." She laughed. "I'm happy you'll be starting a new life soon! I'll give you a call when I know my day off and maybe make it work in the next couple weeks. We'll do it soon!"

"Sounds good."

"I'm sure glad for you – a new neighbor coming. And the new ladies' group – I knew you'd feel at home, find a place. God had a plan, just like He did for Ruth in the Bible!"

After they said goodbye, Sylvia thought of Ruth's story, and smiled to herself. She remembered Lisa alluding to the account of that young widow's life. When Sylvie asked what she meant, Lisa grabbed a copy of the old version of the Bible and read Ruth's words in the beautifully poetic style. "Entreat me not to leave thee…wither thou goest I will go, and wither thou lodgest I will lodge. Thy people shall be my people, and thy God, my God." Lisa had explained that Ruth was widowed at a young age, as was her mother-in-law. Ruth determined to go with lonely Naomi back to her own country. That was when she spoke those words. Afterward Sylvie had heard those words of commitment at two weddings. At one wedding they were read. At the second they were sung so touchingly that it brought tears to her eyes.

When did I begin to drift away from a personal time with God? When did I shove aside that desire inside me to grab the Bible and get alone with Him? – to hear from Him. It wasn't overnight. Just had too busy a life. Too many seemingly important things 'had' to be done. Always some item to tend to… one after another, after another. Things always come up. What is that quote…'the tyranny of the immediate'…does what? Shoves aside the truly important? Although little duty-lists are just a guide, I certainly let them rule. And let slip what I knew was best – my time with God. There's the heart of the problem – finding what is really important, and then sticking with it.

Sylvie made fresh coffee and wrapped her fingers around the mug that said, "World's Best Mother". It was a gift from Nadine a year ago, on Mother's Day. She remembered the long, thoughtful message on the card. There was a struggle in Nadine to cut free. She had been an easy child to raise – a 'secure youngest-born' in position, but in her quiet nature she was not that sure of herself. Nadine's quiet struggle as a teen to be her own person and find herself was not typical of the turbulent teens. It was inward, for the most part. Peer pressure in teen years was very difficult. She had moved away from home last summer to attend university, much more settled after a year of balancing a job and community college. She was conservative in nature and always had her nose in the books. Sylvie thought, *When she was a teen, the book reading looked a lot like an escape to me. But these days study is a 'have to'. She has definitely become more sociable.* Nadine lived in a rooming house with two friends. Once every couple months she made it out for chats with mom – chats and the 'care package' of food and goodies and drug store items that was always waiting for her. Nadine was at ease with her mother this last year. At the moment she hoped to hear about a full time summer job.

Sylvia was glad they were growing closer – slowly. Nadine had such a stable nature that Sylvia pictured the two of them being like two trees, standing side-by-side in the forest. Nadine was reaching maturity and seemed to have dealt with many of her insecurities. Issa was a different matter. The proverbial unhappy middle child, and being very extrovert in nature, she had expressed her thoughts freely. Daughter and mother had their fiery moments, mostly Issa's fire. It was an up and down relationship. Now Issa was gone from home and wouldn't be returning to live. Sylvia realized she would only come to visit, and then on her own terms. Though Sylvia had come to accept that, Mother's Day was coming, and her heart sank with a longing to see Issa. She squeezed her hands around the World's Best Mother mug and felt all of her doubts surface. She could have done so much better with Issa. *Why didn't I recognize what a different child she was?*

CHAPTER FIVE

Seattle - Saturday

The early morning light began to brighten the room. Jenny sat up, thinking. *It's a workday. Ah, it's also Saturday morning with Michael. Len is gone – I wonder if he left a note?* She jumped up and called, "Time to get up!" Michael was awake instantly, bounced out of bed, and started getting ready. They ate a quick bowl of cereal and caught the bus. Michael laughed as he pointed out a dog yanking at its leash "walking his owner". They got off and grabbed warm sausage rolls at a bakery and walked into a small park with a creek. Jenny didn't have to start work for an hour. It was "their time". Jenny was pleased as she watched Michael's delight, running down the path to see if the frog was in its usual place on a rock. She had shared the love of nature with him and it was his own thinking now. This morning he was full of enthusiasm, running over to the play equipment. She joined him on the swings they had a competition for who could go the highest. Then she pushed him high as she could, and left him to carry on. She went to the park bench to sit and watch, and simply look around at the trees leafing out.

After getting 'wound down' he came over to her. "How about a walk, Mom?"

"Great idea! Let's go around the park on the little paths and see if the policeman on horseback is here."

"Okaaaay!" Michael exclaimed. They didn't find the policeman, but they saw robins pulling up worms. "Mom," Michael said, "let's stand really, really still and keep an eye on where they go. If we watch where the nests are from last year maybe we'll see some of the birds moving back in!" Though it was too early see much nest-building activity, they talked of how the birds would be raising their families soon. On the bus back to the Deli Diner, Michael explained about his recent study of the food chain and pond life. He was eager to go learn more at the Saturday children's program in the museum. Today, he informed her, they would get to look through a real microscope. Jenny's mind was on the meeting with Cora's daughter.

At work Jen served the counter, worked the cash register, and kept one eye on the clock as it move toward 9:30, the appointed meeting time. Saturday customers were relaxed, but she was tense as she watched for a lady in a blue jacket who would come up to the till. Mary, Cora's daughter, didn't get that far. Their eyes met with instant recognition as she walked in, looking like her mother right down to the cheerful smile. The only difference was her hair, which was light brown rather than white.

They said, "I'm Mary", "I'm Jenny," at the same time.

"Let's go in the back", Jenny suggested as she grabbed two coffees, called out "I'm on break" and led the way to the lunchroom where Michael would be. On the way Jenny said, "Michael is taken with the chance to be part of this 'interviewing', so he's eager to ask you some questions. He has to go soon, so could he do that first?"

"That's fine," said Mary, with the same relaxed friendliness her mother had.

They walked into the lunchroom. Michael got up and came around the table as Jen introduced them. Mary enthusiastically said, "I am really happy to meet you, Michael!"

"Hello! It is nice to meet you!" He shook the hand she offered, and pulled out a chair for her. The look on his face then became serious and he promptly got down to business. "May I ask you some questions?"

"I'd be delighted to answer your questions." Jenny watched their eyes as they assessed each other. It was a kindly exchange.

"Do the two children who stay with you like to play outside? And do they like to read?"

Mary suppressed a smile at his eagerness. "Yes, they like to play outside, and also to read. They like to watch TV, but I am setting some limits on that. Your mother and I need to find out what the desires are in that matter."

Michael asked if there was a back yard to play in. He explained that he lived in an apartment, but that he didn't mind because he got to play in the whole park some days. Jenny was proud of his positive attitude. She doubted that he got it from her. Must be a throwback gene.

Michael asked questions about what books were at the house, how close a park was that had play equipment, and if it would be possible to go to a library sometimes. He paused. "What are the other two kids' names?"

"They are Steve and Hannah."

"I want to meet them!"

"Well, we'll see what happens here. Your mother and I need to talk." Mary looked thoughtfully at him as he looked eagerly at his mother. *He seems so grown up*, she thought.

"Yes, we'll talk about some things, Michael."

Michael had run out of questions so the three of them chatted.

"Do you have children of your own?" Jenny asked.

"Yes, John and I have two girls, seventeen and nineteen. One graduates from high school in June and one already is away in college. The grad is going to leave for Spokane to work for the summer and then go to school. So we are soon empty-nesters. My husband is manager of Swenson's Supermarket." Michael went out to order his bag lunch at the counter.

All of this seems encouraging, Jen thought.

Mary looked at her watch. "I don't want to go over your break time. You can call me later tonight if you have more questions. John and I will be glad to answer them. Michael is a very nice boy. I'm glad to meet him. You, too!" She gave a light laugh.

"Yes, that would be good." Jenny said. "We need to talk about how much you charge."

"Oh, it will be…and she named a very low figure.

"That's not enough," Jenny said. "I know what day care costs."

"It's good for me if it's good for you. These two kids, Steven and Hannah, need someone else to play with. Real day care, the expensive kind, is high-priced, alright. Babies and young children need constant attention. This is easy because I already enjoy talking with kids. It's not work. I like to be around to discuss a TV program they are watching, or help them with hard words when they read books. They are not a lot of 'work'. I want to limit TV. We can talk about it. I thought one morning program and one or two in the afternoon. I have ones in mind I'd like them to choose from. I'll give you a list I liked that was in a parents' magazine. I provide lunch. I want to work Monday through Saturday, daytime. My mom thought just through Friday, but Saturday is fine for Michael. Steven and Hannah won't be there, though."

"That would be really good for me. The restaurant is closed Sunday and evenings after seven. I usually work till five, though Friday night runs later." Jenny realized she sounded like she was committing to this. Michael did seem pleased with Mary. "If you don't mind, I would like to come out to your place with Michael before we decide for certain. My only day off is tomorrow. In some ways I sound protective, but really, I let him do a lot. He is familiar with riding buses and many of the drivers know him. He would be fine riding alone after he has done it and knows where your stop is. At both ends we would know when to expect him to arrive. Sorry, I'm working out details, and I sound like it's... decided... but I'd like to come out first, then talk to Michael and let you know after." Jenny realized she was talking too fast. Rattling. "Could we come out tomorrow, just to say Hello quickly?

"Oh, I would like for you to come, see where we are, and meet my husband. Ah," Mary paused, "tomorrow we go to church, and we will be eating lunch out with friends. We will be back sometime after two o'clock. Can you come at three?"

"Yes, that is very good! We have an outing planned earlier." Jenny felt pleased. Tomorrow would get this settled. They walked to the front of the restaurant. She was due to get back to work. Michael had his lunch and needed to leave.

"Michael," Jen said, "we'll go out to Mary's place tomorrow."

"Yippee!" exclaimed Michael, hugged her and shook hands with Mary Henderson. He bounced out the door and down the street to catch the bus to the museum. Mary left, and as Jen went to start making another pot of coffee, she sighed and thought how relieved she felt. There was a good possibility that Michael had a place to go. Tomorrow would tell. She felt awful before now, shuffling him around. She had tried to pretend to herself that community programs were the ideal choice, rather than the necessity they were. Even then the program hours just didn't cover the need.

That night Jenny and Michael planned the picnic. They would catch an early bus to the end of the line, past Henderson's, and transfer to the bus for Snohomish county. There was a small lake good for kids' fishing. It was well stocked, and children were usually successful.

After Michael was in bed, Jenny returned to the living room. She settled into her favorite blue velveteen chair, but reading the book she had going failed to grab her interest. *Michael didn't mentioned Len tonight; didn't asked if he was working on an old car, if he was coming home late, or if he was going away on a trip. He asks about him less and less, and Len shows up only "in his own sweet time". What a contrast...Michael helps out. He makes no demands on Len's time. Len, when he is home, never helps with anything. He never spends time with Michael anymore, just gets aggravated at him.* Len's irritable comments replayed. *"Why are you sitting in front of that TV? Why aren't you helping your mother? Don't give me that look – if you could see your face..."* At the table, if a glass of juice spilled, a burst of swearing poured from Len's mouth. He acted like it was sabotage planned against him personally. You could cut the tension in the air with a knife.

Jenny compared the present tension to dating days. She remembered their first time at the beach...how kind and charming he was. He was attractive. He had a youthful vigor, a strength that attracted her. His wavy red hair was the kind you wanted to run your fingers through. When he took her home, he was a complete gentleman. He opened doors and carried the picnic box, though she could have done it. He asked if she felt safe at her apartment. If it had been a lasting kind of caring it would have been wonderful. Unfortunately, his charm was very shallow. Jenny grabbed the book she had been reading. No point mulling over the past. She curled up in her chair to read until her eyes were heavy.

As she got ready for bed, Jenny looked at the triple frame on the dresser that held pictures of Michael – a gift from Aunt Sally. Jen had unwrapped the lovely frame on that day, her birthday. Then her aunt handed her a second gift, a large manila envelope with a bright bow on it – pictures. They were enlargements. Sally had known Jen's skill in taking pictures, and had smuggled her negatives, choosing ones with good lighting and a special pose. Jenny remembered the fun they had had that afternoon as they looked at the photos together. She held the pictures behind the matting and angled them this way and that until she and Aunt Sally were pleased with the look. They marked and cut them and fixed them in the frame. She couldn't count how many hundreds of times since that day she had gotten pleasure in looking at them. The first pose was of Michael, seven months old, four teeth peeking out of a happy grin. In the next he was a year and a half, sitting on a small plastic rocking horse. The third one she had added later, over the top of a toddler picture. That five-year old boy with serious eyes was smiling out at her, but looking so very grown up.

CHAPTER SIX

S unday morning after showering Sylvie came back in the bedroom and dressed. Then she puffed up the pillows, pulled up the spread, and arranged three decorator pillows against the curling vines of the wrought iron headboard. Picking up the soft brown horse with floppy legs and a kind look, she remembered the fun of giving it to Larry. That was after his first stuffy purchase for her – a velveteen rabbit. She had loved the story by that name. She picked up her bunny. Larry had brought it home from a trip and surprised her. That was so many years ago. Setting them down, she arranged Hans the Horse's front leg around Bunny's paw and stroked them both. She loved that man of hers.

At midday Larry stuck his head in the back porch where Sylvia was rummaging through a box, among some little-used shoes. She had just picked up her runners in one had and her flip-flops in the other.

"Say, you getting ready for summer?" He smiled with a light-hearted look. "Want to go for a drive?"

"Sure! Sounds good! Anywhere special? Do I need to take along a lunch? We haven't eaten yet. We're late."

He chuckled. "You are being a good Girl Scout. But let's just take crackers and cheese, some apples. Maybe go north, out past the meadow to Nygard Lake. We can take a walk. Just relax. Take along something to read."

She straightened up, tossed the foot gear in the box and shoved it against the freezer. "I'll be ready in ten minutes."

As they stepped into the car, they commented on the temperature. Though cool, it was mild for April at this elevation. Warm air began pouring from the heater as the engine warmed. Sylvia slipped out of her jacket.

"Are you too warm?" He reached for the heater lever.

"A little. But keep it on a bit. The jacket was too much." She was drinking in the sight of the roadside trees, leafing out. "I can't believe how spring is coming on. Just look! The spring-green color of the tiny leaves is so beautiful."

"Sure is."

"I can't believe how fast the tiny new leaves are sprouting out on those trees. Those tiny leaf buds don't stay tight very long, do they."

"Yes, winter is over."

She nodded, and a 'hmmm' of agreement escaped her lips – a sound Larry liked to hear. 'Sounds contented', he would say.

Larry went on. "I'm glad I'm finally done with winter driving. On the longer trips I knew I'd run into icy roads. It was just a question of where. I'd come to a place where someone had slid right into the ditch, or into another car. I remember once, down near Chehalis, how the river dampness made an icy glaze. I had pulled off the road on a hilly viewpoint to have an apple and coffee from the thermos. When I started again, my tires were spinning. I couldn't make it up the next hill, and I began to slide off the road. I just stopped. Then I remembered that big covered coffee can of sand and fertilizer in the trunk. It worked that time, and I got going. But just a little farther on, there was a car in the ditch, tipping at a bad angle. I was glad I wasn't calling a tow truck."

"Me, too. I worry when you're on the road."

"Now I can do the road trips without wondering where I'll hit black ice." He paused, not accustomed to complaining, but added, "Winter driving is less fun each year." He looked again at the trees and the signs of spring.

"I'm glad for you," Sylvia said as she leaned back and adjusted a small pillow under her head. "I wish you could just stay home!" She closed her eyes.

He looked over. A little smile was playing on her lips.

"You taking a nap?"

"Maybe." Her voice was dozy.

Feeling the car slowing, Sylvia struggled to get herself awake. They were pulling up beside a picnic table. "Hmmm. How long did I sleep?"

"Oh, fifteen minutes. You ready to take a walk?"

"I had better. I'm almost awake. A walk ought to do it."

"A breeze is ruffling the lake. You may want your jacket."

"For sure."

The climb up a steep hillside behind the lake was rough; not just because of rocks, but tangles of growth made it difficult to find footing. Sylvia found herself breathing hard. "I am out of shape! More gardening needed! Maybe get the bicycles out."

"Good idea." Larry stretched out the word ideeeah like the fellow in the movie, "Never Cry Wolf" who showed off his new dentures. As he said ideeeah with a wide smile, he revealed a row of pearly whites where there had been only gaping space in times past. Whenever Larry did this, their shared memory flashed before both of them and they laughed at their private joke. Sylvia remembered the first time they watched the movie; she hadn't caught the dry humor, had taken it too seriously. A couple years later when they rented it a second time she was fully open and involved and simply in a different mood. The stoical main character was an impractical scientist, and the storyline was a mix of ridiculous overstatements seamed together with some truth. Farley Mowat was a writer who brought awareness of the whole "up north" picture, but often drew an impossible scene just for a joke. Sylvia loved good books, though didn't often pick humorous ones. Humor was more enjoyable in movies, though it took her two tries on that one.

The path they chose had long ago faded into the brush. Ahead was a large granite outcrop. No wonder the town of Granite Falls had that name. The nearby river ran among granite boulders that had either tumbled down into its canyon or had been exposed by the heavy seasonal runoff. Larry and Sylvia now heard the sound of rushing water and the air smelled fresh. As they came closer, they saw a creek flowing around the base of their outcrop. It disappeared into a tangle of brush, ferns and thimbleberry. It had to be flowing into the lake farther on. Right here there was a point of land they had seen from the car. But, for today at least, their progress was halted.

"Time to go eat?" Larry asked.

"Sure. Where?"

"A picnic in the car. When you were sound asleep, I got two sandwiches and juice at the gas station! See what a good provider I am." He laughed.

"You are. That's no joke. Always have been!" Her heart was warmed. "I love you!"

"You love me for my sandwiches!"

Sylvia grabbed him in a wild hug, and kissed him. "You are very wrong about that!" She gave him kisses till he laughed aloud.

He held her. "Okay, I cry 'uncle'!"

The wind picked up as they continued back to the car. It was too cold now to sit outside. In the car, they ate enthusiastically while the heater took away their chill. They watched as a storm blew in. The sky darkened, bringing down the temperature. Tree branches began tossing in the wind.

"I'm glad we got our walk in," Sylvia said. "Let's not go back home yet, though."

They read separately for a while. Then Larry read aloud a travel article about the San Juan Islands. Sylvia worked on a cross stitch wall hanging. She was doing it for Mother's Day for Mark's wife, Marie, who loved hand-made things. The daylight began to fade.

"The wind has dropped. Time for one more quick walk, okay?" Larry asked as he began putting the reading material in a cloth bag. Sylvia had sewn it from a hand-loomed piece of material she picked out of an odds-and-ends bin at a yarn shop.

"Okay. Let's go! I'm glad for my warm jacket!" They walked quickly a short way, realizing they didn't want to be outside for long.

Sylvia slid back inside the car, glad for the protection. "I can't wait to get home. Maybe have a fire again, eh?" Sylvia's Canadian "eh" came out now and then, though it had been almost forty years since her family had come across the border and settled in Everett.

"That's a good ideeeah," he chuckled. "I'll set it while you put on something light to eat. All I feel like is soup."

"Oh." She paused. "I can cook something more than that. We

only had sandwiches. I do have leftovers to make the soup hearty."
She was known for her tasty soups. "What else?"

"That would be good. Nothing else."

"A banana?"

"Sure."

"And I have some other fruit."

"That's plenty. We have ice cream in the freezer!"

The drive back brought an even more peaceful feel to the close of the afternoon, and a little pink glow of sunset promised a nice day tomorrow. A sprinkle of rain dotted the windshield and sprinkled the streets as they drove through their little town The sidewalks were quiet, typical of an April Sunday afternoon.

CHAPTER SEVEN

As they began their bus ride Sunday morning, Michael talked excitedly of seeing where the Hendersons lived. But he was looking forward just as eagerly to what came first – their morning at the man-made fishing lake. Soon the bus ride became boring for him. He took out a paper, made a grid of dots, and handed it and the pencil to his mother. They took turns alternately, making a horizontal or vertical line to connect two dots. Soon the grid had many unattached walls of one or two sides. The object of the game was to avoid making a third side on a 'box'. If you did, the other person would mark in the fourth side, enter his initial in the box, and count it as his at the end. Sometimes the fourth side mark started a chain of several squares.

"Hey, Mom, it's getting down to where you have to put a third side, and you know what that means!"

"No, Michael?" Jen said with mock curiosity. "What does that mean?"

"You know, Mom! Hurry and mark it! Then I can claim it! I'll get a point!"

"Yes, I'm afraid you will!"

By the end of the game they each had almost an even number of boxes. It was Michael's turn and he gave a groan. He saw that the only place to put his line would give his mother a long row of boxes that would finish the game. She filled it in and they each counted their own squares. Jenny won, with Michael promising he would beat her the next time.

They arrived at the little lake that had been made into a 'city kids' fishing hole. The young fishermen didn't care that it was man-made. It had fish in it! They didn't make this trip often, though. Usually their outings were closer to home. The lake was already crowded when they arrived. Michael, losing his shyness when he had a purpose, began talking with two boys and their dads. They made room for him. Jenny, seeing him settled, spread a blanket nearby and got out her book.

After an hour, Michael came running over with a small fish, the length of his hand, and a little girl with bouncing blond curls following him. He was hollering, "Look! Look what I caught!" The girl jumped up and down, looking just as excited as Michael.

"Oh, Honey," Jenny said. "That's neat you caught a fish."

She was wondering how to word her next sentence, not to hurt him, when Michael said, "I know I have to throw it back. That man said so. But that's okay. It will grow for next year. This is Kailie. Bye." Off they ran. If it had been big enough to keep, Michael was now able to clean a fish with a little help. Jenny hadn't minded doing it when he was young. *He's growing up,* she thought. She watched the little girl and him, giggling together, trying to hold onto the slippery fish long enough to get it into the water. *How often Michael has said he'd like a little sister, what fun she would be to take care of, and how he'll watch out for her.* He knew it wasn't likely. They had talked, but she hadn't told the whole truth to Michael. Len told her plainly, *after they were married,* that he didn't want children. He didn't want to be bothered with them. She could tell him for certain that they *are* a bother! A *big* bother – and worth every bit of effort! She wished she had known how he felt four years ago…about a lot of things.

Lunch was a great success. They invited Kailie. Though her dad came over to meet Jenny and give the okay, he returned to his friends. The kids threw grapes up in the air to catch in their own mouths. It was inevitable of course, that they all ended up throwing grapes into each other's mouths. After some hard shots and lots of squeals Jenny sent them to run off their energy at the playground. Finally it was time to go. They said good-bye to Kailie, hoping to meet again sometime at the lake, and caught the bus to their important appointment.

Jenny was feeling sleepy as the bus rumbled along, but they were getting close to Henderson's area. Michael was looking out the window.

"Help me watch for the Henderson's street," she said. To her relief, the area had pleasant houses with large back yards. They saw the street sign. When they got off they only had to walk past three houses.

Michael saw the house number first. "Oh, that's easy to find, Mom!" he said happily. For Jenny it was a knot in the pit of her stomach type of feeling. Even though she had already met Mary, she wondered what Mary's husband would be like. The yard was neat, with newly turned dirt in the flowerbeds down both sides of the walk, waiting for bedding plants. Blue, purple, and yellow pansies greeted them from large clay pots on each side of the front steps, and daffodils stood tall in their midst, bouncing their bright yellow heads. Mary opened the front door, dressed in a mint green blouse that set off her ivory complexion. John, tall and fair-haired, stood close behind her, showing the whitest teeth in the happiest smile she had seen on a man in a long time.

"Come in, come in!" the words rebounded as they all stepped inside. "This is my husband, John Henderson. John, meet Jenny Brown and Michael Brown." Mary waved her arm toward the archway to the right, and said, "Let's look around the house before we go to sit down." They walked through the pleasant though simple living room; then entered the dining area where an oval oak table filled the room. "Excuse the finish, or lack of it, on the table," Mary said. "It has seen a lot of wear. John's next re-finishing project." She smiled at him. Surprisingly, Jenny thought, after a possible put-down, he smiled back. She brought them back around through the hall again, and pointed to the front bathroom and bedroom. "Although, Michael, you won't want a nap at your age, this front bedroom is kept as a spare. If one of you children don't feel well, you have a place to lie down."

After showing the two back bedrooms, Mary led them along a hallway. A china cabinet they passed caught Jen's attention. It held, among other things, two miniature tea sets for little girls. Jenny had wanted one every Christmas as a little girl; wanted it so much that she had cried herself to sleep when it was not under their scraggly tree. She had felt miserable *because* it wasn't there. And she had felt miserable and selfish for wanting it – something her mother couldn't afford to give her. Hope. She hoped for it so very many years, a much longer time than what made any sense. She had finally realized it wasn't going to happen. *I'm too old for it,* she had told herself after another disappointing Christmas. Hope not fulfilled. *And anyway, I don't care...*Jenny realized she was staring, standing in front of Mary's cabinet. The others had moved into the cheery kitchen. She followed. Michael and John were going out onto a shaded patio. Mary said to follow them to the outdoor table, proudly pointing out that John had made it in his shop. It was just a practical wood table, but it was nicely finished with some kind of semi-shiny varnish or plastic. She sat down, facing the large backyard. Mary brought tea and cookies. They chatted. The Hendersons were getting to know Michael by asking him questions about animals, what he liked to read, and his favorite activities. The younger daughter came home, stuck her head out the patio door and said Hi, and was gone again. Jenny promptly forgot her name and felt bad. She was too busy sizing up Mary and John – the way they talked to each other. She wondered if they were like this all the time. *If it's real, here is a family who has it together. It's intimidating. Mary will soon find out that our lives are far from ideal.* The word 'dysfunctional' came to mind. She had heard it a lot lately, though without an explanation as to exactly what it meant. *Just go figure – that's probably us.* Listening to them talk, Jenny was surprised that John, an important man who managed a store, was so respectful to Mary. *He speaks kindly to her, like she is somebody... Like she is somebody who counts. But then,* Jenny thought guiltily, *Mary speaks to him with respect in her voice, too.* Jenny remembered many times she had felt such fury toward Len she didn't know what to do. She didn't yell at him – she didn't dare do that. She had no idea what would happen if she did, though she knew she'd be sorry to find out. She had to admit, though, that even if she kept quiet she had been totally frustrated with him and he knew it. She could get sarcastic when she did talk. He needed to *know* she was upset. But that backfired right in her face. He got more belligerent. He jerked chairs around. He clenched his fists and shook them in her face. She just gave up. *Get out of the way, leave the room as soon as you can find a way. Keep the peace. That's the answer. It wasn't peace compared to what she saw in this house. The peacefulness among these people seemed strange. She had a nasty thought! It would be good to be a mouse under the table! Bet it isn't always this way.*

John and Mary were laughing together about their own names, telling Michael they had the two most common names in the English language, passed down from relatives. Then an awkward pause came when Michael volunteered, "My real dad is gone away, a long time ago, when I was a baby. He probably won't come back." They looked at each other, and the guarded expressions on their faces said, *Oh, oh. Sensitive topic – what else can we talk about?*

John pushed back his chair, "I'm sorry to hear that." Then he asked Jen, "If it's okay, I'd like to show Michael my wood-working shop? Just be gone a little while." Before she could answer, Mary spoke up.

"John is very happy to be the father of two girls, but he has a tender spot for boys." She smiled at him. "And for woodworking!"

"Sure, that would be great," Jenny said. The two of them headed for the shop beside the vegetable garden.

Mary continued, "John's dad was killed in a logging accident when he was six. I think he still misses him. He likes to 'be there' for boys. He comes home for a couple hours on some weekdays when the store is quiet. I know he would like to spend a little time with Michael, if that's okay with you. If they go to the shop, I'd be in and out and the door would be left open, just so there are no concerns for either you or us. It's for our protection, too. Sometimes an awful incident of abuse happens to a child, or even repeated abuse. Then there is an investigation and charges and a lawsuit, thank God. You hate to think, though, how the child may have been harmed, especially emotionally. That may not show outwardly at the time unless one knows what behavior to look for. It comes out later. But it has also happened that people were charged with child abuse when nothing took place. Lies are told and their good name is ruined. That also would be a horrid thing to go through, so we have been very careful. I hope you understand it isn't aimed at you. It has simply become our habit."

"I understand," Jenny said, a little numbly. *Not a nice topic to have to think about.* She asked then, with a worried edge to her voice, "Are power tools in the shop?"

"Yes, in the back half, but that's locked. There's a skill saw, a table saw and a drill press, other stuff like that, but they are in a separate room that John keeps locked. He carries the key and I have the spare tucked away. Michael won't have access to those tools. John wouldn't use them with young kids. He only teaches them to use the hand tools that he keeps in the first area, at the workbench. That's where they just went. Later, when Michael is older, if you want, John could introduce how to handle power tools, but not this young. John has never lost a finger, knock on wood!" Mary laughed as she rapped on the table.

"Good idea to keep them locked away. Having the hand tools separate is something I don't think I've seen done."

"Yes, John is cautious. I suppose losing his dad in a logging accident had that effect – that things can go wrong. Of course the worst effect on him was loneliness. He needed a 'dad' kind of man in his life. Though there is no one like the person you've lost, a neighbor man took him under his wing. That really helped." Jenny nodded. How well she knew what it was like to lose a parent, but she didn't need to reveal how her dad had left them or what a shock it had been when word came that he was dead. At least it had been a shock to her. The image appeared before her of her mother's face, with a strange, careless expression as she held out the news clipping and said, "Your dad's dead." Nothing more. Jenny hadn't known then that a woman can harden herself not to feel.

Mary stood up and said, "Let's walk around the yard." Startled, Jenny stood. "We can get a closer look at the flowers. We have a vegetable garden, too. Let's go there first." Jen looked at the neat rows of tiny plants, so orderly. Mary opened a shopping bag, bent down and began to break off the outer leaves of lettuce that looked like romaine. Some of the narrow heads were large, some tiny, and she saw that they had been 'pruned' already. Mary worked on the large heads. "This lettuce and the green onions are about all that's ready. I hope you can use some."

"You bet! That's great. Michael and I enjoy salads, especially now when things are fresh and tasting good, even from the store. I can't believe that I'll be eating greens tonight the same day they were picked!"

"The beets there, showing their little green tops, will be thinned soon; that's mostly to use like spinach before the bottoms develop. The little leaves are nice in salads. There will be more variety to share with you and Michael in a few weeks. Young carrots will need thinning then. Later full sized carrots and beets will come on. Corn and other things that need warm weather will be ready in summer. Also broccoli and cauliflower that take a longer time to grow."

They wandered through the rows as they talked. Jenny wondered if, when the soil was warm, she would get to slip off her shoes and massage her feet into the soft dirt, like she had done at Aunt Sally's when she was a kid. "You folks have a nice place – it has taken a lot of work to get it like this."

"Yes, we moved here when the girls were so small – three and five." She paused. "It's hard to believe that it's been fourteen years." They talked on about what Mary's girls were taking in school and how John and she didn't know if an "empty nest" would bother them. The girls would be home for visits a lot, at least the older one who was here in Seattle, rooming near her school. The younger girl had an aunt and uncle near Spokane who would keep her from getting lonely, and they wouldn't worry as much.

"Oh, here is the rhubarb patch. Do you want any?"

"A little is good. I'll just chop it up and make sauce."

"There you go." Mary stuck in a few stalks after taking off the leaves, and handed her the bag full of produce. "You and Michael enjoy!"

This reference by Mary, as though it was just Michael and her alone, reminded her that she needed to explain. She took a deep breath and started. "Michael hasn't had it the easiest…as far as having, or rather, not having both a mom and a dad all his childhood." She got a wry look on her face. "You know, 'stability' they call it."

"Oh." Mary nodded and simply waited.

"Michael's last name is Hanson. Lennard Brown and I were

married four years ago. He's away a lot - you may not hear Michael talk about him much. He keeps very busy when he is working. He restores specialized old cars. Fixes one and then usually goes away to sell it, like to California."

"Oh. I called him Michael Brown. I apologize for not asking. I'm interested, though, as a casual observer, that Michael seems to have adjusted well to what you call a lack of stability. He doesn't seem insecure. It was probably harder on you. I have a high school chum who has been raising her daughter alone for years. She tells me it's tough."

Jenny nodded. "Yes, it's tough alone. As for Michael he has adjusted, from it being just the two of us, to me being married. It's a good thing that kids are adaptable."

"Well, here come the guys!" Mary said. "I'll get them some lemonade." *'The guys' sounds so good,* Jen thought. *Too bad Michael didn't have...what? What could she say? Fathering? Guess Len just didn't know how. Who would have taught him to be a father? He was thirty-four when they married. How would he have known how to be comfortable around kids? What little he had said about his own childhood was said with a sneer. He had never shared happy memories. Just didn't talk about it, period. They never shared personal stuff. If there were a bunch of guys around drinking beer, swapping fishing stories, he would sarcastically say,* "Yeah, I got to go fishing with my dad. When I wasn't getting kicked in the butt, I was wondering if I was going to be used for the bait." *All the guys laughed. But what was so funny about it? I wonder if he felt loved – maybe by his mother. Maybe she was too stressed to cope with it all. I wonder if his dad provided for them. It's doubtful.* Len had never been a steady provider. He got money, sure enough. A lot of money, all at once. She couldn't ask where it came from. Only once had she questioned. She remembered it clearly. He had grabbed her and shaken her, and said to keep her nose out of his business. It was his money. She quickly grasped that, wherever it came from, it was not gotten for her use, and he was not to be questioned. Later she realized she could get a little if she begged. It was hard to grovel. The scene was the same – she begged, he asked why, she tried to justify, he accused her of careless spending, she denied and explained the bills, he instructed her not to pay some of them, and finally he grudgingly gave her half what she needed for what was overdue. Well, somehow they managed. Collection agencies were usually on his trail, but she couldn't fix that. She almost ceased trying by now.

Suddenly Michael was there, jumping excitedly, not able to stay on the ground. "Look at my boat for the next trip to the lake!" Sure enough, there was a pointed board as long as his arm, with blocks stacked and nailed on to make the cabin. There was even a mast, made with a length of doweling. They had spray painted it blue. It was not quite dry and smudges were on Michael's hands; marks he'd wear proudly, she could see. Michael held it straight up to expose the bottom and Jenny could see his first name and phone number on the bottom in marking pen. "So if it sails away it can be returned," he explained. His face was radiant. "I made it myself, with just a little help. I can build now! I pounded the nails. On the ones underneath, on the first layer, I didn't do so well. There were lots of dents in the wood. But on these ones that show, I did better!" He held it close and pointed for her to see. "Look Mom!" He was so pleased. She realized he hadn't been around tools since they moved from the apartment where he was seven years old. Len's automotive tools were expensive and were not toys for kids anyway. But next door to that apartment building lived a neighbor, a retired man, in an old house. He built birdhouses. He let the neighbor kids put a base coat of paint on them. They knew he would paint over it. They didn't mind. It made them happy just to use a paintbrush, just to do whatever he allowed them to do. They had played with short screwdrivers, a small hammer, and an old tape measure, and sorted nails according to size for the man; that was about it.

"Remember, Mom? When I got to paint and pound tacks into old boards at the neighbor man's? This time I really made something, something real! I made it myself!"

"I see! That is a super boat! We sure will take it to the lake and sail it, even to the little stream at the park near us!" Jenny put her arm around him and gave him a warm squeeze, a long one. It made her heart ache to think of what he was missing. Then she looked at her watch. "I can't believe it! We have to go." She reached down and picked up the bag of veggies and started to look for her purse.

"We've been here for an hour and a half." Her voice lowered in embarrassment. "I'm sorry. I didn't mean to stay this long."

"We are glad you did!" They smiled. They meant it. "It was nice to have a chance to visit; get to know each other."

"I need to make a definite decision here."

"Take your time," John said.

Mary added, "It's a scary thing to entrust your precious child to anyone."

What a nice way to put it, thought Jenny. "So!" turning to Michael she said, "What do you think? I have been watching your face and I wonder if I read it right. You can give me an answer later, at home, if you would like to wait and think about it. Or you are free to say if you would you like to come here every week when I work?"

"Oh, yes, Mom, YES! I want to come! I want to come here!"

"Well, Mary, I'm not surprised at Michael's take on it. I'm very happy with the situation. I feel really fortunate. Is it okay with you and John, or would you like to talk together and think about it?"

Mary looked at John with her eyebrows up. He said, "It's great with me. I won't be here much, but I think that Michael and I hit it off. He'd be a pleasure to have around. When I'm home we could look forward to doing more building in the shop!"

"Well," Mary said, "I am glad for a chance to talk today with both of you, but I really knew – I mean I hoped – it was going to work out after I met you and Michael yesterday. It will be wonderful to have you, Michael!"

Jenny saw Mary's genuine interest as she smiled and held out her hand to Michael to shake. *My, he hasn't gotten that kind of loving look from anyone but me since Aunt Sally moved away.*

"When would you like to start? Tomorrow?" Mary looked at Jen.

"Oh, would Michael be able to start that soon? After school?"

"Sure. You'll get to meet Steven and Hannah tomorrow. Oh, I need to be sure I have your information. Let me have you write down names and phone numbers for home and work. Any allergies?"

"No." Jenny began to write as she asked Michael, "Do you think you can recognize the bus stop?" She knew the answer.

"Oh, sure, Mom. I have noticed that corner before today, when we went to the lake. And for sure I know how to get off at my own bus stop!" They all joined with him in laughter.

"Next Saturday I do need somewhere for Michael. The museum program is over at noon. In fact it's the last week for it."

Mary nodded. "Saturday will be fine. Also, there is a professional day on Friday. No school."

"Oh, I'd forgotten."

"I'll have Steven and Hannah all that day, too. They don't come Saturdays."

"That reminds me; may I pay you on Saturday? That's when I get paid. Since you said you come in to shop on Saturday, would you want to pick up Michael instead of him riding out on the bus? We could meet later and I can pay you then."

"I'd be happy to pick him up. How about I get him before I shop?"

"Yes, sure. He would enjoy that. He helps me. He finds the fruit that's not bruised, and the best vegetables – oh you won't need vegetables! In any case, he's a good shopper. Anyway, here I go chattering. Now I will get 'out of your hair'!"

* * *

Sunday night. It's been a special day – the lake, meeting the Hendersons. What nice people they are; church people, but I can overlook that. I think tomorrow I'll bring home some cheery daffodils – just to celebrate! Jenny wandered through the living room. Michael was asleep. She straightened the pillows, then saw the mini-albums on the bookcase. She picked them up and settled in her blue chair. She opened the plaid album and a small spiral notebook fell out. She had forgotten that it existed – a diary. But not daily. More of a journal. She had jotted down things they had done, and even put her personal thoughts. *Interesting. I wonder what I was thinking back then. Some other time I'll check it out.* She closed it and slid it underneath the little albums.

Jen opened to the first picture. Michael was five years old, and was standing with her on the beach at Alki Point in West Seattle. They had been with her Aunt Sally and her girlfriend Cindy and her son. In fact, Sally had been the one to put the plan together! What a dear woman. Jenny remembered vividly her saying, "We are going to have some fun – some summer beach fun while it's hot weather. We don't get it for long in Seattle, you know! So let's see. You have Thursday off and so does your friend, Cindy. We'll pack a big lunch, so we can eat twice out of it, and we'll spend the day! I'll pay the bus fare."

Aunt Sally hadn't listened to any objections. It was in the works before Jenny could turn around. She pictured how Aunt Sally came the day before, bringing two chickens. They fried them while they chopped up the boiled potatoes that Jenny had cooked ahead for potato salad. As they made iced tea and cut carrot sticks, they talked and laughed. Everything went in the fridge, ready to go into the ice chest in the morning. They sat down to a well-earned rest and still went to bed early, feeling prepared for an early morning. Cindy and her little boy met them at the bus transfer point.

Jenny looked at the next two pictures: two five-year old boys playing in the sand, and Cindy and Michael throwing seaweed at each other. Cindy had just gotten a gob of it on her neck and she had her face scrunched in a "Yuck" expression. In the next one the shocked expressions on the faces of the two moms and the boys, running out of the cold water, shouted Cold! Yes, she remembered how she even swam in that always-chilly Puget Sound water. Then little Michael was chasing a seagull that was taking off, a look of sheer delight on his face. It was good to have that picture captured for keeps.

Happiness filled that day. They ate and laughed and walked, and ate some more! Aunt Sally had answered a multitude of questions the boys asked, and kept them busy playing. That left the two girlfriends free. Free of responsibility, free of worry for one glorious day. They all dug into the last of the picnic food and her aunt bought hot dogs to fill the gap. They rode good old Seattle Metro home at sunset. Aunt Sally again stayed overnight, and they fell into bed. What a memory. *What has happened to me? No fun, ever, anymore. Well, that wasn't exactly true. Like today. Michael and I had a good time. But where is that completely carefree kind of day that we had then? However those years alone with Michael were also tough.* She remembered how she sometimes only had part-time work. They had strange meals – what was left in the fridge or cupboard. Sometimes she went to the Food Bank – when she absolutely had to. She kept her head down in embarrassment and chose the cans and packages as fast as she could. She went only when she had no work and was desperate. Telling herself that it was there for just such needs didn't help; she was still miserable using it.

Jenny flipped the next pages. That took her to Michael's first day of kindergarten, when she had let her aunt know that Michael didn't have tennis shoes to start school. She hated it – not being independent, not meeting his needs. There he was, smiling, ready to go up the school steps in his new shoes. She was glad now. It had been right to ask for help. She turned to the next picture. Len and Michael the day they met. It was spring. It had been a hard winter with little income. Aunt Sally had moved away. A noise brought her back to the present. Michael was stumbling out of bed. She rose, caught up the little notebook, and flipped the stack of albums onto the bookcase. Michael might need help to get his bearings. He sleepwalked.

CHAPTER EIGHT

On Monday morning Larry gathered the toiletries into his kit, set it inside his suitcase and closed it. He inhaled the stimulating aroma of coffee and thought, *Thanks, Sylvia; it'll be nice to share a cup before I go.* On days when he had a long drive he had a piece of toast at home and stopped later to eat breakfast.

Sylvia stepped out on the deck, patterned with shafts of sunlight beaming down through the tall fir trees that stood along the back fence. Looking up, she saw that the sun was rising noticeably farther to the left, or north, than a week earlier. On winter mornings the sun had risen late, in the southeast, making a shallow arc over the garage; that is, when it shone at all through the cloud cover. Even now there were clouds gathering, beginning to block the light. Going back into the kitchen, she thought, *I'm glad I saw the short sunny time. Never mind the clouds. I'll focus on the bigger picture – that age-old repetition of God's steadiness, His plan of revolving seasons. Though it is a worldwide phenomenon, it becomes so personal; timed just right to bring relief when one season becomes tiresome. Soon it's morphing into the next.*

Larry came in the kitchen, set his suitcase down and reached for the toaster, but Sylvia beat him to it. Pushing down the lever, she laughed, and reached up as he took her in his arms, kissing and hugging until the toast rudely popped up. Cradling her coffee as Larry ate quickly, she enjoyed his presence. He hoped to beat the rush-hour traffic. Previously he had been responsible only to troubleshoot for his company. He had dealt with complaints the various outlets received about machines and products purchased by the forest industry. Recently he had been given broader responsibilities and a larger territory. There would be even more trips south, like today, around the heavily populated Everett-Seattle-Tacoma corridor. But he and Sylvia wouldn't think of moving south. They loved this part of Snohomish County, tucked in the hills. Most of his work would still be in the Seattle area. This trip was an exception. Tomorrow he would end up in Portland, Oregon for an industry-wide trade fair. There would be demonstrations of products, including training seminars for computer-programmed machines for the forest industry.

After the mini breakfast, Larry and Sylvia walked outside together. He set the suitcase down on the deck and reached for her, but her mind had started to switch to the day ahead, the jobs to be done – her built-in mechanism to avoid being sad when they were saying good-bye. Larry's pleasant smile, his lips, came close. He pulled her to him. They kissed. They kissed again, lingering in each other's arms. For both of them the loneliness during these trips had grown harder to put up with as the years passed. Now they made phone calls just to hear each others' voices, and they freely admitted it.

Larry murmured, "I love you," as he stroked her hair. "I don't want to leave." He held her close and a warm feeling spread inside her. Knowing that he cared was like having the sun shine. She knew she brought warmth into his life, too.

"You are a busy man, sir." Sylvia put on her coy look. "I don't want to keep you."

"Not much you don't," he laughed. "And I don't want to go, but I must." He squeezed her.

She held him tight. "I will let you go, and then take pleasure in your return."

"My, don't you sound poetic on this beautiful morning. One is reminded it is spring and young love blooms."

"Love blooms, my darling," she said with a twinkle in her eye, "but mature love." She snuggled close. "Come back, and hold me like this." She gave a deep hug and then loosened her arms.

"I will," he said as he gave her one last enfolding, and kissed her full on the lips one last time. "I will!" His fingers ran down her arms, then closed over her hands. He stood back to capture a vision of her to take with him. A boyish grin passed across his face as he gave her a last, quick kiss, grabbed the suitcase and they walked quickly down the steps. He drank in the picture of her face as he backed the car down the drive. At the bottom he waved, then drove down the road, disappearing around the curve. Sylvia held the picture of his strong, kind face in her mental album.

Wandering along the back of the house to the far corner, she thought of the satisfaction of using the time till Larry returned for outdoor work. Looking at the clods of soil she had turned last fall, it was apparent that wintertime freezing and thawing had softened them. *Now I can easily break the clods and chop up the matted grass roots. I'll plant the dried snapdragon seeds I gathered last fall.* She smiled to herself. *Lifeless seeds buried in the ground, seeds that will start taking in the moisture. New life poking through the soil, seeking the sunlight.* As many times as she had seen it happen, it was still a wonder. She remembered that, as a child, she had dug up her grandmother's bean seeds to see how they were doing! Her grandmother came along and, though she asked her not to do it again it was with a kindly tone. She explained about this special time in the life of a plant. She pointed at the sprouted beans in Sylvie's little hand, and told her the white pointer coming out of it was a root, to stretch downward. Another seed had a blunt green sprout. A more advanced one had two tiny green leaves. Grandmother said that they were for reaching up through the soil to get light. Sylvia remembered how awestruck she was to see leaves come out of a bean that had been hard and dead looking! *Yes, I think that as long as I live I will be delighted with the mystery of life renewing every spring. Life and growth.* She glanced down at the dirt clods. *Well, this corner of the house is destined for some flowers, for sure. With lots of time off work, I can turn it into a beauty spot.*

Seattle

Jen walked past the clothing shop window and remembered that she needed to get some casual pants for summer – later. She looked down at her jeans that had gotten too tight. Holes were coming on one knee. Though it might be stylish, her poor knee was getting the worst end of scrapes. A pair of light-weight pants in a mid-calf style – yes, in a nice pastel! Some pants just for fun, summer fun! If she spent time looking around, she might find them in a thrift store. She could look today after meeting Mary. She took a deep breath and let it out. It was good to be off work until Monday.

Coming to the bakery where she was to meet Mary and Michael, she eagerly anticipated the quality coffee. As she opened the door, a lovely aroma waft out to welcome her. She walked up to the counter and asked, "What have you made with that lovely fragrance?" It was payday, after all. She was tired of scrimping.

"Cardamom curls," the plump young lady answered. Deciding to treat herself, Jenny said, "I'll take one. And a small cup of your good dark roast coffee. Don't leave room for cream." This would make up for the lunch she missed.

Jen looked around and decided on a table by the window. She doctored the coffee with raw sugar, sat down and took a bite of the small Swedish pastry. *What a heavenly spice cardamom is,* she thought. Her eyes drifted outside to yellow pansies in a planter beside a bench, inviting a pause from hurry. A little girl with strawberry blond curls cascading over her shoulders came along, plopped down, and pulled on her mommy's hand. Jen looked with fascination at the gorgeous ringlets. Not ringlets, exactly. Softer. The girl scooted over on the bench to pick a pansy. By moving from shade into sunlight, a shining array of colors, from copper to blond, shone in her hair. Jen was suddenly struck by a mental picture of a small red-headed boy – Len must have been darling. A painful question came. *What kind of life did he have when he was that size? I've never known... he never talks about being that young. He just doesn't discuss anything personal. There's no picture album of his childhood. He now has no contact with his parents; figures his dad is dead. When I ask, he tells me I wouldn't want to know them. Who were they, anyhow? What were they like? I've only heard one recollection – the miserable fishing trips he recounted. His words about his mother were not repeatable. I wonder. Was the woman as dumb and useless as he made her out to be? Maybe that was his dad's description of her.* Jen shook her head and focused on the little girl again. What a sweetie. Her mind wandered back to Len, picturing a sensitive little boy with fair skin and bright blue eyes... and as she looked with her mind's eye, she saw terror overcome him... What happened next? She couldn't know. But she could imagine. Probably it was just her imagination working, but...

Mary Henderson called her name, "Jennifer! I'm sorry you had to wait. I'm late."

"Oh, I knew you'd come. After all, you had Michael with you!"

"Hi, Mom. I'm hungry," was Michael's opener.

"Here, Michael," Mary laid a hand on his shoulder. "I'm getting a coffee, and I want to buy you something if your mom doesn't mind." She opened her purse, looked at Jen apologetically, and said, "We didn't have time for a snack. John called and I needed to drive some distance to pick up a clerk for the grocery store – her car broke down. So no snack and I'm late with Michael besides."

"You're here. That's what counts. And sure, Michael can have a muffin or something."

"Mom, there are maple bars!"

"No, too much sugar. Get a muffin." She looked at her plate and felt guilty. "Or you may have one of these cardamom pastries. I guess that sounds more like a special treat than a muffin."

"Looks flaky," Mary said. "Good idea. But I have a favorite here." She shoved three dollars across the table to Jennifer, saying, "I set up the meeting place so that I could treat you, and you beat me here."

Before Jen could object, Mary spoke to Michael, handing him a ten. "I'll stick with the Everything Muffin. Get your treat and a cocoa. You can bring the things here on a tray. Thanks for playing waiter."

Mary settled her purse and jacket and asked how work had gone. Jen told a cute incident involving a bus boy who was a nice kid, but a computer nerd, whose social graces were undeveloped. He embarrassed himself in front of a customer. As Jen talked with Mary, she thought, *How nice to have time together, just woman to woman.* Michael returned and unloaded the tray. Then he dug a book out of his backpack, took his cocoa and goody, and went to sit on the now-empty bench outside. The women talked about the warm weather

and the garden, and how well Michael was doing in school. Mary
had veggies in the car for Jen to take home. While waiting for Mary
to return from the restroom, Jen gazed out the window and thought,
*how long since I've sat having a coffee with a friend and just taken
time for some 'girl-talk'. Have I ever done much of that? This is so
nice.* She felt suspended in time, with the pleasant bakery bustle
going on around her, sunshine outside, and the day's work finished.

Before bed that night Jen took a pencil as thoughts came to her.
She began to write.

Friend

This woman is a friend
Now I know.
A school friend was 'for a day'.
I grew up and thought
'No friend –
Preferable to have no friend.'

This woman is real
This woman cares.
How long is she a friend?
We'll see.

by Jennifer Hanson Brown
after meeting Mary Henderson

* * *

Sylvia's phone rang. She glanced at the clock. Seven-thirty was
kind of early for a phone call. She wondered if it might be Larry as
she picked it up. "Hello, Ford residence."

"Hello, Mom! It's Mark." At the first words a picture of her
firstborn came to Sylvia – capable, strong-bodied but with gentle
eyes and expressions that made people comfortable around him.
"Marie and I are hoping you are free on Mother's Day Sunday.

We would like to take you and Dad out for dinner. That is we, and of course, Emalie," he added with a chuckle, "the most important toddler in the Pacific Northwest. Does that fit with your schedule?"

"Oh! Why, that sounds wonderful! Yes, I'm sure it's okay with Dad. And lately you have been having some weekend time at home – I know you must be enjoying that. How is Marie? Too bad she won't be with her own mother. It's their Mother's Day, too. Just think – it's Marie's second Mother's Day, and she's such a good little mother." Sylvia could picture Marie with Emalie, cuddling her, delighting in her. Mark paused as he heard the words "*little* mother". Marie would feel minimized if she heard that, but let it pass. His mother meant well. Marie felt like a whole person and also had found rich fulfillment in motherhood, and that was what counted.

"Marie is fine. Of course, she wishes she could see her mother. It just can't happen this time, with Mrs. Rodriguez living on the other side of the country. She plans to fly out from New York in late summer. But back to what's happening here. Yes – Marie and I are definitely happy that I have most weekends off. We're agreed that we've both had enough of that overtime business. We are looking forward to spending time together. Not just "couple time" or the three of us, but as an extended family with you and Dad, Nadine or anyone else who's around. Speaking of Nadine, we are hoping she'll come out from Seattle for Mother's Day. It's been months since I've seen that baby sister of mine."

"Yes, she is coming. I just got a call yesterday and she's almost positive she can. Will be good to have you all together. Well... all but Issa." *Her heart gave a little lurch.* She quickly went on. "So this is good news to start the day, and each day until I see you! Thanks. I guess you are heading to work. Better let you go."

"I am. Well, we'll see you in a week and a half."

"Have a good day. I love you, Mark. Bye."

"Love you, too."

Sylvia hung up the phone. *Well, that's enough to make your day!* Then, as though the sun had to shine just to enhance her happiness, the room suddenly brightened. She looked out the kitchen window and saw sunlight beaming on the strip of lawn that ran down the outside edge of the driveway. There were a few tree shadows where the grass sparkled with frost – a sign of the clear sky above. Looking up she saw bright blue peeking through the tiny new leaves of the maple tree across the driveway. *Lovely day. Lovely news! Oh, God, I am thankful. Thankful that you have blessed Mark and Marie with a strong marriage, brought them through the early adjustments. Thank you for this family time we'll have on Mother's Day.*

All of them together in this quiet house – that would bring noise and life into it. Sylvia was glad Larry had come to not only tolerate but to enjoy the disruption to their lives. A real visit! Eat out together for Mother's Day, then come home and lounge around the house. Hug Emalie and watch her play – see how she has changed. Instead of just phone calls, Marie and Nadine and she would get in some face to face talk – real girl-time. Nadine and Marie were good friends. Marie had made her sister-in-law welcome in their home, even having her stay with them when she first moved to the city. And Nadine dearly loved her little niece, bringing gifts, taking pictures of her and going for walks. An inseparable pair that first spring, Nadine would bundle tiny Emalie into the stroller, regardless of the weather, and take her for a walk. Concerned to keep her warm, Nadine first dressed her in a fuzzy coat and hat, then covered her with hand crocheted blankets and, the final touch against the elements, put on a tiny quilt with the mist-shedding side face up. Finally they would take off. Nadine puzzled over the way Emalie fussed after ten or fifteen minutes. She ran with the stroller; she sang. Finally she returned home. Remorse seized her as she picked up the sweaty baby with the red face. Sylvie smiled as she remembered Nadine saying she guessed it wasn't the Arctic. No harm was done to the relationship. They both looked forward to every chance they had together. Emalie began toddling and they were so cute, walking along hand in hand.

Sylvia had a sudden thought. She could still get a card sent to her mother in time for Mother's Day. If it went to her office it could be forwarded. Her 'retired' mother, seventy-four, had a strong bent toward continued success. Even now she was heavily involved in attending meetings, making contacts with people in the know, assessing profits to be earned and, *always* reminding anyone who would listen that she was "servicing people". Now and then she arranged to see Sylvia for a few hours. She grew bored quickly.

Sylvia tried to keep the conversation going on topics that might interest her mother. But inevitably their opposite outlooks would surface and clash. Sylvia knew that the amount of time they could spend together amicably was limited. Her mother realized it in the sense that she often said accusingly that she didn't know why Sylvia had to start fights. It was quite hopeless to straighten out.

CHAPTER NINE

Sylvia stood on the deck and breathed in deeply. Spring air was so fresh. She suddenly shivered and realized that the cold had penetrated her sweater and chilled her. She hurried back into the house and went directly to the coffee pot for a steaming refill. It was "high test" this morning and she wanted the caffeine boost. Filling the World's Best Mother mug from Nadine brought thoughts of Mother's Day – brought thoughts of her three grown children.

Cradling her mug, she walked over to the back kitchen door and looked through its window onto the porch. A line of muddy shoes and boots stood by the outer wall, but it was time for a season change. Soon they would be replaced with runners, and later with summer sandals and flip-flops. Would Nadine's be there, at least now and then? Sylvia was adjusted to the facts – a nest emptied of three children-turned-adults. But her heart was often touched by memories. She could see back to old times – shoes piled in a heap when the three kids were home.

She looked where Issa's air letter was tacked up. It had been too long since one had come. Issa was a great enthusiast of air letters – those neat single sheets of thin paper to write on, fold up, and address on the outside. She told her parents with a knowledgeable tone that air letters were the most secure way to write. They also had limited space. She didn't have the time to "write a book" as she had been accused of doing before she became a far-flung traveler. These days no one knew if or when news would arrive. Touching the letter where Issa had signed, Sylvia smiled to herself. Issa was sometimes one big question mark. It was 'Issa' now, never Isabel. She thought back to when the change came. Isabel had to ask her grade nine English teacher how it should be spelled – she wouldn't accept what her mom said – that one 's', Isa, would be pronounced eye-sa. She gave in to the teacher's suggestion of 'Issa' grudgingly since it agreed with her mother. She didn't want to talk about it.

Issa described herself as a free spirit. Sylvia had always thought that meant being an imaginative, small-town Anne of Green Gables. Now she was getting to know a different Isabel who was more of a literary Ernest Hemingway crossed with Amelia Earhart for adventure. Adventure. What was she doing right now? And where? It was anybody's guess where she was. She was traveling the world with no definite plan. She was probably finished with the Edinburgh, Scotland, theater job. Only when a letter with strange stamps came, would they learn where she was. They were glad for any news – news, at least, of where she had been and what she was doing when the letter was mailed. A variety of choices for the next stop would be mentioned, but Issa was considering, still deciding. Sylvia and Larry read Issa's air letters over and over until they memorized them. They tried not to read what was left unsaid "between the lines", knowing that there were deleted items like diseases and missing passports. It was just as well. Censored adventures were frightening enough – like a wild bus trip in Asia on mountain roads with washouts and drop-offs, hundreds of feet straight down. Or there might be the description of a freight boat ride in the eastern Mediterranean Sea, limping into port with a drunk captain, broken pumps, and the bilge water below-deck rising rapidly. Yes, the minimum of description that they got was enough. It was not that Issa was always in a dangerous place. Sometimes it was tame. She went on low budget tours, usually thrown together with some locals by enterprising friends. Or she made the arrangements, or decided to do her own thing. Though the letters were far apart, joy came with the news as each one arrived. Sylvia didn't let herself consider the alternative – to hear nothing.

Sylvia wandered into the front room. The graduation pictures of their three children looked out at her. She thought, *Now they are each looking out on the adult world. Mark, Isabel, and Nadine –*

each one of them is so different. Though Isabel has managed to train everyone else to say Issa, I'm glad she has quit correcting me, even if reluctantly, when I let Isabel slip out. She surely can allow me some room for error. Sylvia hoped that Issa's present theater work was working out well for her. Issa enjoyed expressing herself; enjoyed people. She was pleasant, unless rubbed the wrong way. As for goals, getting a bachelor's degree had never interested her. For over two years before she left home she had written and submitted many articles to magazines. She was often told she didn't have the depth of knowledge needed. Finally that first acceptance notice had arrived. What excitement there had been for the whole family!

When Issa had last written home, she was considering a couple of possibilities. She might stay put in the British Isles, traveling around for the summer. Theater work in Scotland filled the winter. Although her sightseeing wanderlust might be satisfied with Great Britain, she really wanted to travel through Europe. She might get temp wok, or she could do study art and literature. *She has such artsy, eclectic tastes,* Sylvia thought. *All I know is, it's past time for another letter. We should have had one by now – I keep trying to picture where she is. It's impossible not to wonder. Oh, the nagging thoughts – more honestly, worries – are the hardest part of being a mother. But a letter won't happen by fretting. Well, clearing physical clutter clears the brain.* She fidgeted around the kitchen, bringing order to her mind by picking up and putting away. There were a few dishes in the sink from last night.

Sylvia glanced out. It wasn't bad weather. The few gray clouds coming in might not bring rain. She would finish straightening in the house and maybe have time to get seeds in the ground if she hurried. Working outside would give her a pick up. Maybe it was a low-pressure system, after all, which was giving the day a dull feeling. When the dishes were washed and put away and the house was neat, she still had an hour before going in to the hardware store to work. They had given her an extra day this week. She liked the idea of soon having her own schedule for anything she arranged, like a couple of shopping forays that weren't rushed. Then she would focus on the creative writing that she already had going. Her mind turned to Lisa. She missed her and thought back over the years when

Lisa, Pete, and little Lorene had lived within a few minutes walk. Lisa had always considered the challenges in others' lives. People seemed drawn to her. They opened up and shared their experiences. When Lisa had set herself up with a laptop and started taking credit courses on line, she hadn't been sure of where it would lead. She only knew her hunger to learn and to help others had to be satisfied. This fueled a new career, and then the new role of foster parenting in their home.

CHAPTER TEN

Lisa and Pete's home Seattle

As Lisa gathered her things to leave the house, she smiled at her own eagerness, and thought of how much she loved her work in lay counseling. Years before, when she and Pete had moved to Granite Falls, Lorene was young, and she decided higher education had to wait. Time passed. Finally she began, out of curiosity, with an online class in relationship challenges. She'd had her own as a young person. As an adult she had been glad to help others by listening to them. Though she wanted to do some kind of counseling work, she didn't want to go for a master's degree. Learning the basic principles of dealing with human conflict whet her appetite. Searching online, she read of the fascinating work of the Justice Institute, and went to education sessions.

Lisa realized that there would be opportunities to work under the guidance of a professional if she had better qualifications. She took many classes, including studies in conflict resolution between teens and their parents, and among their peers. But the clincher came out of her own personal pain. Lorene, the daughter she and Pete raised with all the care they knew how to give, chose wrong companions and went down a wrong road. They didn't know what could have motivated such a shift. Lorene broke their hearts when she ran away from home. She gave not a word of her whereabouts – absolutely no contact. Finally she returned to the Seattle area. Lisa and Pete hoped for healing the relationship. Instead they got a shock when they met with her. Lorene's anger boiled out at them. Though Lisa had finished her preparation so that she could work under a social worker, she found it impossible to help her own daughter.

Lisa and Pete had begun a new undertaking in the last two years. First they became temporary foster parents to a one-year old child who was quickly given permanent placement. Then they had a teen come. It was difficult, at best, because the teen knew it was temporary. Resentment was obvious. They had been hoping to give the security of a real home to some young person. It didn't last. That girl left. They could deal with the fact that foster care meant they'd never have full legal adoption. Some teens were neither adopted nor returned to the natural parent. But this felt like a failure.

Soon Yolanda came. She had now been with them for a year and a half. She had survived experiences that had been going on without her mother's full knowledge. She had been removed from her mother's home by the court. A sexual predator was living near, an 'uncle', who had victimized her. She arrived at Pete and Lisa's both angry and withdrawn. This was not her first foster home. Disruptive behavior filled the first several months. Finally she started to sense and internalize the love she was being given. Since she was Latino, she had felt alienated and marked, believing that she couldn't find acceptance. Once she knew Pete and Lisa cared, she begged her supervisors to let her stay with them permanently. They concurred. Though two other children had stayed in their home, Yolanda had truly become like their own.

* * *

Jenny stood in her lobby, holding the mail. It was a large picture postcard of a Corvette. Her heart sank. Lennard. As much as she wanted him to tell her what would be going on in their lives, her stomach went into a knot. Afraid... afraid of what, she wasn't quite sure. She turned the card over.

"Hi, Things are going grete here. I sold the car, but not for as much as I hoped. The guy who bot it is from Warshington. Funy, huh? Come here to sel it to some locol. Wurked out good tho. He has a house in the countree to rent dirt cheap. We can move out there when I get back. It's about an houre north of Seattle. He said we can fix it. You can get anuther job out there easy. People have to eat. I'm caching the bus the day after tomorow. Be there on the weekend. Lennard."

The weekend? Today was Friday. Move? He just decides to up and move? Confused, she tried to get her thoughts together. *What's happening? What does Len have in mind? Of course. He wouldn't even ask me.* Poor Michael – just when he was enjoying going to Mary's home. That would end. He would have to change schools. At least it wasn't in the middle of the year, like other times they had shuffled around Seattle. He could get most of his school work done before they left. She walked up the stairs and entered the apartment. What would the house be like? A fixer-upper, was it. That could mean anything. So start packing. She should look on the bright side. Have a house in the country. Get away. She didn't like being in this cheap apartment, especially with that one creepy man always around. She had a couple of good neighbors that she would miss. People never seemed to keep in touch, once they said goodbye. She'd just have to start again. She looked at her watch. Michael would leave Mary's soon. She would phone after he was on the bus to let them know. She looked around. What furniture would they take? And then there were always the boxes of 'stuff'.

Jennifer held the phone and noticed her hands were trembling. "Yes, Mary. Is Michael gone? Don't say anything." Mary had answered on her cordless. She was in the yard chatting with Michael before he caught the bus. Jen waited while they said goodbye, then continued, "I just heard from my husband. He is coming back this weekend. Please don't say anything to Michael about this now. I'll tell him the news tonight. We will be moving. No, I don't know how soon, for sure. We only have to give two weeks notice here. Yes, Michael was really enjoying being there with you. No. It's too far. An hour away. I am sorry, too. It has worked out so well." She paused and swallowed hard. "Did you say you have some empty packing boxes? If we could. Len has a pickup. We'll come pick them up. No, no need for you to do that. We'll get them. Thanks. I'll let you know the timing when I find out. Yes, it has sure felt good – having

Michael there with you. It's been just great getting to know you. Funny, I remember how worried I was before I met you – worried about meeting you! Yes, it is laughable now. Michael is a good kid. You've cared about him; so it is no wonder he responds to you." Jen felt herself losing it. *I don't want to get emotional.* "Thanks so much for everything. Bye for now." Jenny had tears in her eyes as she laid down the phone. *Oh, how can I just up and say goodbye to this woman? She has become a friend so easily, so pleasant to be with, to talk to. How could this happen so fast? Just when something good comes about...*

Jenny lay in bed that night, feeling sick. Sick for Michael. He had taken the news well enough. He was happy they were going to live in the country. He was looking ahead; asked if there would be farm animals he could visit at a neighbor's place. *How I hope there will be some kids to play with, or some adults who are kind-hearted. What about animals or farms – are there any in the area? What will "living in the country" mean? Is it near a town? Will there be work I can do? A restaurant? Will Len really try to get a forty-hour a week job right away? One with fixed hours and a regular paycheck? What about transportation? If he drives his pickup, then how will I get to work out in the country?* There was a car he had brought home to use but it wasn't running right. In the city she didn't need a car. The bus would do. Anyway, Len never did want a second car for her – too expensive. It hadn't mattered until now. Even if there were buses out there, was there any work? Well, worrying wouldn't solve it tonight.

Jenny drifted in and out of a troubled sleep. She sank into dreaming. *Something is wrong. Mary lives in the country. It's so far, but I have to get there – there is something wrong with Michael. Walking as fast as I can. I've got to get to him right away. The rain is getting heavier. It's so cold. Got to run – keep running. Running. It's so far. So tired. Path is slick clay, slipping. Got to slow down. But I mustn't. Rain is turning to sleet. So cold. Long wet grass drooping over the path – awful, stringy grass wrapping on my legs. So tired – can hardly pick my feet up and put them down. So tired...steeper now. Sliding – oh! No! The edge of the path and I'm sliding – it's a drop-off…so far…Canyon – I can't see bottom; I'm sliding down – so deep. Grabbing branches – but I can't hold on. Michael… Falling… falling…I have to reach Michael.*

Moaning. I hear moaning. Jenny realized it was her own moaning and she dragged up from the dream-depth – grasping for consciousness, trying to clear her mind. Heart pounding and gasping for air, a frightening feeling of danger clung to her. She remembered running, needing to reach Michael. Shaking her groggy head, she got out of bed in the faint light and stumbled to Michael's door. He was breathing, sleeping. *Well, it was a dream.* Jen leaned on the hallway wall, then decided to go look out the window.

Dawn shone through clouds. The wind was blowing from the north-northwest, so maybe it was clearing up. She thought, *It's Saturday. Might as well get up. I've got to get moving. My first Saturday off in weeks. I can pack. It may be a nice day to be outside. There are already some breaks between the clouds. Oh, well, summer is ahead. After we are settled in the new place, we can enjoy the long warm days.* She let Michael sleep. He had lain awake last night with the excitement of moving. After she showered and dressed, she ate a piece of toast and a banana, and had her second cup of green tea with a little honey. She began in the kitchen, reaching up to top cupboards and into the depths under the counter. She filled a large garbage bag with empty containers she had saved for who-knew-what. All kinds of disposable plastic – margarine cartons, cottage cheese cartons, yogurt cartons – they just filled up the empty shelves. Someday she would have the money to shop until the cupboards were crammed full of food and could hold no more! There would be cans of olives, special spices a recipe called for, red salmon, pineapple, and more exotic fruit than that. Daydream. Maybe one day. But now the reality of the black garbage bag called her.

Jen grabbed newspaper to pad dishes and noticed it was yesterday's. A small item caught her eye. "Predator Near Schools", the headline read.

"Children reported a man asking them for directions after school, and then offering 'a ride home'. The man used a 'message from your mom' to coax one boy to get into the car. When the boy began to resist, and said no, the man pulled him by the arm, but he screamed, struggled, and got away. Each child was alone when approached. Students are advised to stay in groups. Parents are encouraged to increase supervision of their children. Police patrols have been increased. As noted by the addresses, these incidents were widely separated. Where this might happen in the future is anyone's guess."

Jenny's heart beat faster as she thought of Michael and how often he was alone. She was pretty sure that if anyone offered him a ride he would refuse. She must caution him not to even go up close to a car if someone called to him. She worried about him on the city buses, the way some people struck up conversations. *If someone talked to him about weird things, I think he would probably go tell the driver. Trouble is that by then he's heard whatever a twisted mind dredged up. Welcome to real life.* She had warned him that people, some people, weren't trustworthy. It was sad – no, it made her mad – that kids have ugly experiences. If only a child could simply enjoy being a child, could be free of fear. *We're moving to the country. Kids should be safer in the country. We have a fresh start.*

* * *

Tucked under a cozy afghan on the couch, Sylvia finally swallowed the last of her coffee and looked at her watch. Eight o'clock. She didn't want to waste her day off. Hurriedly she straightened the afghan and went to the bedroom to shower. While she dressed she planned the day. A walk was the first order of business. As she straightened the kitchen she ate two slices of toast.

Going outside she found that it had warmed up. She went down the stairs, paused, and thought of Lisa. They had often taken walks together. Today Sylvia would take the road. But they had often gone across the back of the property to the creek, or walked in the woods, sometimes all the way up the mountainside to the spring. Sylvia glanced toward the back acreage, and then toward the overgrown path across her driveway. It took off toward the old house next door. It had recently changed hands and was probably beyond fixing. Maybe had been bought for investment property.

She walked down the driveway. A low ridge along her left was covered with both mature and young trees. Typical of this rainy, west side of the Cascade Mountains, an undergrowth of wild shrubs, ferns and grass covered the earth beneath them. She noticed an abundance of flower buds on the large-leaved thimble berry bushes. There would be a good crop of raspberry-like fruit. Once out on the country road, she set out in earnest, walking briskly.

When she came back in the house, a pleasant emptiness hung in the air. *Ah, no obligations to fulfill. No work I have to do. I can work on writing the young teen book. I can just sit down and let it flow. This is such a pleasure – writing for this age group.* She had known she needed help with conversation and found herself listening as young people talked. Her characters were coming to life. Every one was developing individuality, with their own responses, their own desires. She had read when she studied writing that this would happen. It was a thrill to enter into what they were facing, experience it from their own points of view. Up until now Sylvia had a few children's mini-stories published, but only in magazines of limited circulation. She hadn't made much money, but seeing her name in the byline was a thrill. She thought, *Now I'm launching out into an extensive new territory – the book market. Regardless of the outcome, I love what I'm doing! Whether I make money writing or just paper a room with rejection slips, this is what I want to do!*

As she walked over to the sink, she thought of her desire to get back into music; even just playing the piano would be nice if she could find an old upright. *Everything in it's own good time,* she told herself, as she rinsed the plate from breakfast. Glancing up to the bulletin board, she saw her pretty notepad from Nadine, and on it was written, *Visit Grandma Jones.* She thought, *Ah, I will go this week. I get such a lift seeing her, and to think that I go expecting to cheer her up! That's a laugh!* She walked into the bedroom. The sheets could be changed later. For now she'd throw some other things in the washer. There were already clean sheets in the linen closet. She went to the hamper in the laundry room to sort a load. A giant package of toilet paper sat on it. She ripped open the plastic wrapper and stacked up several rolls on her arm. She took them into the bathroom and put the extra rolls in the cupboard. *Why? Why am I doing this now? It doesn't need to be done now!* She smiled as she rebuked herself. *Forget the laundry! Forget the toilet paper! Get to it, Girl! Take advantage of a clear mind to focus on the 'work in progress'. I allow my minutes be eaten away, and then I look at the clock and hours are gone.*

Sylvia determinedly walked over and sat down at the table. The loose-leaf binder had well-organized sections for Characters, Plot, Setting, Background, Incidents, Outline, Problems, Inserts; then the second half had numbered tabs for each chapter. She opened it to chapter five and started reading. Immediately her mind filled with a conversation she needed to get down on paper and she started writing. As soon as that was written, she developed the mood surrounding the scene. *Now,* she thought, *I also need to show reasons in an earlier chapter why the girl feels and thinks this way now. Where do I develop the steps? I don't know exactly where they will go. 'Inserts' – that's where. Later they will be ready to be moved into just the perfect places where they belong.*

CHAPTER ELEVEN

Saturday

Len called when he arrived in south Seattle on Saturday. He laughed at Jenny's request. "You want to give the landlord two weeks notice?" he said incredulously. "You're worried about *that*? *Forget* the two weeks notice. I need to get that truck the man is letting me borrow, and get the stuff moved out there. It will be some time toward the end of this coming week. The apartment's a cinch to rent right away. Stop worrying. You're always worrying." Jen's heart sank. She had been the one who found the apartment and had given her word regarding damage deposit and notice to be given. She felt trapped – she could do nothing to keep from breaking a promise. "Look," he continued, "I'm staying down here in south Seattle for two nights. Got another car to work on. I'll be up there Monday night. So don't look for me till then."

"Okay…" Click. She looked at the phone in her hand and slowly set it down.

* * *

The lingering, richness of wood-smoke from the fireplace reminded Sylvia of last night. It was nice to have Larry home again. She dusted while she remembered how Larry and she had gotten cozy in front of the fire. They talked of getting outdoors for more walks with the weather warming, and of hoping to see family, especially her dad, though his trips were usually in winter. Her mother would be busy, and would only make a short appearance. Isabel was away. Nadine, Mark and Marie, and little Emalie would visit often. While the firelight flickered, Larry and she had cuddled and chatted. Larry asked what was currently happening in her young teen book. She appreciated these times when he could be a sounding board. She told how the development of two of her characters was coming. One was difficult. He listened intently, asking questions and adding a few encouraging words as she described the ease of making one girl 'real' while the other still seemed shadowy. It was taking shape, but she hadn't worked consistently with her changeable schedule. Larry's interest and support had been vital. The passion was there; she loved writing. She had lacked confidence at first about this bold attempt to publish a book, but it grew, largely due to his steady reassurance. *He builds up my positive feelings. No. Not just positive feelings – feelings can be fleeting, though they're important. But when Larry listens to me and responds with his own calm thoughts, it helps me have an observer's eye on people and life. He has insights.* Another topic of importance had come up. Larry talked freely about his upcoming trip. Then he shared that there would be changes in his regional office by summer. He wasn't sure what they were. There was scuttlebutt going around that it might be major. He thought it best not to take it too seriously yet. Wait and see. As the flames turned to embers they had simply sat quietly and gazed into the fire. Soon they were sharing flirty looks, and kisses that became more amorous. She stroked his strong arms. He drew her close and caressed her.

* * *

"Let's go to the show, Michael!" He looked at his mother in surprise. It was Sunday night – school in the morning.
"Really?"
"There is a good one at 6:45." His face lit up as he saw that she really was serious. Jenny opened her purse, smiled with one eyebrow raised, and pulled out two chocolate bars. They slipped them into their jacket pockets, their 'contraband', and grabbed some

mints from a dish as they hurried to get out the door.

The phone rang. "Oh..." *What to do? Shall I go back and answer?...I'd better.* Jen picked it up, hoping it was a short call. "Yes? Brown residence."

"Yes...Hello. I was looking for a relative and I wondered if a Len Brown lives there?"

"Well...I would need to know who you are. I don't know if I should talk to you until..." Jen's thoughts failed her. *How do I explain that I have definite instructions not to give any information?*

After a pause the voice said, "I'm a relative of Len Brown. I don't want anything. I just want to get in touch, to talk with him. Please have him call me. The room number is 205."

Jen wrote down the phone number as she said, "Well... I doubt you will get a call from anyone on that little bit of information. Maybe if you'd tell me who you are...?" Her voice sounded pleading. She couldn't be guilty of letting an important call be lost for lack of her responding correctly. What if Len *did* want to talk to this person? "Can you tell me a little more?"

Again there was a pause and a long intake of breath. "I am a... relative of Lennard's... I haven't seen him for years. I just wanted to get in touch. My name is Sam. You know, like Sam in the Dr. Seuss book. That's who I was named for." He gave a chuckle that lacked humor. "That's it. Just Sam."

"Okay. I can tell my husband that." She quickly added, "I can see if he's the right person. I don't know...can't say. I hope he'll call you if...I will give him the message." They said goodbye and she hung up the phone. *Something strange about this. Why did he hesitate so much. It was like he was deciding how to say as little as possible...like he didn't know if he wanted to say who he was. Curious. Len had never mentioned a Sam; had never been willing to talk about his family. It was like they didn't exist. Who was this man, anyhow?*

* * *

Waiting in the ticket window line, Michael grinned at her conspiratorially. He stuck his hand in his jacket pocket, pushed the corner of the chocolate bar out and slid it back in. He jerked a pseudo-pistol – a pocket-covered finger – toward her, and mouthed, 'Hand it over, lady.' She joined his game – she was caught in the act of smuggling! Or was this a robbery? She rolled her eyes in mock fear. He looked stern. Then he mouthed, 'This is a holdup, lady. Hand it over!' She mouthed, 'They'll get you and lock you up!'

"Aw, lady, I was only joking," Michael said aloud in a repentant voice.

"I'm not," she grinned and jerked her head toward a sign telling patrons not to bring in food. She resented the prices the snack counter charged and felt no remorse at sneaking it in. The difficulty of unwrapping it quietly and savoring it in the dark theater was all part of the fun.

Two hours later as Jenny and Michael walked out of the comedy they were still laughing. Her sides ached. *What fun – we really needed that! A little break was good,* she thought. When they got home there was a message on the answer machine. "It's Len. Be packed. Let you know when I'm coming later." *Got to get this packing done, but not tonight,* Jen thought. Michael was in bed. She suddenly felt drained, and decided to wash up for bed and get some sleep.

In the morning Jen didn't start work until ten o'clock so she went back to wrapping dishes and putting them in a box. *Too bad I don't have that packing paper that keeps dishes clean. I'll not feel sorry for myself though. I am really very fortunate – a house, of all things. What a surprise to be going to a house! I hope we like it.*

Jenny was about to make a call when she saw the notepad by the phone. On it was the number of the man who called himself Sam. *Oh, dear. In all this packing, I must remember to give that to Lennard. I hope he'll take care of it.* She went ahead and phoned Bet, a girl she knew from high school days. It had been ages since she had talked to her old school mate. The apartment phone would soon be disconnected and she needed to let her know. The Oregon number rang and Bet's energetic "Hello" burst on the line like she was standing in the room.

"How are ya doing anyhow?" Bet asked. "What are you up to?"

"We are moving to the country. I'll give you my phone number after we get there. There may be a recording giving the new number, but maybe not. I knew you'd wonder what happened and didn't want you to hear 'disconnected' on a recording and wonder."

"Hey, I hope you like it there, like the new place. So I guess you're busy."

"I was already keeping busy with Michael and work. Now packing. And I had gotten back to writing."

"Neat! Are you still writing that moody poetry?"

"Well, I did write some short poems quite a while back, but not much any more. For the feeling-kind of things I just jot down my thoughts for myself. I am trying to work on little stories for children, mostly about animals. They aren't especially scientific. Tried to keep them interesting and yet have an educational element. Need to check some facts. I tried them out on Michael, but they're young for him. There's lots of interest in animals and the environment, but most parents have very little time to read to kids now. Maybe someday I could get them in a newspaper. If parents knew there was a regular column to share, they might do it. I'd also like to start writing for a bit older reader. Having Michael to bounce them off of helps."

"Good. Sounds good. You can do it. You always were smart."

That was too hard for Jen to respond to. "How about you?"

"I've been busy working at the drive-in and taking care of the kids. I'll be called to work at the cannery soon. Slim is away driving truck most of the time." They didn't talk long as Jen wanted to keep the phone bill low. She hung up, saying she'd call again. She had to get packing; at least tomorrow she had a day off.

There was a knock at the door, startling Jennifer. She opened it and saw Mary's cheerful face. "Come in! If you don't mind the packing mess. What a surprise. Oh, it's good to see you. Here, sit down and I'll make coffee." Mary gave Jen a hug before she realized what was happening. Her usual habit was to resist hugs, but she didn't resist Mary. As she gave her a second squeeze, tears came to her eyes.

"I guess this moving, everything new, is getting to me, Mary. I'm sorry for the tears." She turned to hide her face, and grabbed the coffee pot quickly.

"Yes, I agree. It took me by surprise, really hit me. To have just gotten to know you, to enjoy spending some time with each other, and then…" She left the sentence unfinished. Jen turned from the stove and saw the flowers in her hand. Pink carnations, white daisies, and yellow daffodils bobbed their heads together over the greenery.

"Do you have something to put these in?" Mary asked, as she held out the bouquet. I know it's a strange combination, but the daffodils looked so cheerful I couldn't pass them up."

"Oh, they are cheerful! You're right!"

"I'll finish packing these if that's okay," Mary said, pointing to the baking pans on the table.

"Oh, just set them over there if you would. I use them in the bottoms of boxes. Protects breakables. Though I am almost done with that stuff.

Jen found a tall glass that she hadn't packed yet and put the flowers in the center of the table. "How lovely. Something pretty was needed around here. Packing is an ugly business."

"Have you heard any more about the place you are going to?" Mary asked.

"No. Guess that mystery will be solved when I first see the place. I wish I could move you out there with me."

"I don't think John would go for that." Mary laughed. Jen leaned over the bouquet to sniff the freshness of the flowers, and get her mind off the goodbye.

"Do you think you will get another child before school is out?"

"Oh, I don't think so. The two I had already, Steven and Hannah, are doing better with each other since they've been playing with Michael. I may next fall. Do you think you'll be back down to the big city to do business, and maybe drop in for a visit?"

"Hard to say, but I doubt it. You know how it is." And Jen thought, *We've got to get off this subject. She doesn't know how little I have to say about anything I do. It's too much for me to think about – that I won't see her again.* After having coffee, Mary washed windows, saying she didn't feel bad taking up Jen's time if she could help as they visited. She had only two hours.

The rest of the day loomed ahead after Mary left. *I have to keep reminding myself that this country experience could be very good. I have to think of Michael. It's his first chance to live out of the city.*

Jen pulled the old trunk out of the closet and sat beside it on a pillow. This needed to go with her. The apartment was small; there hadn't been space enough to keep it accessible. In the back of the closet, out of sight, it had almost been forgotten. She thought how the house in the country would be bigger. Maybe it would have a spare room. She could keep the trunk out, and go through the things she hadn't seen in years. She lifted off the antique padlock that was never locked because there was no key. Lifting the hasp, she pushed up on the heavy lid and looked inside. On top was a turquoise plaid skirt she had made in high school. She had kept it because she loved the color. A fond smile played on her lips. She grew, and it hadn't fit any longer. She still took pleasure feasting her eyes on the striking turquoise and grays in the soft wool blend. *Beautiful. I enjoy it every time I see it. But maybe I keep it because I don't like letting go of the past.* She laid it on the floor, then folded back a thin blanket. A ring binder, old letters, a school report with a good grade, and some pictures lay jumbled together. She picked up a piece of paper that took her back years. On it was written a poem.

Alone

No one understands
No one cares...
But what do I know?
Maybe some do.
I don't feel it.

Why can't I be like others
Just enjoy life and friends.
Isolated instead by differences,
Kept in a world where all
I do, say, think, is judged
By an angry God.
How can I trust this kind of god?

I feel lost, lost in the middle
Hanging between this God and people.

Hurt, misunderstood, angry…
No one cares.
Judgmental people – judgmental god.

Her eyes dropped to the bottom, and she read *Jennifer, 15*

There was another poem when she was sixteen. With youthful dramatic flair, it was named "Soliloquy", and began with simple questions about life's meaning. Then it quickly rushed on, in passionate agonizing, to pain over not being loved. In it she was wondering if there might be a certain someone who could, hope against hope, love her. *I remember those desires, and the loneliness. The thrill of the handsome and kindhearted boy in my Literature class – the thrill of him talking to me after class. The longing inside.*
Jennifer remembered how she was riding high on that one conversation. Then, wonder of wonders, he sought her out at other times. He discussed his report on medieval poets with her. Later he looked at hers on British Isles romantic poets. *What sleepless nights I spent, stirred with romantic notions. Then it all came to an abrupt end when he gave a ring to a girl in his math class. How I cried. I lay in my bed alone, so very alone, night after night. Hot tears ran down my cheeks and onto my pillow. Finally, I would turn on a radio talk show so I'd have the babble to take my mind away from loss of what I wanted and couldn't have… I knew what I wanted – to be the girlfriend of that kindhearted fellow – and I was crushed to find out he wasn't thinking of me that way, ever. I condemned myself for my stupidity; how insensitive I was, unable to tune in on another person's motives, or lack of motive. To him it was just school work. I had been carried along by my own dreams, and hadn't picked up on what he was thinking. I didn't pick up on what anyone was thinking.*
Just then a picture slid out. She caught sight of… the edge of a face. Recognition made her heart lurch. The pounding in her chest hurt. She pulled out the picture of a youthful, almost boyish, face. Michael's father, Manuel. A flood of confused emotions swept over her. At first, shock – that he looked so young. He had seemed older then. Had he really been that young? Then anger rose up in her – *how could he deny his own child's life?* If he had been able, he would

have thrown away his own baby.

Even as Jen's heart hurt, a softness toward the boy-man filled her. *I did love him.* She held up the picture. *He was just a kid. Young and foolish.* And sympathy for his childishness came to her. But immediately it hardened against him again. *Selfish. You may have been young, but not that young. When I told you about the baby I saw your true colors. I saw how self-centered you were. To you, Number One was the* only *one who counted. That's what you were really like.* She shoved the picture under letters from Aunt Sally and closed the trunk lid, tears in her eyes.

CHAPTER TWELVE

"I need to get back into music!" Sylvia said aloud to herself, and then laughed. *Yes,* she thought, putting down the magazine article about the Vancouver Bach Choir. *I am going to* listen *to that longing! I have time now to enjoy things I've put off. I've loved singing. I'll join the new choir being formed in Snohomish. It's close. I can attend practices regularly.*

Her mind wandered to her preteens. She had been in a choir. Love of music hadn't kept her from feeling lonely. *I remember it well. I was a social oddity. Young people judge each other harshly. Now I see what happened. I was a nonconformist, unintentionally. Mother said I needed to 'fit into the society of which I was a part'. That was Mother's idea of success. Social climbing must have kept her life full when we arrived in Washington state. Fortunately, at eleven, it didn't involve me much. Not yet. I didn't know how good that time was – being allowed to pursue interests, like joining a book club. I wasn't very successful in Girl Scouts. I think it was colored by leadership from our area. But that choir – I can hear Mother insisting I go to the Hall and join the choir. No joy there. Not at first.*

Even though Sylvia had been told she had a good voice, and was eager to sing, she knew the other girls didn't accept her. They clearly had a sense of their superior status. She wondered what it was based on... sophistication? Their idea of interesting conversation centered around discussing any girl who was not in the group at the time. She knew she was too plain. She simply endured their shunning, whispering, and comments. She couldn't "talk the talk" of the "in" crowd. It seemed superficial. It was irritating. Luckily for her, a new choir leader came and the whole mood changed. He loved music and enjoyed teaching skills that brought improvement in the choir. Recognition was given for anyone who made an effort. Singing became of pleasure. He taught the skills of singing so choir members could develop their ability. Sylvia began singing with all her heart. Though she was still 'strange' by the other girls' standards, the pleasure of making music made up for it.

Sylvia smiled at how important acceptance had seemed to her at that time. Typical of youth. Another recollection came to mind. She saw the smiling faces of a neighbor couple. They invited her parents to their church shortly after the move from Canada. They were getting settled and her parents refused the invitation. A short time later the neighbors inquired if Sylvia could come to a week of children's meetings, Daily Vacation Bible School. She was allowed to go and had fit in easily, enjoying the class time, the group singing, and the kind-hearted people. After it was over, her parents had given permission for her to ride to Sunday School each week with the couple. She learned a lot of Bible stories and enjoyed the people there.

Sylvia's father was glad she had found a church home, but her mother hadn't been very enthused. Later her attendance became irregular, because her mother insisted she participate in "more significant" activities. Finally the schedule constraints caused church attendance to fall by the wayside completely. As Sylvia moved into her teens, she continued to appreciate simplicity, unmoved fancy houses and clothes. She found it a bother to go to parties for the sake of seeing and being seen. It became a burden to have to impress others. What her dad jokingly referred to as the 'upper crust', a term her mother disapproved of. She couldn't sort out this social business. 'Ordinary' people seemed nice enough. They could be kind. They were interested in others. She learned there were also very nice wealthy people. They were kind and caring, generously giving of their time and money, but doing it quietly. They even surprised her by speaking to her as though she mattered. She saw it wasn't money or lack of it that made people self-centered or kind. People were all different, individual. She was puzzled, not knowing what to expect, or how to make sense out of society's rules.

When piano lessons started, Sylvia had taken readily to playing. Her diligent practice pleased her mother, who considered piano playing another sign of refinement. Sylvia lost herself in the well-loved compositions she was taught. Instinctively she felt the intrinsic value of this beautiful music; it expressed her moods. She continued playing, after her required practice time was finished. Compliments she received when she sang and played gave her confidence during the socially challenging teen years. Bringing herself back to the present, Sylvia knew her next move was joining the choir in Snohomish.

Sylvia's heart was singing as she came in her door from the first choir meeting. She walked to the living room bookshelf and tucked in the music folder holding half a dozen songs. She would enjoy going over the selections they had been sight-reading. Each volunteer had been checked for range, and she had been put into the alto section. The camaraderie among all the women made her feel at ease. The choir was going to be fun and satisfying. Tomorrow she would look over the music with a cup of tea when she got home from work.

* * *

"Mother's Day – what a joy it is, having you here! Thank you, Marie!" Sylvia felt her heart being carried on spring breezes. "Let's walk out into the back field. The air is fresh with moist growing fragrances. Sylvia bent down to look into Emalie's eyes. That lasted a split second – Emalie laughed, pulled her hand away and ran a short distance.

"Baa'cup," she called out, and pointed.

Marie said, "Ah!" and turned to Sylvia, who had a puzzled expression. "I showed her a buttercup down along the ditch. She loved playing the 'do you like butter' game. After just one time holding the yellow flower under her chin and saying, "You like butter!", and she kept taking buttercups and holding them to my face. She was delighted. Such simple things children love."

"Building memories," Sylvia said. "That time is never lost."

"I have a feeling that they may not recall such an early incident."

"No, You're right. But that closeness, looking into each other's eyes, is a bond that's never lost." Marie slowly nodded her head in contemplation.

How thankful I am, Sylvia thought, *that our daughter-in-law is such a caring mother.*

Marie continued. "You said thanks for coming out. It's a pleasure for me, too, you know. Having family close means a lot to me. With my mom so far away, I appreciate even more being with you and Larry. I miss Mom. I would love to have her here to share this day with us. But it won't be that long. When she visits, I picture bringing her out here, to your place. She is planning to come in late summer. She'll love the spaciousness of the country. It will be fun to watch you two enjoying Emalie, and getting to know each other better."

As they strolled across the field, Emalie ran in front of them. Suddenly she darted in the forbidden direction of the canyon. Sylvia broke into a run. "She's headed for the drop-off into the creek." She started to say 'I'll get her', but saved her breath.

Emalie saw Grandma coming, squealed with delight, and ran away even faster. Sylvia and Marie were gaining on her. Just in time, Sylvia scooped her up in her arms. Trying to sound gruff, she said, "No, you can't run over there!" She pointed to the drop-off as she stood with Emalie at the edge. Hugging her, she pointed down. "See! It's owie! You might fall. Hurt yourself!" Then she kissed her. Emalie wiggled. "Owie, owie, owie!" she babbled and laughed.

* * *

Jennifer closed the last box, grabbed a marker, and wrote "Thoughts. Jen's box." She set it on the stack outside her door, turned, and looked in at the clean, empty apartment. Locking the door for the last time, she took a piece of scratch paper out of her purse and wrote a note to 'Aunt' Peg. 'So-long – leaving for the country. Thanks for everything you've done. Especially being there for Michael. Goodbye, Jenny.' Peg lived in the next apartment. *I can call and thank her again when I get the phone hooked up. Too bad she isn't home, but I guess I said my goodbyes yesterday. I'll miss her. At least I felt I had some support with her next door – especially for Michael in case of emergency... I felt safe. Now what? It's hard to leave a good job, leave the known. Oh, well, I guess life moves on – 'What will be, will be.'*

PART TWO
FRIENDS

May – June

CHAPTER THIRTEEN

"Lisa, I'm still looking forward to that visit you're going to make out here!" Sylvie stretched out on the couch with the phone.

"Yes, it's on the top of my list. I had to work extra lately."

"I hope you're not doing too much."

"No. I've had to push myself to keep up, and I let stuff at home get behind." She laughed. "How was your Mother's Day?"

"Really, really nice. We had Nadine, Mark, Marie, and Emalie out here. We went to a restaurant, and then had the whole day to visit. They stayed late. It was a wonderful day. How about you?"

"Phil had taken Yolanda to shop for my favorite body spray. She was excited to watch me open it. We ate out and then went down to the waterfront, in and out of shops, The Old Curiosity Shop, naturally. We were hungry again. We ate salmon outdoors from that neat place that the native people have run for years. Watched the gulls and took pictures. Was a really special day!"

Sylvia felt instant sympathy over the unspoken pain of no contact with their natural daughter, Lorene. "So you are doing extra work lately?"

"Yes. But I'm trying not to get burdened by the full schedule.

I had to put my foot down. That's hard in this work. People have problems, but Nora, the counselor, and I can only see them one set at a time. Can't be helped. I've learned that, although I want to give it my all, I must be careful not to burn out. When I leave work, I try to leave the problems behind me. On tough days I have a hot bath when I come home! Then I can be there for Yolanda. She likes to talk. Phil and I enjoy our time together, of course, and we also have a good time with the home Bible study group. Even when I'm tired we go. I am always glad when I get there. I relax. It's a very caring group. We pray for each other. Oh! We got to spend a little time in the book of Ruth!" Sylvie smiled. Even on the phone, Lisa was enthusiastic. "We were in a study on the time period of the judges. The teacher tied in Ruth, since it happened at the same time. I love the life story of Ruth. Now I have some notes. We should look at them together!"

"That's a good idea. We haven't done that for ages. Remember all the questions I had when we started Bible study together? We always said we'd get back to looking up some of those answers. I know you had to move, but I've sure missed you, missed getting together."

"Yes, it's been harder to spend time together than we thought when I left. I'm so glad to hear you'll be working less. I am only off on Sundays and Tuesdays these next two weeks, but the third week I also have Wednesday, a Murphy day. Can we plan for that?"

"Oh, yes. I'm so glad we're going to make it happen. I'll mark that Wednesday on the calendar. Bring your notes on Ruth. I want to find out more about her. You told me a little already."

"Yes, it is a great story of a courageous, caring woman. I love to think of how she, a Moabite, and a young widow herself, decided to move to Israel so she could continue being with her widowed mother-in-law, Naomi. All the while knowing she'd not be accepted by most of the people."

Sylvie remembered their previous conversation and how Ruth said something like, 'Don't tell me to leave you... where you go, I'll go, and where you live, I'll live. Your people will be my people, and your God will be my God.' Such a declaration of loyalty.

Lisa continued. "I'm glad you like Ruth. I do, too. There she is, going to a land and culture she doesn't know, and neither woman has any resources. There was no farm to go back to. There were no brothers to watch out for them. It was just the two of them, alone. She might have had second thoughts, but that's not indicated one time. She knew she would be treated like foreigners often are – looked down on, not wanted. Still she goes. Naomi must have done something right during the hardships in Moab, and Ruth has been watching. Ruth was raised in idol worship. Now she has begun to trust in Yahweh, God, the Creator. Though it's all so new, Ruth believes He is *the* God. She commits herself to faith in Him."

"And what faith that would take," Sylvie responded. "To trust in an unseen God, and then to act on it, following Naomi. In those days, especially – two women alone. Imagine, no social safety net. It will be interesting to get into the whole story. I enjoyed those studies on Romans that we did together. I sure had a lot of questions, eh?"

"Questions make good discussion, don't they?" Lisa chuckled. "I treasured the times we spent together. I miss the country. That's okay, though. Pete likes his job and we are enjoying the church here. We're getting to know people, even though the church is big. This midweek study group in a home is where we make close friends – it's our fellowship, and our social outlet. Discussing anything, all of us letting our hair down and sharing what's on our minds. It's been good."

She certainly sounded happy and Sylvia recalled how it had taken a while for her and Pete to find the right church. She felt a little jealous. It would be good to spend some face-to-face time with Lisa soon.

Sylvia headed out the door for a walk by the creek. Just as she reached the back gate she heard a truck and caught a glimpse through the trees. *A moving truck! The new neighbors are coming. They surely can use help. What a good chance to meet them!* She quickly came back and took the path to the neighboring driveway. Standing to one side, she waited as the truck passed and parked alongside the house. Then she stepped out of the knee-high brush and crossed the drive.

"Hello!" Sylvia called, seeing the passenger door open. "Welcome to the neighborhood!" A woman about thirty jumped out. Her brown hair was bobbed and pulled into side clips, but the back flipped around, red highlights gleaming in the sun. She smiled back at Sylvia shyly. A boy about nine hopped out and came up beside her.

"Hello," came out double, as the woman and boy spoke simultaneously, then smiled broadly at each other. They were amused at their own fleeting duet and Sylvia became an onlooker of the shared moment. *Ah, I like them – they'll be good neighbors!* she mused as they came toward her.

"My name is Sylvia." She held out her hand.

"Hi! My name is Jenny, and this is my son, Michael. He's ten." Jenny stepped forward and shook hands, and then Michael did the same.

"I'm very pleased to meet you! Did you come far?"

"No," Jenny smiled, "just from Seattle."

"I hope you will enjoy country living! Do you expect it will be a big adjustment? "

"Well, I suppose it may be for me, though I like the idea very much. Michael, especially, is looking forward to life in the country! We were in an apartment in Seattle."

Sylvia sensed openness, and was just ready to ask how she could help, but a man with bold red hair walked around to the back of the truck. She said, "Hello."

"Okay, let's get going. You know I need to get this truck back." He only scowled at Sylvia, with not a word, or even a nod of acknowledgment.

I guess he figures I am a bother, she thought. *He's overtired, that's all. Well, I am needed. I can see Jen needs a little support. I'm here to stay and help.* "Hello," she tried addressing the man a second time, with a slightly bolder tone of voice.

A muffled "Hello" came from his turned back, as he lifted the lock on the back door of the truck and opened it.

Sylvia wondered how to react to him. *Should I pursue introducing myself? Oh, just skip it. Leave him be.* She shook her head. *He has a lot on his mind.* She looked at Jenny who dropped her head with an embarrassed look and remained silent.

"Do you need any cleaning supplies?" Sylvia asked, and thought to herself, *There'll be lots to do in* that *house, I'm guessing.*

"No, thanks. I have mine in a box behind the front seat, and the mop and broom are in here, at the back."

"Okay, but if you're short of rags or something in the coming days, just ask. Now, what can I help carry – that is if you want help!"

"Yes. That's really nice of you." Jenny turned and said softly, "Len, may I have the house key so I can see where things will go?"

He grunted, pulled out the keys, and tossed them as he hopped up in the truck. Jenny caught them, then reached in for the broom and mop. Her lips were pressed together in a straight line.

"I live over there," Sylvia pointed north, "through the trees. It will be handy. I can lend you things you can't find for a while. You know – like a pan that is large enough, or pillow cases because yours are layered between the breakables in some box that's at the bottom of the stack. I bet you're eager to get in and get settled!"

Jenny nodded slowly as she felt questions rise in her mind. *What an unusual offer. She's so helpful.* She smiled, her eyes filled with appreciation. "Thank you. That is really nice of you, Sylvia. I may need to borrow for a couple of days."

"Call me Sylvie, if you want."

"Okay. I started out as Jennifer. No one calls me that any more. Now just Jen or Jenny works."

"I do like Jennifer, so I might slip sometimes and call you that."

"Oh, that's fine." Jen turned and stared at the large weather-beaten structure with a serious expression. Her heart sank. There was not a shred of beauty. But the practical concern of the livability was more important. "I am almost afraid to look inside. I haven't seen it yet, and the owner told Len it was a "fixer-upper". Are you willing to take a look through it with me?"

"Sure, if you want."

Jen leaned into the cab of the truck and pulled out a box of cleaning supplies. She passed it to Sylvia, then grabbed another box. She led the way up the short path. Michael came last with a mop and broom, and a large bag of rags.

"Careful," Jen said, approaching the single step before the small front porch. "It looks rotten." She tested the step. Her foot went through a disintegrating board. She shook her head and stepped over it. The porch slanted like an old boat dock. Holding out the key, she mused, "I've never seen a key like this."

"Oh, it's one of the "basic five" skeleton keys used...long ago. They were sold at hardware stores, but I haven't seen one for ages." Jen nodded.

They walked into the cold living room. It stretched to their right, across the whole front of the house, gaping, barn-like, looking down toward the road. Straight ahead, at the back of the house, a narrow archway opened into the kitchen. In the wall at the right were stairs going up, then two open doors. Stairs led down to a basement and next was a bathroom. The old farmhouses had strange floor plans - a bathroom directly off of a front room?

The three of them stood there for a minute. No one spoke. Sylvia hadn't been in the house for many years. The last tenants had been completely unsociable. After that it had stood vacant, boarded up due to damage that they had done. The owner was disheartened and sold. The house cried out, 'lack of care'. Sawdust and dry mud were on the floor. It had a cavernous feeling, exaggerated by dirty windows that barely let in light. Sylvia wondered about the kitchen. What was it like – that room so important to a woman? As if mirroring her thoughts, Jenny said, "Well, let's take a look at the kitchen."

They walked through the narrow archway into a long narrow room. The outside wall to the left held an old porcelain single sink, rust-stained, with large, chipped-off black areas. The short counter to the right of the sink was covered with gray linoleum that had suffered deep cuts. It was only five feet long. A gap yawned between it and a narrow three-burner range that stood alone. It seemed strange that anyone put in an apartment-sized stove when there was enough space for a large one. There was no other counter. Jenny's heart sank. Her silence was notable. Against the right wall a small table stood beside an old fridge. Dirt seemed to be ground into the wooden surface of the square table.

Sylvia looked closer, and said, "I think these circular stains were made from watering pots of plants." The weathering had probably come from being used outdoors. Sylvia wondered if Jenny would need a vehicle to take things to the dump, but she didn't dare bring up the dump right now. Instead she asked, "Do you like plants?"

"Oh, yes. I gave away a couple instead of trying to move them. Just as easy to start some again. Sylvia held back the urge to open the fridge to see if it worked. Surely it did. Anyway, it was not her house.

Jenny set the box down on the counter. "I have a kitchen table. It could go there, at the end of the room, under the window." She pointed to the far wall, and then turned back to the sink. "At least there are windows on both walls. I especially like this window over the sink counter, so I can look outside as I work." She stretched and looked tentatively onto the driveway and the bushes and trees across it. As she did, her face relaxed into a gentle smile.

She has courage, Sylvia thought, reflecting on the big picture, as she called it. She stepped forward and peered out. "You can look over toward my house." She pointed, and spoke in a more cheerful tone of voice than she felt. "Though you can't see it through the trees, it's not far. My kitchen sink faces this direction and has a window, too. We can think of each other as we wash our dishes." Seeing Jen's smile, she thought, *She's tentative, and yet she's brave.*

"That's a nice thought." Jenny said, but turned back to the room. She looked down at the floor, tracked up with dirt and sawdust, and said, "It could certainly be cleaner, but it hasn't been lived in for a long while, I suspect. Apparently men have been doing carpentry somewhere." she mused.

The three of them went back through the living room and out to the truck. After bringing in more boxes marked 'kitchen', Michael said, "This is marked 'M's bedroom'. I'll go up and check out my room."

The two women walked to the back of the long kitchen and hesitated where Jen had said the table would be. To the right was a door. As Jen turned the knob, she wondered aloud, "What's in here? Be nice if there is an outside door." They stepped into a dark, low-ceilinged area that had open studs for walls and no insulation. Jen tried a light switch, and one dim bulb came on, dangling from its wiring. Cobwebs hung about. The floor seemed to be just dirt.

"It may have once been a lean-to woodshed, and was enclosed later," Sylvia said. She considered other possibilities. Cardboard boxes were everywhere. Some were stacked. Some were coming apart, spilling out dirt-caked canning jars or newspapers gathering dust over the years. Peering into the darkness, the women detected shelves along the far wall. All kinds of junk was on every shelf, on the floor, stacked around.

"Michael will want to explore all this. I wonder if it's safe. Don't tetanus germs live in dirt?"

"Yes. But I guess barnyards are a more likely spot, or stepping on a nail. In here it's papers and jars, more than anything. I don't know about rusty tools."

They turned and noticed a door to the outside just as Michael reappeared. He tried the door, after slipping a bolt lock. "Look! Look at the big back yard!" It was over-grown with blackberry vines that even reached up to choke two old apple trees with a few blooms.

"Can I go look around out there, Mom?" Michael pleaded. "Please?"

"Sure, for a little while. But we should unpack."

"I will. I just want to see this first! Oh, there are new steps." He hopped down to the ground, and then cautiously walked along the path, stepping over the brambles that blocked his way. An old shed had moss growing on its shingled roof, and was succumbing to an overgrowth of blackberry vines. Michael opened the door without much strain. "It's empty," he called in a disappointed voice.

"Probably won't fall in on him," Jenny shook her head. "At least not for a while." The two women gave a last look at the mess inside. "I guess could be flattered with the name, storage," Jen said. "But I won't bother dealing with it. There is a lot of extra space inside." They turned back into the kitchen.

"Would you like me to wash out the fridge and wipe down the cupboards? Get the shelves ready so you can put your dishes in place? I'll sweep first."

"That sounds like a good plan. But I want to go see the rest of the place first. You want to come, too?"

Sylvia hesitated. *I hope she doesn't get embarrassed, the way things are. It's interesting that, thought she is young, she seems older, for whatever reason.* "Sure, I'll come," she said simply.

They went downstairs first. To the right, a laundry area led under the front of the house. The clothes dryer was vintage, and had two heat settings, high and low, or maybe scorching and cold. The washer, set apart from it, looked a little newer. An ancient, wood-burning furnace stood like a black octopus with ductwork stretched out from its body. In the shadowy recesses under the living room floor, clotheslines dangled their stained wood pins from the floor joists. Thick cobwebs hung everywhere, keeping the women at bay. They backed out and returned to the foot of the stairs.

Jen opened a door on the left to a refreshing contrast. A clean, usable room with cement floor, and walls recently covered with plasterboard invited them in.

"My, this house has all kinds of room." Jenny said, with a touch of awe. "I'm used to an apartment. Second-hand furniture will help fill it, but then, who wants a place all cluttered. This room could have a couch or extra bed and a chair. Be a retreat."

They proceeded to the last basement door and peeked in. There was only a dirt-floor. Old canning jars spilled out of two broken cardboard boxes. The room was basically empty.

"This was a cellar, I think," said Sylvie. "Cool, but protected, to store vegetables in winter. Well, I should get to those kitchen cupboards." Sylvia turned toward the stairs.

"There is still the upper floor," Jen said. I'm going up to see the bedrooms. Do come with me."

At the top of the second floor stairs was a landing. Doors opened three ways. A small bedroom straight ahead looked over the back yard. A large bedroom to the right was over part of the living room. A small room on the left caught their attention. It had one tall window.

Jenny walked over to it, wondering aloud, "Maybe this window faces your house. Yes! I can see the top of your roof!" She beckoned to Sylvia. "Come look!" As Jenny gazed out the window, she took a deep breath and thought, *I have a neighbor, a woman.* She turned quickly to leave, saying, "I'm glad there is someone next door, but I guess I'd better get busy." At the doorway she looked back and thought, *I might curl up in a chair and write in a journal again. I might even write poems or something else that could be published!* But that was her secret. She paused on the landing. "The larger room to the southwest will be ours. The middle room will be a good one for Michael. I bet he's already picked it, and put his boxes in the

119

closet. Nice for a boy, with that window facing toward the woods in back. A place to look out and dream."

Sylvia thought of the city boy delighting himself in all the open space. "Behind us is an open pasture that Michael is welcome to play in. There is a gate beside our garage. One thing, though. There is a creek and right now it's full from spring rains. I think at his age he'd be safe enough if he's cautious, but you may want to take a look at it before you let him go there on his own. There is a path down the steep bank, but you have to pick your way down. He'd be okay unless he slipped at the top, fell, and hit his head. I don't mean to scare you."

"Oh, I appreciate the warning. I'll check it out with him before he goes alone. He's good about not taking chances, but this is a whole new world for him. A little more "in the rough" as the golfers say." Jen got a dreamy look. "Michael's going to enjoy it here very much. He loves the outdoors. So do I."

"Ah," Sylvia said. "We have something in common there. We'll have to take a walk and I'll show you my favorite spot. It takes longer than going to the large creek. You cross over that, walking on two large logs, and hike up the small mountain. A lovely little creek flows down through the woods. It takes a while to get to where there's a beautiful natural clearing. A spring bubbles out of the mountain there, and forms a small pool. That glade is so moist that the bright green moss is this thick on the nearby trees." She spread out her fingers, and smiled at the memory. "If you approach quietly, especially at sunset, you will see deer. For sure you'll hear the little frogs this time of year. They make a tremendous choir for their size."

"Ah...it sounds lovely. And frogs – I've gotten kind of attached to frogs since Michael found one at the city park. First he crept around to learn its hiding places. On later visits it would be sitting out on a rock, like it was waiting for him."

"That's neat – seeing them enjoy a new experience. I know how a mom gets involved because of her kids. Mine loved showing me frogs they caught. In spring they would find the eggs in their jelly-like blobs and watch the wee balls change, getting eyes and tails, until the day when they hatched into polliwogs. They kept some in jars, watching, fascinated, as they grew little legs. Then letting them go so they'd live. Even now I think of the kids when I hear their chorus."

"Yeah, kids." Jen looked wistful, but saw that Sylvia wondered why. She quickly said, "When I get time, I'd like to go with you to that place up the mountain."

"Right. It makes me think of my grandmother who loved natural beauty. Say...remind me and I'll tell you later about her. I mustn't take time now. And as far as walks go, we can take a shorter walk first, when you need a break from unpacking. Just to the large creek. Then, when you are getting to the end of the boxes we'll do the long hike up in the hills to the spring!"

Jen stopped at the bottom of the stairs. "When I'm getting brain-dead I'll remember that." She looked at the stack of boxes. "You know how it is; after a while you look at the thing you just took out of a box and you can't think. You don't know if you want it, or you should repack it, or, better yet, give it to the thrift store."

"Oh, there is another thing. I can take you to the thrift stores. We'll go to the town of Snohomish. We can go at lunchtime and eat by the river. I love watching the deep waters of the Snohomish River moving along powerfully, with only a few miles to go before they reach the salt water. Seagulls wheel and cry overhead."

"Oh? Does this creek here flow into it?"

"No, it empties into another river a few miles north of Everett and Marysville – the Stillaguamish."

"Wow, that's a name and a half." Jen attempted pronouncing the long name. They laughed when she put too long an oo in the gu part. "I'll work on that one! So we can find more shopping in Snohomish than here?"

"Yes. It's not a city, like Everett. But I think you'll like it. You might find something for the house. Then there's alway books!"

Jen laughed out loud as they went into the kitchen. "I will have to be careful there. My favorite second-hand item – books! I could become a book store owner or a collector. I even buy one I don't intend to read right away, but I keep it there on a shelf, beckoning to me. And I do get around to reading it eventually. I donate them back when I get too many!" They went into the kitchen.

"Me, too. Maybe I can lend you some I have already. You can

take a look. Well, here I am, just talking," Sylvia said, taking a bucket and a cloth out of the box of cleaning supplies. "I need to get busy. Get to cleaning these cupboards and not distract you anymore. If you need me to do something somewhere else, just say so."

"Thanks." Jenny looked up and saw Len carrying in a box.

"What in the world have you been doing? Nothing is getting done." He cursed. "Get busy." He dropped the box down loudly for emphasis.

"Yes, sorry. Of course," Jenny said timidly. Sylvia, feeling like a heel for wasting Jen's time, took the bucket of sudsy water, stepped up on a chair and stuck her head and arms in a cupboard.

Jen asked, "Do you need help with the couch and chair?"

"Of course. What do you think?" Len turned abruptly. Jenny followed.

CHAPTER FOURTEEN

Sylvia put the clothes on top of the washer and made up her mind. *I'm sure Jenny needs to get out of the house to clear her thoughts; too many boxes can make one stir-crazy.* She peered around at the kitchen clock and wondered if it was too early. A phone call wouldn't be invasive. Good thing that Jenny and Len had gotten their phone hooked up right away.

"Hi, Jenny. Sylvia here. Are you able to get away for a walk? I would like to take you to the pasture and creek behind us, or maybe along our road so you can take a look at your neighborhood."

"Oh, I don't really have time. There are so many boxes everywhere. We are still tripping over them. I do need to borrow a dustpan, though. I broke my plastic one, banging it on the garbage can."

"Sure! I have an extra."

"Oh, dear!"

"What? What is it?"

"Oh, I just saw a phone number of some man, scribbled among other messages. I'm sure Len didn't really see, or was too busy to let it register. I need to remind him to call tonight. Sorry! Where were we? Oh, the dustpan!"

"Why don't you come over here to get it, and I can show you my place. Once you've been here, you can't be a stranger at my house. You'll feel "at home" and want to come back!"

"Oh, thank-you. As for making a person feel at home, I can imagine you would do that. Thanks so much for the help cleaning. I appreciate all the hard work you did. Sorry I can't be sociable until later. I'll come get the dustpan and stay for just a minute." Sylvia hung up the phone, glad that at least Jenny could take a break.

A knock came, rat-a-tat-tat-Tat. The kitchen door stood open, and the porch door was ajar. "Welcome!" she called. "Come in! Actually, wait a minute." She hurried out where Jen stood, and gestured. "I want, first, to brag on Larry. He built this deck! He did it last summer. It's our 'relaxing room' in nice weather – bounded by the whole outdoors. Or rather unbounded. We lean back and put our feet up, and let our troubles shrink to a manageable size as we look at the tall trees and the hillside behind us."

Jen could see the happiness in her eyes, and thought what a pleasure it would be to unwind here. "Wow, Larry built this deck, eh?"

"Yup! Say, I hear that "eh"! You have some Canadian influence from somewhere!"

"Oh, not much. Just picked it up from a cousin who had lived there," Jenny said.

"I have a cousin there. He and his wife are in British Columbia, in the Lower Mainland. I'm overdue to go see them."

"Oh. What's the Lower Mainland?"

"The Vancouver urban area and the cities around it. The lower part of the Fraser River Valley. I can drive to their place in two and a half hours."

"I've never been," Jen replied, as she continued looking at Larry's enterprise. She spotted a long window box sitting on the deck, empty. "Where will that go?"

"Down at that end on the rail. Larry wants to anchor it securely before I fill it. I hope he gets to it soon. But let's go inside." She turned and held the screen door open. "Go on through this porch. It's a catch-all. Handy, but it gets cluttered quickly. I was sorting through this box of summer sandals and tennis shoes." Sylvia shoved it with her foot.

Stepping into the kitchen, Jenny looked around. There was a relaxed, cheerful atmosphere. The sunny colors of the wallpaper caught her attention. *Those yellow and peachy colors would warm a dull day,* she thought. *And with only the one window over the sink it could be gloomy without that brightening effect.* She followed

Sylvia into the living room with its large window that showed the expanse of the front yard.

"Oh, what a sweeping view!" Jenny gasped.

"I do enjoy that – looking out on the stretch of land across the road. I'm glad our house sits high on the property. Yours does, too."

"Yes. But trees are blocking the view. It's nice to see across that farm field, but it's your *yard* that is really something." Jenny stepped closer to the window. "The flower beds, the lawn rolling down to the road, so thick – like a carpet. Then, along the ditch, the tall grass. It's so... so country. What are those big bushes that are growing here and there, all the way to the road?"

"Rhododendrons. They have large blooms. They are just starting to show color on the buds, and will open soon. There are two peach-colored azaleas also, here in this bed near the house – these small ones with a more open, Oriental look. The largest rhodies will have huge pink blossoms. They are the old faithful ones. The newer varieties, closer to the road, come in many more colors – purple, cream, apricot, deep red. They are the most recent to be planted. We started with the standard pinks. Then we bought two more each year. But I'm ahead of what really took place – we spent the first couple years just getting a real yard. When we came it was more like a gravel pit in places and rough pasture in others. Several piles of trash were covered with tall grass. All the ground was uneven, with mounds and holes that made it hard to walk."

"What a lot of work!" Jenny stretched close to the window to look out better. "Oh, I see a bit of peach on the buds of these close ones. And pink bud tips farther on. I can't wait to see them completely opened up!" *It looks like a park.* Jen felt overwhelmed at the thought of the hours of back-breaking work. *These people have lived here long enough to put in new flowering shrubs year after year, ever since their grown children were little. Long enough to care for the shrubs and bring them to maturity. To think that, as a child, we never had a garden. Too much moving I guess. Ah, to stay in the same place...*

"Would you like a cup of tea or coffee? Oh, have you found your kitchen things, like your favorite mugs, or a teapot?

"Yes, I mean, No." She turned from the front room window.

"Ah... yes, I found the basic mugs, but I can't take time to sit down now. Sometime, though. I need to get back. Everything is still kind of upside down. In my head, especially." She laughed. "With Michael in school I can get a lot accomplished."

As Sylvia wished her success with the unpacking, Jen walked through the kitchen to the back door. Putting her hand on the knob, she falteringly said, "Ah... I think... if I could... I need to borrow a dustpan. If it's not too much trouble." *How embarrassing,* she thought.

"Oh! I am so sorry! That is what you came for! Of course. I'll get it." Sylvia returned, saying, "Keep it as long as you like. In fact, keep it period. I have two."

"Oh, no. I'll return it. Thanks very much." Sylvia went with her to the outer door, saying a walk would be nice any time she wanted a break.

Outside, Jen craned her neck as she left the steps. She hoped to see the whole house but she was too close. Not wanting to be obvious by walking out into the back lawn, she continued across the driveway, thinking, *I do want to take a mental picture of it. I want to be able to picture Sylvia here in her house.* She glanced back once more as she pushed through the damp bushes that hung in the path. Coming out onto her own driveway, her eyes went to the broken porch step. *What an eyesore. What a run-down house and even the yard shows total neglect. I feel embarrassed to think of anyone coming here.*

Jen walked up the drive and went behind the house. Someone had left boards scattered there, and she flipped over a few of them, knocking off bugs. She found one wide enough for the front step, but it would be too long. She dragged it to the front yard and laid it over the step that was rotted out. It hung over at both ends, but it would be safer than having a large hole that would twist an ankle or trip someone. She stood up and looked at the house. *I should stop complaining. To think – I have a* house *to live in! Sylvia has an old house, too, and she doesn't mind. Of course, there's no comparison. A lot has been done to hers. I wonder if our landlord will pay for more repairs? Like a new porch!* She looked at the lower part of the two small posts that held the little roof. The bottoms of them were rotten. *Maybe he'll consider doing it. He did have the back threshold fixed before we came...*

Larry looked out the back door, wondering where Sylvie had gone. *I'll bet she is over saying hello to the new neighbor.* He crossed the drive and heard voices as he came along the path. He called, "Hello!".

"Hello, Larry!" Sylvia answered.

He came out of the bushes and paused, smiled at the young woman with Sylvia and said, "Hello."

"Jen, this is my husband, Larry. Jennifer Brown, our new neighbor."

Jen nodded. "Hello."

"Glad to meet you, Jennifer," Larry held out his hand, but noticed her hesitation to take it. "I'm glad you'll be living next door." Jen nodded again. "I know my wife is happy to have another woman to visit with – she told me so! I hope you enjoy the area."

"I *am* glad to be out of the city. I guess this area is changing fast. I imagine there is a lot of land speculation for development."

"Yes. But we aren't going to let that change our minds. We didn't buy in order to speculate. We'll pretend the land is still a couple hundred dollars an acre like it was when we married."

"It must have been only farms then. Did you just want some 'space', rather than land to farm?"

"Yes. We talked during the first few years of marriage, how we would like to move out to an area like this. We wanted to raise our kids in a rural setting. You know – having a horse to ride, joining a Four H Club." He paused and shook his head. "Seems like a long time ago now. Have you been living in the city long?"

"Yes, pretty well all my life. I've visited in the country and I loved it."

Sylvia spoke up. "Talking about the country reminds me of Michael. I wonder where he is? I'd like Larry to meet him." Just then she caught sight of a movement and looked up. Michael was waving from the second floor window in the spare room. "There he is!" she said as she waved back. He disappeared from the window and soon was running up to them. He stopped beside his mother and looked at Larry.

Larry didn't wait for an introduction. He stepped forward and held out his hand, saying, "Hello, young man. I am happy to meet you – Michael, I believe!"

Michael's face showed the surprise of a child receiving an unexpected honor. He shook hands and responded, "You must be Mr. Ford. It's very nice to meet you." He felt older, special, at being called a young man. "Your wife is a good neighbor. She helped my mom."

Larry chuckled. "Yes, she is a nice lady. I like her, too." Jen giggled and Michael's big brown eyes danced at the comment. "You must find it interesting to ride a school bus and have a school with fewer students."

"Yes, I like the school. I can find my way around easy because it's small. And I like my teacher. I'll only have her a few more weeks, though, until we're out for summer." Larry went on chatting with Michael, asking questions about school and his interests.

* * *

The insurance office had a line-up of customers. The receptionist told Sylvia it would be a ten minute wait. She sat down and picked up the Everett paper. She skipped over the foreign news, since she'd heard it on the radio that morning. A header on an article declared "Woman Beaten". The details were gruesome. Jane Doe's severe injuries were from blows with a blunt object. She was unconscious. The husband, who was missing, was the prime suspect. Nausea churned in Sylvia's stomach as she continued to read. The woman's three-year old child was given x-rays that showed old broken bones that had mended without benefit of medical attention. Sylvia wondered how much threatening, intimidation, and then beating, she had gone through. And what had the poor three-year old had seen and felt? What was his life like? How could he trust anyone? *How awful not to feel safe with the very man you live with, the one who, supposedly, is your "caring protector".*

Sylvia got out of bed thinking of Jenny. She stood at the kitchen sink looking south, in the direction of her house, as she made coffee. Maybe she would phone later. By calling, she wouldn't have to tiptoe around, hoping Len wasn't there. He still made her uncomfortable. All she had ever gotten from him was a scowl, and she turned that over in her mind, as she pictured his face. *I guess it is none of my business that another woman married a man I wouldn't pick. It probably looks worse than it is; he was exhausted with moving and he was concerned about getting the truck back on time that first night. He has still had lots on his mind since then. I sure feel lucky to have Larry for a husband, the more I see of other men.* Sylvia ate breakfast, poured a warm-up in her coffee mug, and kept wandering by the south-facing kitchen window. She couldn't get the little family out of her mind. *That house is so far gone. Doesn't look like the landlord will be doing much more to fix it. Oh, dear God, watch over this family! If a fire started with them upstairs it would be...I really should warn Jenny. Suggest she might want to get a rope for each bedroom, tie an end around a bed leg and have it ready for escape. At least they could throw it out the window and climb to safety. Lord, just keep them from harm over there. I wonder what they'll do for heating once it is cold in the fall. Does that old wood-burning furnace really work? Maybe they can get a good heater for the living room before winter. But at least that is months away.*

Sylvia stepped outside with the plan of going down to the creek. She had phoned Jen but there was no answer. She wondered if she would catch sight of her, get her to come along. Where the path split to the creek or Jen's house, she paused. She saw movement in the yard. Jenny was outside.

"Hello Jenny!" she called.

"Hello."

"Want to go for a walk?"

"I can't. Haven't got time."

Sylvia came across, and saw Jenny was struggling with a broken shovel that had a taped handle. "Can you get much accomplished with that shovel? It must pinch your hand."

Jenny looked embarrassed. "It does pinch and, no, I'm not getting much done." She walked over and leaned it against the house. "Might as well give up."

She looks so tired, Sylvie thought. "I have garden tools. You are welcome to borrow them."

"Thanks. I guess I need to." Jen wondered if she'd ever be able to just go buy them.

"How are things going? Other than with shovels, that is!"

"Okay I guess. How about you?"

"I'm looking forward to us getting together. I bet I could help some more inside with unpacking."

"No. It's at that point where everything is a decision. Keep or throw or where in the world do I put it. I'm sick of it. Would just like some order in my life." She saw the concerned look that came on Sylvia's face. "I don't mean to spoil your morning with my grumbling."

"It sounds kind of like you need a break. Why not?"

"For one thing, Michael stayed home from school this morning. Guess it's the flu. Felt listless, worn out, and didn't eat breakfast. Just went back to bed." The conversation paused while Jen smoothed the ground with her foot. It had holes in it where she had removed weeds.

"I'm sorry to hear he's not well."

"Yeah. I'd better go in and check on him."

"Tell Michael I hope he'll be feeling much better soon."

"Okay." She attempted a smile. "I'll tell him."

"Well, we'll make it one day soon – getting together."

"Yes," Jenny answered without energy. "That would be nice." She turned toward the house.

Sylvia went slowly back to the path. *Motherhood,* she thought. *It's worry-some and draining, but a real blessing.* Her mind jumped to her own mother. She had sent the Mother's Day card. It was doubtful her mother was around to get it, with all her business activity, even in so-called retirement. Always full of busy-ness, though who could fault her since she brought in good money doing what she enjoyed. *I wonder if she ever thought of sending a Happy Mother's Day card 'to a daughter who is a wonderful mother' or 'to a daughter who is precious to me'. Silly. I'm being selfish and silly. She's just busy.*

Her mind returned to Jen. *What is going on there? Jenny doesn't seem herself. What is it? Is she tired from the unpacking, or is it Len? Or Michael being sick? She seems dragged down by something. She doesn't owe* me *any explanations. But things are different and it's nagging me.* She knew that she and Jen had only enjoyed surface things together – nothing very personal. But she cared that a woman with such excitement in her eyes could be made dull and listless... by what? Maybe Jenny was just coming down with the flu, too.

Sylvia walked to the creek without paying attention, and slid down the bank. The noisy gurgling of the water invaded her mind. This time it was mere background noise. She was troubled. She looked at the flowing water. *I wish that I could take Jenny's troubles and plunge them into the clear stream; they would go swirling away to Puget Sound like children's stick boats, never to be seen again. Oh, my, I am getting melodramatic. It must be my new freedom – having time to think, to puzzle over things. Here I have just hit fifty, and I'm sinking back into the emotionalism that tossed me around as a teenager. It's not only time to think, though; it's having time to* feel, deeply. *What a thought! Maybe it's that old diary/journal that I ran across the other day. I'll get it out and read it. Tune in on the feeling side I've been ignoring. Hmm, I should give Lisa a call.*

* * *

Jenny returned to her high school ring binder of poems and jottings, laying on top of her trunk. She set it aside for a moment, and went to the window, drawn to gaze out at the sudden storm. Rain was pelting the leaves of the thimble berries and alder trees till they rattled. Louder yet was the drumming on the roof above her second floor retreat. She watched the wind bend branches, wondering how many powerful storms had swept over the Puget Sound lowlands.

It took her back to high school, when storms made her feel small. They were awesome. She had learned in a special writing class how to gather her thoughts. She found she was able to grab a pen and get her emotions written down as poetry. A storm was pure drama. It still brought a feeling of awe now, as she watched. The first wildly tossing, racing clouds were billows like surf thrown off the ocean. Then the clouds built overhead until they were a darkening shroud. It was an overwhelming display, yet she also felt an affinity to the storm, attracted by its outpouring of energy. She opened the window and leaned out to feel the fresh wind blowing in her face, free... and freeing.

The display of the elements was stimulating – the wind whipped across the defenseless land, tearing at the branches of trees. Jennifer remembered how, as a teen, she had felt whipped and torn by life. She remembered being caught up, watching a storm – could see herself – grabbing a sheet of paper, dashing off line after line of potent, rhythmic phrases in blank verse. The words were like the unpredictable storm... words pouring onto the waiting paper as a scrawled torrent. The flood of ink, barely readable, was a flood of emotions finally expressed in tangible form. She had been surprised by the mysterious kinship between the tempest and the expression of her surfacing turmoil, coming from deep inside. Her inner passions had come forth like a sudden flood, and, in their release, their intensity diminished. Just as the storm clouds emptied, fled, and the sky-pressure lifted, the tension bound within her eased.

She picked out and read one of the 'storm poems' from the high school binder. There was deep satisfaction in finding this way to make sense of her emotions. Or, if not make sense, at least articulate them. She had needed, then, to describe the pain that was filling her heart, pain that had built up inside.

Young as she had been, she had known these expressions of her own emotional storm were hitting some illusory mark of literary expression. In her loneliness, later in the night, she had felt overwhelmed by life's burden. She lay awake for hours in the darkness, asking herself what she had to live for. What was she doing with her life...her lack of life. To use feelings and words as a creative tool brought joy, but the joy was fleeting. In those years life was not just up and down. It was mostly down.

Jen had left to put a second load of clothes in to wash. Now, when she returned, she came across another notebook. It was from after high school. She opened it and read.

Baby

Tiny nose and fingers
Curled in your sleep
Eyes that dream now flutter –
What secrets do you keep?

You and I have secrets
And some of them are good.
For now I'll wait and long
To see my dream unfold.

We'll have a home that's warm
We'll laugh and talk and read –
As to a man you're growing...
God help me meet your need.

Jennifer Hanson
Michael is three weeks old today.

Jen read it again. She thought of Mary. *She would understand those new mother thoughts I was having. I wish could have shared it with her. What an amazing event a baby's birth is – there's just no getting around it. Funny I thought of asking God to be part of raising Michael at that time. I wonder where God is right now? I guess Mary would have had the answers.*

All of the sorting through old writing, poems, jottings or journaling, if it could be flattered with that name, had Jennifer thinking of high school. *That time period was... what was it? Rather, what was I like? I was so tentative, uncertain. I remember how I felt when the infatuation over the literature classmate was done. I was desolate. It was winter. I dragged through it. Then summer came. The end of that summer I truly fell in love.* The meeting came at the swimming beach. The place to be invisible among a hundred teens, or be viewed. She wasn't sure what she wanted. Laying on her mat to dry after a swim, taking another dip and sunning herself, hiding herself in the radio's sound waves, listening as the DJ's voice carried her along.

The voice seemed to begin speaking to her. It was just the people nearby, chatting, she had thought, and ignored it.

The voice said her name, and she jumped. "Oh, hello," she muttered, embarrassed about everything. She couldn't look up because of the bright sun. She had ignored him, her hair was a mess, she couldn't think of a word to say – "Want someone to talk to, Jennifer?" he asked. She came to her senses and spoke. "Someone to talk to... say, how did you know my name?" "It's on your radio." "Oh," she had answered weakly. He was so good looking. He had nice eyes. His name was Manuel. That was the beginning, and what a romantic summer it had been. True summer fun, most often by the water. She remembered taking him home to introduce him to her mother. She was shocked at the reaction. *My mother is jealous!* She couldn't believe it. After that it was harder than usual to please her mother. She heard constantly that her hair looked awful, how her clothes were out of style, how she slouched, that she didn't help enough around the house, or she had better get her schoolwork done. She spent hours on Saturday catching up the family's laundry and doing the cleaning. Her resentment built until she didn't speak at all, or became rude. When she walked with her boyfriend she felt like somebody. She was somebody. Her senior year began. The summer days on the beach faded with the sunshine. Manuel was working two hours away. They didn't have time to sit talking.

That school year flew by quickly, especially after Jen had moved out of the house for the third time. The message she got was unmistakable – her mother didn't want her. She told her mother that if that's how it was, she didn't need her either. She rejoined her bohemian friends – they always welcomed her. But she found herself looking at their casual attitude with a more critical eye. None of them were making an effort to reach a goal; didn't even have goals. People came and went and no one cared. They were drifting. She didn't want to lapse into not having goals. After finishing high school she made good money waitressing. When she went back to see her family with some gifts and practical items she had for them, the relationship with her mother was still the same.

Jenny was a failure. She fought it. Though arguing was limited, she could strut her defiance – and her mother read it very well. The visits were short.

Jen stood up, and dropped the notebook back into the box. Yes, I was defiant. So what? She deserved it. Right now I have other things that need attention.

CHAPTER FIFTEEN

Jenny lifted the last of the bowls out of the box, ones she used infrequently. She placed them on the counter where she could get up later and reach the higher shelves of the cupboard. *Living out here is beginning to feel a bit like home. Sure great to live where Michael is able to stretch and run. I'll even get time to enjoy being outdoors. I may not be able to stay at home for more than a few more days, though. Hopefully that café calls me to come fill in for waitresses on vacation. Well, even to waitress part-time helps pay the bills.* She picked up the dustpan. There was shredded debris on the counter from unpacking and she used her hand to sweep it over the edge and catch it. She shook her head, remembering how uncomfortable she had felt reminding Sylvia that she was going home without the dustpan she had come to borrow. Then how Sylvia made her feel at ease. *I am sure lucky to have a neighbor like that. Friendly – or at least she seems to be. I stumbled all over myself wondering how to tell her I needed that dustpan. She didn't act offended. To think, we even enjoy the same things, reading and walking.* A doubt crept into Jenny's mind. *Well, I'll just wait and see what develops with her. See if her friendliness lasts. Or if I'll find out she's the kind that gets right in your face. And I may get so busy it won't matter.*

Moving expenses and utility hook-ups had taken the ready cash and the bills were behind. This landlord had given Len permission to paint the walls, but they wouldn't be buying any paint for some time, so the permission didn't have much benefit. The truck for moving had cost something after all, though Len thought he was getting the use of it free. They had the phone installed right away because he needed to get calls in order to get a job. The phone bill, including deposit, had arrived immediately and should be paid. She hoped she could find a job soon, a secure job. She didn't really want to use up her savings from tips, tucked away in the bank. The account had been in her own name in Seattle and was transferred here when the joint one was moved. It should be kept for emergencies or something special. Hopefully they could pay off these bills without it.

Len had applied at the mill, and seemed quite hopeful. But they said they would call him, nothing definite. He had even talked to the owner of the gas station about a job. She was surprised he would do something menial, but maybe it had potential for some mechanic work, too. He didn't explain anything about it. He had borrowed a pickup from Joe or Joe's friend in south Seattle for a while. When he drove the car out to the house, Joe drove the pickup and made sure he got there. Len went back with Joe after he warned her he had barely gotten it running. He said it wouldn't last, and not to drive it much. He was "working out something" for buying the pickup on time – something about doing work for Joe or his friend. She had a hard time keeping up with it.

Jenny realized that she was wandering around getting nothing done. Back to boxes. She sliced the tape and pulled open the flaps. There was the Scrabble board. *Ah, I'll have to show this to Michael when he gets home from school. We'll try again and see if he takes to it this time. He was a little young before.* She placed one of the wood racks for letters on the kitchen table as a reminder, and put the box in an upper cupboard. Thinking of Michael at school made her wonder if he really was adjusting to a new teacher and classmates. Probably was doing fine. He was a good student, but socially he was a little shy.

It made Jen feel good to have clean laundry to put away. She had a tall stack of folded clothes in her arms. She reached the top of the stairs and turned into their room, but stopped short when she saw Len. He was standing with his back to her, facing the window and holding something in both hands. It was the triple frame with Michael's young pictures in it. She waited quietly. And wondered.

After what seemed like several minutes Len went to the dresser and placed it there carefully. He turned and suddenly saw Jennifer. She'd never seen him speechless – he was.

"What?" he barked as his face changed from pensive to angry.

Jen shook her head and answered softly, "Nothing. Just laundry." She had seen it. As much as he had quickly covered it, she had seen him looking at those little boy pictures with a contemplative look. *Was he thinking of something besides the pictures... like his own childhood?*

Jen sat on the front porch, on the board that covered the broken step. Surprisingly, she had grown to love this spot, broken board and all. She looked up at majestic fir trees on the front of Ford's property. On their own property there were two tall firs on the south side of her house that cast constant shade over it. She could only see the tops of them. Looking west again, toward the road, she saw only young trees, growing thickly in front of the house, down both sides of the driveway. Certainly not as stately as Ford's, but at least they provided a screen from road dust. She wished she could see out across the meadow. But they were a shelter to countless sparrows, chickadees and juncos.

From morning to night, during this breeding and nesting season, the birds chirped and sang happily. Absent-mindedly she watched. Michael had scattered seeds, and several birds scratched, pecked and quarreled with each other. Time to raise their young. Into her mind came the picture of Len holding the photo frame in the bedroom. He'd had the strangest look on his face – until he was seen. Then he snapped into a covering-up mode. *Contemplating... what?* she wondered *Do I dare ask? Yes, I must ask.* She pondered the possible outcome for a minute. *No. I don't think I'll take the chance.*

Jen felt light as she walked down to the mailbox at the end of the driveway. The air was fresh with spring. A light breeze was blowing – a pleasant change from the cold wind that had blown for three days. Coming to the road and out of the trees shading the driveway, she saw the sun was peeking through the clouds.

"Hello!" The male voice startled her. "Hello, Neighbor!" it

repeated.

Ah, Jen thought, *it's Larry!* "Hello," she called as he came into sight on the driveway parallel to hers.

"Beautiful day, isn't it!"

"It sure is!"

"Getting your mail, too?" he asked.

"Yes, well, what there is. Store ads for now. Guess it hasn't been switched to this box. It still seems funny to think of someone actually driving along the road, filling the mailboxes one at a time."

"Actually, community boxes are being put in place now by the post office. They have enough compartments for a whole area. Facilitates quick filling."

"Oh. Efficiency, I guess. Are you based at home now, for a while?"

"A short while. I had to do paper work and make phone calls this morning. I'm going out for the afternoon, doing the rounds of nearby outlets. Though I'm home tonight, I leave tomorrow for three days. How is it coming for you? Are you getting settled?"

"Yes and no. You know how it is. Confusing. No, I guess you haven't moved for a long time, so you're not confused." Jen laughed a little. But inside she realized, *That sounded so forward. I hardly know him and I sound like I'm assessing him – whether he has mental challenges.*

"Well, I may get confused, but not due to moving. Good luck getting it all sorted out! See you." Larry walked away, thumbing through his mail. She went through hers. There were the usual advertisements. She had hoped that by now the post office would have changed the General Delivery personal mail to this box, but there was no sign of it yet. *But maybe I'm not getting any personal mail, anyhow. Who would write?*

The phone rang. Jen picked it up to hear the voice of the man who was a mystery. "I'm sorry to bother you. This is Sam Brown. I wondered if Lennard Brown would be able to call me? I would just like to talk with him on the phone."

Jen felt confused. She had neglected to keep on reminding Len about the need to return Sam's call. "I'm sorry no one has contacted you. I guess you realize we have moved because you found the new listing. It's been a busy time. Sorry. I just don't know what to tell you."

"If he doesn't want to get together with me in person, that's fine. I'll understand."

"Oh, well. I have the number written down. I need to think to mention it."

"Don't worry. If it doesn't happen, it doesn't. Just please tell him I don't want anything – just wanted to talk with him. And the phone will do. Thanks for trying. Bye."

Jenny shook herself and looked down at the poem she'd been reading. Seated on a folded blanket in what she'd come to call the Quiet Room, she had papers spread around her on the floor. *I guess it's a waste of time to be spending all afternoon going through such old papers. This poem... I haven't written poetry like that for years, but it seems like yesterday.* She recalled her teens and early twenty's and the deep mood swings. At times she had felt very high, but then there were the depressing lows. No one told her she was depressed. Jenny brought herself out of the past by consciously looking out the window. It was getting dark. She was late. Dinner would be late. Life again seemed confusing, like then. But she reminded herself, looking at these poems and jottings, that she could gain release, even escape, as she wrote. But escape didn't seem like the right word for now. A sense of order and direction was more needed. She got up stiffly.

CHAPTER SIXTEEN

S ylvia came along the path and took the branch to Jen's house. She hoped to encourage her to come on a walk.

"Hello? Jenny?" she called out.

"Hello!" a voice came back.

Sylvia stepped out of the wet ferns. Jen was peering down through the brush toward the road. A Golden Retriever came bounding up the slope, oblivious to the prickly Oregon grape, and cut across the driveway toward Sylvie. The shabby coat didn't disguise her skinny ribs. She was wagging her tail vigorously as she came running up. Sylvia stretched out her hand. The dog cringed and pulled back. "Oh. She's been beaten. Poor thing."

"Yeah, I don't know whose dog she is, and she *is* scared to death half the time. The other half she wants to lick you to death. Can you believe she wants to get in your lap, big as she is? Michael wants to adopt her."

"Well…" Sylvia had a mischievous look on her face… "you may be the proud owners of a dog. I've seen her around recently, even in the town, but never with anyone. I think she's a stray."

They watched the dog push her face into the brush along the driveway. She pulled it out and turned, smiling at them – her tongue hung out and her lips pulled up in a lopsided grin.

Jenny said, "hmm, I don't know. If Michael gets attached to her and then the owners show up… and anyway, I doubt that Len will put up with having a dog. Michael sure likes her though. Threw a ball for her after school the last two days."

"Bet she likes to take walks with Michael! How about you? How about the walk we've talked about?"

"Oh. I don't know. I wanted to get this lawn cut. Well, not lawn. I mean tall grass. I think you could dry it and make hay!" She laughed.

Sylvia came closer and looked at the old push mower. Jen's effort to cut the lawn with it had only resulted in moth-eaten patches torn out of the tall grass. The remaining grass had already fallen or else the mower had flattened it to the ground. Glancing at the mower she saw the problem. Nothing could be expected from those dull blades, speckled with rust. The wooden handle was weathered and rough with slivers. It belonged in a museum. "Isn't the grass too high for that old thing? *Where* did you get it?" Instantly Jenny dropped her eyes, and Sylvie regretted her bluntness, knowing she'd hurt her feelings.

"We didn't. It was just here. The landlord said we could use whatever was around. Said he just wasn't supplying anything more because the rent was already low." She awkwardly ran her fingers through her hair to pull it off her perspiring face. "Yes, it is too high to cut. And the mower is about as sharp as a board. I might as well give it up." She gave a discouraged sigh, flipped the handle over, and pulled it backwards to the side of the house.

"You look worn out, Jen."

"I am. Say, I like that – calling me Jen in stead of Jenny. Len says jenny is a female donkey. I need a change, a change in my direction. Maybe that's symbolic."

Sylvia could just imagine Len calling her jenny the donkey, or worse.

Jen went on. "I *am* taking a new direction in my life, making this move." She coughed. "Agh, I am so dry. Come in for a minute; I need water. I'll make iced tea for us and think about that walk." She hopped over the board covering the rotten step and went in the front door.

"Hey, you have unpacked a lot!" Sylvia exclaimed. "Such a small stack of boxes left to go! How are things going? Are you finding all the things you need to function?"

"Yes, it's good that way. It's no longer overwhelming. Now I'm at the point of pawing through these boxes that have only a few odds and ends left in them. I'll try and get them completely empty and gone." She pointed. "The evidence that we're getting settled is growing – the growing height of that stack of flattened cardboard boxes. How about you? Are you bored yet, now you're not working much at Granite Falls Hardware?"

"Not at all. I'm glad! *So* glad. No problem with having enough to do. Except I would like to get out for walks more. I called you a couple times, but I guess it was poor timing. I only got your answer machine. I need someone to walk *with*!

"You know," Jen said with a determined expression, "I will go with you *now*, not tomorrow! You keep saying how pretty this area behind us is. I'd like to see it! Agh, I need moisture." She ran a glass of water, handed it to Sylvia, and drained one of her own. "Before we go I can make that iced tea, or maybe you'd rather have something hot? Or after?"

"Yes, after. Let's go for a walk first, if you feel like it. Then come over and have something at my place instead."

"Well, thanks. That would be a good plan. Making sure the walk happens. Sorry about the answer machine. I had to take Michael to the doctor. He was getting too tired in gym class to run laps. I've had that on my mind – just didn't get around to phoning back. Sorry. Tomorrow he has to go in to the lab for a blood test."

"Oh, dear; I hope it isn't serious."

"Yes, me too. Probably just run down anemic. Anyway, I'll come with you now." Sylvia was opening her mouth to ask more about Michael, but she sensed that the topic was closed. They went outside. Sylvia expected the dog to join them, but she had taken off.

"Wow!" Jen exclaimed as they entered the field. "I haven't taken the time to come back and look at this big field. Didn't picture it like this when Michael told me – didn't think that it would be so open. Really feels good back here, eh? The sunshine pouring down." Jen's thoughts wandered. *I am so glad for this place – Michael is having his dream come true, living in the country. It's how a boy should be able to grow up.* A picture of Len as a boy came to mind. She could see him...He had grown up in the country, on a poor farm. His dad worked away from home. From the few things Len said, it seemed like there had been more back-breaking work than a boy could get done, or would even have been capable of doing. Then, when his dad did come home, it seemed there was constant drinking and fighting. Len said very little. Jen shook her head. *Sad,* she thought. *But I'll clear out these sad thoughts by looking around, living in the now. I won't let this perfect day be spoiled…still, the image of a little boy working hard, then being beaten by a drunken man twice his size… it's haunting.*

They heard croaking from what was either a toad or a frog. Sylvia guessed it was a toad, being in the dry field. "Michael would want to catch it and hold it if he were here!" Jen laughed. "How wonderful to have all this space around us!"

"I love living out here. Larry and I call it "having elbow room", and we seem to be people who need it. It isn't always sunny, but you lived in Seattle so you know about the drizzly weather. Could be worse. At least we don't have winter blizzards like in the east; just snow." Sylvia started walking again. "If you like this, wait till you see what's ahead." They zigzagged their way across the field, getting off the path to examine wildflowers or unusual grasses that would dry and be pretty in an arrangement.

Sylvia pointed to where the hill dropped off into a gorge. "We'll go over there."

"Oh, I hear it! I hear the creek!" Jenny trotted ahead. The ground became rough and she slowed, then the path disappeared where the land dropped away. She was looking over the edge, down into the boulder-strewn ravine. "It's beautiful – all the lush green grasses along the banks of the creek! But how do we get down there?"

"It does look like it's too steep, but you can do it – come over here. It's less steep. Hold onto a handful of weeds." Sylvia demonstrated by grabbing onto them and making a full-circle wrap around her hand. She squatted down. "If you get low, better yet, just sit, it's easier. Scoot along on a slant, grabbing the weeds as you go, till you get to that little ledge." She went first and Jen followed.

Trying to look around at the beautiful surroundings while she kept one eye on where to scoot and slide, started Jen giggling. Gasping as she laughed harder, she called, "Wait! Let me catch my breath!" She grew quiet as her gaze lifted and she saw giant evergreen trees rising above them on the far hillside. She looked below, silently watching the creek. "This is so beautiful...so beautiful." She shook her head in wonder. "Peaceful, isn't it?"

Sylvia wondered at the puzzled look on Jen's face. The "peaceful" part was not a statement, but a question, *Is it truly peaceful?* It was as if peace were a feeling foreign to her. Sylvia sensed that Jen wanted some kind of profound reassurance. But Sylvia was at a loss to respond. She couldn't get a handle on what she vaguely sensed, and dared not probe.

Jen started sliding downward again, so Sylvia moved on in a low crouch to the bottom. They stepped over boulders and onto flat, soggy silt at the edge of the creek.

Sylvia pointed to it. "The creek level has dropped since the end of the last rain. This shoreline has recently been under water. Nice and moist. I may have mentioned the frogs already. You may hear some, and there are even more up the hill by the spring."

Jen nodded, taken with a thought, and turned to her. "Did I tell you we used to walk in a small park in Seattle and look for a frog? He was often waiting on a rock for us – at least that's what we said – that he was waiting for us!"

Sylvia grinned. "Yes. Michael was all excited when he told me. I'm glad he likes the country lifestyle. I can't wait to take *you* to the clearing and the spring! That will have to be for later, when we have more time. It's a real retreat. I can understand why the deer seek it out, and the frogs sing. Any wild creature would be happy there, surrounded by the moist air and plenty to eat. I like the calming greens. It's quieter there." Here the water churned loudly over rocks. They found dry boulders and sat, breathing in air that was rich with the oxygen given off by the surrounding undergrowth. Water-music filled their ears.

Time ceased for Jen as she sat in the cool shade. She breathed deeply of the fresh air and listened to the spellbinding sound. Finally she spoke. "I *have* to bring Michael down here. Until now he hasn't come this far; I asked him to wait till I could come with him. He just *has* to see this. Feel it."

"I'm so happy for you both – coming to live in the country!"

Jen nodded slowly, thinking. "Yes, living in the country. It hasn't been what I expected in a couple of ways." She looked up and smiled. "The house is the first one." She chuckled. "I might as well laugh. It doesn't fix anything to cry! And it's coming together, feeling more like it's livable. And I am *so glad* we ended up here. Look at this beauty. But speaking of country, you were going to tell me about your grandmother helping you appreciate natural beauty. When I saw the creek I thought of my Aunt Sally. She was full of Robert Lewis Stevenson's poems. She often said the one about the boats going down to the sea."

"Oh, yes. I know it. My grandmother quoted it."

"Tell me about her. Did you grow up in the country?"

"On the edge of the city. It grew around us. At first the nearby roads led to nice walks, but later Grandma took me in her car where there was enough open space for long walks. Wherever we went, she taught me to notice, to *really* see what's around me. And to let it uplift my mood. She pointed out beauty spots with unabashed enthusiasm. With her I began to make full use of my childhood imagination."

Sylvia paused, filled with memories. "Even if we were only walking by a country road, she would point out a tiny rivulet flowing along in a grassy ditch. We'd pause and she would to listen, saying, "it's making music!" I loved the shared moment, listening with her. Because of her I listened better, hearing even the soft sounds in nature. She helped me take in so many things that were around me. We might talk about frogs as we walked along the edge of a pond – how they enjoyed living in the safety of the water, cool in summer, mud to sleep in during winter. We would step along quietly, straining our eyes to catch sight of one before they all hopped into the water."

"Like Michael's frog friend did at first." Jen laughed.

"Yes, like Michael's frog did. I remember taking our kids for walks here, pointing out the same things my Grandma had. Michael's lucky to have you, your interest in the things that he takes to naturally."

Jen just quietly nodded her head. Sylvia noticed a small smile passed over her lips. She went on. "The first time we went on a walk in the deep woods, she spoke of her awe of the towering trees. She tromped along boldly under the dark shadows of the giants that towered over us. I think she was bold because she sensed I was afraid. It was so dark. She would point up at the impressive canopy and we would stretch our necks back to see the treetops far above. She told how those very trees had been there when the area was settled by the first people who followed the explorers. Then we began to walk along again. I wondered where the path would lead. Grandma was going to where a small stream burbled. She said "Listen to that sound. What are you hearing up ahead?" I answered, "This one makes more music"! Sure enough, it was a sizable stream. It gurgled and splashed in a small waterfall onto a bed of pebbles. With Grandmother helping me to imagine that it was a roaring river, we dropped sticks and leaves into the various eddies. They were swept along. We pretended it was thundering and splashing over boulders, rushing to the ocean far away. Our imaginations, Grandmother said, could carry us down the stream pretending we were going to far away places. She made it magic. Then we left the stream. She showed me another place, a sheltered, mossy hollow. She said, "You know the story about the shoemaker and the elves that helped him while he slept. This is one place where the wee little men, the leprechauns, play. They come out when no one is around and dance while one of them plays tunes on a tiny flute. They dress in soft suede made from plant fibers and sewn into tiny pants and vests. Their shirts are made of woven dandelion down. They play games, laugh and talk, and enjoy their time together. They feel safe as long as they are certain they are alone. One is a 'watcher', always on guard. If he hears a noise, and especially if it is a human noise, he gives warning and they all scurry away. No one ever sees them." Even though she let me know by her twinkling eyes that it was a story, I loved being caught up into a secret fairy world. Imagination – what a gift it is for a child. There were some problems between my parents, like in most homes, so I was very thankful for the escape provided by the gift of imagination – thankful that Grandma stimulated it very early."

"Ohhh, thank you for sharing your memories of her." Jen thought of Aunt Sally wistfully. "And for the description of the spring and the pool up here – I'm looking forward to taking that longer walk. I'll keep the pictures with me. Like reading. Sometimes I like to read in order to escape into a world that has nothing to do with what is around me. You took me right with you, describing those scenes! I can almost see it." She got a philosophical look. "You know how reading books is like unbolting a doorway and stepping into a whole new world."

"I know what you mean. I love a good book – a good escape!"

The dreamy expression on Jen's face revealed her imagination was still at work. "I hear people scorn the idea of 'escape' but they're not going to convince me!"

"Right!" Sylvia reached out and touched Jen's arm but she pulled away without seeming to notice she had done it.

"It will be nice to think of more walks while I work. And I'll think of you when I'm reading a good book." Jen looked down at her watch. "Oh, I've got to get back and get to work. And speaking of work – I'm hoping to get a call from one of the restaurants to come in and waitress as a spare." She got up.

"Well," Sylvie said, "we can come back here anytime you want, or feel free to walk down by yourself. If you wander about back there, the neighbors don't worry about property lines." Sylvia led the return up the bank. "The way you were working in the yard, though, I think I need to get you some more liquid. You'll be dehydrated."

"Okay. I did say I'd come over, didn't I? And I did put in some effort on the yard, so I can sooth my guilty conscience with that thought." She gave a wry smile. "This time has been revitalizing, even if it was short. Your kitchen is a good-feeling place, too, so it's not hard to leave this and go there." She flashed a relaxed smile.

As they walked along, Jen said, "You have been doing some moving of furniture, too. You said on the phone that your dad shipped his desk to you and you've put it in the living room."

"Yes. I'm so glad to have it. When I look at it, it's like having him in the room, or somewhere nearby, ready for a face-to-face chat. I put the desk against the front wall, between the window and the front door that leads outside – the one we rarely use. As I sit there I can stretch over and look out the window at the flowers in the front yard."

They walked into the house and Sylvia paused in the kitchen to fill the kettle. "Go on in and take a look."

Jen entered the living room and gave a soft "Ah," and stopped. She raised her voice to be heard in the kitchen. "It looks so nice there, with the old brass floor lamp beside it." She went over to the desk and stroked her fingers across it. The sunlight was penetrating into the depths of the pecan wood. Light brought out the rich grain and the dark flecks seemed to float as if in liquid in the light-brown wood.

"That is quite a desk." She paused a moment. "I'm glad I got to see that picture of your dad. Glad you told me about him. It will be good to meet him when he visits."

"I'm glad, too," Sylvia said, coming into the room. "I look forward to introducing him to you." She looked up at his picture and said, thoughtfully, "I believe you can understand a person better when you meet their parents. It's like part of their context. Have a seat. I'll get the tea."

The kettle was whistling and Sylvia left the room. Jenny thought of the word 'context' and she looked up at the pictures on the wall. The Ford children – Sylvia had named them off – Mark, Isabel, and Nadine. Old-fashioned names. She studied their faces. They looked like nice people. She shook her head. When Sylvie returned with the tea, Jen asked about the kids' years in school. Then Sylvie pointed out other pictures on the wall, especially pausing at her grandparents' pictures.

Jen played with her spoon distractedly, then turned abruptly to Sylvia. "What did you mean by that, ah... statement?" Her voice faltered.

Sylvia was puzzled. "What statement?"

"You said you think we understand a person better when we meet their parents – it's part of their context." Jen took a breath.

"Is that a bad thing?" Sylvia asked. She couldn't see a problem, though a problem was definitely written on Jen's face.

"I think context helps us get the big picture. My parents said a lot, well, mostly my mother, said a lot more with her life than she realized. Said it loud and clear. But what she thought certainly has no part in my thinking. Their lives shout that children don't matter, that they should be out of the way. That they're not worth the trouble. Then there are others in the family, one aunt in particular, who speaks in a way that reveals her philosophy – that people should be demeaned, 'put down', so she can feel superior, and...and...a lot more. So that is a context, right?" Jenny was agitated.

Sylvia wondered, *what in the world? – what 'can of worms' have I opened up?* "Oh... why, no doubt we can think differently than our parents did. By context I guess I was meaning what we come out of and react to in one way or the other. I agree with you. We decide to hold the ideals that *we* choose. We decide how we will treat others. It may be the opposite of what we saw or felt. I didn't mean to hurt you. There is no doubt in my mind that you value Michael highly as a person. And it shows in him. It proves that you obviously made important decisions about parenting."

"Yeah...I suppose." Jen was quiet. She looked up and pointed. "I look at Nadine's picture and I think of my little sister, Patsy. I haven't heard from her for half a year. I worry. It may be a long time before I do hear. Or, who knows – any day she may phone. I hope she will soon, while she can still get the recording for our new number. Patsy didn't have much going for her as a kid. Not what brings out the best." She looked at the pictures again. "You know, your kids have a good chance...a chance for a good life I mean. I hope they make the most of it."

Sylvia nodded slowly, quietly saying, "I hope your Patsy does get in touch. And thank you for your wishes for my family." She wondered if Jen would say any more, but she remained quiet.

Jennifer walked home slowly, thinking of Sylvia, of her yard, her home. She enjoyed both freedom and order. The way she pointed out the beauty of a flower in bloom, or the peace in the creek canyon...*it seems she looks with a different viewpoint than I have*. It provoked thoughts about the unrestrained life she had admired as a teenager. She hadn't been daring enough to live as a real Bohemian. She had dutifully worked and paid her bills. She was proud of that – no, arrogant, really. But at the same time, she felt enslaved to... something. What? The easy life of the others seemed free. But it was not so admirable as it seemed at first. It held lasting appeal only to those who were unwilling to take responsibility. They seemed to go down hill, becoming grubby, not caring what they ate, turning their sleeping hours upside down. They talked of the great creativity flowing out of them. But it was a lot of hot air, as her Aunt Sally would say. So was she resentful that she couldn't do that – couldn't live that life. Hardly. She couldn't make sense of it. There were many free-spirit types still around, doing quite well for that matter. But they were the hard-working ones. They kept a free spirit about enjoying beauty and fun and creativity. Sylvia had some of that free-spirit enjoyment in her. But there was a deeper reason for Sylvia's freedom that Jen couldn't put her finger on. What was it?

Sylvia had been unusually quiet after they sat down to dinner. Larry took another bite of his potatoes, as she asked his impression of Lennard Brown. Then he said, "I don't know. Len seemed okay when I met him by the road. We didn't talk much, just a welcome to the neighborhood."

"You're probably right. My impression of him on moving day was skewed – he was worn out, I'm sure." Sylvie shook her head. "It's just that he doesn't even look you in the eye."

"Oh? He did me. Of course, I was pulling out of my driveway and he was pulling into his, talking from his pickup. It wasn't really an 'eye-to-eye encounter'." Sylvie saw him raise an eyebrow, as if pointing out her skepticism. He smiled, and went on. "Len seemed happy with things since he's moved out here. He's pretty proud of that pickup. Said he hopes to buy it."

Sylvia nodded absently. Her mind was not on pickups; it was absorbed in pondering Len's personality. Why had he been rude to her? Didn't he know any better? Maybe it was just his upbringing. Or did he not like women – women who were responsible for getting his wife off track. She remembered that their chatting had gone on too long that first day. He needed help to get things inside and unpacked. Well, she was sorry for that. It was wrong.

"The northwest regional manager from Tacoma spent the whole day at our office. He spoke to me about a larger territory." Larry waited for a response. There was none, so he said, "I might be gone from home longer in the future." He waited.

"Hmm? Oh, I'm sorry," Sylvie said. "What did you say? Something about the future?"

"Yes, the big boss wants me to take on more territory as a regular thing."

"Oh." Sylvia looked at him. "Do you mean more than just this Puget Sound corridor?"

"Yes. It would mean being away from home longer stretches."

"Oh, no. Just when I am off work, and we can spend time together without me being worn out." She scowled, though she usually tried to let Larry have her support in job decisions no matter what.

"I know. That's how I felt about it at first. He says he'll give me a good pay increase. You can enjoy your early retirement! And one more week of paid vacation per year. That would be nice! But he wants me to travel all the way past Portland Oregon regularly. At first I'd stay on this side of the Cascades – only do the western part of Washington. But when I asked if I'd have to go "east of the mountains", he hedged. Said I could decide that later. I'm sure that means he plans to ask me to do it. The upper end of the territory is northeast to Darrington, and straight north to Bellingham and the border. But that's not bad. The traffic problems are south." He pushed his zucchini slices around on his plate with a fork.

"Well." Sylvia stopped. *What do I say?* "That's a decision. I guess it's a promotion. One more week of vacation is nice. Do you want it?"

Larry had a wry, crooked smile as he chuckled, "The vacation time?" Sylvia felt her irritation rising. She was trying to find out how he really felt. He was making light of her, making it difficult.

"No. The new job description."

"Guess I have to consider it...think it over." Larry changed the subject, and that was the end of the conversation.

* * *

"I saw you when you got the mail." Lennard's face was intense. His tone of voice held a warning.

Jen thought, *Oh, no. What have I done now?*

"You think we have a pretty nice neighbor. Friendly fellow. And you're friendly."

"Friendly?" Jen echoed. "With Larry?"

"Yea, friendly." He stared at her, then slowly said, "Just watch out."

Jen puzzled over what she was suppose to watch out for... Larry making advances? She doubted that. "I... sorry. I only chatted about ordinary things. There was nothing to it. I didn't mean anything by it."

"Yea, sure. I was watching. Just don't give him the wrong message. You don't even know him."

"I... okay. I don't think I did."

"You don't know what it was – to him. Don't know how a man's mind works."

"Well, no." Jen tried for a little humor. "I'm sure I don't know first-hand how a *man's* mind works." Her laugh was weak.

"Don't be mouthy. Just watch yourself."

CHAPTER SEVENTEEN

Jenny looked out the front room window on the horizon to the southwest, and saw a heavy bank of wet-weather clouds coming. She thought, *More rain. Oh, well. This is spring, after all.* She returned to pondering what Len said about Larry. *Larry is a man, but he's a good person. I don't know what Len's worried about. Maybe I missed something. I need to be more careful not to upset Len.* She looked around at work to be done and felt like taking a break, phoning Bet in Oregon. She needed to give her the new phone number, and she had ended the conversation last time without asking how her summer would be spent. She entered the long-distance number and listened to it ring as she thought about Larry.

"Hello."

"Hello, Bet. Jenny in Washington again. I just wanted to give you a shout. Thought I would give you my new number."

"Oh, a surprise to hear from you twice in one month!"

"Yeah," Jenny continued. I wanted to hear how you and the kids would spend your summer, too."

"Oh, the usual. Trips out to the ocean beach; loll around on the sand. I will work four long night shifts at the cannery, then I'm off three days a week. If I'm not at home to get a "come in, we need you desperately" phone call, then I will have the whole three days. Enough time to make it worthwhile to go somewhere with the kids."

Bet took her phone number; they chatted about the everyday things. In their school days, Bet had been a lively one. She always seemed to enjoy learning the details of the latest news on everyone in school and outside.

Bet questioned, "What do ya think of our latest scandal?"

"What do you mean? Which scandal? Remember Bet, we live a whole state away from each other. The media knows public interest – only what's "in my back yard" is important to most of us."

"Gotcha. Well, there is a big hubbub over an eighth-grade teacher here in Smithton. He's being investigated. He's accused of seducing a thirteen-year old girl. She can't be identified, but people seem to know who she is." Jen's stomach churned. "Now, did he really seduce her or did she seduce him – that's what the talk around town is. People who know are questioning whether she is believable or maybe is just a party girl."

"I think they ought to listen to her." A sick feeling came over Jenny. "I doubt that a girl that age seduced her teacher. Come on, Bet."

"Yea. Well, anyway he is being scrutinized up one side and down the other. It's gonna ruin him. So you think her story is valid, huh? But here's the question – should you always come to the defense of the girl? Do you think she didn't have a single thought toward him in her head? I say she probably asked for it – flirted."

"What? So *what* if she had a crush on him and flirted! Don't you imagine he had a little more understanding of life than she did? Getting a crush on teachers is common at that age. Teachers are mature adults."

"But can you imagine what this will do to his reputation?"

"If he's innocent, I feel sorry for him."

"Me, too. I doubt she was thinking of his reputation when she flirted with him. I still think she asked for it. She just threw herself at him and got what she wanted."

"Come *on,* Bet! How awful to say she "asked for it." Hot anger was rising in Jenny. "You mean a man his age, an adult, shouldn't be responsible for his actions? That he isn't able to ignore or at least resist an eighth-grader's interest? He had *better*! And in a position of trust – I can't imagine. It's especially horrible when students can't trust teachers, or other authority figures." *How,* she thought, *could anyone defend seducing a child?*

"I still say she threw herself at him."

"Did she?" Jenny's voice was cold. "What did she want? Him? For what – a possible husband? Maybe for a boyfriend to take her to the prom in a few years? Get real. Ask yourself some questions. What is going on in her life? Has anyone come alongside her and asked that? Does she have parents? Is she a foster child who, for whatever reason acted out. Then went through a bad time – shuffled around from home to home? Is there stability? Have the adults she is with really loved her and cared for her unselfishly, or is she shifted from pillar to post?" Has she been molested? If so, did she reveal it to someone who listened and then said, 'oh, you'll get over it; that happens'? That gave her pain no importance – minimized the situation *and* her. Someone who should have acted, believed her, and helped her. She should have been supported – that it really did happen and it was wrong, and it *mattered*. Did she see herself as a thing, a sexual object, instead of as a unique, significant person? Maybe she thinks of herself as just some "thing" to be used, to bring someone else satisfaction. Have they asked?"

"Whoa, I can tell that this is a touchy topic for you. Sorreey."

"It's not that I'm upset with you, Bet."

"Oh, I didn't think so. It *is* a hot topic for you. I can see that. So you think every girl who gets in trouble was raped when she was twelve or eight or four?"

"No. I don't." Jen could hear her own anger. "But I do think various levels of sexual abuse happen. This happens to more girls than you think." She recalled her tension, almost panic, when Maggie said girls needed support no one gave. Abuse was a favorite topic of Maggie's, even at the lunch table at Deli diner. She'd been through it all. Jen calmed herself before voicing her thoughts to Bet. "The girls should be asked questions and then really listened to. Not just police-type questions for a report. Sometimes a poor girl ends up in an interrogation room, questioned by a man with no woman present. She's embarrassed."

"Oh, I don't think that happens anymore."

"You're probably right. I think that is changing. Even then, if there's a woman officer, she may not have given heed to the training – "How to put a victim at ease and get accurate answers". Maybe some women officers are out to get a promotion – thinking an appearance of being capable, which to them means blunt and tough, is admirable."

"Give the women officers the benefit of the doubt. A lot has changed."

"Okay. Whether a man or woman is taking the info – I guess it's not that – it's just to have a questioner who cares. Who shows concern; who asks and hears with the heart. I do think it has gotten better. But later, she'll be faced with enduring questioning in court. That's a high-pressure scene. A defense lawyer is getting a fat fee from the teacher and his supporters. He's well-known. She's a nobody. I don't know if a kid is going to survive that kind of cross-questioning, putting doubts in her mind as to what happened, what she or he said, what her behavior was, how the teacher showed his intent." Can't you see her wilting?"

"I suppose. You sure have it in for a lot of people, though – teachers, lawyers, police women...

"No I don't. I just think the girl is powerless."

"Okay, I can see your point. You want to know that her side is heard. I do still think you'd be surprised to know how many girls – and I admit they are looking for real love – are jumping into bed with every Joe and Pete and Bill around."

"I suppose. Whatever," Jen said tonelessly. Looking for real love – that was saying a mouthful. "Guess it will be a while before the case is settled."

"Yeah, I suppose. Well, I didn't mean to push your buttons. Sorry. How about Len and that old Chevy he was working on? Did he get it running?"

"Yes. He finished that a while back. It sold. Now he's going to Los Angeles to sell another one." She didn't speak of her doubts about the trip, but she thought, *Who knows when he will be back? Seems to take his own sweet time, except this last one, when he arranged the house – without me. Who can guess what's next? I can't. But Bet doesn't need to hear it.* Jen prodded her brain into another path. "So, your kids will sure enjoy the ocean beach – which part of the Oregon coast did you say you plan to go to?" The talk went on a while longer, but Jenny became weary. Things were about the same. She brought the conversation to an end. She had taken care of the nagging thought to call Bet with her new phone number.

Jen sighed deeply after explaining about the girl in Oregon. Looking into Sylvia's eyes, she saw agreement as she added, "She'll have a hard time maintaining a clear mind in the witness stand. It's horrid to think of her even being put on the stand – like a deer dragged down by wolves – when the defense uses witnesses as he tries to destroy her credibility." Jen shook her head. She went on, heavy-hearted. "That girl is still a child and should be defended against exploitation. Now, in the present, no matter what her past was. She needs help. And anyway, I don't believe that part about her reputation. Just because a girl dresses unwisely doesn't always mean she realizes she's provoking attention she can't handle – it doesn't mean she knows the outcome. Until it's too late. She wants attention, for sure. Unfortunately, she'll get it. The wrong kind."

Sadly, Sylvie nodded. "You're right. She is still a child. Sometimes I wonder if a girl has even been warned about attracting unwanted attention, or told how susceptible men are to visual stimulus. I guess some mothers haven't been guided themselves, so it's hard for them to know how to go about it."

"Yes, it would be hard to have a teenage daughter. I'm not sure what I'd do. When she is pushing her mom to be allowed to dress like a friend, or wanting to go where others go and you know it's not safe. Some just sneak and go anyhow." She remembered schoolmates. She hadn't sneaked, but she cringed inside, thinking of the past. The ugliness when she left home...the force of anger when she and her mother argued. Her own mother had sent her away at the end of one of those arguments. Her anger had become a shell of toughness and independence. Thinking back on that, Jen questioned it for the first time. *Maybe that toughness was not all good.* She looked at Sylvie with a fleeting fear that she'd been discovered. "I don't know how I'd deal with raising a girl."

"It's true that it's a huge challenge. I am still dealing with the fact that one of my two daughters is unhappy with me." Sylvie stopped. "With this girl in Oregon, I wonder about a lot of things. I wonder about her vulnerability. Does she have guardians or parents? Have they set some guidelines to protect her? If they say she has to be in at a certain time, it tells her friends that there's someone who cares. Kids fight curfews, but it's a protection. Does this girl have a strong, loving father figure? It could be that she flirted with the teacher because she was looking for affection, for a dad. Not necessarily the kind of attention she got. Like you said, no right-acting adult would take advantage of her flirtation. And a teacher of all people – you would hope that, rather than exploit, he would see a need and get her some counseling." Sylvia sounded stirred up.

"That's right!" Jen said. "When I think what a good counselor could accomplish..." she shook her head. "I wonder how many kids, boys or girls, fall through the cracks and don't get help?"

"I have no idea."

Jen had a far away look. "A lot of hurt."

"You're so right – a lot of hurt. When it comes to a child's perception, one wonders if this girl learned guiding principles for her life. How she should think about herself, what she fills her time and her mind with. Does she feel she has worth – to anyone? Does she dream about the potential within her? Does she get direction and encouragement to get busy and work to reach her goal? Does she understand that real love is lasting, that the Hollywood kind is not real? That love is much more than being cuddled in someone's arms for a little while?" While Jenny sat there, deep in thought, Sylvie pondered the worst case scenario. "I wonder what that girl has been through? Has she been molested?"

Jen raised her eyes. "That's exactly what I said. You have to wonder how she could be manipulated by a teacher. Maybe by threats or put-downs, or...if she had already had experiences that made her think she was a piece of trash. Something was wrong," Jen said emphatically, her eyes full of pain. Sylvia saw it and wondered. *There is something personal to this. What do I say now? Or do I keep quiet?* A strange feeling went through her. *What deep pain has Jen been through?*

Later, as Jenny scrubbed the toilet, her mind drifted to the girl in Oregon. She rubbed her sore neck. It was stiff with tension. *Talking about girls and their problems upsets me so much...Sure, I had my own share of unpleasant events happen to me when I was a girl.*

Wasn't anything like that – like a teacher overwhelming me – that I know of. Funny though, that it drains me so much. Well, enough of that somber subject. She set aside the bowl brush. *There must be so many abuse victims. I wonder if, maybe, I could help...* Standing up, she stretched, then walked out to the living room window. Through the trees she could see that clouds were coming from the west. They were rushing across the sky toward her, their undersides dark, heavy with rain. She felt the gloom of the low pressure and the approaching storm. Then a bright patch of blue in the south caught her attention. *What a pleasant sight that little patch of blue is. I am so lucky to live here in the country. I see more sky now instead of tall buildings. So nice to be able to notice what the weather is doing throughout the day. A patch of blue – someone said there was a good movie by that name.*

Eager to see more, Jen climbed the stairs. *I can get a view of the sky all around from up here.* She went to Michael's room and looked east. Nothing notable was happening. From the master bedroom she saw the same view as the living room. Then she went to the north-side room, her own retreat. Clouds were beginning to cover that part of the sky, releasing a fine mist. She stood quietly, gazing out at the tossing trees and the immense sky. The vastness shrank her sense of weighty problems. The window was open, letting in the fragrant, rain-freshened air. She breathed deeply of life-giving air that was beginnning to clear out her mental 'cobwebs'.

Refreshed after standing several minutes, Jen reached down and picked up a spiral tablet she was using for a journal. Sitting down, she rapidly wrote her mixed feelings. Nature's power and beauty; melancholy feelings – sadness for the girl in Oregon, sadness for herself. *What do I have to feel sad about now? It's spring. The weather is warming. The trees have leafed out in their fresh greens. I have a good neighbor, and Michael loves it here. Len even seems better.* She put down both sad thoughts and happy ones. As she did, more came. She stopped and re-read. Thoughts seemed more significant on paper – if not to anyone else, at least to her. She was pleased. *That free flow I once had has returned – more like poetry than journaling. When I first visited with Mary I wrote again. I'll have to keep paper handy. As I look at my written words I can sort out my thoughts better. Even when they are confusing, I see it easily. I fix it. I feel the strength that comes from having my ideas make sense. I can't believe that I'm still finding out who I am at thirty.* She giggled.

Jen slipped out of the house. The mist had stopped. In spite of rainclouds threatening, she walked slowly across the back field. The sky was dark. When an unexpected shaft of sunlight shone brightly on a hilltop, she stopped and gazed for two or three minutes until it disappeared. She quickened her pace toward the canyon ahead as she heard the cadence of high water, roiling around boulders deep in the creek. A physical sensation stirred inside of her, and she recognized it – anticipation – as strong as the pleasure of arriving. At last she stood on the edge of the canyon, watching the creek rushing, hurrying around the bend and out of sight.

Sylvia picked up the ringing phone – it was Lisa, greeting her with a cheerful "Hello Sylvie, how are you doing this week?"

"Great! I hope you're calling to say you'll keep our date for a visit on Wednesday!"

"You guessed it! I can still come. I'm bringing the notes on Ruth. Maybe we could cover some of the Bible questions you mentioned, too. I have a new study video I just got. If we don't watch it, I can leave it behind."

"Sounds good. I hope you have plenty of time. The new neighbor, Jennifer, is really nice and I hope she'll plan to be home and come meet you! I've enjoyed getting to know her. We took a walk down to the creek, and she appreciated its beauty so much."

"Oh, I'm so glad for you to have another woman nearby!"

"Yes, and she has a ten-year old boy who loves country life – they lived in Seattle before. It's nice to have a child in the neighborhood. But that awful old house... I feel sorry for Jen. It was supposedly 'fixed up' before they moved in."

"That is really too bad – that place was a wreck. I guess that one of the sheds fell down! Pretty sad. Well, maybe the landlord will do more, or if she has a husband he can work on it and take it off the rent."

"She has a husband, ah, but he's not around much. It would take a lot of work. Guess the out-of-town landlord must think that. He has done as little as possible. Just covered over the obvious problems. I think Jen can look trouble in the face. She didn't say much, but she looked disappointed. And the way she talked, I doubt the landlord would take anything off the rent for repairs." Sylvie wanted to say that the husband didn't seem the sort to do any work on the house, but held her tongue.

"I'd like to meet Jennifer. I hope she stays, in spite of the house." They chatted a while even though it was long distance, but finally had to bring it to an end. After Sylvia hung up, she made sure that she had marked the calendar. There was a note on the date already, 'Lisa coming'. A warm feeling filled her just thinking about it. She'd give Jennifer a call.

* * *

"What! You did *what?*" Len's scornful laughter filled the room. "You put cookies in the oven to bake and then went outside and stayed there until they were charcoal?"

Jen shook her head. "I started looking in the yard, where I could put flowers, and I guess I just got to daydreaming."

"Daydreaming? You were out of it – *that's* what I'd say. You *are* out of it. You don't know if you're coming in or going out."

"I just lost track of time for a few minutes. That's all."

"You just lose it, period. You don't know if you're coming or going. The kitchen is filled with stinking smoke and you say 'that's all'. What a waste. And you could have burned the place down."

"I don't think a house fire would start from the oven."

"You don't *think* so, huh? Don't tell *me* what you *think*, Mouthy. What do you know? And you gripe and complain about wanting to buy more groceries. Then you go and waste them!"

"I know. I should have been more careful." In self-disgust Jen averted her eyes, and recalled how she'd meant to keep a close watch on grocery spending.

Len swore, "You're so stupid!" He reached into the fridge for a beer. "You weary me." He stomped off to the front room.

Jen picked up the ringing phone. It would be Sylvia. So few people knew her number.

"Hi! I'm hoping you can come over to my place this coming Wednesday! You'll have a chance to meet Lisa, that friend I told you about who used to live out here. We'll have some girl time!"

Jen hesitated. It did sound good. "Okay. I will." *I don't have a job. I'll try out the fun side of this woman-at-home role.*

As Jenny puttered in the kitchen afterward, she thought about this Lisa she'd heard of. So she and Sylvia had been reading the Bible together. Sylvia seemed to think that Lisa knew a lot about it. *Well, I have some questions for her!* Jen thought. *I might not be brave enough to bring them up now; just meet her. I'll keep them in mind for another time.*

CHAPTER EIGHTEEN

Jenny quietly closed Michael's door with a sigh. It was still dark out; too early to stay up. Her back ached. It would feel good to go back to bed, lay down. It was four-o'clock and the sun wouldn't be up for a while. She decided to take a chance that she wouldn't wake Len. Going carefully across the squeaky boards, she gently took hold of the bedroom doorknob and turned it quietly.

Tiptoeing across the room she slid slowly into bed without touching Len's back that was toward her. Suddenly he turned, muttering angrily, "Have you been up with that kid again?"

"Yes," she said softly, hoping calmness in her voice would soothe him.

"It's wrong. Dumb. You know better." His voice grew loud, forceful. "Don't you?"

"Michael was crying. He was in pain." Even as she gave the answer, she knew he wouldn't accept it as valid.

"That's an excuse. It's just to get your attention, get your sympathy. He's a wimp." He gave a disgusted snort. "So now that you've ruined my sleep…" He left it hanging in the air. He tossed for a while. Jenny lay tense and silent, wondering if he'd start in on her again. When snoring began, she hoped to relax. But her muscles were stiff and she had a headache. The clock measured the passage of time. She stared into the darkness and her mind returned to the figure of Michael in his bed, finally going to sleep, but whimpering softly.

In the morning after Len left, Michael was still achy. After getting a soak in the bathtub with Epsom salts he felt better. "Do you think you feel like going to school?" she asked.

"Yes, I think so. I'll know if I walk around a bit. It's late though. The school bus will come in a few minutes."

"Well, maybe Sylvia feels like taking a drive and would take you in. I'll call."

Sure enough, Sylvie was happy to give him a ride to school. Jen wrote him a note. As she sent him out the door, a riddle book he carried caught Jennifer's eye. *That's good to see. He tries to outsmart me with his riddles, gets delighted. Good that he's into something lighthearted. It's an outlet, and it will help him be more sociable while he's adjusting to the new school.* Then, as her mind wandered, she remembered getting in bed at four a.m. and having Len chew her out. *Oh, well,* she thought. *I knew I should have gone downstairs. It was dumb to go in there. Next time I'll know better. Get a blanket from the basement room and curl up on the couch.*

Saturday, Jen answered the phone. Sylvia's voice asked, "Would Michael like to go to town with me? I'm shopping. I'll be gone an hour. Just thought, it being that he's home, he might like to get out, and you might like to work on the house."

"Oh, how nice of you to think of him! He probably would. I'll ask. Hold on." Jen came back to the phone. "He says he'd like that. He might be shy to say, but he likes you! I'll say it for him."

"I like him. Good to have a boy around again. My son, Mark, is long since grown up, so this is nice for me. I'll pick up Michael in twenty minutes."

As they drove along, Sylvia asked Michael if he had seen her children's pictures on the living room wall. When he said no, she described them.

"My oldest is Mark. He was an only child for a while, like you. Then he had two sisters, Isabel and Nadine. Mark lives close, in Seattle with his wife and little girl, one and one-half years old. His sister, Nadine, is also there, going to college, but in a different part of the city."

"Where is Isabel?" Michael asked.

"She's far away. I don't know, right at this moment, where she is. That seems strange, doesn't it?"

"Yes." Michael was quiet for a minute. "Do you miss her?"

Sylvia didn't expect the direct question. It hit her. She swallowed hard and said, "Yes, I do. I love getting letters from her. When you grow up and live far away, write to your mom, even if it's just a note or a postcard."

"I will. But I'm not going to leave her for a long time yet. When I do go away, I'll send her something pretty from where I am. She'll like that."

"That would be nice. Sometimes Isabel writes a letter from far away, and it makes me very happy. I had my other two grown kids here on Mother's Day. It was great."

"Ohhh..." Michael's voice trailed off sadly. "I missed Mother's Day. I guess we were moving." Michael got a cheerless look on his face. "I missed it," he said again quietly.

Sylvia pulled up and parked. The hardware-variety story was in front of them. "Well, it's not too late! You can get your mom something here, and make your own card. I'll give you five dollars to spend any way you want."

"I wouldn't take your money. I budget my allowance for buying things."

"Oh," Sylvia said, surprised at his grown-up, managerial tone. "If you don't want me to give it to you, then I'll lend it to you. You can pay it back later, out of your allowance. But now is a good chance to shop and surprise her, if you want to."

"That's a great idea! I have four dollars at home I can spend four and pay you back today." He looked at her, a little unsure. "If it's okay, that is..."

"It sure is. Take the five and use it all. I know you're right next door and won't leave town owing a bad debt!" She laughed, but he didn't.

He looked at her like he was trying to be sure of what she meant. She gave him a light smack on the shoulder and said, "Well young man, I have some shopping to do and so do you!" She quickly got out of the car, saying "Let's go!"

Michael methodically shopped, walking down every aisle, going back around the store, carefully deciding what would be best for his mom, while Sylvia browsed in other aisles.

* * *

Sylvia set out her porcelain mugs on the kitchen counter, remembering how many times she and Lisa had visited like this. She could hardly wait. They had become close as neighbors. Even though Lisa was younger, Sylvia quickly learned that she had a good understanding of life, and the closeness grew between them. After a time, Lisa shared her own pain – the misunderstandings between herself and her daughter, Lorene. The strain of wondering how to be a parent had taken a toll. She had regrets, and Sylvia listened. Then they balanced the serious talk with pleasant activities. Confessing a mutual abundance of words, they laughingly referred to "cussing and discussing a problem to death". Theirs was a meshing together that neither had expected. Lisa also shared thoughts Sylvia had never considered – a different outlook on life. As she dealt with her parenting difficulties, she gained an equilibrium, trying not to blame herself morbidly, knowing Lorene had responsibility. Sylvia was encouraged by Lisa's insights into Biblical truths. In pre-teen years, the Bible had been a totally new book to Sylvia. She began to learn about God's promises and blessings which she could claim in her own young life. Too quickly, she had quit attending church. Lisa was excited about a Precepts Bible Study, a course she was taking. Sylvie was surprised to read how she might incorporate the course's principles into her own daily life. It wasn't just Lisa's point of view. It worked. She was encouraged as she began to apply God's thoughts to real life. Then Lisa moved and the studies were over.

Sylvie looked up, startled by a noise, and hurried to the back door. Lisa pulled into the driveway and energetically popped out of her car. She was a large-boned young woman, closing in on her fortieth birthday. With healthy energy in her every move, she gave a youthful impression. Sylvie hurried down the porch steps. Lisa grabbed her and they hugged and stayed arm in arm up the steps.

Lisa swept her free arm toward the periwinkle blue pansies. "I see how the yard, and even the porch, are bursting forth with color again this year. I see the rhodies are budding into loveliness. It looks more beautiful than ever!"

"It is coming along nicely, isn't it? Come on in, and make yourself at home! I can't believe how long it's been!"

"I shall do just that!" They entered the house and Lisa strolled into the living room while Sylvie put on water for tea. Lisa wandered over to the window, looked out on the yard, and raised her arms in a stretch, envying country life. She went to the pictures of the three kids on the wall. "It feels so good to be here!" Coming back in the kitchen she commented on Sylvia's desk.

"Oh!" Sylvia was startled, remembering. "I must call Jen and see if she made time to come over. I've looked forward to introducing you two to each other."

"I would like to meet her. However, I'd like to catch you up on Yolanda and Lorene. I don't want to say some of this stuff later. I do hope Jen is still able to come."

"Yes. I'll call in a bit." Sylvia carried a tray with the tea pot, cups and sugar to the deck, set it down, and indicated a padded chaise for Lisa.

Stretching out on the padded lounge, with a pillow that Sylvie had readied for her, she said, "It's so relaxing here. I haven't felt as free to share with others what's going on, the way I have done with you, except for Rona. We've become friends. But the tension sure builds up. Sorry I couldn't bring only good news."

"I'm sorry it's that way. But I'm glad to listen to the news, good or bad, you know."

"I know you are. I appreciate it. I'll share it, but first off, I want to hear how you and Larry are doing."

"You know…" she gently shook her head, "Larry and I are doing just great. I can't thank you enough for recommending Marriage Encounter."

"I'm glad for you! But that's just like you, Sylvie – understatement about your own efforts! Giving someone else the credit."

"You told us! And Larry worked at it. Remember him? Before, he couldn't talk about his feelings at all. Now, though it's not daily "love and feeling letters", we talk. We do give each other notes, too.

168

We're getting better! Correcting misconceptions." She scrunched her head down like an embarrassed turtle, pulling into its shell. "For one thing, I don't interrupt Larry when he's talking. I learned it takes a man more time to get a hold of the right words before he'll begin talking, or continue."

"How true! Pete's that way, too."

Sylvie said, "I was re-reading our notebooks. It was nice to remember how the light came on. I had been frustrated, felt I wasn't finding out the deeper stuff that was going on inside him. And felt, too, that he wasn't interested in my feelings. I appreciate being heard now, and being able to *hear* Larry. It is so much better – when we practice it!"

"I remember you two... the separateness. How you seemed alienated from each other. After you attended, I saw the looks, the communication, even with just the eyes... Yes, you worked."

"Ah. We did. But you are the one who brought the tools to us. We weren't quite at war. But for sure, we lacked a sense of teamwork. We're learning! Now, that said, I want to hear how it's *really* coming with Lorene and Yolanda."

"Unfortunately, as I said on the phone, Lorene's antics didn't stop. She ended up involving Yolanda. After the unpleasant Christmastime incidents I told you about, there was one more. Sometimes I wonder how many years this will go on with Lorene before there is a change. Anyway, two months ago she came back and read us the riot act *again*. The counselor has encouraged us to play hard-ball with her, since that is her style. After she had vented to us, we quietly emphasized that she had responsibilities that she needed to face. We told her this was her opportunity. She could take steps and change how she looked at life; see where she was at, where she was going. If she'd let go of bitterness, she could heal. Easier said than done, I know. But it can be done. Whether she feels our sympathy or not, I can't tell. In any case, she didn't like what we said. We ask her, what is your goal? As a young adult you can get help and get an education. Then you can make a living and run your own life, just like you keep saying you want to do. If you continue to be involved with people who don't have their own lives together, who knows? You could end up surrounded by an even worse crowd than you can imagine – end up feeling used all over again. Pete and I hoped that she would see this and get honest. Take responsibility. We felt bad but we believed we were saying what was needed. Sadly, she wasn't listening."

"How *did* she respond?"

"You wouldn't have wanted to hear all she said when she left – cussing us out. We were the worst. We understood then. She wasn't ready. We didn't know when we'd see her again..." Lisa paused, and put her hand to her face, overcome with tears. "Oh, Sylvia, there was so much hatred in it." She heaved a sigh, brushing at the tears.

Sylvia reached out and pressed Lisa's arm. "Here I thought she might be ready to start some healthier communicating with you and Pete – less blaming and more adult."

"Well, she's not there yet."

"She's such a bright girl. One day she'll be ready to have a more mature attitude."

Lisa nodded slowly, then went on. "After the goodbye scene, we felt that she would likely disappear again. Wrong. She waited until Yolanda left the house, followed her, and then she verbally lit into her with all she had. She picked her time and place, knowing that we would never allow her talk to Yolanda that way. Then she began pulling Yolanda's hair and hitting her, but just then, fortunately, three girls came and pulled her off. She took off running. I was so angry. What Lorene said made Yolanda feel like dirt. Besides that, Lorene implied if Yolanda weren't living with us, Lorene would have come back home to live. It took the poor girl weeks to get over it. I kept assuring her that Lorene knows that we have room for both of them. How can Lorene say that when she always talked about wanting a sister. Yolanda believed us when we finally said that the only thing stopping Lorene is that she doesn't want to have any rules. She especially doesn't want rules about respecting others. Nor does she want to deal with her attitudes and her 'baggage' and let go of it. The fact is, that her only freedom will come in forgiving us, and those who have hurt her. I hope she comes to see that we could only give what we had to give to her at that time. We made mistakes and we've apologized for them. If she'd let go of this blame game, she could move on with her life."

Sylvia slowly shook her head, incredulous. "I have trouble picturing that this is the same polite little girl I knew a few years ago. I'm so sorry, Lisa. It's sad to hear that Lorene still is hurting you and Pete, and now, on top of it, Yolanda. And herself."

"Yes. It hurts. Pete was overwhelmed by her earlier verbal attacks, but I thought I was doing okay. Then that latest aggressiveness aimed directly at Yolanda happened. Well, I found out I wasn't okay. I was so angry – I wanted to find Lorene and straighten her out. I asked around but didn't get a chance to talk to her – just as well. I talked it out with Pete's counselor. So...anyway, that's where it's at now. It could be a long time before there's healing." Lisa grimaced wryly. "'Patience is a virtue', they tell me." She took a deep breath, reached an outstretched hand to squeeze Sylvie's, and said with a smile, "I'm in the mood for something *non*-serious now. Let's see if Jen can come over and we'll have some 'girl time'!"

"You've got it! I'm so glad you're here. Maybe you needed this day as much or more than I did! We've started, and now we'll get together often. I'll give Jen a call."

Jen arrived, coming up Sylvie's steps to the deck with hesitation, and shyly said, "Hello." Sylvie had gone in to get a plate of snacks.

"Hello!" Lisa jumped up and held out her hand. She restrained herself from her usual hug. "I'm glad to meet you, Jen! It's so nice you live here by Sylvie. When I moved away I was hoping and praying for a woman to move nearby. Do you miss the city?"

Jen described the move and meeting Sylvia. Her pleasure in seeing the creek and experiencing the sense of peace, away from the city rush and pressure.

Lisa shared how she had enjoyed Sylvia's friendship. "After I moved away, it was lonely for both of us. At first I was busy learning a new job, so the phone calls were short. After the initial confusion of unpacking and the job adjustment, I really missed being able to pick up the phone and say, "I'm coming over!"

Sylvie came out with a plate of veggies and crackers. "Back in one minute. Jen, I have coffee almost ready for you. And I'll make a fresh pot of tea."

Sylvie returned to find Lisa talking about her search in the city for quiet parks amidst the bustle.

Sylvie said to Jen, "Out here we don't need to look far, do we?" Jen shook her head with a look of satisfied appreciation. Then she asked Lisa, "Where did you live when you were here?"

"Farther down the road. I prefer old farm houses, if they're fixed up. Ours had been modernized enough."

"Do you miss living in that house?"

"Oh, life moves on. It's Sylvie I miss. And Larry. He and Pete got along well."

"And," Sylvia interrupted, "I really missed Lisa when she left, more than she knew. I didn't tell her too often. Make her sad. She had helped me a lot. We were talking just a few minutes ago of how she directed Larry and me to Marriage Encounter. That weekend was hard work, but it changed our outlook."

"You mean *you* changed your outlook!" Lisa piped up.

"Okay. It's true. Thinking of where Lisa lived, I remembered Jeremy, and his mother, too. You and Michael would enjoy meeting them. I'll introduce you soon." "There are a lot of nice neighbors to get to know," Lisa said.

"Yes, "

With a raised eyebrow, Lisa asked, "Have you introduced Jen to Mrs. Weltam?"

"Oh, Lisa!" she laughed. "You're bad!" Turning to Jenny, she said, "Mrs. Weltam lives about a mile down the road. She's... unusual."

Lisa laughed out loud. "Is that what you call it! Unusual, is it?" She turned to Jen. "Mrs. Weltam is the most negative person you'll meet here. Maybe ever. Just so you're prepared. Otherwise she might have you overwhelmed. Hmm. Weltam overwhelms. That works." She chuckled. "Sorry to gossip. I'll leave it there."

"There is one funny incident I have to share with Jen," Sylvie said. "Once when the three of us were together, Lisa told us her cat had given birth to kittens. Mrs. Weltam was scandalized when Lisa said that she wished Lorene had been awake to see the birth. Mrs. W. asked, 'Whatever for? That's an awful thing for a child to see.' I had never seen Lisa speechless before. She looked confused, and I was ready to burst, holding my snickering as well as I could, not daring to look at her. Finally Lisa replied, 'So she could see the miracle of birth; see how the mother cat loves her babies, how she purrs all the while. How she releases each kitten from the membrane holding it like a little package. To see how she cuddles and licks the kitten dry.' Lisa couldn't stop. She said, 'It's a wonder to me how even a "first-time" mother cat knows to do those things. Purring constantly for joy.' I thought Mrs. Weltam was going to upchuck her lunch. It really was funny – until that point. Then Mrs. W began to lash into Lisa with her tongue, how coarse and indiscreet she was, et cetera. But that's enough. I *am* gossiping for sure, now."

"Here I was being positive, telling Jen I prayed for a woman friend to move by you, and we're dragging her down already!" Lisa laughed and turned to Jen. "All banter aside, I am very happy that Sylvie has you so close by. You *are* an answer to prayer, you know!"

Jen laughed. "I don't know. That's hard to believe! Have *you* found a woman friend in Seattle since you moved?"

"Yes. Rona. She's been great." Turning to Sylvie, she said, "I'd like to bring her with me another time."

"That would be great. Jen and I can both meet her. So Jen, have you had any calls from the restaurants for waitress work?"

"One. They said they needed someone on the spot – right then. I couldn't get there fast enough. I have a bus schedule and I could at rush hour, maybe. But in between there are big gaps. I can't just stand by the road, wave my hand, and make a bus appear."

"Oh, no! Too bad you missed a shift. I would have been glad to take you."

"I appreciate that. You had told me so. I might have asked, but I knew you were gone that day. When I told them how much time I'd need to get there by bus, they said they'd get someone else. I said I'd like them to try me again. I think it was just an emergency that time. Too bad. I'd have liked them to see that I can do the work. Ha, I should go in and say, 'I'm going to put in a four-hour shift free, to show you what I can do!' They'd fall over."

"No," Lisa laughed. "I think they'd say, 'You can't do *that*. You need to fill out all this paperwork. We'll send in your Unemployment Insurance form. Then there's the Labor Board. We don't want trouble...' My eyes have been opened to the complications of working in the city. Here, too, I'm sure. And anyway, you should be paid."

"I was in the city a long time." Jen dropped her head and smiled to herself. "Once upon a time in the city… But that was then, and I love living out here. I have to admit though, it was sure easier getting a job there. I miss the pay. Especially the tips. To think that I'm missing the tourist season – busy wasn't the word for it. Exhausting, but the tips were wonderful. At least I have a savings account with tip money in it." She looked down. "Lennard doesn't know there is much in it though, so please don't say anything to him. I'm glad I have a little cushion. Right after we moved I was able to pick up a few things with money I'd drawn out in Seattle. That was before Len got work." She looked up and smiled weakly. "Don't worry. He got on at the mill. He'll have regular paychecks now."

Sylvia's eyes met Lisa's, then she stood. "I'll fill the tea pot again. I'm sure glad he got a job." Turning to Lisa, she flourished her hand toward Jenny, "This lady needs the coffee for a stronger lift. All that unpacking and getting settled into a new house. Jen, you have made a big difference over there already."

"I don't know, but thanks. Say, speaking of getting settled, I'm ready to go to the second-hand store with you. I've made a list of what I need to look for."

"Do you want to go now?" Lisa asked. "All three of us can go."

"Oh, no."

"We can. We'll all go."

"It can wait," Jen said. "It may take me some time and this is your visit. In fact, I'm very glad to meet you Lisa; I shouldn't have stayed this long, taking up your time together."

"Oh, please," Lisa countered. "Part of the reason I came out was so I could meet you!"

Jen felt the old grab of fear come over her. *Why did Lisa want to meet me? To find out if Sylvia was misled in making friends? But it's silly to be afraid. Lisa seemed to say it genuinely.* She responded. "I've been looking forward to our meeting, too."

They decided to stroll around the yard, enjoying the rhododendrons. After walking down the country road a way, they came back and sat out on the deck to rest.

Agreeing on a walk across the back pasture, they strolled across and sat down on the bank above the creek. Lisa said, "I have never forgotten the first day we met, Sylvie. You were so excited about this creek!"

"Yes, I guess I do go on and on about it, don't I?"

"Well," Jen piped in, "it's worth getting excited about!" Surprised, she thought, *I'm more bold being around Lisa's enthusiasm.* "I've just begun to enjoy it. I'm planning to spend a lot more time down here. We plan to go up the mountainside to the pool, too."

"I haven't forgotten! I'm waiting until you have the time, so you let me know."

"I will; and it won't be long." She gazed across the creek to where the small mountain rose out of sight.

Unwilling to see the afternoon end, the women slowly started back to the house.

"I am so glad to meet you, Jen! This is wonderful, knowing that Sylvia has you to keep her company." Turning to Sylvia as she opened her car door, she said with a laugh, "I'm inviting myself out again. You said you didn't mind, so I'll bring my friend, Rona, and the four of us can have a good visit. Oh." She reached in her car's back seat. "Here's that video I said I'd leave."

"Okay. I'll look at it. It will be so nice to have you and Rona out. I've been missing women friends and now it's all happening at once! Give me a call when you have the day figured out between Rona's work schedule and yours. I'm eager to meet her."

Saying a reluctant goodbye, Lisa drove off. Sylvia turned to Jen and said, "Well, now you know Lisa. I'm so glad! After she finds out their schedules, we can set a time for another visit."

Jen meandered home with a dreamy feeling. It had been special to be included in the afternoon. Two long-time friends... Her cheerful mood left her as soon as she saw that Goldie had dug a hole under the edge of the porch. Len would beat her for that if he came home now. She got the shovel to fix it. The poor foolish dog was probably after a mouse.

CHAPTER NINTEEN

Jen started out the door with her list in hand. *I know Sylvie can answer my questions about gardening.*

When Sylvia opened the door and Jen waved her list of questions, she grabbed her jacket, saying, "Good! I'll get the seed catalog. It has pictures. We'll take a look in the garden." They walked along the beds, springing to life with green. Sylvia named them. A few were already blooming. She pointed to one clump of chopped-off brown stalks. "That's a late perennial. Perennials come up year after year with very little care." It looked dead, but, as they got down and looked closer, Jen saw that green sprouts of new growth were pushing up among the dead brown stuff. "That one will bloom in August and September. Old reliable," Sylvia nicknamed it. "Perennials are expensive initially, but last for years. To get color in your yard now, you can start with sowing seeds for the fast-growing annuals, and you may also want to buy some plants already started, ones that wouldn't sprout on their own in the early season cold. Our temperatures are cooler than the Seattle-Everett area, because we're at a higher elevation. They also have the moderating effect of the water, the bays and tide flats. Our nights are not reliably warm for a while yet. You aren't behind."

"Good," Jen nodded, and thought that there was so much she didn't know.

"To have perennials, get divisions from a neighbor – me!" The quiet enthusiasm in Sylvia's voice revealed again to Jen an earlier insight. That under the subdued surface of this woman lay depths of emotion. Sylvia continued, "Get a deeply prepared flower bed ready for perennials by adding to the soil, after you get out the rocks. Then we'll just dig in with a shovel and take 'divisions' at the right time. Some things can be moved right away, others later."

Jenny began to express her appreciation, but Sylvia interrupted with, "It's nothing. I've been given so many plants. It's nice to know you'll enjoy them."

Sylvia opened what looked like a dirt-smudged magazine. Flipping the pages of the catalog, she pointed out which items she already had in her garden. Turning pages of color pictures she said, "Here is the section on annuals – the ones you can buy for quick color." She pointed to some. "These are good in poor soil and don't need much watering." She pulled out a stub of a pencil. "Go ahead and put check marks by the ones you like." They strolled along. Jen asked questions and Sylvia nodded, or sometimes shook her head, explaining a plant's fussiness. Just looking at the pictures excited Jen as she visualized how she could brighten the yard around her home.

"Let's go in the house for a cup of tea." At the table Jenny made a list of possible bedding plants to buy. It was exciting to know that the only thing that lay between her and a colorful garden was hard work.

Sylvie commented, "One warning – it's normal to bite off too big a chunk the first year. Breaking up and preparing soil is very hard work. Literally, as in hard soil! I have had a neighbor, Jeremy, a teenager, helping me for the past several years. You might want to consider hiring him for part of the heavy work. So take it slow; it's a 'work in progress'."

Jen wondered just *how much* work it would be. "More than a year?"

Sylvie nodded. "More than a year."

As they went back outside they heard the school bus pull up on the road below. Soon Michael could be heard coming up his own driveway, calling Goldie. Then he appeared at the edge of Sylvia's driveway, calling, "I have a riddle for you, Mrs. Ford!"

"I'm ready for you, Michael! I'm an old riddle solver from away back. Three kids taught me well!"

His delight was obvious. "Oh, Mrs. Ford, I doubt that I can confound you then." Sylvia supressed a smile. He felt important as he flipped open his small book. He showed her the page with the picture of a table on it. At the top was a question he read aloud. "What do you put on the table, cut and then pass around, but would never actually eat?" He smiled impishly up at her, his brown eyes dancing.

Sylvia thought. "Cut...hmm. But never eat." She pondered a while. "I don't know. I just can't think of anything."

"A deck of cards!"

"Oh, Michael! You are too clever for me! I never thought of cards." He went running off with Goldie, saying, "Thanks. I'll find another one for tomorrow! Come on, Girl!"

* * *

Len hollered, "Barmaid! Give me a beer! It's hot outside, and I'm getting hotter under the collar by the second. What's the matter around this two-bit joint? Can't you get off your backsides?" He pounded the bar with the next words. "Give a thirsty man some service?"

The barmaid appeared and came sauntering over to him, her face tilted as if to size him up. "Got a problem? We serve nice men here. Can you be a nice man?" Her look was half flirtatious, half irritated. "I might get you a beer if you're nice!"

"Sure, Baby. I am a nice man. Now get me a beer – I'm hot and dry."

"Okay, Big Boy. Okay. We've got hot wings today. Do you want some of those, too?"

"No. Just the beer. And hurry up. I'm thirsty."

As she poured, she looked over at a customer sitting quietly at the end of the bar. "Say, Joe, do you need another?"

He looked directly at Len and said, "No, I don't, thank you. But I *can* set an example of basic courtesy for your mouthy customer there. If he gives you trouble, let me know."

Len turned on his stool and looked directly at the man. "You an English teacher or something? Got a problem with the way I talk?"

"I just like to hear a woman treated with courtesy, that's all."

"Yea, well, I can be as courteous as you any day, fella. So just come down off your high horse and relax."

"I'm relaxed." The man turned away. Len figured it was over. Suddenly the man was standing nearby.

"I don't think I've seen you around here before. You just passing through?"

"No. You wish I'd be movin' on? Is that it?"

"Hey, don't *you* get on *your* high horse. I'm just greeting a new face in town, that's all."

"Oh, yea? I'd be glad to make sure you *don't* forget this face. You got a problem with it?"

"Greeting, I said. I didn't say problem. You been in the area long?"

"You know – I don't need to *answer* your nosy questions."

"Oh, you're the friendly type. The way you ordered this barmaid around I should have guessed. We really *don't* need your type here. If you think you're going to come to our town and make trouble, buddy, you've got another think coming."

The barmaid came over. "Hey, fellas, can you just drop it? We got a nice place here and we like to keep it that way."

"I'm nice," Len said. "Your man Joe, here, is the ugly one. He told me to get out of town." Turning to Joe he said, "I don't think I like you bein' the reception committee. We ought to change that. Elect someone else to the post." Len glanced around. Two men were sitting at a table eating hot wings. They looked away with feigned disinterest. "You over there. Are you friendly?" They didn't answer.

"I said YOU! You deaf? This guy thinks he owns the place." The men looked nervously at Len. "I'm gonna name him Mr. Joe Friendly. He has decided he's the big shot around here. We'll see."

With all eyes on him, Len, quick as a cougar, swung around with his fist carrying all the weight of his body into Joe's jaw. He went sprawling backward onto the bar stools and slid off. Rolling over as he fell, he spread out his hands to save cracking his face on the floor. Dazed, blood running from his mouth, he lay there – then shook his head. Len heard his low muttering.

"You still feeling friendly?" Len kicked at the bottom of Joe's shoe. No answer. Joe gathered himself in a crouch. Suddenly his shoe shot out and clipped Len in the shin bone. In a flash Len grabbed and twisted the leg, then kicked the man hard in the ribs. He curled up in pain, unable to take a breath.

"Guess I shut your friendly mouth for a while." He grabbed his beer, downed it, and threw money on the bar. Looking at the barmaid he said, "There's enough there for a nice tip. But you ought to be paying *me* for the entertainment. Be glad to bring you a little excitement again, any time." He walked out.

* * *

The letter lay open on Jen's table. *What a time for a visit by Aunt Gertrude. It couldn't have been worse. And now she's waiting for an answer. How will she be picked up at the airport? I'm not even sure I can get to Everett in that car, let alone through Seattle and halfway to Tacoma.* Jenny considered the distance to Sea-Tac Airport. It was impossible. She dreaded writing the letter. No, writing wouldn't do. It would have to be a phone call. The date of Aunt Gert's trip was too close. It had taken extra time to forward the letter. *Oh, why does it have to be a phone call? It will be worse trying to explain it on the phone. I can hear it now – I'm telling her why I can't come down to pick her up while she's trying to tell me why I can. Oh, Aunt Gert… oops, I had better start now to say Aunt Gertrude, or I'll slip and then I'll be in trouble. After she has to make the trip out here on her own, she'll already be in a doubly bad mood toward me. Oh, why did it have to be now? One bright spot; Len will probably be away, selling a car. But how can I deal with a visit when this house is like it is? She won't put up with any of it.*

Jen's mind went back to her 'family of origin', as it was called by the professionals. Aunt Gertrude had been married to her father's older brother, Wilbur. She was a widow for some time now. In the early years of their marriage she had lived in the east among the elite and the social climbers. Jenny didn't know when they had moved to San Francisco. She was well-groomed and proper. That was fine. But her properness was pompous, and one could see that in the woman's haughty facial expressions. She *knew* she was a "lofty" person. Her haughtiness, and the disdain in her voice as she scrutinized another's efforts, conveyed the message – no one, that is *no* one, measured up to her standards. Jen had become acquainted with this proud woman's contempt for lesser beings under very trying circumstances. It was during a visit by Aunt Gertrude, just after Jen's dad had left them. Gertrude showed up with her husband, Wilbur, or Willy, in tow behind her. Jen could still hear the harsh, domineering voice accusing her mother, "You drove him away. You *know* you did. And to think you could have been a proper wife. If you had some class, you might still have a husband. He will never come back now. And why should he?" As this tirade continued, Jen could see her mother's tight lips, head bowed forward, not in humility but in an effort to keep her anger to herself. She knew she could find no defense in the face of this woman's scorn. Gertrude had left and gone to a hotel. Jen's mother had stormed around the house, yelling, "Who does she think she is? Coming in here in her self-importance, presuming she can just lord it over me. That's what she's saying – that she thinks she's *somebody* and I'm nobody. Well, I could tell her a thing or two about that so-called happy husband of hers. Willy doesn't have a life, and he wouldn't have one single idea of his own if he tried – and he never will even *try*." Jen's mother held a level of contempt for Aunt Gertrude that was equal to – no, it surpassed what she had received from the arrogant woman. Though they rarely spoke of Aunt Gert afterward, Jen knew there was corroding bitterness in her mother.

Aunt Sally had spoken only one time to Jen about growing up with Wilber and Carl, Jen's father. It had been during Michael's babyhood. They talked of the challenge of parenting. She had turned to Jenny and sadly told of the unhappy relationships in her childhood home. Uncle Willy was a brat, spoiled by their mother. She not only gave him unwarranted privileges, but also enabled him to evade responsibility for his actions. When a dispute arose, she was partial to Willy. She reproached Carl – he enjoyed his father's kindness. The father had seen through Willie's self-centered ways and caught him giving deceitful answers. Aunt Sally recounted how, when their dad had been killed in World War II, they fell into financial ruin. Their mother was angry after being left to raise three children alone. She seemed to want to punish her dead husband for dying. She had never forgiven him for not favoring Wilbur, or Sweet Willy as she called him. She became more disparaging in her treatment of Carl, while continuing to favor the 'spoiled brat'. As Jen thought on these things that Aunt Sally had shared, she saw that, to Wilbur's detriment, it was a set-up for a manipulative, domineering woman like Aunt Gert, who ran his life, coming in where his mama had left off. Sure, he had still wanted his own way, but she knew how to please his self-centered appetites while getting everything that she wanted.

Jenny sat down and ran her fingers over the expensive but overly-ornate paper of Aunt Gertrude's letter. How her dad's sister, Aunt Sally, had come out of all the conflict in the home with such a kind spirit, Jen thought she would never know. Sally, or actually Sarah, had been close to her father. Maybe the security that her father's love brought had made the difference. Though young, she had learned to divert him from confrontations with his big brother.

Aunt Sally had said, "I learned to sense when the trouble brewing between the boys had become serious. Willy was ready to take off running to Mother with his story, blaming the trouble on Carl. Mother would believe anything he said, so there'd be no fixing it once he played the informer. I found I could bribe Willy not to tattle. He was self-indulgent so when I asked him to be quiet, all that was needed to smooth things over was do what Mother did. I'd give Sweet Willy a piece of my candy, or I'd tell him, 'let's get cake from the kitchen maid.' It's too bad that, as they became young men, bigger problems were not so easily solved. My only lasting regret is that there was no life insurance money left to give Carl an education after Willy received his. Mother had run out of money. As you know, your dad took up the trade of halibut fishing out of necessity. The rough conditions took a large toll on his health. He was not prepared to handle that life. He joined with men around him in heavy drinking. On the home front, Mother, who had always 'put on airs', found lack of money very difficult, emotionally, especially. The time came that she could no longer pay the help, and had to dismiss the housekeeper, the maids and the cook. She had only one half-time maid who helped her. She was getting older and could barely cope with the hard work of keeping her own house. It was very large. The best furniture was sold in order to get by. This was overwhelming for her. Carl found work on land and he and your mother married and were very happy at first. But he had to go back to fishing. He struggled with life on the fishing boats. As time passed he became an alcoholic. Our mother constantly, until her dying day, reminded Carl he was inferior, a lowly fisherman."

Aunt Sally spoke of all this at one sitting. When Jenny asked questions on a different occasion she had little more to say. Simply, "I am sorry it was that way for your father. Carl would not have left his family if he had thought differently about himself. He could no longer provide by halibut fishing. His health broke. I have explained the situation so you won't hold things against him. Your mother was a working girl; they were very much in love. She was doing okay when they were first married. This need for the background picture is the only reason I've told you these difficulties – so that you will understand your parents, their marriage breakdown, and also..."

After a pause, Aunt Sally continued. "There is no reason to hate your Grandmother Hanson. She – my mother – came out of great difficulty, though it took me a lot of years to find out the story and even more time to understand it. There was a lot to overcome, and she just never did. She was one of the Home Children. She was brought from England and placed in a home in Ontario, Canada, before World War I. Some of those children were taken in by families to do farm work and housekeeping. Some of the homes were good, and the people were loving. But in others the children were made to feel they ought always to be grateful, yet they were treated more like slaves. In some homes they were made to eat separately. I suppose their food was different from the family. They could "see that they were inferior", at least in the eyes of their 'benefactors'. Inferior to the natural-born children in the household. In her whole life, my mother never spoke of that time period. I later researched it. I think the humiliation of it scarred her deeply."

Aunt Sally's eyes look off in the distance to that long-ago situation. "Can you imagine, being taken away from your home, your sad mother, your country? Being thrust into a strange household? One where they don't love you and even enjoy humiliating you?

Her school days must have been filled with teasing about her shabby clothes. When she was at school, I wonder... I don't know if she would have been ashamed and easily humiliated, or if she became defiant toward those around her. But I imagine that her attitude left something to be desired. She struggled all her life to prove that she was 'somebody'. When she reached her teens she left that first household and worked as a domestic servant in several others. She finally worked for my grandparents, who were very lovely people. She fell in love with their son – my father – and she married him. That's interesting and unusual – her employer's son became her beau. She had apparently picked up some social graces from the families where she was a maid. His was a wealthy family who had been able to survive the Crash of 1929. When their son fell in love with her they did everything they could for Mother. She told me of how wonderful it felt to be the belle of the ball. As the new bride they helped her settle into her new life. She was on good terms with her parents in law for some time."

Here Aunt Sally stopped, as though wondering how much to say. "Mother had a chip on her shoulder. She thought she was looked down on. I never sensed that she was, certainly not by her husband's parents. Maybe by others. But I can understand how she would have created some of her own problems. She became huffy and defensive easily. The whole "class conscious" matter, even in America, was a big factor. In England the attitude about good "blood" or "breeding" was mixed up with a lack of understanding of the pathetic situation of those in poverty, especially the lack of educational opportunity. Her mother would have endured being thought of by some as "worthless scum". If you were uneducated and poor, you were from "vulgar stock". I never heard my maternal grandmother's story, and, if Mother knew any of it, or about her father, she said nothing. Mother may have erased her mother's situation out of her memory when she was sent to Canada. Not understanding the forced removal of children that was legislated, she probably felt abandoned by her mother. When she arrived, she had too much to deal with, I would guess. Isn't it unfortunate that she rejected the one avenue of help she had. I would say bitterness was to blame.

"Anyway, our Hanson grandparents, Dad's parents, helped us.

After Dad, their son, died in World War II, they helped Mother and us children even more. Then their business failed and they could no longer give us any financial help. Mother had to go it alone. Frightened to death, she continued with her blaming. She believed they were lying to her – that they chose not to help her. I remember her saying "They would only help their son, but not us, their poor relations – Oh no! Now that he's dead they are done with us." This didn't sound right to me. I knew my grandparents' love. I remember the last time I visited them before they moved away. Grandma Hanson reassured me of how much she loved me. She had shown it, too. She regularly had me come over to show me how to do needlepoint or knit or bake, and, best of all, to simply talk with her. I learned a lot about life and about people. She was broad-minded and kind-hearted. On that last visit she told me, "Be patient with your mother, Sarah, my Sally. Your mother is very lonely and unhappy. You are a good girl, and even though you are young, you are a big help to her and your brothers. When you feel lonely, remember the songs we have sung together. Especially remember Jesus Loves Me. Sing those songs when you feel alone or when life is very difficult. I will pray for you. God will watch over you." Then they moved away. Though Grandma Hanson sent letters and cards, Mother read only small portions to us in sarcastic tones. Then came her censure of both my grandparents – their high-class ways, their lack of concern for us, and, as always, their failure to give us money. It was sad. I never saw Grandmother again. I always believed that she was praying for me and loved me."

Jen came to herself. *I certainly replayed that whole story. What a family we are. What a story, if only it were just fiction.* She glanced down at Gertrude's letter, shook her head slowly, and went to the phone. As she dialed the number she realized that there was no way she could do this visit, but she wondered how in the world to say so. Gertrude answered and as soon as she learned that the timing was bad – that Jennifer could not pick her up at Sea-Tac, that if she came, she would have to take a combination of airport bus, city bus and Greyhound – she angrily said, "Fine. I'll wait until you can sort out your confused affairs. Then I'll come. Get yourself together. I will come in July. It is a good month to travel. All the noisy children are in camp or wherever they put them when school is over. I want to see your new home. Pay a proper visit. It has been a long time. You will have yourself in order by then, won't you?" *What could she say. Aunt Gert had her plans.*

CHAPTER TWENTY

J en's thoughts were going too many directions after she ended the phone call to Aunt Gert. *This house – how will I have it nice enough, fixed up enough, for Aunt Gert? In July or ever? How in the world can I go down to Sea-Tac and pick her up? Oh, my. Hopefully she will change her mind, or at least make her way up here from the airport somehow. Still…the house…*

Jen sighed. Her mind was a-swirl. *I need to think about something else. Collect "my wits" as Aunt Sally used to say. How I miss her.* Climbing the stairs, she headed for her retreat. She had planned to use the remodeled basement room for summer, but it wouldn't be ready. She turned into the Quiet Room. *I like this better, this upstairs feeling, as though I am in an artist's garret. Besides, I look out over the trees and can see a bit of Sylvie's house. Nice to think of her just being there. And beyond are the hills rolling upward to the sky…* even her thoughts got a skyward lift from the sight.

Jen gazed for a while. The clouds and her thoughts drifting along together. She looked down; beside her trunk were a yard-sale end table, and a self-help book. She had bought them both one day when she was out with Sylvie. She had thumbed through the book a few times, randomly, and read here and there. She rebuked herself. *That's no way to read it. Should start at the beginning. Seems to have some good self-esteem ideas. And here sits my notebook for journaling. Not much written in it for the past month. Nothing of value, at least. I wonder what is in the trunk…haven't looked since we moved.*

Jen pulled up the hasp and lifted the lid. She shuffled through various paper layers. "Poems" was written on the cover of an old spiral. Realizing she had forgotten about that notebook, she opened it curiously. On the first poem she had crossed out many words and squeezed substitutes above. Opposing arrows indicated sentences that should trade places. There was no title except a note in parenthesis at the top. (Title: 'Cream' or 'Take a Helping of All') and Cream was crossed out. Jen remembered the day she had come home and written this. She had been at a museum where pioneer life was being acted out. She watched how the women had made butter. Yellow cream had risen to the top of a large container of 'settled milk'. She watched as a woman skimmed the cream off the top of the milk and put it in a glass churn. She announced that they would be turning the churn for a while before they got butter, so Jen wandered around to other displays. When she came back, flecks of yellow showed in the cream as the paddles swirled it against the glass. The woman turned a hand-cranked mechanism that was part of the lid. The butter flecks began sticking together in larger globs. A little longer and the woman stopped, and poured it through layers of cheesecloth in a sieve, catching the whey below. She rinsed the butter with cold water repeatedly, and then patted it into molds to chill. Cold butter made earlier was for sale, but Jen didn't have a cooler in the car to get it home. She *had* taken home something of more importance – thoughts. Thoughts to write down, prompted by learning that the "buttermilk" or whey was thrown, along with the skim milk, into a slop pail for pigs.

She read the poem.

To live and yet not to really live
To skim but the "surface of life"
As a housewife who gathers the rich cream
From off the settled milk.

As that housewife saved but the
Cloying cream and threw the rest
To feed the hogs – all those
Good minerals and protein!

Is this what we desire while we're here?
The high "surf" of a rich menu?
What does Life offer? Only cream?
Or shall I take a helping of all that comes my way?

Just days before, Aunt Sally had explained to Jen that her grandmother, who was mother to both Sally and Jennifer's father, had been unable to sort out life's hard blows. Rather than finding a solution, she had struggled against her challenges. She had put on airs. After Jen saw the skim milk thrown away, an analogy became apparent – that her father's mother was unable to drink the skim milk. She wanted the cream. Jen had sat down and written this poem. Now she noticed a surprising slip-up in the last line. Without noticing it at the time, she had dropped the general "we", used throughout the poem, and switched at the end to I and my – "all that comes *my* way". *Interesting,* Jen thought. *I know that my perceptions at the time were like my grandmother's. I wondered, "why have I been caught and the guy gets away. I'm pregnant, not him. I have to deal with this. He doesn't care."* Her eyes again went to the top of the page, and she reread the poem.

I can see that I rebuked myself when I wrote this. I was considering the situation, realizing that I indeed had to take what life gave me, and deal with it. She shook her head. Michael had come to be such a blessing in her life. Though getting pregnant was a natural result of a hasty, passionate situation, she had not been caught and punished. She had Michael. If she had been younger she might have adopted out the baby. But she had felt sure she could raise him. She had not been dealt with in a cruel way – though it was hard. His life was a gift.

As she thought of that difficult time, she thought of another word-picture. The great pressure that she was under made her think of peat bogs and coal. Pressure on the bogs for thousands of years turned the peat from decomposing vegetation to useful coal. Good thought. Then a fuller picture came into her mind. That same coal, under some tremendous, unknown pressure, was turned into diamonds, sparkling in the sunlight. Diamonds! – well she certainly wasn't a diamond. A wry smile turned up one side of her mouth. *Maybe I am still peat! And maybe, just maybe, someday I will be useful coal, be of some value to others.*

She turned the page of the old notebook, wondering what else was here.

I wonder what's become of Sally
That old gal of mine...

Jen had to chuckle. The song was missing some words, even whole lines, but she remembered how Aunt Sarah, nicknamed Sally, had sung it for her. Jen had written it down much later, but couldn't recall it all. She shook her head, regretfully. Too bad they lived so far apart. The good old days were over, but they had had some great times and good laughs together.

Then Jen's eyes fell on a manila envelope. She had mailed away for a money-making opportunity, addressing envelopes. It was just an initial step. They would send more lists. Looking at the instruction sheet, she at first felt guilt over a missed opportunity. However she also remembered timing herself, and she realized she couldn't make a decent wage working at it. She needed a computer and printer – which was the way most people would do it now. She thought, "*It is surprising that there wasn't a mechanized method. They will be sending their lists off to India soon. But instead of giving up, I might be able to earn something if I just tried. Suppose I'd never get the bonuses they promise. What if it is a scam, just to get a person to buy the lists?* Jen shook her head and laid the paper down.

* * *

Jennifer answered the phone. When she recognized the voice as Sam, her heart sank. *Oh, this poor fellow. He's never going to get a call back from Len. So what do I tell him?*

She began, "I'm very sorry that my husband hasn't returned your call. I don't know what to say."

"That's alright. That's the way these things are sometimes. When I say "these things" I have to admit that I'm not letting you have the information you deserve. I might as well tell you. I am Lennard's son. I was raised by my mother. I have almost no memory of my biological dad. At this point, I just wanted to get to know him. But

190

maybe he doesn't want that. They were married for a short time. My mother said things were difficult. He told her he wanted to 'try the family man thing', and later he said it 'didn't work'." He laughed ruefully. "I can understand that he might rather forget it all. Maybe because of it, he'd rather forget I exist – but I do! And for sure I don't want to go into the past and hash it over. It's certainly not to blame anyone. If he doesn't want to talk about he past, I don't either."

Sam paused. "I need nothing; I have a good life. My only desire is to see him. We could meet over a coffee – keep it casual, just sit and talk about the present – what is going on in our lives now, as two men. I could get to know him, and he, me."

Sam quit talking, and Jenny felt a blur of confusion. Len had never said he had a grown son. Was this for real? This young man didn't sound like he was making up a story to benefit himself. There was no benefit she could see for him. He wasn't pushy. Nor did he sound dishonest.

Jen attempted a reply. "I...ah... excuse me. I didn't know that Len had a son. I'm sorry; you have given me a bit of a shock. I gave him your number to call last time you phoned, so that step has been tried, and as for any other way... I don't feel comfortable taking it in my own hands, telling you to come out to the house. Len would not appreciate it...in fact he'd be very angry with me for arranging anything. You are welcome here anytime, as far as I'm concerned. So I guess... if you are able to set up a meeting with him yourself... that's the only way it can happen. And I have my doubts about that. I can't do it, though I wish I could. You seem to be asking so little."

"Yes...well – all I can do is try. I don't mean to bother you. And I'm very sorry I gave you shocking news. I have had it on my mind to try reaching him for the past year. Sometimes this re-connecting can turn out very well. I've known it to help both the parent and the adult child. I guess I'll think about this some more. Maybe I'll call back again sometime – catch things just right, when my father is home. You never know! He may take the call." He chuckled softly. "But, realistically, I think in this situation... it may be a long, long time before a *real* connection happens. I have to say, though, that I feel we eventually will meet. Thank you very much for your effort, and for taking the time to talk to me. It feels like a bit of a link to my dad. Thanks."

"You're welcome. I'm sorry I'm not able to help you set up a direct contact with him."

"That's okay; you gave him the message. You did what you could. Thanks. Goodbye, and God bless you."

"Goodbye," Jen said. Even after she heard the click, she stood, numb, holding the phone in her hand and staring at it. *This fellow seems so genuine in his desire to just talk, to be able to relate as an adult to his own blood father. How sad. Len isn't going to like this. Do I even dare tell him that I know he has a son?* Fearful memories came to mind of times that she had given Len unpleasant news. She considered, *Even if I do tell him his son, Sam, called, he is not going to respond and return the call – that much I'm sure of.*

Jen worked hard to get things put away. She was looking forward to the next visit she and Sylvia would have with Lisa and her friend. She wondered if they might even want to come see her place. A scary thought. The way it was, with so many rooms to clean, she thought she'd never be done. Some closet shelves were still coated with thick dust. Now, at last, most of the hanging closets were clean. She could finish putting away their clothes. The house was in a livable enough condition that if she heard a knock on the door, she didn't have heart attack.

That day Sylvia phoned with the news. "Lisa and Rona are coming. We'll have our four-some!"

Sylvia was pleased about this visit with friends. As she waited for her guests, she stirred the soup, turned it to low, and noted that it was five to twelve by her watch. She looked out the window, even though she couldn't see them until they came up the drive. The anticipation was fun. They would have plenty of time to visit in the afternoon, since lunch would be right away.

Hearing Lisa's car, she smiled and went out on the deck to welcome them. Just then Jen appeared. She walked around the front of the car as Lisa and tall, blond Rona got out. Lisa introduced Jen to Rona and they came up the steps.

The old friends hugged while Rona and Jen shared basic

courtesies about the beautiful day, and warmed to each other. Rona exclaimed, "I can't get over seeing all this open space after being cooped up in the city. It's been far too long since I felt this much elbow-room."

"I agree! Nothing like open space!" Jen said. "I'm enjoying living here with acres of trees and grass for a 'neighborhood'."

"You lucky duck! I'm jealous." Rona teased.

They all trooped into the house and sat down at the large kitchen table as Sylvia put on a green salad, crackers, a plate of cheeses, and a large shiny pan of hearty soup. She ladled soup into bowls and, as they ate, they had laughs and a time for getting to know each other. Sylvia gathered up the empty bowls and they continued picking on olives and pickles. She put out a plate of tarts for dessert. As they passed them she asked, "Is Rona your nickname?"

"Yes. It's Ronhild, really. It seemed unnecessarily ethnic. I like my Norwegian heritage, but I didn't want to make a big deal of it. Also I like things simple"

Jen spoke up. "My last name was Hanson – Swedish. And Dad's mother was Norwegian. His parents were in business, but Dad went back to fishing. Good old tradition, fishing, as you know."

"Oh? Halibut?"

"Yes. Gone all winter."

Rona nodded. "I was glad my parents farmed. It wasn't much of an income. But I remember my school-mates whose dads were halibut fishermen. They really missed them."

"It's true – I missed Dad a lot." Jen said no more.

"So let's all farm! Stay 'home on the range'." Lisa said brightly. "Sylvie, here's a plan! Pete and I will move out and help you on your farm. Dig up the weeds, and put in your veggie seeds! Then all of us will harvest. Pull up your carrots when they're big and have a 'feed' on them! We'll eat steamed carrots, curry-carrot soup, and bake carrot cake!"

"Don't forget the tub full of hot corn on the cob," Sylvie said.

After a good laugh, Sylvie turned to Lisa and said, "I am so glad for you – you said on the phone that you and Pete are truly happy in the church you're in now. Rona, you've had a lot to do with that, I think."

"She certainly has!" Lisa piped up. "You know quite well, Sylvia, what we've been through with Lorene taking off. When Yolanda came, it was tougher than we thought it would be." She turned to Jen and said, "We have a foster daughter, Yolanda. She gave us quite a challenge from day one. She played mind games – she'd developed some of them for a long time. Rona and Scott, her husband, just took us to their hearts. They simply said, 'Tell us about it.' And then said, 'We'll be praying for you. The Lord will get you and Yolanda through this. He has a plan in bringing her into your household.' And they did pray with us. They had the three of us over to play games, and daily they held us before the Lord. Very special people in our lives."

Rona looked embarrassed. "Sounds like a big deal, but it wasn't. We enjoyed Pete and Lisa and we became friends. Simple as that."

Sylvia said, "Friends. That's a wonderful word." She got up to grab the coffee pot and refill their cups.

Jen turned to Lisa. "What do you mean, Yolanda played games she'd used for a long time? When she came, wasn't she glad to have a home with you?"

"Actually, no. She'd been through terrible things. We came to realize that she didn't trust anybody. She was also sure that it wouldn't last. Figured we'd get tired of her and ask that she be sent to another home. She was in pain, and she was a pain. It's like she was going to take control and force the issue – get herself kicked out. Actually part of it was that she was afraid to get attached to us. She couldn't afford the loss, emotionally."

"What do you mean, 'loss'?"

"She loved her mother. She was taken from her for her own protection. Her mother was too weak to provide needed protection for her. There was an 'uncle', just an acquaintance who was called that. He was bothering Yolanda. Her mother couldn't stand up to anybody, couldn't 'stand on her own two feet', so to speak. She wouldn't believe Yolanda, who at first said he was bugging her. It got worse. He threatened Yolanda that he'd take her kitten out and kill it if she told what was happening. When she resisted him, he did kill the cat in front of her, made her look at its body. Then he told her if she told anyone, he would take her little brother out fishing and make sure he ended up in the river, drowned, 'accidentally'. He said no one would know anything different. Of course she took it seriously. When finally a neighbor reported things she saw, a social worker came. But even she couldn't get things opened up with the mother or Yolanda. By talking to the girl over time and letting her just play with dolls and tell stories about them, it turned out she knew things no girl her age should know or could know normally. Not from TV even. The social worker couldn't get the mother to believe that Yolanda had been repeatedly sexually assaulted by the man." Jen and Sylvie both shook their heads and groaned.

Lisa continued. "So her home life hadn't developed trust. She had been in two foster homes before we were given our chance. Those situations weren't successful, mainly because Yolanda sabotaged their help. Yolanda was very angry. She had been taken from her home, after all. And her anger about the abuse was just beginning to surface. Also she couldn't afford the loss of another trusted person, like I said. The lack of trust still crops up now and then. As a young child she had trusted her mother totally. Later she started to find out that what was 'normal' in her life was not normal – a huge eye-opener. That's called homeostasis – what's usually happening. That's hard for us to understand at first why a child would be uncomfortable with a change for the good. Until you think it through. She lost her home, her mother. She hadn't been able to trust anyone to help her when she tried to tell. Then she was thrown among strangers. In the teen years they throw up walls. Some say 'never again' – you can all go to Hell."

Sylvia quietly said, "It's hard to know if a teen is suffering abuse when she acts out, or is just going through the normal teen things. They have their bursts of hormones, and they find out that they can make adult choices and no one can stop them. I'm sure Issa hasn't been through anything like that before she left."

"Well, they each have their individual personalities. Some just have strong wills, like Issa, and it seems like they have to struggle against something as they develop. Too bad when it's their parents. There is an expression in counseling. It's a person referred to as your "Safe Person". It means someone who loves you so much that you know you can treat her or him badly, and they will keep on loving you. It's a sad thing that a human gets in that mode of hurting someone who loves her. But I do understand that it's a feeling of being so safe that she can test that love to the limits."

"Hard to figure sometimes." Sylvie wiped a tear away. "Hard to endure." Lisa squeezed her hand as she got up for another trip to get the coffee pot.

Rona spoke up. "You said that Yolanda is thinking about others, getting outside herself. Can you explain how?" Though Rona had encouraged Lisa in times past, she hadn't heard much of recent developments.

"Well, though she has only been getting stable for a few months, we are broadening the 'neighborhood' so to speak. The three of us have volunteered in what's called the Kids Neighborhood at church. We go into that department once a month when the parents are invited to come. Some may not be attending church, but they do come to that special day. Extra hands, like mine, are needed to go with the kids to another room and help with crafts. During that time the parents are then told of something special, a gift their kids will receive. One time it was even Bibles of their own. The Bible would be presented to the child on the following Sunday. An older man got up and told the parents what a similar Bible had meant to him. His dad had written in and given it to him. His dad died in an accident later, and that Bible came to be a big comfort. So these parents were given time to write in the front of their child's gift Bibles whatever their thoughts were. It was so neat that loving thoughts were expressed in writing. Most of us parents fail to find opportunities to express our thoughts in writing that sometimes aren't said aloud.

"So Yolanda and Pete and I help with those days. The three of us have been talking, and maybe we'll do some other neighborhood volunteering. Yolanda likes the idea. Our church helps regularly at the gospel mission downtown. In summer there are "kids' days", with lunch, and then there's time at a park including skits that older kids do, and singing with a guitar to finish. Yolanda would find her niche quickly I think."

"I bet she would," Rona said. "I can see her getting involved in the skits. Drama is a good way to test your own emotions while you're pretending to be someone else."

"I remember that," Jen said. "I had a good high school English teacher. We spent time acting out parts. Sometimes we would only read a poem, or a scene from a book. but I liked that feeling of becoming that person. "

"Does Yolanda like kids?" Sylvia asked.

"Very much so. She had wanted a baby brother or sister. I'll share a big future possibility with you. It's a ways off, yet. We are considering taking in another foster child, a young one. Yolanda says she'd love that. We don't want to rush it. We will wait until we're really sure."

Just then Larry walked in. "Hello, Ladies! Did you leave anything for me to eat?"

"Oh, poor Larry," Lisa said. "You didn't have any lunch!"

Larry looked sheepish, and said, "Actually, the regional manager took me out to a wonderful lunch." Jen looked up in time to see easy rapport between the two. She thought at first that his comment was a complaint that his wife had spent too much having friends come. But he had a twinkle in his eyes.

After being introduced to Rona, Larry spoke again to Lisa. "How are things going for you and Pete?"

"Really going well. We've now found a church we are thoroughly enjoying, and Rona here, and her husband, Scott, are the ones who made us feel at home." Lisa knew that Larry had been through a hurtful and discouraging time in a church, but she was not one to shy away from a touchy subject.

Larry simply took it in, and said, "Good." He turned and said, "Rona, I hope you are enjoying your time out here in the country."

"Very much so!" she said.

His big smile for Jen cheered her, as he suggested that she could tell Rona just how good country life was.

Lisa stood. "Say, ladies, it's been good! But Rona and I have to get on the road. Traffic, you know. Sorry to break this up, but we may be into the thick of it now. But I don't mind. It's been such fun! So nice to get to know you better, Jen! Now that Sylvie will be off work, we'll all get together again soon. I'll bring sandwiches and salad next time, if you don't mind being host again, Sylvia. Sound okay, everyone?" They all responded enthusiastically. Lisa and Rona hurried to the car. Jen helped Sylvia with the dishes, just to have a little more time together.

CHAPTER TWENTY-ONE

Jenny pondered the thought of a child being out of his own home, needing foster care. She hoped nothing ever happened to her. That's the fix Michael would be in. Even now, things were tough for him. He probably knew that Len was sorry he ever took on a child – that he was a bother. What a feeling for a child. Yet she was afraid to even comfort Michael or talk about it, in case he tried not to think of such a thing. *Imagine…here Len has had a son of his own all along. How could he not care? I guess I shouldn't tell Len I know this man who phoned is his son. That would cause such an upset…*Her mind went back to foster care and Yolanda and Lisa. The girl had been in care in a home where it didn't work out. Imagine that feeling. Not having a home where someone cared.

It wasn't long until an opportunity to get to know a neighbor presented itself. Hearing a knock one morning, Jenny answered and found an eager, sharp-eyed woman holding a package in her hands. "Good morning. Are you Mrs. Brown, by chance?"

"Why, yes." There was a pause. Jenny hesitated, not knowing if she should ask what was, to her, the obvious question, 'And who are you?' The woman had the look of one who would respond well to exaggerated courtesies, as, 'And to whom do I have the pleasure...' *How can I feel that way? Shame. I know not one thing about her.* Jenny chided herself.

"*I* am Mrs. Weltam." With that announcement she extended her gloved hand.

"Oh." Jennifer Brown was speechless. What she had already heard of Mrs. Wheltam tumbled around in her mind. Confused, but realizing that her first impression was right, she just stood there, overlooking the woman's rigid hand pointing at her. Then suddenly she thought, *The hand, Dummy. Take her hand!*

"Oh," she said again, and reached out. "I'm glad to meet you." She reproached herself, '*You liar! You're not glad.*' Mrs. Weltam stood stiffly, and Jen froze.

"Well. I thought I *might* come in and welcome you to the neighborhood."

"Ah, yes, of course. Please come it. Come in and sit down. I'll make a cup of coffee. Or do you prefer tea?"

"I prefer neither. I will drink a cup of my own tea that I brought with me. It is a special herbal mixture to promote calm."

"Oh. You brought it with you?" Jenny asked in an incredulous tone. She looked down at the box – *could it contain a teapot*? "You brought tea you've made with you?" Realizing her mouth was open, she promptly shut it.

Mrs. Weltam answered. "No, you *foolish* girl. I only brought bags, not the liquid tea. This box contains cookies I baked to welcome you."

"Oh, thank you. Here, have a seat here on the couch." Jenny took the box and backed up. *I am foolish. She has me sized up. I can already see what kind of a visit this is going to be. The assessor and the fool.*

After boiling water in a pan, Jen poured a mug full, brought it in and set it on a coaster on the coffee table. Mrs. Weltam put in her own tea bag.

"Do you live in the area, Mrs. Weltam?" Jen asked, knowing very well she did. But it was a start on a conversation.

"Of course I live in the neighborhood. I have come here to welcome you to it. Would I be living elsewhere?"

"Ah, no. I guess not."

"I live in the large brown house a mile farther down the road. I live there with my son. Poor boy. He lost his father, you know."

"No, I didn't know. Was that recent?"

Mrs. Weltam continued with her story as though she hadn't

heard. "He was only nineteen years old when he was abandoned by his daddy, left fatherless. It was quite a shock as you can imagine." Mrs. Weltam settled back in the couch.

Jen could see that she was going to get the whole history. Just as well. It might mean she would be relieved of the effort to keep the conversation going. "How is your son adjusting now?"

"It is getting a little easier. It's been fifteen years. Actually, my son was much closer to me. 'Dear Mother' is how he refers to me. So, it is a good thing that he didn't lose *me*. We have kept each other company these fifteen years."

Jen nodded. She didn't know quite what to say. Losing a loved one was terribly painful. She still missed her father. But she had a feeling that, in this case, it was not only a matter of the loss itself. It hinted of Mrs. Weltam using it to strengthen an unhealthy cord between her son and herself. It seemed strange.

Jenny asked a question occasionally. Mostly Mrs. Weltam was giving forth with glorifying her son's history and telling pieces of detrimental information about others in the community as they had any relationship to him. There was no need for Jen to work at keeping conversation happening.

Mrs. Weltam suddenly spoke sharply to Jennifer, her eyes probing, and asked, "Did you want to open the cookies?" The box sat on the coffee table.

Jen jumped and reached for it. "Oh, yes. I didn't know if you wanted me to open it now."

"That would be customary."

Jen felt the sharp rebuke and wondered, *What else can I do wrong?* She went for a plate, placed the cookies on it and offered them to Mrs. Weltam.

"No, thank you. I have tasted them at home. These are for you."

Jen took one, saying, "Thank you, very much." She bit down. Rather she tried to bite it. To her horror, the cookie, held between her teeth, was as hard as cement. She might never succeed. Finally it broke. What a relief. She quickly looked around for her hot drink and realized she hadn't made herself one. With her mouth full she glanced at Mrs. Weltam, whose eyes were boring into her. She attempted a weak smile. Rising, she went to the pan she had left simmering and poured herself a cup of hot water. Returning, she took a sip and burned her mouth. *This is disgraceful. I'm insulting her and her gift. I'm being rude jumping up. What next?* She returned to the sink and ran some cold water into her cup. Drinking and chewing, she managed to get the cast-iron cookie eaten.

"Well. Thank you for bringing the cookies. Sorry, I just got thirsty and realized I didn't...I hadn't... I just needed some water."

Mrs. Weltam grimaced. "The cookies are hearty – they are from a special recipe I developed myself. I combined various recipes and came up with these, for good health. How do you like them?"

"They are really different – they're nice." *Oh, why did I add that? Why can't I just be truthful. But how? At least I could think of some way not to exaggerate, and do it without insulting.*

Jenny began to wonder, as the conversation lagged, what else was there to talk about. She had endured Mrs. Weltam's surface questions, her long personal history and the glories of her son. She found herself hoping that the lady had somewhere to go soon.

A knock at the door startled Jen. *What a serendipity. Someone is here.* "Excuse me, Mrs. Weltam," she said. "While I see who that might be at the door." *Or is it whom?* she thought. *Oh, Jenny, get real. You don't have to impress her. Do you?*

Opening the door, Jen saw it was Sylvie. She almost squealed in delight and hugged her. "Come in, come in!" Bringing her around the couch, she said, "Mrs. Weltam, I'd like you to meet my neighbor, Sylvia Ford. Sylvia, Mrs. Weltam." Then Jenny realized they knew each other and they were all aware of that. *Boy, am I rattled!*

"Yes, yes," Mrs. W said with a dismissive wave of her hand. "We know each other *very* well. Hello, Sylvia. How are you?"

"Fine, thank you, Mrs. Weltam. And you?"

"I am very well, thank you. How is your fine husband?"

"Very well, thank you. And your son? Is he in good health?"

"Oh, yes. With the care I give him you can already assume that he is in very good health."

Jenny waited out these formalities, and then cut in to ask, "Sylvia, may I get you a coffee?"

"Some of whatever you are having will be fine, Jen."

"There is ordinary tea or coffee. Mrs. Weltam is having her

special medicinal herb tea. My ordinary tea is very ordinary – last time I bought the cheap stuff."

Sylvia was delighted at Jen, at the way she wrinkled her nose in a sprightly way.

"That's fine. I'll take a cup of the cheap stuff!" She laughed. She watched the odd look on Mrs. Weltam's face and had to glance away to keep from grinning. *A dose of purgative for 'overdone sophistication' is something that woman needs. How does she ever mix with the poor, or the poorly educated? Sometime I'd like to take her to volunteer with the mentally challenged. They can be such fun. Oh, well – her loss.*

Jen returned with the teapot and a cup, set them down, and looked ill at ease. Sylvie could read her question-mark expression, saying, *What will we talk about?* Sylvia solved the problem by quickly asking how Michael was, and how school was going. As Jen answered, she realized that, in their 'getting to know each other', Mrs. Weltam had not even asked if she had children.

"You have a child? In school?" Mrs. Weltam asked in a severe tone.

"Yes." *Oh*, she thought, *here we go. I don't like the direction this is heading.*

"And you said that you were married four years ago." Her brows came together, severe. "How could he be old enough to be at school?"

"He's very smart for his age!" Sylvia cut in. Jenny appreciated her effort. *Sylvie hopes to save me from embarrassment; hopes that we'll start talking about* who *Michael is, rather than the difficulty of the date of his birth.* It didn't work.

"But it couldn't be that he is in school already!"

"He is in grade five." *So there*, Jen added, silently, and felt her ornery streak rise to the surface. Still, she grasped at the slim possibility that Mrs. Weltam would have the courtesy to let it go.

"Grade FIVE," she exclaimed. "Oh. I *see*."

"Yes," Jen said resolutely. "I had Michael before I met Len and married him."

"Yes. I see," Mrs. Weltam repeated. Jen considered where this might go. But that was the end of comments on Michael. The visit lasted only a few minutes longer.

Mrs. Weltam departed, and Jen thought, *Good riddance. I believe that you won't trouble me again. You'd not like to be tarnished with my germ of immorality. If only you knew how I'd like to live that part of my life over again. Marry first. Make a good home for my boy. Be able to hold my head up and look people in the eye. Well lady, I will just look 'em in the eye anyhow.*

Sylvie laid her hand on Jen's arm as she sat down. "I'm sorry you got cross-questioned. Consider the source." She looked tenderly at Jen, who finally managed to look up.

"It's okay. Nothing new." It wasn't okay. Jen was shaking so hard inside with anger that she felt she was vibrating. "I need some fresh air." She opened the door.

"Well!" Sylvie said it in a cheery tone. "It is good that you got to meet Mrs. Weltam. Now that is done, and out of the way... among your new and unique experiences in our little valley!" *Might as well make light of it, though it's heavy for Jen to be put down. Maybe she can just let it go.*

"Yea. Right." Jen took a deep breath, stood up, and grabbed her used tea cup. As she started for the kitchen she said, "Tea isn't going to do it. I'm making some coffee. Or considering how my heart is racing, maybe I should drink herb tea – should have some of Mrs. Weltam's calming herb tea! She left her bag." Jen held it up between two fingers with a grimace and answered her own question. "NO, thank you! It's gonna be coffee!" She turned abruptly before Sylvie could see her eyes filling with tears.

Sylvie followed into the kitchen. "You know, when you meet people who are *so* perfect – like they had never had a complication in their own lives... Well! What can you say? There's nothing to be said. May as well accept their self-assessed perfection." Jen, still teary, didn't turn around to see what Sylvie's expression was.

CHAPTER TWENTY-TWO

Sylvia pulled the weeds from around the post that held the mailbox. As she straightened up, Jeremy, a boy who lived down the road, came bicycling toward her. Waving, he called out, "Hello, Mrs. Ford. How are you?"

"Fine, Jeremy, just fine. I'm loving this weather. It has really warmed up. School will be out soon, won't it?"

"Yes, you bet it will! Do you have any jobs, like the yard work last summer, that I can do?"

"Oh, I've been doing it myself now that I'm not working at the Falls Hardware. I may have something heavy to do though. If so, I'll call you. You were a big help!" She enjoyed his company. He was a pleasant kid in his early teens, and a good worker. After seeing her children become active out in the community at twelve or so, she had seen how broadening the interaction with adults in other families was. "There is a boy, Michael, who just moved in next door to us. He's younger than you, but acts older than his age. I don't know if his mother could use any help. But, in any case, maybe you'd like to meet them. Are you on your way somewhere or do you have time now?" She realized she had left out Len, but then, he wouldn't be hiring any help with yard work, she didn't think…and he wouldn't be interested in meeting a neighbor boy, from what she'd seen.

"I have time now. I'd like that. I bet he's lonely. Hard trying to find your way after moving."

After arriving at Jen's house and making the introductions, Michael took Jeremy up to see his room. In a few minutes they thundered back down the stairs and out the back door.

"I bet they're gone to check out the little shed and Michael's rock collection inside," Jen said. The two women moved to the window and looked out. Jen continued, "The ones on the ground all around it are ones he has found and brought from all over – the roadside and the field, and by the creek when we walk down together. I'm a little nervous about him going to the creek while the water is still high, so he has to have someone with him for now. That's where he found some "specially valuable ones", as he calls them. He keeps them inside the shed. Plus another project. He's building a wood frame to hold panes of glass that were out there on a shelf. He is super gluing, and will caulk it somehow, he says, and make an aquarium." She shook her head. "An impossible project, I'm sure. I can't imagine… when he realizes that it's too cold in winter and he wants to bring it inside. I can't have an aquarium that is going to leak or burst a seam sitting here in the house. It will mean a confrontation. Ah, me. Imaginative kids are a challenge!"

* * *

"It's supposed to be sunny Saturday. Perfect picnic weather," Sylvia said with a pleading tone into the phone, hoping for a 'yes' from Jen. "The men are both off work." She had the menu items already, except for potato salad.

"A picnic. It does sound good. Saturday, eh? I'll ask Len and phone you back if you'll be home." Jen hung up and thought, *Sylvie is making it easy for us to say yes. She's bringing ham she already has, and hot dogs. I hate to be needy, but there's barely enough grocery money right now. I do have time to get the potato salad made – oh I hope Len says yes. Maybe the men will get to talking. Larry seems like the kind of man who could deal with Len and his moods, and even be an influence on him for the better. I can't pressure Len to go. He will have to like the idea himself.*

Michael stood in Larry's back yard, pointing, both arms stretched out. "Was it from here to there?" He wanted to know the exact location where an old shed had stood. Larry had been telling him how he tore it down when they took over the place.

"Yes, but not that big. It only came to where you see these stubby stumps from some small alder trees." Larry stood by the small stumps. "They had seeded themselves along the front edge of the shed." Larry took three long steps and stood. "This was the back of it, here. It was used for different purposes over the years. Who knows all it was used for? Maybe the first man on this land lived in it alone while he worked to get the land and a cabin ready. Once that was done he could marry his sweetheart."

Michael looked at him. "Really?" His eyes were big with imagination.

"I don't know. Just guessing. But you might ask the librarian if there are personal accounts written down. Many of those are collected into a local history book."

"Okay! That would be so cool to read about. Would have been even better to be him – to live here and cut trees and build the cabin and plow a field for a big garden." He looked away, across the back field, dreamily.

"It was hard work, but it must have been very satisfying. A man would have to know how to do many things well. Couldn't afford to hire others to plow, do the building, or care for animals when they got sick. Sometimes cows ate nails off the ground. I've seen a vet put a magnet down a cow's throat to retrieve some junk. I'll show you something." He went in the shed and picked up a jar. "In those days they made and used square nails. I guess a blacksmith made them. I have found a few here."

"Oh!" Michael held the jar, then jumped up and down. "Could I look in the dirt and see if I can find any of them?"

"Sure. Get that small shovel. You can dig around for them. Slice off the top sod and set it aside. Then go through the dirt and put the sod back when you're done. Water it afterward. I'll show you how." Larry thought, *If this kid goes into any field requiring imagination, he'll do very well. It would be nice to have a chance to talk with him more. Maybe I can help him find some 'treasures' right here. I bet he'd enjoy going up to Monte Cristo, daydreaming of the gold prospecting that used to be. If it were an outing maybe Len would come, too.* Larry nodded to himself, as if agreeing to his plan, and tucked it away for the future. He should ask Len first if he'd be interested.

"Do you think Len would want to go to Monte Cristo?"

Sylvia turned from the sink and looked at Larry curiously. "I have no idea. Why?"

"Oh, I was just thinking…" He had a preoccupied expression. Sylvie merely shook her head and went back to rinsing lettuce.

Larry worked through his plan in his head. The focus of the boom town of Monte Cristo had been gold. But he always thought the lives of the people were most fascinating. If they stopped at the ranger station, Michael would see items on display. He'd learn the hard circumstances the first settlers lived under, how the snow piled up and they couldn't get out to buy food or take a badly injured person to a doctor. Clues to those long-ago days were in pictures. But to Michael it would come to life outdoors. There were old buildings, though some were now flattened by last winter's heavy snow. An acquaintance was trying to buy a place in the town site, so they could get permission and see some of the mine equipment that was on the property. Michael could imagine how it worked, seeing an old ore car and smaller things. Then Michael could read more about the area's history if he wanted. Len would like seeing the old cars. There were rusted-out vehicles abandoned on several properties. Kind of far gone, but someone might know stories with local color.

Larry said, "Yes, I can see both of them enjoying an outing up there. Michael will be busy at the picnic. I'll get Len aside and ask him about going. In case he wants to say no, it won't be in front of Michael."

Sylvia called to Larry from the foot of the stairs. "Come help me move something heavy." She led the way upstairs and pointed to a large pot that held a sturdy succulent that was like a small, odd tree.

"What is that?" he asked. "It has odd…I don't know what. Do you call them leaves? It looks like it belongs in the desert."

"It does! You're getting just too smart about plants. It's a jade plant. I've been bringing it along here until now. The nights are warming up outside, so I'm going to put it on the deck for the summer. It will have enough shade there to adjust. At first I can cover it at night, if it's cold. "

"Oh. Well, I'm glad you know what you're doing. If you just want some muscle power to lift it, I can give that."

Sylvie came over, stretched up, and kissed him full on the mouth. "That's what I need! A strong man!"

Larry worked his way down the stairs. He went through the kitchen doors, trying not to knock branches off. He set it down on the deck and stood up.

Sylvia said, "Mmm, my strong man!" and kissed and hugged him again.

Coming into the yard, Jen said, "Oh, oh. I think I interrupted something. Sorry." She gave the tone of mock apology to her voice. They saw the delight on her face, and laughed.

"Oh, we'll behave," Larry teased. He stood back from the large pot and eyed it. "Is that where you want it?"

"Well…it would be better a little closer to the wall for protection – at least for now. You can move it out to the edge of the deck later, when the weather is warmer."

"You don't want much, do you!" Larry laughed. "Sounds like I have a job as permanent yard man!"

Jen laughed, comfortable with their easy-going relationship. She thought, *I wonder if they know what they've got? Nice to see people be together and … be* glad *they're together.*

The three of them were looking at the decorated pot, and Sylvia spoke up. "I got that ceramic planter at a hardware store clearance in Everett last fall. I like those tulips that are on it. Makes it seem like a springtime item. It was sure marked down." It was apparent she was pleased with herself.

Larry said "Yup. Feels good to get a bargain. You know what I'm wondering. Is that the plant you showed me last summer? In a pot this size?" He made a circle with his hands. "If so, it's sure grown."

"That's the one. The only jade plant I have. It is doing well, all right."

Jen kept looking at the pot. It was nice. The plant was healthy and well shaped. It draped over the edges of the pot, softening the line and bringing unity. But something was wrong. There wasn't "unity". *They're wrong together. That is what it is!* she thought. *The spring motif on the pot is pretty... pastel colors... but it has tulips on it! No 'desert feel' at all.*

"What do you think, Jennifer? You are being so quiet – what is it?"

"Oh. I guess I was." She didn't say any more.

"Well, something is going on in your head," Larry had a wry smile and raised an eyebrow.

"Something you aren't saying. Come on! Out with it!" added Sylvie.

"Yes, well... I guess I see the thick leaves of the succulent and it makes me think of the desert where it's hot and dry... I guess I picture red clay pots for planting something like that. I..." she looked uncomfortable.

"Say, you're right!" Sylvie looked at the pot and back at Jen. "I guess you have been around this kind of thing before! That's very true! I have those pansies on the steps in big plastic pots. I could have used this pot for pansies, putting it at the top of the steps. Pansies are cool-weather loving, and spring-like. I have a large old clay pot in the shed that I need to sterilize. I could use that for the jade plant."

Larry rolled his eyes. "Thanks, Jennifer! Now she'll want me to carry that pot of pansies back down to the grass. Then bring it back here. Then this jade plant will have to go out there to be redone, too. Then carry it back here. You gals need a gopher."

It disturbed Jenny to be causing so much trouble. Then she caught a glimpse of Larry's expression. He laughed. She looked confused. "You're teasing me, complaining about all the carrying, aren't you!" She shook her head. "But why would a gopher be wanted? I thought gophers ate plant roots and caused trouble in a garden?"

"Oh," Sylvie laughed. "He means a go-fer, like go-for! 'Go for this, and go for that' – an errand boy."

Jen was embarrassed, but got a big grin on her face. "Oh, okay. I got it! Just slow."

"No you're not", Larry cut back in. "But I'm wondering. Why would you have to move the pots to the grass? Can't you just fill them with plants and dirt right where they're going to sit?"

"No, I make too much mess. Soil all over. That area is better."

She pointed to the yard by the northeast corner of the house, far from the driveway. "Then I won't make a mess where it will be seen. The potting soil just works down into the grass. It's not by the steps where people will track it inside. And for sure I don't want to make the deck a mess."

"Hey, I'd be glad to hose the grass and sweep off the deck and hose it for you afterward." Larry had both eyebrows up and an appeal written on his face.

"Hmm." Sylvia was considering. "Well, they are awfully heavy for you to lift. And I'd like to get it all finished." She stopped to think about it.

"As for the dirt," he said, "I'll be sure to hose it off well; the steps, too. It will settle right into the ground."

"Oh, you're right. That would work."

"See," he said. "That's what you have me for! I can be your gofer *and* your idea-man!" They all laughed.

"I think I caused a lot of trouble," Jen said. "Should have kept quiet!" But she was smiling at the compromise.

"Ah, you wouldn't get away with keeping quiet – once I saw you had something on your mind!" Sylvie smiled. "You've got to say what you're thinking!" Larry watched the the two women exchanged an understanding look. Everything was good.

CHAPTER TWENTY-THREE

The drive to the lake for a picnic was bright, with stripes of shade and sunshine shining through the trees. Sylvia looked behind them to see that Jen and Lennard's pickup was still there. Len said he wanted his own vehicle so he could leave early. Michael, riding in the Ford's back seat, broke into her thoughts.

"Thanks so much for letting me come with you, Mr. Ford. And I'm really glad you let me dig in that dirt where the old building used to be. Did you say the square nails were made by hand? How did they do that?"

Larry answered him while Sylvia wistfully thought how nice it was that Michael could be with him. Larry was sometimes gone overnight or longer for his work. He didn't see much of Michael. The boy was always eager – he had a great interest in *the way things used to be'* and Larry loved that topic. The stories of early Puget Sound days that his parents had told him were happily shared with a young listener. They would be retold to Michael. At the moment Larry was launching into the need of settlers for blacksmiths and other tradesmen as the communities developed. He had already told Michael some of the jobs that needed to be done in the early years to tame their property.

The wooden sign pointed off the road and Larry turned. He parked near the path to their favorite picnic table. Len parked and everyone clambered out and shared in carrying the ice chest, bags of food, gas grill and boxes to the picnic area. Larry said, "I figured if at all possible we would light a wood fire, but I wasn't sure if the fire rings were still in place." Walking ahead of Sylvia and Michael, he stopped at a table. "Sure enough, there is one!" He pointed to a large metal truck rim with a rack welded across it. "I'm glad; it's probably too early in the summer for restrictions on fires. Though they wouldn't take that heavy thing away, there'd be signs up saying no fires. We're okay." Len helped carry firewood, and Larry got it ready to be lit later. Just then the neighbor boy, Jeremy, arrived with his friend Martin. They had been at ball practice and Jeremy's mother dropped them off. Impatient to see the lake, the three boys trotted down the path and the men followed.

As the guys came out into the sun on the lake shore a fisherman was rowing away from a dock in his small boat. Larry said, "That looks so good! Just a quiet rowboat and a fishing pole. This lake is restricted; no motorboats. Not that I mind them elsewhere, but we need some peaceful spots like this."

Len was strangely silent as they watched the three boys racing up a hillock to an overlook. Coming to a standstill, they stood shielding their eyes with their hands, looking like three shipwrecked sailors, yearning to be rescued.

Larry chuckled. "In the car on the way out, Michael described a predicament from Treasure Island, when the marooned crew hoped for rescue. I figure Michael is telling it again. He has a good imagination!" Len just grunted. Larry watched the boys. He was glad the the older ones were considerate of Michael, considering the tensions in Len and Jennifer's family. Larry let his mind wander over possible topics of conversation with Len, and thought of Monte Cristo.

"Say, Len, there are a couple of old vehicles up at the foot of a mountain east of here. Monte Cristo is almost a ghost town. It was a population center in gold prospecting days. Some people lingered on a while and old relics are left behind. Some people part-time on their property. I think there is a vintage Oldsmobile. Another is a pickup, a little 'newer', if I can use that word! How would you like to go there with me some time?" Larry waited, but there was no response. "We can take the boys and check it out. Sylvia packs a good lunch to take along. They'll get hungry – after we park it's a bit of a hike. I'll bring a camera and get some pictures of the vehicles, since they can't be disturbed. Want to go?"

"Hmm," was all Len said. Larry was determined to be patient. Then Len spoke. "Yeah, maybe. I'll see how my schedule goes. I'm going out of town again. Maybe after that." He turned and walked the path the boys had used. They were gone. Len reached the top first and stood looking out at the small rowboat moving slowly through the water, a fishing line trailing behind.

"I'm glad the fire is not giving us any trouble. Some of the wood was wet." Sylvia put on a dry chunk of wood, and asked, "Do you want a quick coffee, Jennifer?"

"Oh, sure. I'll set up that percolator you brought. Sounds good."

"Here!" Sylvia held up a thermos. "I mean I'll pour you one right now to get you going. But it's a good idea to put on a fresh pot. This will be gone as soon as the men get back."

Sylvia held out the mug of coffee. Jen took it, then exclaiming, "In a mug, even! Thanks."

"Yeah, 'No thank you' to foam cups."

"Look how well the fire is burning now." Jen looked into it dreamily. "Feels good here in the shade."

"Still flaming up a lot, though." Sylvia set the percolator over the edge of the flames.

"Nice, isn't it – all the varied colors." Jen looked intently into the flames.

"Let's do the hot dogs on this old griddle. Just set it over the fire. The bars of the grate are too far apart and the wieners will fall through." Sylvia chuckled. "And I feel lazy. We can roast them on sticks next time. When the boys come, they can roll them around to brown, and, if they must, they can put them on the grate over the fire and accidentally drop a couple into it. They like excitement...or mischief!" Sylvia poked apart the well-burned pieces of wood with a heavy stick and spread a wide bed of coals. Now the green wood she put on would catch well, and slow down the fire.

Jen laid out the paper plates and opened the chips. "I'll leave the potato salad and ham on ice till we're ready."

Sylvie rolled the hot dogs over and pulled the griddle back. "Let's sit and relax. It's a day off from the usual routine. Right?" She pulled two folding chairs to the fire and they settled in. Conversation flowed easily from one topic to another. The visit to the second-hand store had brought out their common interests. They talked of how they'd both like to get into some furniture-rescue projects in the distant future. Small stuffed chairs that were battered but nicely shaped for a lady. A little sanding on the wood parts, then learn how to attach new webbing. Get the right foam, and finally, cover it with beautiful, expensive fabric. Voila! The piece de resistance to enjoy, or sell through an ad in a crafter's co-op. They laughed at how rich they would get selling to the tourists seeking memorabilia.

Sylvie pulled a magazine out of a food box and flipped to an article. "I saw these beautiful hand-loomed scarves in an issue from last winter. Look at this one – the deep forest greens and rust."

"Nice. Oh! I like that dark blue and purple, some of my favorite colors. And it looks so soft. Is it part angora? Does it say?"

Sylvie checked the text. "Yes, it is. Warm, for sure." She closed her eyes and gave a satisfied mmm as she imagined the comfort.

Looking at one picture, Jen wondered, "How can anyone like that ugly gold yarn worked with the greens in that scarf?"

"Have you noticed that color on a redhead?" They enjoyed the stimulating differences of opinions they discovered, and debated whether a true redhead could wear pink.

"Oh-oh." Jen exclaimed. "The hot dogs."

"I'll get them. I'm closer." Sylvia said. But Jen had jumped up and began rolling them over to the side of the griddle.

"I'll call the men, then," Sylvie said, and grabbed a pan and wooden spoon. Jen reached into the ice chest and took out the the food. Sylvie walked down the path to the beach, beating out a rhythm and calling, "Yoo-hoo! Lunch time! Yoo-hoo! Come and get it!"

The men turned at the sound. Larry waved. He came alongside Michael and Jeremy; Lennard and Martin came behind.

"Do you enjoy cars, Martin?" Len asked.

"Oh, yes!"

Len gave him an appraising look, considering the eagerness. "Would you like to help me do a little work on one?"

"Oh! Yes!" Martin was doubly excited now.

"Come over some time. We'll see what you can do. Larry

mentioned that your mom is gone for a while. Does your dad work Saturdays?"

"He does a couple times a month. Maybe I could come then. It gets boring at home."

"Sure. Sure it would. Well, you come. We'll see how much you'd like to learn. There are lots of things I could teach you."

"Would Michael be there? I bet he enjoys learning about cars!"

"Michael? Huh," Len didn't notice Martin's surprise at the scornful tone of voice. "He's too young." He saw a puzzled look on Martin's face. He dismissed it with a disparaging wave of his hand. "You're eager to learn. I can see that! Yes, I can teach you lots of things."

* * *

Everyone ate heartily. Len sat down in front of the fire with his mug of coffee and stretched out his legs. Larry came over and started to sit down, but saw Sylvia trying to lift the ice chest. "Wait, Hon. That's heavy." He set his mug down on a rock and went to her. After putting the chest on the picnic bench, he made room beside it so she could cut and serve the cake. Picking up the dirty glasses and flatware and putting them in a plastic tub, he said, "I'll fill this with some soap and water. You can add that pan of water on the fire when it's heated. The boys will be glad to wash up things for you." He smiled persuasively at Michael, Jeremy and Martin.

When he sat back down Len said, "You teaching my boy to do women's work?"

It was hard for Larry to tell if he was teasing or serious. "I figure a guy who knows how to take care of practical things, won't get married for the wrong reason."

"What wrong reason? Having a woman do that work is how it ought to be."

"Oh, well, a guy needs to help his wife. Usually starts when she has a baby. I remember I wasn't very familiar with the kitchen when our first one was born. So that was a bit of a struggle. Found out there was no mystery to the washing machine. And there were lots of diapers to wash before disposables. Sometimes the women are just plain tired. I think a guy can feel comfortable coming alongside."

"Aw, women. They're tough."

"They're strong, but not the same way we are. Anyhow, the boys won't mind helping out after they have some cake. Right boys?"

The boys, at that moment, were watching Sylvia cut large pieces from the large rectangular cake, dark with raisins and spice, and covered with a broiled caramel frosting.

* * *

"The clean-up is done. Let's walk down to the beach together," Larry said. He shoved the mostly burned sticks of wood apart. Though the fire was low, he took the used dishwater and doused it until there was no more smoke rising. They all strung out single file along the path through the brush. As they came into the open, Jeremy went to Larry and asked a question about Douglas fir trees. Len moved over to walk by Martin's side.

Michael grabbed his mother's arm, saying, "Let's skip rocks!"

"Sounds good to me," Sylvia piped up.

"Me, too," Jen joined in, and they stooped over like berry-pickers in the field, looking for flat stones.

Larry finished the explanation, and looked around. Seeing Len and Martin together, he walked over to join them. An uneasy feeling came over him. He wondered about the warm attention Len was showing the boy. *Why doesn't he flash some of those smiles toward his own son?*

CHAPTER TWENTY-FOUR

The creekside park was damp. Overhanging trees made deep shade, but it had a peacefulness that seclusion can bring. Jennifer was glad she had brought Michael. She opened the car door, grabbed her jacket and quilted tote bag and got out. Michael ran to the swings. She had paper with her to capture any poetic inspirations, and a good book to read. Walking to a bench under a tree, she noted the damp moss on the water-soaked boards and was glad she'd worn old jeans. She pulled out a plastic bag, pressed it on the seat, and sat down.

Jen caught sight of a child, about two years old, emerging from the wooded creekside path into the clearing. A young couple followed. She felt lonely, but shoved the thought away. An older girl in a red outfit ran from behind the couple. About six years old, she raced to the swings and began chattering to Michael. First she tried to push him with little success, then she hopped on the swing beside him, still jabbering. He nodded now and then.

Jennifer, thinking a nap would be nice, leaned her head back against the tree trunk, but the bark hurt. She rummaged in her tote for something cushy. Nothing. The bag itself would have to do as a pillow. She arranged it, settled back, closed her eyes and let herself drift. As she grew kind of floaty and mellow, and a pleasant lakeside scene came to mind, a jangly noise assaulted her. The girl was attempting to sing. With no musical ability, the ditty of repetitious words sounded like a machine-gun. Jen stood up, irritated, and barely caught her bag before it hit the dirt. Oh, for peace and quiet.

The two kids were jumping out of the swings.

"Michael!" she called. "Michael!"

"What Mom?"

"Do you want to take a walk?"

"Sure!"

"Shall we go down the path along Canyon Creek?"

"Okay!" The little girl had bounded over, and stood by Michael. "Hi! I'm Penny. Where you going?"

Inwardly Jen groaned. *We don't need her along.*

"For a walk along the creek!" Michael answered.

"Can I come? If you ask my mommy and daddy, they'll say yes!"

Miss Enthusiasm, Jen thought. She couldn't read Michael's face – *did he want her to come?* "I don't think so."

"Can we ask if she can come, Mom?"

Looking into his eyes, she saw kindness. She didn't feel any. *Shame on me*, she thought. "Okay. We'll ask."

Getting permission, they started on the twenty-minute circuit in the deep woods. At first the path was near the river. The constant roar of the water vibrated in the moist air. Stones pushed up above the surface of the dirt path were slippery, and Michael stepped carefully. But this Penny was fearless. She *ran* along the path.

"Maybe we will see some frogs!" Michael bent and peered into the thick growth. *It's so green in here*, Jen thought. *Rain-forest feeling to it.*

Penny slipped on a mossy stone and fell. She let out a howl, but only momentarily.

Jen had to give her credit for toughness, but she said, "Slow down, Penny. I don't want you to get hurt. You can take my hand."

"I'm not hurt." She hurried out of reach.

Ahead of them the path climbed into a rocky area. Just then Penny slipped and fell on her side onto the rocks. Jen winced. Penny gasped, then cried. When Jen stooped beside her, she looked up, rubbed tears from her eyes, and tried a smile. She pushed herself up off the ground and stood.

"Oh, Penny, that hurt. You'll be bruised. I don't think your parents want you to come back hurt. Take my hand."

"They don't care about an old bruise. They say I'm tough. And I'm strong!" She showed her tightened bicep and grinned, one tear still on her cheek.

The path narrowed ahead, and Michael walked carefully. The edge dropped off into the fast-moving water.

He turned, and said, "Careful."

Penny giggled and ran up to him. Jen shouted, ineffectively, "Stop!"

Michael hurriedly backed onto some rocks. Jen ran past and grabbed Penny's hand.

"I'm okay. I don't need to hold anyone's hand."

"Yes, you do!" Exasperated, Jen held her hand tight. "Because I want you to! This is too dangerous, otherwise."

"No, it's not!" She gave a mischievous look and tried to pull away.

"Yes, it is!" Jen insisted, holding on tighter. "We are going back now." She turned, tugging the girl's hand, and Michael followed.

Later Jenny sat in the car as Michael took a final turn on the swing. Penny's family had already left. The day was spoiled for Jen. *Why do I feel so angry. I'm afraid of what I might do to a kid like that. She was only being headstrong. Sure doesn't know to come when called, though. No sense of safety. Len says I turn Michael into a wimp. Maybe I do.*

* * *

Michael stood drying the lunch dishes while his mom washed. He had a very serious look on his face, and he said quietly, "Mom, how could I not sleep for ten days and not be tired?"

"Not sleep for ten days? Why?"

"I don't know why, Mom. Please, just tell me, how could I not be tired?"

Jen thought a while. "I don't know. How could you not be tired?"

"I didn't sleep for ten *days*... because I slept at night."

"Oh, Michael! You got me again! I didn't know you were joking! Trying to buffalo me! And I fell right into it! I'll be on my guard next time, Young Man!" She reached out and grabbed him suddenly, and lovingly enfolded him in a hug. "I think you're just too smart for me! But I've got your number now." He hugged her again tightly. She thought, *I wonder how long this will last – my little boy hugging me. He'll grow to a teen and he may not want to. I'd better enjoy it now. How does a mom keep it open – the hugs, the talks and walks, and just being together. Though he'll spend much less time with me then, I want to be part of his life, even a small part.*

The dishes were finished, and Jen took the wet dish towel from Michael and hung it to dry. "I know what, Smarty Pants. Let's play Scrabble! Last year you got discouraged. But you are doing so much reading I'm sure your vocabulary has caught up to mine!"

"I don't know, Mom!"

"If we play, you won't get discouraged, will you?"

"No! I would like a chance to beat you!"

As she got up on a chair, she said, "It's Saturday afternoon and we've both gotten our chores done." She brought down the game. "I looked at your room. It looks neat enough, since you worked on it this morning. I was especially glad to see you had set out your rocks. That moss you found yesterday – you might want to lay it in a dish and keep a couple teaspoons of water under it, so it stays green. Nice to see that your room reflects your interests, that you're making it your own."

Michael opened the game board. "Do you think we'll live here a long time, Mom? I like it here."

"I imagine so." Her casual tone of voice belied her concern. "Oh, I saw that you found that picture of you and Mary and John. Nice that she gave you that." As she handed him a wooden rack for his letter tiles, she saw his face get serious.

"Mom…" Michael looked up, his large brown eyes sad. "Will we ever get to see them again?"

"I don't know. I can't say." As she spoke a thought came. "Maybe someday they'll want to come out and see where we live!" It was probably a long shot, though. She sat down to play.

"Really?"

"Oh, Michael, I don't know. It's just that it could happen." She paused. "I have their address, come to think of it. Would you like to write to them?"

"Yes!" He jumped up and retrieved a notepad out of a drawer. "What is it?"

"Oh, slow down! Let's play. Leave that pad out on the table so I remember, and I'll find it for you after our game."

For his second word, Michael put down 'hooey'.

"Hooey? What is that?" Jen protested. "That's not a real word. Let's look it up!"

"Do you *really* want to lose your turn if it's here?" Michael had a confident air as he thumbed rapidly through the pages of the dictionary. Holding it out and pointing to the place, he said, "There it is, and it means nonsense!" Michael was triumphant.

"Well, what do you know!" Jen shook her head. "Learn something every day."

"I saw it in the dictionary at school when I looked for hootenanny last week. Our teacher gave us the assignment to make up a challenging spelling list. It was like a contest. I came in second for the 'worst' word – hooey!"

"Good for you! Jen said. "Your turn. I lost mine." The game progressed and she saw the delight in Michael's eyes when she teased him for getting too smart. He was learning needed skills for the game, like taking advantage of a high point tile so he got more than just face value. He laid down a word containing a four-point h and got it on a triple letter square. When Jen played, she ignored the h he had put down. Then on his next turn, he played off from it easily. They both decided to check the spelling of yep for yes, and found it could also be yup. She protested, with a laugh, that the dictionary was too new. Though his mom won, Michael took it in stride.

The next day they played another game of Scrabble as soon as the breakfast dishes were done. Jen was glad to see Michael's continued pleasure when he made a good score. He made two words in a row crossing pink double word squares. She did place her tiles to give him a chance at the red triple word squares on the edges, but she couldn't give him noticeable help – he'd be upset. She was impressed that his vocabulary had indeed grown. Though he was behind, he kept his score climbing, and wasn't discouraged. Finally she won. They talked about some of the words and their meanings or how they could be added to. He pointed to words that were his, and seemed pleased. *Yes, indeed,* Jen thought. *My little boy is growing up.*

* * *

Jenny parked the car in front of the Post Office. She would get the mail first. Then go look at the greenhouse items that were brought into town. It wouldn't hurt to just take a look at the bedding plants, even though she wasn't ready to buy. The last stop would be to get milk and bread. *First hot day we've had all spring. Sunshine to make the flowers grow. I'm glad I'll be able to buy plants right here in Granite Falls. Maybe it won't be a large selection. But, after I find out what they have, I can keep a mental picture of them blooming and beautifying the yard as I work on that rocky soil. My own garden! I can't believe it – flowers of my own! How many times have I passed the displays of cut flowers at the store, and told myself I mustn't splurge on something we can't eat. So what that I've never had a garden – launching into the unknown is good for the soul! I can do it!*

Jen had a list of all the possible plants, colors noted beside each. It was tucked in her pocket like a secret plot. She pulled it out and grew excited as she thought of how the yard would look with flowers blooming. She had already spent three days digging and sifting out rocks in the hard ground on both sides of the front porch. Flowers would be cheerful at the entrance. There was not much sun because of the trees, especially where the porch roof shaded that corner toward the driveway. But Sylvia said it had enough light for shade-loving flowers like impatiens.

Tomorrow, Jen determined, she would do much more in her battle against the resistant, hard-packed clay. If she couldn't get waitress work, she could make a home. She pictured bringing flowers into the house – a vase full of blooms standing regally on her coffee table and another one in cheerful colors on the kitchen table. Out of doors the bright flowerbeds would greet everyone who came. First ones visible would be along the far side of the driveway. Against odds, she planned to get something blooming over there. Besides the rocks, blackberry vines were thick, even brushing against the car. Hacking them back would have to do for this season. She hoped she could beat the odds, though Sylvia seemed doubtful about fighting the established roots of those vines.

Jen thought of the pleasant times spent with Sylvia, "talking flowers". Sylvia was becoming a friend – the friend she had wanted and thought she'd never have. Yes! – it would be such fun to make up a big bouquet of her own flowers and give them to Sylvia! Thinking how she had wanted a true friend also brought to mind the fear she'd had of making friends, keeping her distance in case she would regret letting down her guard. *That sounds silly,* she said to herself. *It doesn't make sense. But after all, not everyone can be trusted to be what they seem at first.* The apprehension the night before she met Mary came to mind clearly – how she had felt trapped when Cora was 'making arrangements' on the bus. The feeling of wariness she'd had...well, she had been wrong about that one. But wariness could be good. And it hadn't kept her from becoming friends with Mary. She smiled to herself. That had turned into much more than just finding adequate child-care – Mary also became a good friend – and in such a short time. But that was over. Sadness swept over her. Mary was gone...out of reach. She might never see her again.

Jen realized she was still sitting in front of the post office, daydreaming. She worked at cranking the windows down – dumb old car. She turned to get out and had to push with both hands on the door, which dragged on its hinges.

Jenny reached out for the mail and returned the postal clerk's smile. Turning away, she saw the top item in her hand had General Delivery on it – missed the forwarding order. General Delivery – she couldn't wait until all their mail came to the box, to an address of their own. General Delivery always felt shiftless. It reminded her of childhood, after her dad had left and her mother began to move every few months. She thought of her younger brother and sister. Painful memories. Just before she had Michael, her brother had died in a speeding car crash. So pitifully young. *He didn't keep in touch. I was caught up in my own problems. Didn't really know what was going on in his life. He wasn't even licensed yet; just a kid – he didn't think there would be consequences for drinking and driving – he thought he was invincible.*

She leaned against the front fender of the car, looked up into the sky, and blinked away the tears that sprang to her eyes. Squeezing back more that were threatening, she pushed aside the thoughts. Things she couldn't change. Her sister Patsy got in touch once or twice a year. In fact, it was about time for a phone call, or maybe even a visit. Mixed feelings filled her. Patsy was so touchy that she was hard to have around. Jen needed, wanted, to find out what was happening in her sister's life. But it seemed like visits inevitably ended in misunderstandings and accusations.

Jen looked down and started to thumb through the mail. Two envelopes from the bank. Ah, the statements for both accounts. The joint household account was barely in the black. But she knew what was in her savings account. She felt good, proud of herself for carefully putting away her tip money during the last few weeks in Seattle. At first she had felt awful when a large overdue bill for the car business went to collection, but Len had said, 'I'll take care of it. Stop your nagging.' He hadn't – so it did. She probably should have tried to pay it. It hadn't been right to owe money and not pay.

When she had talked to Maggie, another waitress at work, she told her, "Smarten up! It's normal to expect a guy to pay the bills he runs up. You had better take charge of a few things in your own life, including money. Considering Len's attitude and his track record, do you think you can count on him? You have to think of yourself. Think *for* yourself. Not go around trying to fix Len's problems – problems he brought on himself." At first Jen had thought Maggie sounded harsh, like she didn't care about Len, and wasn't concerned about unpaid bills. After they talked more, Jen started to see her point. She also saw how vulnerable she was as a result of Len's irresponsible decisions. It had been a good feeling when the savings account in her name grew. When the spring weather warmed and tourists poured in, tips had doubled. Her attitude changed. She had always been down to the coins in her purse, with nothing in reserve. It seemed strange to have money in the bank, waiting. But, though she had been tempted to get it out, she resisted. Especially recently. A day might come when she would need it worse than now. Maggie had also given her a booklet that she said would help her see where Len was at – so she could understand him objectively. Of course there were things she hadn't told Maggie; couldn't tell. She wondered where that booklet was – probably in some packing box upstairs.

Jen's thoughts turned to the present and the pressing need – a job. This money would disappear fast once she dipped into it. She badly needed some new clothes for waitressing as they didn't supply uniforms out here. She could shop in a thrift store in Snohomish. Maybe wait till she had a job. Sylvia might go with her, or, realistically, take her when she went to Everett. She needed a reliable car. Though this old car had functioned today, Len said it was done for; not to drive it far. The transmission was slipping badly, and he said it could go out on her at any time. She wondered if he was planning to bring a better vehicle out from Seattle. Dismissing the thought, she considered clothes again. *After I get a couple nice blouses and pants, I'll feel better. I should go back to that café at the shopping center on highway 9. Let them know I'm serious.* It seemed the most likely place. She would be a fill-in at first – if only she could know ahead and go by bus. Well, those problems wouldn't get solved now. Maybe Len would get a functioning car. In the mean time, what a pleasure the garden would be!

Jen slid the bank envelopes to the bottom of the stack. The next item of mail was a picture postcard with deep pink flowers covering a shrub, as big as a a double garage. The caption read "Rhododendrons – University of Washington Arboretum". She remembered little rhodies in the city, smaller than Sylvia's. These were gigantic. Who would have thought?

Jen flipped the card over – it was from Mary! She eagerly read, "We miss you both and hope you are settling in well. Nothing new here except that the garden is lush – a real jungle. I wish you could drop over and fill the trunk of your car with veggies! We love you and are praying for you. Keep in touch! Mary" The loving concern in the message brought tears to Jen's eyes. She ached inside. At the same time, her heart was filled with warmth. What a wonderful woman. It was hard to understand why that situation, so good for Michael, had to end. She sighed. However, he was living in the country now. He could play in open fields instead of playgrounds. How could she whine?

* * *

Jen walked into the hardware store. "I understand you have bedding plants?"

"We sure do," the pleasant-faced man said. "Right on through the back of the store." He led the way down an aisle and out a door. "You can have a look around. Here is a cart for your selections."

"Oh, I'll just be window-shopping today. I have to do some more soil prep first."

"That's fine. Take your time." He left. Jen couldn't believe how many little plants were jammed onto the shelves. A lathe "roof" was over the area, and strips of sunlight alternated with shadow. She got out her list and lost herself in a world of plastic name tags, pulling one out of the pot to read, pushing it back in, going to the next flat. At this stage they all looked the same – green. No flowers, just lots of little leaves, some finely cut, some broad, some palmate as if they had fingers. That was where her terminology stopped. The next aisle was a surprise. The plants had blossoms! The buds on the impatiens were opening enough to show color, and the pansies had wide open faces, purple, periwinkle blue, rust and yellow. Pansies were an absolute must. Such happy faces!

* * *

Len opened his front door. "Come in, Martin. Come in. Glad you made it over. I'm washing the pickup and waxing it. You want to help?"

"Sure Mr. Brown. What can I do?"

"Fill this bucket half full of water in the kitchen sink. It has the soap in it. Bring it outside. I've got the sponge and cloths."

Martin brought the bucket outside, but was startled to hear Len's angry voice and rude name-calling. What was up? He saw Michael with a cloth and bucket, and Len waving his arms.

"How could you scratch that finish? You idiot! You're not supposed to grind dirt into it, Stupid. Can't you be careful? Oh, so you didn't *know* the cloth was dirty? You could *see* it was. What an idiot."

"I didn't mean to scratch it." Michael ducked away from Len's waving arm. "I was just trying to help." They both caught sight of Martin.

Len called out loudly, "Good thing you're here. This moron used a dirty cloth and scratched the hood." Len turned back to Michael. "Get out of here. Go play. We don't need a little kid to help."

When the pickup was clean, Len threw Martin a fresh rag and showed him how to use a buffing compound. The boy worked up a sweat, rubbing, and stood back with a happy smile.

"There Mr. Brown! The scratches on the hood came out. It looks okay now, doesn't it?"

"Looks great, thanks to you." He gave him a congratulatory slap on the back.

Michael stood at the window, looking out at the shining pickup, and Martin and Len.

CHAPTER TWENTY-FIVE

Jen pulled out the chair and sat down in Sylvia's kitchen as she brought the teapot of Red Rose to the table for them to share. "Thanks for having me over, *and* thank-you for prompting me to check out the bedding plants at the hardware store. A few were already blooming. I enjoyed seeing them and dreaming. Now I want to get the beds ready immediately so I can go back and pick them up."

"I'm glad! I figured you'd need an incentive to finish the hard job of digging!"

"I have plenty of incentive after seeing them. Of course I have the reminder of how much work it takes – my aching back!" But Jen was smiling as she sipped tea, took a deep breath, and relaxed into her chair. "Your home is comfortable – a person wants to just come in and enjoy!"

"You're encouraged to do that anytime! Especially when you need to get out of your four walls. It can be gray this time of year. You get cabin fever."

"Ah, words and their meanings – what do you mean "cabin fever"?"

"Oh, it's a northern or pioneer expression. Explorers, prospectors, and early settlers used it. Actually, anyone who was outdoors most of the time. In winter they endured being cooped up. The long hours of darkness didn't help. It all began to get to them. I can imagine that the homesteaders who'd been used to long days, tending gardens and working their farms, became irritable. I guess there seemed to be a personality change when friends lost their tempers with each other. They called it cabin fever 'cause they realized it was like a sickness."

"Hmm. I can understand that. Ha – you used two other expressions. "Cooped up" and crabby. Limited to a chicken coop, and I know about crabby! My Aunt Sally had a crabapple tree in her yard. The little apples made good jelly, but oh, what awful tartness to eat them fresh – especially when I tried before they were ripe. So I can see your homesteader being "crabby"! In my imagination he has a sour expression from eating unripe crabapples! Aren't words fun?"

"Sure are. I'm writing a story for young teens or pre-teens. I'm finding I need a new vocabulary. At the mall I listen to the expressions the teens use. I'll be having coffee and a group of them sit down near me, enjoying their iced cappuccinos. I listen. Sometimes it's all girls and sometimes it's a mix of boys and girls. That in itself is interesting. I am surprised at their interaction. Surprised that they have some compassion when one of them has a serious problem. Seems better than when I was young."

"Oh?" Jen's eyebrows shot up.

"Not always! If it's a bunch of boys they harass each other. Once one of them spilled hot coffee on himself. He got teased for being clumsy. Yet even their banter has a certain... well, if not affection, closeness. It's all very interesting. Back to language – I especially like the way they make up their own. I hear the changing expressions – what used to be labeled "hang out" is now just "hang". They are creating their own language."

Jen nodded. "I remember a teacher talking about how English is a living language, changing constantly. She said if you were to read a book in a dead language like Latin you would know what the words mean because they haven't changed in 2,000 years. But our language is changing all the time."

"True," Sylvia nodded. "I guess I must be old-fashioned. I especially enjoy hearing people use old expressions. The ones I heard as a kid pop into my mind unexpectedly. It takes me back to another time. I miss them, and feel sad when they are lost. If you say "You hit the nail on the head", it still makes sense, but using a hammer is not a common experience. Few people pound nails now.

And it's rare to pick up a needle and mend socks, so "A stitch in time saves nine" is another outdated one. We don't spend hours knitting socks, so we rarely mend them. We buy new ones."

"I suppose each generation has it's own special sayings." Jen looked thoughtful. "Some last, I guess, and are still understood. Expressions my folks used still paint vivid word pictures for me." She laughed. "'Sweat like a horse!' is one. I rode horses with a friend as a teen, so I've seen a horse lathered up. They certainly do sweat." Her expression became quizzical. "So – you like words...I remember you saying if I took you to buy second-hand books you might fill up your shelves with dozens of them!"

Jen grinned sheepishly. "That's right."

"Our public library has a great selection. I'll take you to get a library card. You can have a free-for-all, then take them back and get more."

"That would be great. I didn't have much time for reading while working full time. I'll take advantage of this little break."

"I may have a hard time not commenting, pointing out books on the library shelves that I've read. But I'll try to control myself! No comments unless I think it was a waste of time. Even then, 'To each his own'! You can browse the library shelves to your heart's content."

"It will be great to have access to so many books *and* have the time to read them."

"Yes, our lives have seasons. The library is on the far side of town. I'll take you on a drive around the area. I know the town is very small after living in Seattle, but some things are tucked away. Nice to get oriented."

"I'd appreciate that. Get the lay of the land."

"Did you have a chance to unpack any of your own books yet?"

"I took out a few books in the upstairs room. There's another box downstairs. I don't have that lower room fixed up yet, but I do want to."

"Oh yes, the renovated room in the basement you thought would be a good get-away. Say, I have a couple of wooden chairs in the shed. I moved them out there to save space. We'll take a look. See if you want to use them. One has been in the family and brings memories. I'm glad if you can enjoy it in the meantime and you can give it back when you're done with it. You can keep the other one."

"Thanks. That'll be a help. Yes – in the "mean time"! You said another one of those expressions! How mean is it?" Jen laughed.

"Right! Thinking of 'mean' as ornery. But mean time? I guess it's more like "in between", like mean numbers in math. Seems obscure. Sometimes we simply take the idea of an expression for granted, without thinking about what's behind it."

"Funny, I remember the terms 'mean' and 'average' in math class, I can't remember the difference! Math wasn't my strong point! As for the downstairs room, I did like its remote feeling, away from everyday activity. I dream of reading, losing myself. Then again, I especially like that room on the upper floor that has a window facing your house. Except, the only drawback, it'll get hot in the summer. I can't believe I have options – two rooms to pick from!" She smiled, then went on. "I needed a bookcase for the basement. Decided to set up one right away to empty some boxes, so I picked out boards from the woodpile in back. The dirt came off using a broom and a bucket of water. But they are so rough I wonder about painting them. Could cover them by tacking on roll ends of wallpaper. I plan to use cement blocks or stacked up bricks between the shelves. It'll be a good-sized bookcase. The one in the living room is small, and anyway, it's needed there. I want a private place for my notebooks for writing. Have things at my fingertips in a quiet place."

"Oh! Tell me about your writing!" Excitement filled Sylvie's normally calm face.

Jen dropped her eyes and didn't speak. *Caught in a lie. I'm not published. I'm not a writer. Just a wanna be."*

"What do you like to write?" Sylvie persisted.

"Just thoughts. Not real writing, like an author." *Do I want to share this?* Jen wondered, looking up into Sylvia's eyes. *My thoughts aren't for others to see – there's lots of anger.* Considering what she should say, she began, "I put down my feelings. Later, when I re-read, I ask myself, *Does this make sense?* My reason for writing most of it is only so I can get my thoughts clear; get them on paper. When I read it later I see that it's garbled in places, so I scratch out and fill-in words that clarify. A lot of it is worthless.

Most of it. I stick it in the back of a folder, or in the bottom of a box with a stack of other stuff. Probably never look at those again. Sometimes though, I take out one and think, *Yes, other people must go through this – just the same experiences as I've been having. I need to develop this someday.* So I tuck it away, thinking that I may use it later as a starting point, maybe for a poem."

"Oh, you write poetry, too! And you journal – some people never do, you know. How nice to have a woman living right next door who has a real love for words. So nice to have something like *that* in common! It's my good fortune. So tell me about your poetry."

"Well…" Jenny hesitated. "I used to write poetry – most of it was when I was in my teens. I started up again a while back. Funny. It was different. The teenage poetry was volatile, explosive with emotions. Haven't done that kind in ages. Recent ones were calm by comparison."

Sylvia nodded her head. "I can identify with that!"

Jen went on. "A while back I sketched out some articles about small animals and the outdoors for children. It was a good exercise. When Michael began reading, we read together. I got back in the reading habit, too. His coming home excited from his Saturday at the museum got me going on the animal stories. I did finish a couple. I doubt I'll pursue that, but it was fun."

Sylvia had watched Jen's face brighten as she talked, her excitement bringing a rosy bloom to her cheeks. Then it faded. *I wonder if one of the smaller papers in the area would print the animal stories, or maybe even the poems? I think Larry knows the editor of the Snohomish paper. I can take her by to meet him. Then I can encourage her to bug him until she gets herself into print. Better not say anything now. It's not the right time.* "Would you let me read any of your children's articles, or the poems? I'd really enjoy reading anything you've done. Only if you'd like to share them."

"Really? Well, I'll take a look in my stuff. See if I can find something among the poems. I have stories in my head, but I don't usually write down any, other than the ones for children. I guess the journal is similar to stories. And," Jen smiled wryly, "that's for private consumption. Whether the poems are worthwhile for reading…I don't know. I'll check."

233

"Just whatever you'd like to share; I don't mean to press you. *However,* my idea of 'worthwhile' may be less critical than yours! Creative people are hard on themselves. I think it's a God-given gift that we humans have creative minds. And that we have language, too. You know, in a writing class I joined once, we read our own writing aloud. That works well, because the voice inflections are right. I'd like that, if you'd like to read yours aloud. That class was a couple years ago. We met here in the library. It ran for sixteen weeks in the winter. No one put on airs. We simply read anything we'd written, without worrying if it was "good" as we thought of good writing. Just had to be on paper! Some did very dramatic readings. Others were quiet and contemplative."

"Oh!" Jen let the word hang in the air. "That must have been quite an experience."

"Yes, a really good one."

As they sat drinking tea they continued chatting about the writing class until shouts and a bang interrupted them. Hurrying to the window over the sink, they saw Michael and Jeremy throwing a baseball on the driveway. Jen called vainly to Michael to stop, but wasn't heard through the glass. She reached up, rapped on the window, and pointed to go out back, in the field.

Sylvia saw the marks on her outstretched arm, she exclaimed, "Oh – what happened?"

"What?"

"Your arm! It's all bruised."

"Oh. That...It's just... I banged it with the shovel handle when I was digging."

"It looks so painful."

"No. It's fine. I bruise easily." Jen turned abruptly. "Well, I should go. I need to make sure the boys know to throw the ball elsewhere, not by the windows."

Something about the abrupt change and Jen's uneasy manner aroused Sylvia's concern. *A shovel didn't made those marks,* she thought; *they are the imprint of fingers.*

* * *

What a pleasure a hot shower was! Jen let the water beat hard on her back. Breathing deeply, she considered how simple an act this was. Her muscles were sore from gardening and she let the hot water massage her as she thought over the little pleasures of life. Pleasures like seeing the colors of a sunset, a field of flowers, or watching the delight of a baby taking in the activity of a public market and the expressions on grown-up faces. She especially found pleasure when that baby saw her smile and responded, face lighting up in open sweetness.

Looking at the bargain vinyl shower curtain she had found, she thought, *not exactly the pattern I would have liked, but it's a good feeling to be getting things more organized.* At first she had put up a sheet to keep in the water. She noticed a dark patch in the corner of the seal around the tub. *Oh, oh. That mold is back. I scrubbed and bleached till I was sure it was gone. Just have to do it again. Oh, well!* She couldn't stay glum while showering, her favorite 'creature comfort'. She lingered until the hot water was running cool, turned it off, and stepped into the small room. No fan. She wiped the fogged mirror. It seemed dark. A good dose of paint would give a sense of light. The ugly lime green was so intense it swallowed up the light. She grabbed a pretty dusty rose towel to dry, and recalled running across the set as she packed up the apartment. She had bought them for a wedding shower gift for another waitress. She took off for Las Vegas and didn't return, and the shower was canceled. At first Jenny kept them, unused, *'just in case'.* In case she needed a gift for another occasion. Mostly she was reluctant to take out something brand new and use it for herself. But when she unpacked them and considered the ragged-edged towels they normally used, she hung them up. The lime green walls clashed terribly with them. *But,* she thought, *it's my incentive to cover up that paint!*

* * *

Jenny was sweeping the upstairs rooms. She came into the one she privately called her artist's garret, looked at her trunk and thought of all her "scribblings" over the years. Journals she had kept. Poems written on notebook paper. Her mind wandered to her mid-teens when the urge to be out on her own had grown strong. She had wanted to join any group, be with any person who had poetic sense, and spend her days being creative. People who resisted expressing their emotions had totally baffled her. Though it was true that she now kept her feelings to herself, she still couldn't understand the complete restraint of some people. Not restraint exactly. It was as if they never felt anything. They seemed to her to never have had joy in living, or, if they once had, they decided against it. The aura of her teen idealism returned and she remembered how she believed that a person should feel free to do, free to go. Yet at the same time she had held back. Big-sister responsibility had done that. Responsible. Always responsible. Until the day she left.

Shaking her head, Jen remembered how she had hated "properness". Tired of life as it was, or existence, during her last year of high school, she had the dream of moving out from "home", if it could be called home. *Out,* she thought. *Why the word out? It's away from, not out. But it's true. I felt like a captive, a Cinderella who was a captive. It wasn't responsibility. I could do the work. No...It was so depressing. I was a failure, a nobody. I had to escape from a black, depressing pit. I dreamed of living with people who were creative. People who painted beautiful works of art, or who wrote as and when ever they felt moved, day or night. I needed to be with like-minded people who could feel; who knew they didn't have to fit into a stilted form. So what if that ideal life I longed for might be a Bohemian life? What was so bad about that? It was just a simple life – one in touch with nature and oneself.*

She did find friends who thought her way. Things at home were worse. She left and got a job – not quite the kind of job she had in mind. She washed dishes in the back of a dirty restaurant all evening. She was tired from lifting stacks of heavy plates and working long hours, getting up early and going to school. There wasn't time or energy for creativity. And she looked around at her 'mates' and perceived that the truly creative people were few in number. Some of the others were hopeless, helpless cases who could ramble endlessly, sound intellectual, but couldn't remember to take a bath or eat. They had fried their brains on drugs. It was hard not to get tangled up in their exhausting rehearsal of problems.

They talked endlessly. She watched the effects of their immersion in alcohol and drugs and knew that she didn't want to muddle the good mind she had – about all that she had. Fortunately, among these 'free-thinkers' she had the encouragement of knowing a few truly creative fellow-travelers. She enjoyed the times they spent singing, quoting poetry, or intelligently discussing the world's problems. Sometimes she watched others heatedly challenge one another to consider a new viewpoint. She was too insecure to enter in, but it was stimulating to listen.

* * *

Two days of heavy rain had brought a chill to the air. In spite of the fact that mud was thick and puddles were everywhere, the threesome decided to take a walk. Michael slogged through a deep puddle, dragging his feet. Jennifer and Sylvia skirted around and got back on the sidewalk. He trudged along behind them, as if to wear a hole in his boots. "Man alive, I'm sorry I brought you along, Michael." Jen shook her head while he ignored her, and kept dragging along. "Can't you pick up your feet?"

To Sylvia, he looked so weary she wondered if he'd make it home. "I have a proposition for you two. How about something to eat? There's a nice little bakery with goodies and coffee *and* hot chocolate just around the corner." Michael looked up, doubtful.

"That would be good." Jen felt a tad remorseful that she'd been cranky. "Fortify this boy. I guess he needs it. I'm sorry, Sylvia, that touring the town ended up a wet hassle."

"Oh, I'm not! If you don't go out in the rain here, you don't go out at all!"

Jen laughed. "You're right. And I sure appreciate being in and out of the shops and the library. Seeing artwork in the book and gift store was an eye-opener. I wouldn't have thought an area that's, ah, out of the way like this would have so much art."

"You mean out in the sticks?" Sylvia laughed as she pushed open the bakery door. "Yes, you can say it. Maybe the boondocks, even! Actually, with creative pursuits being popularized for fulfillment, I think more people are trying it. All talents are appreciated here, I think. Crafts, too, that rural people have been good at by necessity in early times."

"Yes. But those paintings were professional. Not a quick flight of fancy by someone fooling around. They were good."

"All kinds of people out here. It's a real mix. Being out in the sticks is not what it used to be. Now it's called 'the urbanite's answer to the rat race'!"

"You're right about a rat race. I can't believe how much I've slowed down since I moved here. I even breathe deeply and walk instead of constantly rushing around."

They enjoyed thawing in the warmth of the bakery, then decided to take what was left of their bag of chocolate chip cookies and walk some more. The air felt fresh now, instead of chilling.

"Look! It's baby Jesus." Michael pointed to a Nativity scene in a second-hand store window. "Mary said it's not just for Christmas. She's the lady where I went after school. She talked about Jesus being real. That He wasn't just a baby, or just a story, but grew up to be a man. He walked everywhere, teaching people good stuff."

"That's nice you learned about Him. Well, when we decorate for Christmas, I guess we know now, we had better have a Nativity set in place!" Sylvia poked Jen with a wink.

* * *

In her "upper room", as Sylvie had named it, Jen pulled out a paper holding a May - June poem. She read through, set it aside, and opened one of two spiral notebooks and flipped through. Reading a half a dozen different ones, her mind wandered. She looked at the notebook on the little table. There were many poems in that notebook from her teens – all free verse, all her personal feelings. They ran the gamut: intense anger, loss of hope, sadness, and bursts of joy. Attempts to capture the ecstasy and agony that she felt in her teenage years. Personal. But the later ones, from her pregnancy and Michael's delivery, were even more personal. She went back to the two spirals. She'd find one that was alright to show Sylvia. Not too revealing.

PART THREE
FEAR

June – August

CHAPTER TWENTY-SIX

Jen looked up at the kitchen clock and then stood watching the gray light creep through her windows. *It's not too late to crawl back in bed. I could get another hour of sleep. But I shouldn't.* In her weary state it was hard to sort out. *The movement will wake Len. Is it worth it? He'll start asking if I've been up with Michael. And when he finds out, he'll be angry.* Nervously she paced the kitchen floor, thinking about the drop in their income. At least, she consoled herself, short on sleep as she was, she didn't have to face eight or nine-hours of waitress work, on her feet, running. She paced the length of the kitchen again. It would be such a help to have a job, have the income. She puzzled over a conversation earlier in the week. Len had said, "You might as well stay home, since Michael is sick." But why? His change of mind totally surprised her. He was sitting, reading the paper. She guessed he was holding the Help Wanted ads as he said, "Don't worry about job hunting. It just isn't gonna happen here. So stay home." *I'm a dreamer,* she had thought. *He certainly must mean a very short while. Does he have money coming in soon? From where?*

She looked at the clock again, and thought, *Better stay up.* There was a deck of cards on the table. She sat down and shuffled them absentmindedly and dealt out a game of solitaire. There were no moves with the seven face-up cards to get it started. When she went through the deck the first time, there were still no moves. Even the second time she only played two cards, and then it went stale. She gathered them up, re-dealt, and the next hand was better. She got eight cards to the top, and then it stalled. She played several more games, until an hour had gone by. *"You should call Len,"* the clock kept taunting her. She wouldn't acknowledge it. *I don't have to call him yet. He will be glad for the sleep...I'll play another game.* But after that it was definitely past time. *I'll finish this game. I really must call him. Ah...soon enough after this game, it's going so well. Once I get up from the table – that's it. Just once more – I'll just go through the deck once more. I've almost won.*

Crash. Upstairs Len threw open the bedroom door hard, and she heard the knob smack the wall, deepening the hole in the plaster. Unintelligible shouting echoed and something heavy hit the bedroom wall. A loud bang with the sound of wood splintering was accompanied by swearing. Must have been a dresser drawer breaking. Quickly she gathered up the cards, hid them under a stack of old mail, and ran to the refrigerator. Grabbing the deli meat she tossed it on the counter, then laid out slices of bread.

Len's feet thundered down the stairs, and he ran in, yelling, "Couldn't you get off your lazy rear and wake me?"

She was buttering bread fast, being as careful as she could not to tear the bread. "I...I forgot to watch the clock." It was a lie. But how could she say she didn't *want* to wake him? Dreading his morning moods, she had only made things worse.

He yanked open the cupboard door and threw the lunch box on the counter. She jumped as it clanged against dirty glasses. One shattered. He grabbed the metal box and flipped it open. "Would it be *too much* to ask, Your Highness, just to have you call me?"
He jerked her around. Her arm hurt as he twisted it. He was right in her face, glaring down. She turned her eyes aside. He grabbed her jaw, pushing her against the door jamb. His eyes pierced into her. "Maybe you don't care whether I get to work. Maybe you don't even *care* if I bring home the paycheck."

Silently, trying not to struggle against the pain, she thought of their finances in the past. *There have been months at a time when you earned nothing. But how can I talk? Now I'm earning nothing.*

"You're lazy. You don't care, do you? It's all on me, even footing the bill for that brat of yours." She winced at mention of Michael in that tone of voice. He loosened his hold as he went on. "You'd be in a fine mess if I weren't working." And on he went. Something had changed. It wasn't like she actually saw his earnings coming in – quite the opposite. A chill went down her back. Would they return to Len being out of work, and her, too? A memory came – he talked like this when he was restless, bored, wanted change. He always had wanted excitement out of life. *Would he quit his job?* she wondered. *No, surely not. Not another job down the drain. Not moving again. NO. This may not be perfect, but we're settled.*

Yelling again, he said, "You lay around all day. Ever since you quit working…"

"I did NOT. I didn't quit. I had a good job in Seattle and now I can't find one. You got the bright idea to move here when you were in California." Len grabbed her shoulder with one hand and raised a clenched fist. "Owww," Jen cried out. "Your fingers are digging in. Oww, it hurts."

"So it hurts. It's meant to hurt. Get you to think before you yap your mouth. Gonna call you The Mouth. Can't keep your mouth shut. You say it's *my* bright idea, do you? We could use some bright ideas around here. How many bright ideas have you had lately?" He cuffed her on the side of her head and shoved her away. Muddled, stumbling, she heard the yelling as foggy background noise. Grabbing the counter, she caught her balance.

"A lousy excuse for a sandwich – turkey. I wanted beef." He stomped from the kitchen, swearing. Pawing through the shoes by the front door, he said, "I can't find my shoes. This house is a mess. Can't find a thing." He threw shoes, slippers and boots in every direction. Dried dirt came loose in hard gobs, then broke into dust as fine as powder. He put on his flip-flops, went out to the pickup, and returned – with his shoes in hand. He found them where he had left them.

Jen watched him sit down on the arm of the couch to put them on. She turned away and went to finish packing the lunch, thinking how often Len had jerked Michael off the couch arm, saying, 'Stupid, you don't *sit* there. You'll break it. A shrinking feeling contracted Jen's chest. *He'll never admit he has a problem. If only he'd calm down, he'd think more clearly. He's so hurtful. I don't expect him to say he's sorry to me, nor will he ever apologize to Michael. He'll never apologize for anything, to anyone. Certainly not for knocking dirt all over the floor. Larry Ford would.* She closed the lunch pail. As she turned back, insight came like light. *I have been hoping, wanting, a better life here. It could be so much better. Since he doesn't choose to change... I guess I don't expect anything. Apathy. It doesn't matter. Nothing matters.* It was a hopeless feeling. Darkness settled down on her. She set the lunch pail on the floor.

Shoes laced, Len jumped up, threw open the door and stepped out. Then he remembered his lunch pail. He turned, grabbed it, and left, slamming the door. *More anger,* she thought. *So what's new.* She looked around the cluttered room. *I could have called him to get up on time, though. I blew it, for sure, not calling him.*

Jen took in a deep breath but it didn't relieve the pain and tension in her neck. Her head ached from being smacked and jerked around. She walked over to the kitchen table. The corner of a solitaire card peeked out. *What a life – when my highest pleasure is to hide away, play solitaire. Michael is growing up. What am I teaching him?*

Discouraged, Jen trudged up the stairs. She felt oppressed by a weight. Sylvie talked about a sense of guidance. *I have no sense of direction. How can a person have direction? How can I teach Michael to have that? I'm plodding, mired down. I have such a sense of aimlessness.* Turning into her upstairs space, she wandered over to the window. Looking north above the roof of Sylvie's house, her eyes rested on clouds. They were sweeping in from the left, off Puget Sound, heavy with its moisture. Moving east, they would collect against the hills to shed life-giving moisture. But she was as dry as desert sand. She stared at the countless trees without seeing. *Sometimes...* she thought. *Sometimes... I wish I could fly away...* She sat down, picked up a pen, and began to put thoughts on paper.

Sometimes

Sometimes, I wish I could fly away
on the wings of a bird
Or snuggle into a burrow with a field mouse.

Sometimes, I wish I could transport myself instantly
to some other place, some other time.

Sometimes this world with all its struggles, this life with
all its burdens just seems too much to bear, and
I wish, just for a little while,
to see... to feel... to think no more.

But this is only Sometimes...

Other times, I see my child's face and
I could get lost in his eyes forever, or
I feel his arms around me and think
"there's nothing better than this!"
Then there are times I feel so confused
about what to think, or how I feel...
that Sometimes the tears come
and I don't always know... are they tears of happiness
or sorrow... memories of joy
or grief... or maybe, a little of both.

Sometimes the despair is all there is.

June – Jennifer Hanson Brown

* * *

Work was a cure, wasn't it? Jen forced her shovel into the hard ground. Sylvia and she had looked at pictures in the garden book. For the layout of the beds, perennials were permanent and best in the back, Sylvia said. They needed deeply prepared soil. Jen put her foot on the shovel, shoved with every ounce of strength and tipped it up. She bent down and rolled a large rock to one side. *The annuals will go in front and give quick color,* she thought. *I'll use money from the "Penny Jar", and buy petunias and geraniums, besides my favorite pansies. Probably even a sunflower or two.* She was dreaming. Sunflowers had caught her attention in the city. Bright yellow heads of a short variety bobbed from sidewalk planters. Jen's mind wandered happily, thinking of how the plants would burst into bloom – like a party happening. Her mind jumped to grade school days, and a colorful surprise party. The birthday girl had squealed with delight as her mother led her into the room filled with girls who also burst into squeals. She danced up and down, grabbed the girl next to her, and then turned and hugged her mother. A nice family. A good party. Maybe when Michael got to know the kids at school she would give him a party like that. Maybe, in the fall.

Using both feet, Jenny jumped up and onto the shovel with all her weight. It stopped dead. Her feet stung. Must be a huge rock underneath. She glanced at the long edging of stones down the driveway. The yard *was* a gravel pit. Scraping with the shovel, she worked around the rock. She couldn't pry it. Squatting, she worked with both hands and a trowel, and finally got it loose. She was barely able to lift it out. She rubbed her back, and stood and surveyed the scene. At least, near the front door, there were less rocks. Sylvie mentioned that subsoil might have been spread around when the basement was dug. The ground in the back yard might be better.

Thinking of sun and shadow, Jen was reassured that this flower bed along the drive would get plenty of sunshine since the tall trees were on the north or back side of it. The trees across the drive wouldn't matter. They were small and went down the hill from the house.

Turning another shovel full of rocky dirt, Jen looked at the poor soil. So much soil improvement was needed. She appreciated Sylvie's donation of old leaves become leaf-mold. Some was piled, waiting to be worked in. For years Sylvie had collected wheelbarrows full of leaves from the woods, mixed them with other compost, and let it all decay. Peat moss, Sylvia said, would give porosity and hold moisture, and the leaf mold gave lively bacteria and nutrients. Jenny had peat moss on her list to buy.

Jen cast aside a large rock and pictured the early settlers building stone walls. She would have enough cast-off stones for her own wall at this rate – if she fulfilled her plan for all the garden beds she wanted. She stooped and sorted stones, and threw them in a bucket. Her back ached. She stood. For now, it was time to quit.

CHAPTER TWENTY-SEVEN

Though the morning air was still cool, Jen felt the sweat running down her back. She stretched and slid out of her vest. Looking around, she was pleased. *I've accomplished a lot. That grocery money I sneaked into an envelope will get me some bedding plants.* Another half hour passed when a noise came from the brush along the driveway.

"Good morning! Hard at work I see!"

"Oh, Sylvie! I'm glad to see you! Now I have a reason to take a break. She used the back of her hand to wipe the sweat from her face.

Sylvie laughed. "Do you usually wear mascara on your cheek?"

"Oh-oh, I bet I'm a mess! Need to scrub these hands. Let's have tea, if that sounds good." She laid the shovel by her bucket, and led Sylvia into the house.

The living room turned out to be cool, so Sylvia opted for hot tea. Jen was having hers iced. She poured Sylvie's mug full, downed her iced tea, and held up the empty glass. "At least this helps me cool off. Whew, I'm still thirsty, and tired. I think I'll get water, and then turn this in for hot tea." They walked to the kitchen. She took down a mug.

When the cupboard door was open, Sylvia noticed Jen could use more mugs, and thought that would be a nice surprise.

She looked closer at Jen. "You have been working way too hard. Let me see your hands!" Jen held out her hands and Sylvia turned them palm up. "Just as I thought. Blisters. Blisters and calluses. Do you have garden gloves?" When Jenny shook her head, she went on,

"Okay, it's my treat. We're going to the hardware in Granite right now and get you some. Can you get away?" Jen nodded. "While we're at it I'd like to stop in at the thrift store and see what's new. Are you okay with that?"

"Sure! I'll revive. Sounds like fun. I'll get the smudges off my face and clean my hands better. These nails...they look awful."

"I know it sounds funny, but if you put some hand lotion on before you go out to garden, it keeps the dirt from getting ground into your skin and under your nails."

"Ick. That would feel funny."

"Well, at first it does, but it's not so bad. When you're wearing gloves the dirt still seems to get in and make your hands grubby. The lotion works. Your hands wash up easier afterward."

"Okay, I'll try it next time. For now it will take some work with the scrub brush. Help yourself to more tea. There's still some in the pot."

* * *

Jenny wandered down aisle after aisle in amazement, thinking what a conglomeration of merchandise this was for one store. "How did they ever decide to stock such a variety of things, like nylons, horse salve, kid's color books, imported dried food and sewing notions?"

"It's because they have been here for fifty years. Then people didn't 'go to town' often, the way they do now. Active farms meant they stocked what the farmers needed. Then they added the modern things as they came along. It's quite an inventory, all right!"

"Do you miss working here?"

"No. I was ready for a break and some freedom with my hours."

"Do you think they will be able to sell all this stuff? Seems like there would no longer be a call for some of it. In fact I see quite a bit of dust on certain items... like packs of artist's brushes."

"Oh, that's my fault. I encouraged ordering them. I had talked to several tourists interested in painting, and encouraged them. I paint some, so I also bought supplies here. We had to bring in a minimum order, and I admit, we are overstocked! I should say *they* are overstocked. There it all sits – paper for pencil drawings, small sets of oils, watercolors and paper for adults, and of course the usual for children. The tourists' craze tapered off. Now kids use markers. I think they are going to send the stock back or clear it out at reduced prices." Sylvia wiped her finger over a package of paper. "Yes, pretty dusty, isn't it!" Jen grinned, and Sylvia thought how pretty she looked when the lines of worry and strain left her face. Her blue-green eyes sparkled.

They wandered through the aisles toward the garden products in the back. Here, too, everything one could imagine was available – seeds, powders and sprays for bugs and diseases, both chemical and natural. Jenny reached up and took down a diatomaceous earth powder for earwigs. As she did, the neckline of her blouse pulled open and Sylvia saw a large bruised area over her collarbone. *Funny place for a bruise,* she thought.

Surrounded by leaf rakes, hoes, and shovels, they finally saw a rack of gloves near the back wall. Sylvia pointed and said, "Take your pick. I got you into this garden thing. You're brave to bite off such a big chunk. Oh, and here is the peat moss to improve your soil. I need some, too. I'll get this large bale and split it with you."

Jenny's expression changed from one of relaxation to concern. "Oh, I don't want you to do that. Just get a small bale."

"No. There's not much difference in price between the large and the small. Makes sense to get a bargain. Please just let me do it."

"Well...okay." But Sylvia could feel the reluctance in Jenny's tone of voice. *It's hard for her to accept favors. I wonder how much kindness she has received in her life?*

When they reached home, Sylvia pulled up in Jen's driveway and they unloaded the peat by the outside faucet. Slitting open the plastic, they shoveled some into a large cardboard box for Sylvia, and flooded what remained in the bale with water. As Jenny stretched up, Sylvia saw that she was still sore. "You may want to take it easy, and let your back get used to this shoveling and bending. No point in getting stiff."

"I think you're right. Let's go in the house. The other day when you said you were working on a children's book, I think I said I would show you a poem I had written. Do you have time now?"

"Oh!" Sylvia's face lit up. "Of course! I've been looking forward to hearing them."

"Well, don't expect much." After they got in the house Jenny told Sylvia to wait, and she disappeared upstairs. She came down carrying a notebook-sized beaten-up spiral. She sat down, opened it, and some loose papers slid to the floor. "I have scribbled things over the years. This was my earliest notebook." She shoved the loose sheets in the back, flipped pages, and hesitated. "I wrote this when I was twelve." She began reading.

Rainstorm

Hammering, hammering
The pounding of the rain
Pelting on the leaves
Beating on my brain.

Slashing at the grasses
Pouring down the street
Birds and helpless puppy
Cower. Not a tweet.

Tails between their legs
Cows and horses bow
Wind tears over the pasture
Controlling all for now.

Rain jumps on the roof above
Glad I am to be
Safely under cover
Though soaked and shivery.

Into hot bath water
Comfort over me flows
Forgetting those poor creatures
Gloom still rules outdoors.

Jennifer Hanson, age 12

"Oh, I enjoyed it! I'm surprised. Twelve years old, and writing that! You let me share your experience of that rainstorm, cold and wet, shivering. You pictured for me the miserable animals in the field. And I could feel being chilled to the bone – the perfect cure – a hot bath!"

Jen nodded and smiled, but said, "Well, it's just a childish poem, really."

"It's very well-expressed for twelve. The hot bath water coming up to one's neck – I could just feel it warming me! It has rhythm, flow. I think it's well done. I feel privileged that you shared it with me."

"It doesn't say much. Nothing profound."

"But life *is* like that. Made up of ordinary experiences the writer shares with the reader. Creative people are sensitive, and are able to put it into words. The reader feels 'with' the writer – shares the thoughts or experiences, maybe gaining understanding or enjoyment."

"Reading *some* of my stuff would not bring enjoyment. It's grim." She paused. "Pretty personal. You know how that is."

"I understand. Do you have others that you feel you can share? Maybe another that you wrote when you were young?" Then Sylvia raised her hand, shaking her head. "Sorry. If you don't want to share any more, it's fine. I guess I'm putting pressure. I didn't mean to. I shouldn't even ask."

Jen hesitated. "I haven't really looked through much of the old stuff. And I haven't written much lately." Then she remembered the one about friends, written after she met Mary. "I may have another, if I can find it. Come on upstairs with me."

As Jen climbed the stairs she felt daring, opening up her private self. They turned into the room, and she said, "First, come look out the window."

Sylvia went to the window and exclaimed, "Oh, what a nice vantage point. You can see the hills behind us and to the north."

"Notice something through the trees over here?" Jen pointed and Sylvie's eyes followed.

"Oh. It's my house. How about that."

Jen smiled sheepishly, and thought, *It doesn't mean much to Sylvie. It does to me, though.*

As Jen went through papers, Sylvie looked around. There was almost no furniture in the room – a trunk, a chair, and a small table. Maybe that gave clarity to one's thoughts – a kind of oriental simplicity that helped the mind focus. She noticed Jen had a handful of papers and she was smiling.

"What's that?"

"A bunch of sheets with articles for children about animals. Some are finished. I saw Michael's enthusiasm when we talked about animals. I enjoyed listening to things he told me from his books. But when I read them, they seemed stilted, too informational. So I made up stories with facts and kid-type fun, too."

"Oh, that sounds interesting. I hope you can get them published some day."

"Maybe. That would be nice. But here it is – the poem. It's only blank verse." Jen held out the hand-written sheet. "It's called "Friend". I met her when I was needing someone to watch Michael. I hated having him alone even though there was a nice lady in the next apartment. One day on the bus a woman mentioned that her daughter, Mary, did child care and could watch him. Though I was worried, it just worked out so neat. Michael and I met Mary and John, and agreed on arrangements. He went there after school. Mary actually became a friend, if you can do that in so short a time. She was special. I wrote this after a visit with her." Sylvia read.

Friend

This woman is a friend
Now I know.
A school friend was 'for a day'.
I grew up certain – knowing
No friend is real –
Preferable to have no friend.'

This woman *is* real
This woman cares.
How long is she a friend?
We'll see.

Jennifer Hanson Brown
after meeting Mary Henderson

"Oh, Jennifer. That's very touching." She paused. "I sense a lot of emotion in it." *I'd better be quiet,* Sylvia thought. *What is this part about doubting how long?*

"There was feeling." Jen's voice interrupted Sylvia's mulling. "You know how it is as teens. Lots of cliques and gossip and surface stuff; lots of pretend friendliness and you get stabbed in the back. It's discouraging. But Mary was a truly nice person."

"Oh – I wish I could meet her. Is there any chance she would visit?"

"Ah, I don't think she'd want to come all the way out here. Too far. Then again, I guess...who knows? She did send me a postcard. I should respond." Jen got a wistful expression in her eyes. "It was so nice to hear from her."

Taking the sheet of paper, Sylvia reread Friends. She softly said, "I like this. It's very good."

"Thanks." She paused. "I didn't think I'd move out here and meet someone who cares about things I like – reading, poetry." Without waiting for Sylvie to speak, she said, "Now I have some time, so I'm wanting to do more reading, get more insights. I want to understand people, and why they do what they do. Then write – I've buried that desire. Maybe, when I have the inclination, some more poetry. Kept it to myself..." She almost said, 'because life was heavy, and no one was interested'. But caught herself and said, "I was busy...but now it's nice to find a like-minded person. Find out that I'm not abnormal!" She laughed.

"I know for certain you're *not* abnormal. You have a real gift for expressing heart-matters, and you have your own special insights, of course. You are unique!"

"I guess that's one way to look at it." Jen chuckled, but it sounded skeptical.

Sylvie went on. "It's hard to have energy for anything creative when you're working long hours."

"I definitely didn't have time to get involved in a writers support group, even if I'd found one. Didn't have time to even think of looking for such a thing!"

"It's true that work takes the energy out of you. I had a long gap of not writing anything. I was working part time in a medical office. The kids were small and took a lot of energy. Could barely keep up with ordinary activities. And then I went full time. As far as being creative...well, there was nothing left."

CHAPTER TWENTY-EIGHT

"**I** *am simply going to keep trying until it works,*" Sylvia thought, as she rang Jen's number. They hadn't found the right time for a visit recently.

"Hi Jen!"

"Hi."

"It's me again. I'm hoping today you'll come over and see me!"

Jen said, "Well, maybe. I was going to do laundry while Michael rested this afternoon. "

"Oh, come over and do it here! I'll make some Red Rose tea for you! Michael can rest here on the couch. I checked a book about dogs out of the library. Thought he'd enjoy that. And Larry picked up a few DVD's of the old TV programs – things we watched as kids."

"Hmm... I can skip the laundry. I think that's just... that it would do us good. Thanks, Sylvie. Thanks a lot."

Sylvie, that's neat. She's using my nickname all the time now.

Jen continued, "We could come about two, if that's good. Some time out of the house is... is... sounds great."

"Okay! See you then."

The good-byes faded, but the unfinished sentence hung in the air. *"Some time out of the house is..."* Aloud, Sylvia finished it. "Is just what the doctor ordered". That was an expression Jenny used often, but she hadn't said it this time. Did she not want to think about a doctor? What was Michael's doctor saying? How serious was it?

"Michael, Hello!" Sylvie curtsied. "What would make your royal highness happy? I am your humble servant. Enter!" She swept her hand in an arc, bowing, and he laughed. He was an enjoyable kid to be around, and had a good sense of humor. He fit in easily with adults, having grown up without siblings.

"I am honored to be invited to your castle, Madam!" Michael responded in kind.   Suppressing a grin at how cute he was, she led the way to the living room. He sounded like an adult when he carried on a conversation on a subject he knew well. But there were other times Sylvie noticed he seemed unsure of himself. She could guess that he might be less confident with other children. Socializing would only get more challenging for him as time passes, especially when he entered the world of teenagers. She caught herself as the thoughts rushed through her mind

"Here are the DVD's Larry just got." She pulled them off the shelf. "Do you want to pick one to watch? They have some old TV programs from when I was a kid."

"Yes! That sounds neat! I've wanted to see something from the old days!" Sylvia smiled, wondering what his mental picture of her childhood might be. Maybe he pictured her taking a stagecoach for long journeys!

"You can pick from Lassie, The Lone Ranger, or.." She had the DVD's fanned out and his hand flew to the one of Lassie.

"Oh, may I watch Lassie? She looks so friendly."

"Sure. I know you love dogs. Also I picked up this book about dogs at the library. It's checked out for three weeks. If you want to watch Lassie, you can come back some other time and read the book." He busied himself thumbing through the book first.

Sylvia went to the kitchen and saw Jenny was leafing through a magazine. She returned to Michael with a tray of crackers, cheese, baby carrots, cookies and milk. He settled on the couch with pillows and an afghan. When the program began, and Lassie wagged her tail and barked her friendly greeting, he looked delighted. *Poor kid, he really is thin. Physically, he doesn't look ten. And yet he looks older in the face. Why? Is it his hollow cheeks that give him that look of being older and wiser?*

In the kitchen, Jenny looked around, and thought, *I like wallpaper!*

I wonder if I could learn how to hang it? There are plenty of flaws to cover on the walls of that old house. Start small. One wall in the kitchen could be papered.

"Ah," said Sylvia, coming in, "it's good to see you settled at my table!"

"Yes. It feels good – sitting in your kitchen, taking in the cozy feel."

"Well, it's meant to encourage you to relax." Sylvia felt at home with Jenny. Hard to believe they had only known each other since May. Some friendships just clicked. Sylvia sat down to pour the tea into two tall porcelain mugs, and said, "I'm thinking of changing the kitchen somehow – in what way I'm not sure."

"Oh, it's perfect. Don't...oh, I'm sorry." She hesitated. "I shouldn't say anything."

"You can say it!"

"It's just that I enjoy it the way it is." Jenny looked around. "I guess, most of all, I enjoy the cheerful colors. It all goes together. And it's so large to me, after an apartment." She reached out her hand and touched the sponge-painted wall, the subtle suggestions of flower petals. She studied it as though she were seeing it for the first time. "Impressionist – a nice impressionist feel; delicate. You are an artist. You've picked up the wallpaper colors perfectly – just enough of the peach, apricot and yellow of the flowers, but softer. Did you study decorating and colors, or is it instinctive?" Jenny didn't wait for an answer. "Your combination of old and new is so right for a farmhouse. Like the old wall clock and the sponge painting. But here I am, talking like I know something. I don't. It just feels right. Don't get any ideas now, and sell!" Suddenly she raised her eyebrow and looked Sylvia straight in the eye.

"Hah! You flatter me!" Sylvia laughed. "I didn't study. Just read a lot of magazines and books. I can't promise that I won't change anything, *but* we are definitely not selling! One thing I thought of doing. It involves Larry. He could put a narrow shelf up across this back wall. High, above the porch door and pantry opening. You know?"

"Yes. Good idea!"

"He could cut a groove in the shelf. I could display platters and nice plates and enjoy them. I don't have expensive ones, but they have memories over the years. I don't bother, now, to get up on a chair and take out a nice plate or bowl. It would be nice to use those things I enjoy, and I would if I saw them."

"A shelf would be nice. Since that wall is plain, how about a miniature wood rail to decorate the edge of the shelf?"

"Yes! That's a good idea! Larry can buy it ready-made and attach it. I'd like that. Thanks." The approval warmed Jen. Sylvia turned back and gestured to the wallpaper. "You know, this is old and I had been thinking of changing it, but you're right. If I did, I would need to redo the whole color scheme – so I probably won't."

"Right! You'd just have to change everything. I've been looking at that wallpaper and wondering. How difficult is it to put up? I'm daydreaming of fixing up at my place."

"Not very hard." Sylvia went on with hints and explanations.

Jen thought how it would improve the funny old barn of a house. "This reminds me that I have a problem. My Aunt Gertrude said she'd be coming sometime in July. I'd like to call her and say it isn't possible yet."

"Well, she'd probably understand if you can't have her right now. Let me know how it works out. If you want, I can help you. We could paint, do some wallpaper. It grows on you once you start. I was frustrated at first. Made mistakes. But I enjoy it now."

Two Lassie episodes had finished. Michael came into the kitchen carrying a book, and said, "I looked up collies and read how they were used in Great Britain. The book said the collie was especially popular there. And in Australia they have their own kind of shepherd dogs. They have lots of sheep." He was obviously fascinated.

Jen said, "It's nice Sylvia had that out of the library for you to read. But it's time to go home now."

He persisted. "I wonder if Mr. Ford knows about dogs. Did he have a dog he could tell me about?"

"Yes, he did. He'd be glad to talk with you. I had one, too."

"Oh! You know how much I like Goldie then! What kind of dog did you have?" He held out the book. "Please show me."

"Ah, I wish I could." She laughed. "He was such a mixture that I would never find him in there! He looked odd. Considering where

257

we lived, the way he looked was especially funny. It was a wealthy neighborhood and he didn't have a purebred pedigree. You could tell he was a "Heinz 57". Sometime I'll tell you about his antics, but now your mom has to go."

"I'll remember to ask you! Mom, what's a 'Heinz 57'?"

"Come on, Michael! We need to go. I'll tell you on the way home."

* * *

Sylvia hurried over to Jen's. She paused before knocking long enough to see the tiny bedding plants. She knocked vigorously on the door and looked at the business card in her hand.

When the door opened, she held the card up. "Guess what? This is the name of the editor of the weekly newspaper in Snohomish. I talked to him. He is interested in meeting you and seeing your children's animal stories. He was very impressed that you had a series already outlined. He said that often people write a good article, but then fail to keep material coming on time for each issue and readers are let down. So he is very interested in your writing. I mentioned that you are capable of writing good poetry, too. I didn't think you'd mind if I just said that much. It's an opportunity. What do you think?" Expecting a positive reaction, even joy, Sylvia's heart sank when she saw Jen's face go hard.

"I couldn't possibly get involved in promising a regular column. And I don't know I could in the future. I've come to realize that I write for myself, mostly. I hope you didn't tell him I would do it." An edge of rebuke was in her voice.

Confused, Sylvia couldn't form an answer for a minute. *Have I overstepped my bounds? By doing what?*

Jen asked again, "Did he think I was going to agree to a series? I hope not."

"Oh, no, he didn't think that I was answering for you. I'm sorry if I have made you uncomfortable about meeting him. He just would like to meet you."

"I don't want to meet an editor. I'm not interested. It's a real obligation. I couldn't fulfill it. I don't have many stories ready to be in print. Who knows when that would ever happen."

"I guess I didn't really find out how you felt about publishing. I suppose that, since I want to publish... I must have transferred that desire to you in my mind. I apologize for mentioning it to him. It's just that, well, I was in there, and the topic of creative writing and writers came up, and..."

"It's okay. Just so I don't have to meet him, there's no harm done."

* * *

Laughter rose from Sylvia's deck. The two women shook their heads as they talked about the pitfalls of word usage. Sylvie was thankful that the tension, after she talked to the editor, was gone.

Sylvie said, "Just this morning I thought of 'wishy-washy'. Where did that come from?"

Jen pondered a moment. "Washy could be like an item in the wash. Not one that is dried and stiff and 'stands up for itself'."

"Yeah, and wishy is just wishing for something, but not working for it. Then there's 'crazy as a loon'. I thought it seemed unkind to those birds; like, what's wrong with them? Then Larry and I visited my Vancouver cousins, and after, we were on a trip around southern B.C.. We were at a lake and heard loons in the evening. What a sound! Kind of a loose, descending laugh that's eerie. I love the sound because it's interesting and I wonder what they're telling each other. But if you thought humans made it, you'd say they were crazy."

"Some are out of context, like 'smart as a whip'. The smack of a whip smarts the skin. It hurts, but that thought doesn't figure with being intelligent."

"There's one my aunt used for years, so I never thought it odd as a kid. When she'd talk about getting a lot done, she'd say, 'I'll shell these peas while you practice your spelling words. Bring your list. We'll kill two birds with one stone.' I always knew what she meant – that she wasn't going to kill any birds. Then one day she was on a bus, talking with a young woman. She said it, 'kill two birds with one stone', and the young woman looked at her absolutely horrified, and said, 'Ooh. No! Who would want to kill birds?'"

Jen laughed, picturing their faces, and Sylvia went on. "I can see my aunt's puzzled look, wondering what the problem was. And there's another old expression like it. 'There's more than one way to skin a cat.'"

"Eek," Jen said, with a grimace. "Now *that* is not a nice picture. I'm too visual. Well, it goes to show you, the world of verbal people, writers, can be a minefield or a mine full of gems."

"You are right on!" Sylvia laughed. "Oops, our favorites are almost gone," she said, picking up the depleted cookie plate.

Jen stood. "I think I need my sweater." Following Sylvie into her kitchen, she glanced up at a motto, 'Friends are friends forever'. "Did you say that your friend Lisa made that, and gave it to you?"

"Yes. She hopes to drop out soon. We'll all get together again and have a good visit."

"Oh, I don't feel right, interrupting your visit."

"Hey, I wouldn't ask you if I didn't want you to come!"

Jen blushed. "Okay. I believe you. I guess I'm cautious about not pushing myself forward.

"Really? I can't picture you being pushy."

"Well, I guess I must have been. I was told that as a kid. Anyway, like you said the other day, I'll try to stop being unsure of... of myself, I guess." She grinned. "I'll really try!" Jen saw Sylvie's smile and she had a warm feeling come over her – *acceptance...almost...*

* * *

Lennard grunted as he shoved up out of the couch. "Guess I'd better get the battery terminals cleaned." He raised his voice. "Michael, you need a lesson. Come on. I hope you haven't been using any of the tools in the toolbox."

Michael looked up from the jigsaw puzzle he was working. "No, sir. I only used the screwdriver in the kitchen drawer – the one that belongs there."

"Good. Come outside now and watch me. I can show you how it's done." Len's ego-filled voice irritated Jennifer.

Sylvia came across the driveway as Len stepped out of the house with Michael right behind. "Hello!" she said in her brightest manner.

Might as well be cheery, she thought.

"Hi" Len snapped, as he walked right past without as much as glancing at her.

"Hello!" Michael said. "We're going to clean the battery terminals. I'm gonna learn how!"

"That's great! You could have a trade when you're big. You can work on cars when you need to earn college money!"

His face lit up as he considered. "Yeah, that's right!" He hurried after Len, and she went into the house.

After drying the dishes while Jen washed, they sat down to have a cup of coffee. Jen seemed tense to Sylvie. But then, she seemed to have days like that. They chatted.

"Jeremy came over a few days ago to visit Michael. Nice kid. He and Michael went rock-hunting a little while. He knew how to look for special ones. Said he had an uncle who polishes rocks. Michael had a boy from his school class come, too. He seems more content, now that he's starting to make friends."

"Good! I'm glad."

"It surprises me that kids here don't seem to mind age differences as much as in the city."

"True. I used to think it was having fewer kids to choose from. Also, families here visit as families in another home. So the kids mix, regardless of age."

Yelling interrupted them. "You *did* take it! I know you did. We'll go look and if you're wrong you're in big trouble, boy!" Len came blustering through the living room, muttering. Michael trailed behind. "That stupid kid of yours..." He yanked open a kitchen drawer, pawed around, and threw utensils on the counter. He grabbed a screwdriver, looked at it, cursed, and threw it down. Slamming the drawer shut, he turned abruptly. Grabbing Michael by the arm, he shoved him forward and said, "You find it. I know you lost it." They left.

Sylvia felt numb. Can I stand up for Michael? How can you tell someone else how to raise their child? But this is not normal. It's meant to frighten Michael; intimidate him. The least I can do is be a friend to Jennifer. Get her out to enjoy her life here. What else can be done?

Sylvia held the phone before dialing, hoping she'd think how to encourage Jen to get out of the house.

"Jen! Come on over for a little while, won't you?"

"Oh, I don't know... I have work to do." Jen sounded weary as her voice trailed off.

Sylvia thought, *Lord, help me find words. Maybe, if I'm upbeat, she'll pick up my mood.* Cheerfully, she said, "Just for half an hour, okay? Even though it seems not long enough to bother, can I convince you to take a wee break?"

"Oh, all right. Just for a little while."

On the way over Jen thought, *It's silly to bother. I should go back home and phone my apologies.* But she continued on the path. The moment she stepped into the kitchen, she was enveloped in a warm sense of relief, being there – she would get a badly needed breather for body and soul.

"Welcome!" Sylvia held up a pretty forget-me-not mug and said, "I have the tea water on to boil. Have a seat."

Jen looked at the table and reached out to touch a small, worn booklet. It was square in shape, and had a few strange characters of some foreign language on the cover. "What do you have here?"

"I came across it, and boy, did some old memories came flooding back!"

Jen picked up the booklet and opened it. "What is it?"

"An exercise book I bought in north India to use for a diary. I went there at the end of my first year in community college. Had the chance to stay with an aunt and uncle."

Jen turned the pages. They were full of Sylvie's writing, in normal Roman letters, with some of the strange script here and there. One page had words in stanza form, like a poem or song. Though they were in normal abc's, they were certainly not English. She held it out as Sylvie set down the teapot.

"What's this?"

"That's a song a villager on the Nepal border taught me." Sylvia sang the words softly in his language. "I remember very little Hindi, and even less of the Nepali man's language, except for a few words. But I can still sing this song. Yesu in the song is the name of Jesus.

This tells of a common experience there – how Nepalis come to a river where there is no bridge and need a way across. In fact, it happened to me. A man is there, called a taranhaar manchi. That means "carrying-across man". He takes you up on his back in a deep basket, and carries you safely across the river. The people learned that Jesus is a, or rather, He is *the* Taranhaar Manchi."

"You mean there are Christians there?"

"Yes. Long ago there was a high-caste man, Sundar Singh, who trekked all over telling village after village that he'd found out that Jesus was real, was the Son of the one God who made us all. Many heard what he said, and some believed. I suppose that was a hundred years ago."

"Back to that man at the river. How do you mean Jesus is *that* man?"

"Jesus is the carrying-across Man who is the only way to the other side, to heaven. It's by what He did. He came to earth for that express purpose – to pay for our sins on the Cross. When those people heard this, they realized that, compared to Him, their gods don't care. The people spend much effort and money trying to appease these immoral, cruel gods. They never would expect to be loved by them – it doesn't happen. They wrote this song when they learned that Jesus cared. He came down here to make the way to heaven for them."

"So if He made the way, it's like a path. I have to walk on it, and get to the other end, to heaven."

Sylvie was puzzled. "What do you mean?"

"You're saying it's up to me to live a good enough life so that I don't fall off the Jesus path."

"Oh!" Sylvie exclaimed. "No!" She shook her head. "As soon as you trust Him, he has taken you across and put you on His path. You belong to Him from then on. He walks the path with you. He's the Strong One. The Bible says you are "in Christ". We rely on Him. You may stumble on the path, even resist His direction. But in all circumstances, He is directing things for your good. When you trust Him, you are His "born one". You are in His family for keeps. You can't get un-born. Even if you are acting like a wayward child, you cannot get out of the family. You have new life in you, because the

Holy Spirit dwells in a believer. There is no disowning with God. There are phonies, but there have always been religious phonies. They just acted the part. Once you are in His family there is no rejection by Him. You're His child forever. He says in fact that He is the way, the truth, and the life."

Jen sat quietly a moment, then shook her head slowly. "I wish I could believe like you do. It just sounds like a story to me."

"I hope that one day it will be the best true story you have ever heard!"

Jen picked up the ringing phone. Sylvia said, "Hello! How would you like to go with me to meet a lovely old lady, Grandma Jones?"

"Sure. You've mentioned her before."

"Have you got time now?"

"Yes. Michael is playing and helping down at Jeremy's and won't be back until dinner time. This sounds like fun. I'll meet you down at the road."

Jen hopped in Sylvia's car, and they drove in to town. A neat yard held a tiny house with a rocking chair on the porch. When they knocked, a voice beckoned them inside.

"Hello, Ladies, how nice to have company. Sylvia, you've brought a friend. Who do we have here?" She smiled and the wrinkles on her face formed round, plump softness.

The twinkling blue eyes sparkled at Jen, who stepped toward the seated lady. Grandma Jones extended both her hands as Sylvia introduced them. Clasping Jen's hands in both of hers, she held them for a moment, gave a warm squeeze, and looked into Jen's eyes with a tender expression.

"I'm glad to meet you, Jennifer! Very pleased indeed. Any friend of Sylvia is a friend of mine. Have a seat. I'm too crippled to get up and down much." The three of them talked about Jennifer's move in to the area, and how she liked it. Grandma Jones asked if she had children.

There was a moment of sadness on Jen's face, a hesitation. She answered, "One. A son, ten years old." Sylvia was struck by it, but couldn't quite absorb the look. What was the meaning of it – the way it had come over her face?

They talked about local happenings. Grandma Jones spoke of her children, and Sylvie asked about the grandchildren and their individual happenings. They touched on Mr. Jones' death. Jen enjoyed sitting back, relaxing as they talked. She entered the conversation now and then. When possible, she stole a look around at the quaint old art prints on the walls, an upright piano, and an oval mahogany occasional table that held a crystal vase and two fine porcelain figurines. The room was not well lit, but there was no gloom to it. Soft pinks and blues in the flowered wallpaper were brought out in pillows and a finely knit afghan on a rocker. Jen studied the woman. Her face was cheerful and her voice loving, as she answered questions about her family. Jen noticed a yellowed motto in a frame over her head. She silently read the old script: "Ye know not what shall be on the morrow. For what is your life? It is even a vapour, that appeareth for a little time, and then vanisheth away" James 4:14. Though the wording was in an old-style English, the meaning was plain – too plain. She read it again. *It's true. I don't know what is happening tomorrow.*

Grandma Jones studied Jen as she read, and then broke into her thoughts. "I like that verse. It reminds me that life is fleeting. When I think of a vapor, I can see steam rushing vigorously from my teakettle. The steam is hot enough to burn me – it's very real. But it quickly rises, cools, and then it's gone. My life has moved along so rapidly… it is hard to believe it's over. Childhood years were the slowest. It moved faster when I was busy raising my children. I didn't even think about time, I was so busy. The first one left home and soon they were all grown. That was a surprise – happened so fast. But I was busy with work, my hobbies, my husband and neighbors. And now I'm done. The vapor has cooled and faded. The verse and the speed of a lifetime remind me that it's God's perspective that counts." Jen thought the lady's smile was wistful, or maybe only thoughtful. Grandma turned to Sylvia and asked if she'd heard from her daughter overseas.

Jen looked again at the verse – she realized that it was a Bible verse. "Ye know not what shall be on the morrow. For what is your life?" *What is my life? My life is… confused? Yes, somewhat confused. But mostly, it is confusing me. What's next? It's too much to figure. Live one day at a time. ...a little time, it says. For a little time, we live.* She looked at Grandma Jones who was accepting life as it is, sitting so contented, even though she winced when she moved her arthritic limbs. *Seems she's had a good life, maybe an easy life. But she could still complain about being lonely. Certainly about how her husband died a painful death to cancer. Instead she looks peaceful. Happy, even. Well, my life is different. I have to fight my way through it all, and hope to make it.* Resentment rose up in her.

"Don't feel bad about the arthritis, Sylvia. It's my time to go soon. I am looking forward to that day." Jen tuned in again on the elderly lady's words. She wanted to assure her that she wouldn't die soon. But, looking at the woman's expression, she realized she truly was looking forward to it. "I'll join my dear husband. I'm so glad he has relief from his pain and is with the loving Savior. God bless his memory to my family. May they benefit from the example of his well-lived life."

They talked a bit longer. Sylvia asked, "Are you still knitting, Grandma?" When she got a 'yes', she went out to the car and brought in a bag of yarn.

Grandma said, "Ah, this is very good! Thank you! I'll use it for the Eastern Europe orphans' clothing project. They said good-bye and left.

As Sylvie drove down the road, picturing the yarn that would end up keeping orphans warm, she shook her head, thinking, *Grandma is still working for the good of others.* Then she asked Jen, "How did you like Grandma Jones?"

"How could anyone not like her?" Jen asked. "What a sweetie." Her mind began to work. She pictured Michael there. "Sylvie, I wonder if I could bring Michael to meet her? He likes older people. Always looking for a grandma, I guess. Or, more likely, someone like my Aunt Sally. He sure loves and misses her."

"Grandma would love that. She enjoys people of all ages. She'd love to share her own experiences and those of people she's known. I'll drive you two over to see her. Just tell Michael to ask her about 'the old days', as he calls them, and he'll hear interesting stories. Let's plan that for as soon as it's do-able for you. You let me know when."

Sylvia pulled the car into her driveway and turned to Jen. "I could have driven up your drive, you know."

"This is just fine. Thanks for taking me. What a neat lady."

"I have something I'd like to give you, Jen. I hope you'll take it – no strings attached. No need to comment on it. I just want you to have it." She reached over, opened the glove compartment, and pulled out a little book. "It's a New Testament – the part of the Bible starting with the time Jesus came to earth as a baby and then on into the next one-hundred years. I thought if you have this to read, you can look for whatever. You can find answers to your questions for yourself." She held it out.

Jen looked at it. *It's contrary to my good sense to take it. But it's true – I'd rather look for myself.* Hesitantly she took it. "Thanks. I don't make any promises."

"I wouldn't want any. It's for you, no questions asked. The book of John, the fourth book, is a good place to read. It shows who Jesus is. I put a bookmark in it. I like Psalms – that's at the back. Actually, it's from the Old Testament, a thousand years before. But it's a favorite of a lot of people. I read Psalms when my emotions are in need of expression – any emotion you want to name seems to show up in Psalms."

"Well... thanks." Jen pushed the door handle to leave. "I'll take you up on that invitation to visit Grandma Jones with Michael sometime."

Sylvia came in the house and wandered around, thinking of the visit, feeling restless. In her mind's eye she saw the visit unfold, with Jen and Grandma Jones getting acquainted and talking about family. *I wonder what kind of mother Grandma Jones was. Must have been very rural out here then. Except for my walks with Grandma, my childhood was citified. And not very warm.* Her mind wandered to thoughts of her mother. *Maybe my feelings of separation from Mother came from as early as the baby's death. It seemed like Mother was detached, almost alienated from us. I never questioned when it started, or how it felt to Dad or my big sister. Now Mother is totally immersed in being successful.* Sylvia felt ashamed at that thought, at being critical. She recalled the nursery rhyme book and the feelings it brought to her. *I wonder what my sister is dealing with? She tries to "do it all". It's hard to hug a porcupine they say – my mother or my sister. Really, they're not that prickly; they're just involved with their own affairs. I could forgive them that.*

Michael launched into telling his mom about Sigurdsens. "Jeremy knows them. He says they're real nice. They have a boy, Kyle, that's an 'only', like me. Jeremy's mom wants to take us over to their farm, if it's okay with you."

"Well... I trust Jeremy's mom; that's nice of her. I'll give her a call. Get the details."

So it was arranged, and Michael went to Kyle's for the afternoon.

At dinner, Len was gone. Michael came home excited, ready to share all the details of his adventure at Sigurdsens' farm.

"I like Kyle; he's nice. He showed us all around the farm. There was a real nice dog, black and white, and he even understands how to herd sheep. They don't have any sheep. They have just one milk cow, and some chickens. But we got to go into interesting sheds, and a barn, too. I thought that was all the buildings, but Kyle said there's an old abandoned house. It's back behind the woods. We didn't have time to go there."

Jen listened to the non-stop description, smiled, and shook her head. "Sounds like you had a good time. I hope it didn't make extra work for Kyle's mom."

"Oh, Mom, Sonja was glad to have us. She gave us homemade apple pie and big glasses of milk for a 'snack'." He grinned. "Just a snack. It was huge! But Sonja said we were hard-working farmers who'd been walking and running all over the fields."

"That's nice. Does Sonja want you to call her by her first name?"

"Oh, yes, she asked us to. She said that even though she'd been married, she had lost her husband. So she didn't want to be called Missus. Kyle was in the bathroom, washing up. She put her finger up to her lips, pointed to the bathroom, and told Jeremy and me that it made Kyle sad, so not to ask him about it. She wants just 'Sonja' because she feels like she is a Sigurdsen again, being back with her dad. Kyle remembers his dad a little, she said. But they are a family again, since his grandfather is like a dad to him."

Jen thought that a person sure got all the details from kids. "I understand from Sylvia that Mr. Sigurdsen is a very nice man."

"He is, Mom. You should come meet them. Jeremy's mom said you'd like Kyle's grandpa, and his mom, too. She'd probably take you over to meet Sonja."

"I'll think about doing that." Michael seemed to have a bit of color in his cheeks, just from being outside at the farm. She remembered how, when they lived in the apartment, he and a friend had visited the grandfather's farm. She felt, not for the first time, a sense of amazement that they were living out here in the country. Who would have ever thought?

Two days later there was a Craft Fair down in Snohomish. Sylvie insisted on taking Jen and Michael and treating for the admission and eats. The three of them piled into Sylvia's car and prepared to make a day of it. Though lunch time was far off, they weren't there half an hour when the smells of fresh baking drew them. They discussed choices and decided to share a pecan-topped cinnamon roll and two spicy ginger-peach muffins that had chopped-up bits of fresh peaches and candied ginger throughout. As they sliced things for sharing, the aroma made their mouths water. They ate and talked about what there was to see, and what each was especially interested in. Jen and Sylvia noticed Michael losing interest when they spoke of embroidery and quilting.

Just then a voice called out, "Hello!" A friend of Sylvia came over. She introduced her son, Jimmy, who was twelve, and he began telling of the carving and wood-working he'd seen. His mother added that they were going to the displays of handmade children's toys and replica airplanes. She offered to take Michael along.

Sylvia turned to reassure Jen. "I've known Jimmy's family since he was two." She grinned at the boy. "I even babysat him occasionally." Jimmy grimaced and objected that *that* was when he was *little*. Michael had lunch money. Off they went with Jimmy's mother hurrying behind.

Jen's thoughts turned inward. *It's a different world from the city. I'm trying to learn to feel safe among these friends and neighbors who are so well-known to each other.*

Joan, another of Sylvia's friends, came over to say hello and meet Jen. She invited them to needlework demonstrations being done by friends from her Ladies' Bible Study group.

Jen was already nodding at Sylvia, and gathering up the trash as Sylvie said, "I would love to see that!" They strolled through the crowd, talking. Turning to Joan, Sylvie said, "I was thinking the other day about you. I really wanted to come again to that Bible study you had in the spring. On the book of John – that was good. I was simply working too many hours at the hardware in Granite to come much. But now I'm free. Can you imagine? A lady of leisure!"

"I'm so glad for you! Nice that you were helping Nadine with school expenses, but it's a good thing she got that student loan."

"Yes. Takes the pressure off. She has always worked hard at her studies, but it's good for her to know the monetary value of her education. When do you start up again with a Bible study? And what's the topic going to be?"

"Ruth."

Sylvia exclaimed, "Ruth! I love that story. I just got a set of notes on it from my friend, Lisa." Getting out her date book, she wrote the September start-up time and the address of the home where it was to be held.

They arrived at Handcrafts and Joan had to leave them to oversee a display. Gorgeous handwork lay on tables and hung on the walls. The crewel wall hangings, done in yarn, were dramatic. Most were bold, done in fall colors, though some were in purples and blues.

Next, the Victorian style quilts caught their eye. "Look at these!" Jen exclaimed. "I can't believe that fancy embroidery on them!"

"Yes! Look at this one. See the velvet pieces, how there is feather-stitching on every place they meet! It got first prize!"

Jen could only shake her head in wonder, and, in spite of the sign, she stroked the soft, lustrous velvet. It deserved top recognition – it was simply elegant. They moved on. Many quilts had a carefully planned scheme of compatible colors, even to the binding on the edge and the embroidery floss used for decorative stitching. Others were machine-sewn "crazy quilts" with irregular shape pieces. For an even more casual mood, one had a seemingly aimless scattering of colorful children's prints. Order was brought to possible confusion by placing plain-colored pieces between the prints. Though machine stitched, careful detailing had been applied throughout using lace, narrow rickrack, and tiny buttons.

Needlework was in the next section. There was a wealth of fine traditional embroidery and the newer Brazilian style. Jen was fascinated by a tatting demo. The lady said, 'This lace is nothing but knots!' as her tiny shuttle flew. Lace had also been made with a fine-tipped crochet hook, and some was knitted. A video showed the fading art of making antique Belgian spool lace. Jenny retraced her steps, and oh-ed and ah-ed as she hung over the embroidery. She especially liked a decorative pillow showing nine small 'window panes', each framing bouquets of dainty flowers. Embroidery books lay open to show the step-by-step methods for each style stitch. There were stacks of free sheets with basic instructions.

Jen filled her tote bag with a half dozen sheets. "I'll learn to do these stitches. Someday I'll practice until I can make my work nice. How I'd love to create something that beautiful."

Sylvie nodded, wondering aloud how she would get back to doing some handwork. "It's early for thoughts of Christmas, but I'd like to start something for giving. Hand-made gifts are special. Too often I pick ones that are too hard, or wait until too late. Then I don't get them finished. Hand work *can* be a nice way to relax."

They walked out into the open. "Let's get something to eat," Sylvie said. "We can have hot dogs and coleslaw. It's the best home-made slaw around."

"Oh, you shouldn't," Jen said.

"Why not? Give me one good reason, since it gives me satisfaction."

Jen couldn't resist her relaxed, generous spirit. "Okay. Thanks! That will taste so good." They stood in line, hearing conversations buzzing around them. A lot of the talk was neighbors, catching up. Jen heard their concern for each other, but she was sure that people were the same everywhere – some getting along, and others, not.

The next morning Sylvia wandered back and forth along the rail of her deck. Her thoughts, too, went back and forth in her head – thoughts, and pictures – like the large bruise on Jen's arm, another bruise on her collarbone. *I feel like things are unhealthy over there.*

She entered the house, went to her file, and pulled out a small pamphlet. There was a fund-raising effort to start a safe-house in the area for battered women and their children. She searched it, but there was little information. It was about the organizing and operating of a safe-house. There was no info that she needed right now. *How do you even bring up battering in conversation to a woman who might be suffering it? From what I've heard, she may make light of it. Maybe Lisa understands the possibilities of abuse...*

Later in the day Sylvia still couldn't get it out of her mind – *if Jen is being hurt I've got to help her. She could be in serious danger. But if she won't tell me... If I show too much concern and she is fearful that Len will notice...I'd best not force it. The door to help her might close. I just don't know. I need some response from Jennifer. Then again, it may be that it's my overactive imagination. Len was nice at the picnic.*

CHAPTER TWENTY-NINE

The next day Jen arrived, waving a book in her hand. "I can't stay, but look what I found! I was in the upstairs closet and saw this. It's an oldie I had picked up in a Seattle second-hand store, and then forgot it." She held it out. The corners were worn off. The gold-lettered title was so faint on the pale red cover that it was unreadable.

Sylvia took it in her hands carefully and opened it. "Why, it's a very old Roget's Thesaurus! You have quite a find here!" Sylvia saw that it was laid out in the original, two-part form. You had to look in the back portion and choose from a list of the various uses or connotations of the word. A number was given for *that* use. Then you turned to that number in the front section where synonyms were compiled. She flipped the pages and stopped at VOLITION - INTERSOCIAL VOLITION. A center column line separated synonyms and antonyms. Liberation, 750, was on one side and 751 Restraint was on the other. After her thoughts about Jen's situation, it was strange to read. After Restraint was [Means of] 752 Prison and 753 Keeper, which continued a list: custodian, ranger, gamekeeper, warder, jailer, turnkey, castellated, guard, watch, watchdog, and even *chokidar* and *durwan* (*Anglo-Indian*). *Fascinating!* she thought. Turning to the back index she found "deter" *dissuade/* It was also under volition: 616. Dissuasion N. She skipped to the verb DISSUADE: 'cry out against, remonstrate, warn, dishearten, disenchant, hold back, keep back, restrain, repel, turn aside, throw cold water on, cool, chill, blunt, calm, quiet, quench; deprecate". It seemed to Sylvia a grim picture of a maiden in distress in a Romance novel. Her eyes went back involuntarily to *warn*. Again a warning flashed in her own mind – *is there danger for Jen? How can one know? I'm a worrier, it's true.* She pushed it aside.

"This is special," she said. "It's rich with such a variety of meanings. What a stimulus for writing!" She stopped flipping at the entry, INTELLECT, on the top left page. On the right page was RESULTS OF REASONING. Farther on in that section was COMMUNICATION OF IDEAS. Closing the book she stroked the cover and said, "It's a real treasure. A little awkward to use, but a wealth of helps. I can see how thought-provoking it is. And a big help when looking for just the right word."

A little plaque caught Jen's eye. "O Lord help us to become masters of ourselves, that we may be the servants of others." She pointed to it and asked, "Who said that?"

"Oh, I don't know. I think it was some monk in the 1300's."

"Ugh."

The harshness in Jen's voice surprised Sylvia. "Why? What's wrong with a monk saying it?"

Jen's expression was hostile. "Well... I'll tell you sometime. I have to get home."

"Oh. Alright. Well, let's look at this thesaurus again."

Jen started out the kitchen door. Sylvia looked at the phone book where she had tucked the pamphlet, "Local Safe Home Needed", and thought, *Yes, I will.* She slid her fingers around it, then tapped gently on Jen's shoulder. "Here! Did you see what is being organized?"

"What?" Jen turned. She read the title and her face went pale.

"It's about a local effort to make a place in the area for women who are being beaten or emotionally abused – so they can find a place of safety."

Jenny looked quickly up into Sylvie's eyes and back at the pamphlet. "Oh." She paused. "Well." She paused again. "I doubt it's needed here. That's just for the slum areas, isn't it? For the down-and-outs who live that way. I mean who would need it out here? I've really got to go. Bye." And she was gone.

It kept pressing on Sylvia's mind – was Jennifer Brown safe? Her neighbor's strong face had begun to show uneasy expressions, and her blue-green eyes were often anxious. *What is really happening in her life? I guess the best thing I can do is ask her over; just keep things open.* She picked up the phone.

"Jenny! Are you free this afternoon? Can you come over for tea and a visit?"

"Hmm…no. Not today. Michael has an appointment with the doctor this afternoon."

"Oh, nothing serious, I hope?"

"Probably not." Jen kept her voice even.

"It's good school is over."

"Yes. Well, I have to go. Thanks for calling."

Sylvia looked at the phone in her hand, surprised at how quickly Jen hung up. *She's not telling all. How I long to spend time with her, give her a chance to talk. She has a lot on her mind…We must get together.*

Larry positioned the pruning saw on a dead branch of the willow tree.

"Hey, what are you up to?"

"Oh. Hello Len," Larry answered, turning to him. "I'm cutting this branch. It's dead."

"How did that happen?"

"In the winter. I'm just getting around to it. Kids from down the road swung on it, not knowing that branches are brittle in winter."

"Yeah, kids are destructive. They don't even have to try. They just break things."

Larry wanted to respond, defending kids from such a blanket accusation. *Do I let this pass, or confront it? I guess I might sound like a know-it-all. Len can be so negative, so down on people. I guess that's just him.* Larry decided to simply minimize it by not responding. "The tree will do fine. Willows grow fast." He set down the saw. "So how are you enjoying life in the country?"

"Really do. Really do. It's freer here." Len sounded self-assured, stuck out his chest and sucked in a long breath of air. "It's different." Len surveyed the trees overhead.

Larry wondered, "Different... in what way?"

"It's wholesome out here." His eyes glittered with enthusiasm.

"Good for Michael. He likes it. I think I'd like to leave city life behind. Problem is, if this job at the mill just holds out. The hot weather has come on with a vengeance. The loggers have to get out of the woods before noon – danger of sparks setting forest fires."

Larry nodded, and said, "Hoot owl." These shifts were well known to him.

Len went on explaining anyhow. "The fallers are limited to morning hours. There's less time for them to work. So there's less logs coming in for us to cut into lumber. Next they might shut down the woods completely. We'll run out of logs to cut. On top of it, there's less house-building going on. I may be laid off."

"That's tough on the paycheck." Larry nodded thoughtfully. Len snarled about idiotic management, about stupid rules. As he ranted on, Larry pondered how the two different Lennards, one pleasant, one angry, could be within one person. And it was a curious thing that he mentioned that Michael liked it here. *It hasn't seemed like Len cared much what Michael likes. Strange he'd bring it up. Then again, maybe Sylvia has just read Len wrong about the boy.* In any case, Larry figured he had to accept Len as he was, not as he'd like him to be. Len's diatribe on management ceased, so Larry asked, "How's Michael been feeling?"

"Oh, same-old same-old. But he'll snap out of it. He'll get better."

Larry nodded. He considered what this family faced. *With a layoff threatening them, I'd like to help out. Len seems too self-sufficient for it, but maybe...* "Say, if you do get laid off, let us know right away. Though you'll get U.I., it doesn't cover enough. It can be a difficult time. I know. We've been there. Sylvia and I enjoy sharing, now that we can. It wasn't always that way – we've been down to the last can of beans. Now Sylvie stockpiles like a squirrel. It's a good feeling to 'pass it on'. Gas is another drain. One of us can take Jenny to town for shopping, or take Michael to the doctor. We go to Snohomish and Everett frequently anyhow."

"We will *not* need any help." Len said flatly. "We're just fine. I can take care of things. It's damned aggravating to wonder if you have a job, that's all. Stupid regulators. So that neighbor boy, Jeremy – I haven't seen him around lately."

So much for that topic, Larry thought, then replied. "Jeremy got a job running errands and doing odd jobs for a couple of businesses. He's a good kid. Helped Sylvia with the yard the last couple years. Why? Did you need yard work done?"

Len nodded. "Oh. No, just wondered."

Larry parked the car, still thinking about Jeremy, who he'd just seen on his bike; wondering why Len asked about him earlier. He walked into the kitchen and Sylvia looked up, startled. Her scattered pages of writing covered the whole table. "Oh, hello, Hon! I didn't even hear you drive in!"

"You must have been deep in thought. You'd been hoping I'd have a chance to chat with Len. I did, earlier, when I was pruning."

"Yes. What did he have to say?"

"He mentioned he might be laid off. Fire hazard in the woods."

"Oh, no. Jen is so worried because she's not bringing in anything. How soon?"

"It depends on conditions. They're doing hoot owl shift now. I offered our help, but he wouldn't have any of it. I said we'd give rides to Jen and Michael to the doctor or to go shopping."

"Of course."

"Mentioned we had plenty of groceries you had squirreled away!"

"Oh, you're teasing me! Did you really say that?"

"Yes! And I have to admit it's great you do. We can certainly share; could feed all the neighbors for miles around during combined volcanic eruptions of Mt. Baker and Mt. St. Helen's."

She enjoyed the twinkle in his eye. "But back to the Browns. I'm worried about that family. Jen seems stressed, but not only about the obvious work and money thing. There's something more."

"Oh, you're just worrying again."

"I think with good reason."

"Like what?"

"She had a bruise on her arm a while back. When I asked, she said it was from the shovel handle."

"So?"

"Didn't look like a shovel handle mark. I just didn't feel good about it."

"You can't go through life on your feelings."

"I'm not!" He could be so irritating when he refused to tune in on feelings. "There's more. When we were at the hardware store, her blouse opened. I saw a large bruise on her collarbone."

"And what did she say about that?"

Sylvia felt the jab of conscience. "I didn't ask. She acts funny; upset. Like I'm invading her privacy."

"Maybe you are. She's giving you a message. You're probably making a federal case out of nothing."

Gee, thanks, Sylvia thought. *You are a big help.*

After dinner Sylvia's irritation toward Larry had eased. *That's what food can do for you,* she thought. *Relaxing.* With Bengal Spice tea in their cups, they stayed at the table, talking.

"You had the tabletop thickly papered with your writing today. How is it coming?"

"Really well, if you count the number of pieces of paper, as you saw. But I need to sit down to the computer and enter them in."

"Oh, yea. You said that the creative ideas flow better with a pencil in your hand."

"For initial ideas, yes." She laughed. "Mostly because I get them just any time, anywhere, as you well know. In the car, on a trip, in the store parking lot, and even in the middle of us playing a game!"

"Um-hmm" A little smile curled one side of his mouth.

"Later the whole thought comes back if I have part of it down. But the computer – well, once I get going, it won't be distracting."

Larry reached out his hand to touch hers, but she paid no attention, still thinking of the cluttered table. "It makes such a mess when I work at the table. And I'm always having to pick it up. Now that I have my dad's desk, I need to get switched over. Guess I'm feeling disorganized."

"Darling, I can't imagine you being disorganized!" It was a private joke from the challenging years when the kids were little. For the most part, she had lived it down.

She cast him a mock disgusted look, wrinkling her nose, and focused again on her thoughts. "I'm wondering. I should buy a large file box for the creative writing. Hanging-type file folders will work. I have waaay too many loose papers." She shook her head and laughed. "Once it's filed, there will be no chance of it getting scrambled. I can quit picturing my nightmare! I have it every time I pick everything up. As I alternately stack the layers on my arm, criss-cross, I can see this catastrophe..." She looked at Larry and gave a rueful laugh. "...I see myself dropping the whole armload. I see jumbles of papers, strewn across the floor – a proverbial "fifty-two card pickup". Yes, that's probably the answer. Buy the file."

"Well, what's stopping you?" He stood. "I have to make a couple phone calls now, while it's early."

Sylvie sighed. *What is stopping me? He's right. Nothing is stopping me. Just going in to town and doing it. I'll go to Everett. I need a few other things, too.* Sylvie felt discouraged. *Sometimes I drag my feet. Don't get things done that are on my mind.*

Today was a day in Everett. Sylvie parked the car for one last stop, and thought, *I'm glad I've had the day to shop. It gets so crowded later in summer.* A large grocery shopping for non-perishable items filled the car. She had run other errands, and then gone to the office supply and found what she needed for filing her writing.

This last stop at the fabric store was her treat. Though Granite Falls was growing, it didn't have 'specialty stores.' She walked in, thinking that usually she had an excuse, like needing good thread or sewing machine needles. Today she didn't even have an excuse. However, she didn't have much time to linger, either. She loved looking through the interesting quilting cottons, and especially the marked-down remnants. Checking a bargain bin of notions, she found several cards of pretty buttons, and chose some pre-made appliqué flower patches to trim the yoke of Emalie's new dress. Ideas always came as she browsed, but it was time to head home.

She slid into the car seat and felt the accumulated warmth, and thought of the long, chilly spring. *Ah, feels good. Really too bad the timing of this trip didn't work out for Jen to come. That doctor would go and change the appointment.*

The drive home was uneventful. She pulled into her driveway and stopped at the mailbox. Thumbing through several pieces, she saw the hoped-for air letter! From her vagabond daughter, Isabel!

Oh, Isabel! She hurried around the car, sat down, and slit it open. Energetic writing scurried across the pale blue paper.

"Dear Mom and Dad, I am sorry I have let so much time pass. Finished in Great Britain, then a couple of girlfriends and I started a Europe tour. Got rail passes, good for three months. What a neat deal – not cheap, but worth it! We have seen most of France, Belgium, and Germany, and as it got hot we went to Switzerland. It was so lovely up there by the cool lakes. The breezes were blowing off the mountain glaciers. They are shrinking year by year, so I'm glad I saw them! I can say now that it was worth it – all the hard work last winter and spring in the cold rains and miserable conditions at second-rate theaters! The pay was low, but I saved every bit that I could. This 'playing tourist' has been great. We sleep in hostels and eat cheap out of the open markets. It's wonderful to see... so much! I wish you and Dad could come enjoy all this."

Sylvia stopped. Her eyes were blurred by tears. *Issa is safe. And imagine – she is thinking of us! How thoughtful that her desire is for us to enjoy the same experiences and sights.* Sylvia read the rest of the letter, then laid it on the car seat. Parking the car, she hurried into the kitchen, sat down, and read it again. What a relief. *Thank you, God, for watching over her.* Tears of release flooded her eyes and ran freely down her cheeks, all the tension slowly washing away. *I didn't realize how tightly wound my nerves were, worrying over what was happening to Issa. Concern to the depths of my being, and I've been burying it.* She rotated her shoulders and felt the muscles ease up; then she took a deep breath, and another. A few lingering tears slid down her cheeks as she laid the letter on the table where Larry would see it immediately when he walked in.

* * *

Len yelled, "No bills, you hear? We have to face the facts. If I lose my job, it's curtains. That's all. No bills." He snarled one more time, "No bills." The door slammed so hard the windows shook.

No bills. Jenny couldn't think of any bills she had made. All she had done lately was grocery shopping. Maybe that was it – she had asked Len for grocery money. Oh, she had charged underwear at

Sears in April for Michael when his were falling apart. But she was sure she had paid that and another bill with her wages just before they moved. *That emptied bank account – how could he have? What happened to the money, really? Now here we are, broke again, and I can't get work.* She realized he had just said 'lose' his job. *Why? Why does he say lose it, not just have a short layoff? Has he done something at work? Losing a few days because of hot weather, well, it was not the same thing as having no job. Was he being fired? Or...* She thought about it... the usual length of time had passed... when he either lost a job or quit. Then he ended up working for himself again. She couldn't count the number of times he had changed jobs just since she knew him. Foolishly, she realized, she had thought this job would last.

Len drove the long way into town. Wary, he kept his speed down and watched the sides of the road ahead. He knew the word was out. He'd overheard another laid-off mill worker talking in an Everett bar. The police had been around asking questions. Had come in the bar where the man was, looking for a man who started a fight – a fight in *that* bar. Len remembered, and listened. No mention of an arrest warrant. But he wouldn't make himself visible, just in case. One couldn't be too careful.

CHAPTER THIRTY

Jen washed her dishes and Sylvie dried, as they talked. "You say your Aunt Gertrude called and canceled her trip out here herself?" She walked around Jen and set the soup bowls in her cupboard.

"Yes! I was so thankful. I wasn't looking forward to it. I don't like to feel under scrutiny, and she always makes me feel that way. Points out what could be done better."

"I guess some people don't even realize what their words do to others. I suppose we are all guilty at some point. I know my daughter, Issa, tells me how hard I was on her; how she felt guilty, felt like a failure, when she was a teenager. I've apologized. I definitely was too critical – first daughter, you know. Trying hard to be a good mother. She didn't accept the apology. Seemed to want to stay mad at me. Hopefully, she is working through that now. I felt disapproval from my mom when I was still at home. Later I realized it was hard for me to take criticism. I was unsure of myself. I needed to get out on my own, figure out who I was, and get some confidence." Actually, the word Sylvie wanted to use was understanding. She went on. "Becoming a mother myself helped."

"I suppose." Jen didn't agree, but she didn't want to explore it, either.

Just then Len's voice exploded at the front door. "WHAT are you doing?"

Sylvia flinched. *Oh, oh, Michael is in trouble again.*

"What in *Hell* are you doing?" Sylvia looked, and saw Michael, frozen, holding a box. Len was shaking him with a vise-grip on one shoulder, and continued yelling. Michael cringed, curling forward as the angry words fell on him.

"I...I thought you said you wanted me to take this to the basement...I...I'm sorry."

"You *thought*. No, you didn't *think*. That box has some of my best tools in it and I don't want them rusting in the damp basement. I *said* to take them out to the truck. Truck, Stupid, not basement. The cans of oil go to the basement."

Len shoved the boy toward the open door, and then followed. Sylvia was numb. *I should have done something to help Michael. What could I do?* She felt cowardly. *Why do the words never come when I need them?* She turned to look into Jen's eyes, to read this situation, but Jen had turned away to look in the fridge.

As if nothing had happened, Jen looked up at the kitchen clock and said, "Well, I should start dinner."

"Yes," Sylvia said, and a heaviness pressed down on her chest. "I need to go home and do the same." *I feel paralyzed.* She moved toward the door. "See you tomorrow, maybe."

"Um hmm."

As Sylvie walked slowly along the path, Len's words filled her mind – raging words, striking out at Michael. Words so furious that she wondered how anyone could live with that much anger inside of him. He seemed to be overcome. Again his words rang in her ears. "What in hell..." and she wondered what he was thinking when he said hell. What did the word, the concept of hell, mean to him? The complete absence of Love...that was her first thought. Len didn't claim to believe in God. Maybe that's why he didn't believe in Love. He couldn't feel it. So hell – to be where there was the absence of God – was a constant for him. He was living every hour of every day without God, as far as he could tell.

Sylvia had known others who didn't believe in God, but they weren't as negative as Len was. What a contrast it would be for him – if he only knew what he was missing. If he knew the joy he could have – the joy of being secure, being valued, of a love that lasts forever – then he would want it. Wouldn't he? Len seemed oblivious to the contrast between God and Hell. He could inflict pain on others. Sylvia ached, thinking of him making others miserable and living a self-centered, lonely existence himself. There was none of the joy she felt, knowing to One who created the beauty of the gorgeous countryside, looking up toward heaven in thankful praise to God for His goodness. How sad. Len was experiencing the complete absence of kindness, of love…of God. Just emptiness and anger, lusting and longing for whatever, and ending up with emptiness. Yes, Hell.

Sylvia busied herself as she waited, but she kept looking up at the clock. Finally she heard Jenny's familiar ra-ta-Tat Tat! Jen called, "I'm here", as she opened the door, knowing she was expected. She came in and put her car keys in her pocket.

"Oh, you drove the car?" Sylvia asked.

"Mm-hmm," Jenny nodded. Her glance was direct, with a little tilt of her head toward the door…a warning look, not to talk about it. Sylvia was still wondering why she would drive such a short distance, when Michael stepped in.

"Oh," escaped Sylvia's lips, when she saw the deep circles under Michael's eyes and his white skin. She realized she'd better change the subject.

"Here, Michael. This tray of snacks on the counter is for you. There's some juice." She poured a glassful and set it on the tray. "You can stretch out like a leisurely knight in his castle."

Although Michael flashed her a big smile, she was dismayed at his hollow eyes. He didn't look himself. She decided she'd better carry the tray into the living room. She gave him the afghan, handed him the remote for the DVD, and returned to the kitchen.

"I got a call from Lisa. She's not sure when, but she will be out this way again. She's having a hard time getting a weekday day off. I'll let you know when she calls back. I hope you're planning to come."

"Oh, yes. I enjoyed the visit we had before. It would be good to see her again. Let me know. Today has to be short. But I hope I can come then. I'll see what my schedule is with the doctor appointments. I may need to take Michael in to Seattle for some special test."

Doctor appointments seem to be taking up a lot of time, Sylvia thought, but rather than ask, she sensed that Jen needed some cheerful conversation first. "How are the flowers coming along?"

she asked.

"Some are doing fine. The ones close to the house are going to make it. I really feel bad about the bed along the driveway, though. Remember how you warned me about that soil?" Jen gave a pained look. "Poor things. You said, 'It's gravel underneath, like a sieve – it won't hold water.' And you were right. Even with the decayed leaves and peat moss, the poor things droop their heads and look dead by mid-afternoon. You mentioned the soil improvement takes place over several years. I'll put in another bale of peat next year. Every day they need water. Twice a day if it's hot. I get out there with a bucket because my hose isn't long enough. Who would imagine they'd need water that often."

"It's true. This area truly should have been a sand and gravel pit! Say, we have an old hose that is just laying in the garage. Even though it has a couple leaks, I bet we can tape it. You can keep it. I have some black plastic tape."

"That would help."

"Say, friends dropped by. They had been to eastern Washington and picked up peaches. I had them bring a box for me, but I see they are ripening up fast, so I put some in this bag for you to take. I can't make jam or freeze them fast enough."

"Oh, they're beautiful. Bet they taste good! Thank you very much. Though Len doesn't like to accept things, this will be okay. He's not home much to eat with us. I'll put them in the back. He won't ask."

"Oh. Okay. I don't want to cause a problem."

"No. It won't be."

Just then, Michael came in the kitchen with the tray.

"Thank-you. That was good!" he said.

"You haven't eaten much for a knight riding his steed!" she joked. A sad look crossed Michael's face, and she felt like a dummy. She had touched a tender place, and hurt him.

"Oh, it was just great, thanks. I haven't been exercising much lately. Say, I sure like these stories about Lassie and the boy. Kyle's dog is like her, really smart. I'm training Goldie to be a dog like that." His voice trailed off as he turned back to the living room.

"I didn't mean to hurt his feelings about being an athlete. I just didn't think. I'm sorry. What is the situation now?"

Jenny looked down at her hands. "We don't know. He has had tests. Got results on some. Waiting on others. No answers yet. He is scheduled for more tests. That's one reason I was happy we could come over today. Keeps my mind off it. Getting out may help him rest better tonight. Sometimes he tosses at night. Seems to be running a fever. Not much shows up when I take his temp, though. He sleeps so restlessly." Jen looked troubled.

Sylvia couldn't think of anything to say that would be the truth and also comforting. "I'm sorry. I hope they find some way to make him feel better soon."

"I wish he had more energy. It comes and goes. It's not normal for a ten-year old child. He used to enjoy baseball and basketball. Now he has absolutely no endurance."

"Ah. It must be discouraging for you."

"Yes. And I think it's bothering him, too, wondering what's going on. Do you know, he asked about going to Sunday School. I thought I'd ask you if there's somewhere he could go."

"Sure. Lisa introduced me to a couple of good churches. I don't know about their children's programs. But I can phone and ask. Or we'll drive by. Check for the time on the info board that's out front."

"Okay. I guess it won't hurt him. He liked Mary, the woman that took care of him. She had Bible story books he'd read. He hoped to go to Sunday School with them, but we moved."

"I hadn't gone to Sunday School until after we made a move. I believe God was at work, that He arranged that. I hadn't been raised to think church needed to be a regular part of our lives. My mother felt we were fine without it. Dad respected the Bible. I picked up that much. I realized he thought differently, but he just let it go. When I talked to him later, after I was grown, I found out he believed in the Lord, personally, as his own Savior. He believed the Bible is God's word, and he knew quite a bit about it. He was just a person who didn't like to rock the boat. He wanted to keep peace with Mother. "

"See!" Jen said sharply. "Religion caused trouble in your home. Religion always causes trouble. Do you think God – if there is a God – arranged that?"

"Yes, I do. I am not what you'd call a religious person, but I have learned some things in the Bible about God and Jesus. That he cared enough to reach out to me. He was at work in my life when I didn't even know it."

"Well, I wish he had been *'at work'* in mine." Jen knew her words had the nasty sting of sarcasm. *Why do I have all this frustration and anger inside? Yet, those people deserve my anger.* She knew that her words were revealing, and yet hiding, so much. *It's hard, even for me, to know why my feelings run so deep. So how can anyone else?*

"God was drawing me through the very move that put me into the social climbing I disliked. The new house was next door to a lovely couple. This neighbor lady took me to a summertime Daily Vacation Bible School. It was every day of that week. We sang songs, had a Bible story, learned verses, and did crafts. The people there were so happy. I couldn't get over that. I hadn't heard the Bible stories before. I was one of the older children. I tried to learn my verses, but I struggled. One day a teacher who was listening to my memorization talked with me. She said, "The Bible is different from other books. God is the Author, and it is a living book. It speaks to our minds *and* to our hearts.""

"It never spoke to mine," Jen's inflexible look was hard to decipher. But she waved her hand and said, "Go ahead." *You will anyhow, I suppose,* she thought.

Sylvia continued. "This teacher said we can't understand the Bible with our heads or our hearts until we know the Author of it personally. Then she asked me, "Do you know Him?" I asked her how anybody could know God when He was up in heaven. She said that Jesus, the Son of God, came down to earth to live just like we do. He lived as an ordinary human, so we would see that He understands us. He showed us, at the same time, what a perfect life looked like. Then He took all our sins and died for them – He took our place, as though He had done them himself. God the Father would look upon any of us who trusted Jesus as *our* Savior as if we had never sinned. When I would accept Jesus as my substitute, God would see me through Jesus' perfection. I was struggling with that reality – that I wasn't good enough for heaven. I wasn't perfect, no matter how much I tried. I sinned. I wanted forgiveness." Jen was silent. Sylvie went on. "I prayed and asked God to forgive me. I was sorry. I trusted Jesus, and I thanked Him for taking my place. I knew in that moment that it was *true!* Jesus *had* paid for my sins! I was forgiven. The teacher then explained that Jesus sent the Holy Spirit to be in each new believer's heart – in my heart. That He was there to stay, and to help me pray and understand the Bible and live by it."

Suddenly they both realized that Michael was standing in the doorway, listening. As they looked up, he said, "Mary explained Jesus just like that, like you said, Sylvia. Jesus came to die for my sins. He wanted to. He died to take them away, and He showed He could do it when rose up again, alive." He stopped. Jen looked blank.

Sylvia waited to see if Jen might debate Michael's statements, but she didn't. "You have a good understanding about Jesus, Michael." She looked at Jen, and thought, *I might as well ask.* "Did you mind that Michael was hearing about Jesus at Mary's?"

"Well, no. I knew they talked. She asked me right off if it was okay for him to read a Bible storybook that she had. Sometimes he came home and told me the story. I never thought about it being bad...or even that it was *that* religious. It wasn't, the way Mary told it." She looked puzzled. Then her expression changed. In a low voice she said, "Wouldn't that be something – if my own son ended up in church."

Michael wondered at the strange flatness in his mother's voice. *I wonder what's wrong?* He saw strong disapproval on her face, and a shudder ran across his shoulders. *Why would Mom mind that? She thinks the Hendersons are so nice. John teaches some men at their church, but Mom knows that, and she still likes him – likes them both. But being in church sounds like something really bad. Hendersons aren't bad.* A puzzled expression lingered on Michael's face. Jen changed the subject. She stayed a bit longer before she took Michael home.

As she left, Sylvia thought she seemed sad – understandable with Michael sick. Disturbed by their talk of Jesus, too. It was hard to know if she would still want Michael to attend Sunday School.

* * *

It was Friday morning, and Sylvia had been writing for two hours, when a knock came at the back door. *Oh well. I guess no more work. Who could that be?* Again it came, and then she clearly heard Jenny's special ra-ta-Tat-Tat pattern. *Ah! Good! It's Jenny. Maybe she will have some news from the doctor.* Sylvia opened the kitchen door as Jenny came into the porch. She smiled, her eyes weary, and stepped into the kitchen. She paused, catching sight of the file folders on the computer desk and living room floor.

"Oh, dear, I'm stopping your creative flow."

"Not at all. I'm getting up early, writing while I'm fresh. I always look forward to a visit with you. It's never a hindrance to my writing."

"But with Larry coming home tonight, you'll want time to wrap up fresh thoughts that are coming to mind. I'm sorry."

Jenny looks totally down and discouraged. "You're giving me a break. In fact, I've put in enough time for today. Have a chair. I bet you enjoyed the walk over. How is Michael? You're alone."

"Yes. My old neighbor from the apartment, the one we call Aunt Peg, phoned and came yesterday on the bus to visit and see where we live. Nice to see her. Mostly, she wants to cheer up Michael. In Seattle she enjoyed 'neighboring' with him. They'd chat." Jen smiled. "And he's happy for her attention. I would have stayed but she insisted that I have some time away." Jenny hung her sweater over the back of a kitchen chair and sat down. "I left your phone number with her, in case she needs me."

Sylvia put water on to boil for tea. "Good. You can stay without concern."

"As for the walk, I noticed the feel outdoors has changed. Last night I stepped outside for some fresh air. I was surprised how it's cooling down. Though the calendar says it's still summer, the days are getting shorter, and there's a sense fall's coming. I notice nature more than I did in Seattle. I do love that little walk. Living out here in the country is just the best. These months have flown by. I wish I could live here always. You never know, renting."

"Oh, I don't think you have to worry about being asked to leave. The owner probably doesn't want it for himself. Just bought it as investment property. It is *so* good to have you living here." *Jenny seems so vulnerable. I hope my words can sink deep in her heart to encourage her. She needs it.* "What is the word from the doctor?"

"Oh, there is very little new information. Just more tests to be done. This on-going fatigue puzzles everyone. At first I don't think our family doctor even believed it was real."

"You know, don't hesitate to come over. This a difficult time. However I can help, I want to." Though she cared about Michael, her immediate concern was the dark circles under Jenny's eyes. She filled the tea pot and set it on a tray with two pretty mugs in forget-me-not pattern. "How about you – are you sleeping?"

"I get sleep, though it's always broken up."

"Have you thought of taking something to sleep, just for a while?"

"Oh, I'd rather be alert in case Michael cries out with a bad dream."

She looks so worried. I wonder if it's more than Michael's sickness. I'd like to know what's really up. Sylvia picked up the tray. "Come on in the front room. You are more tired than you're letting on, aren't you? There, grab that afghan and get comfy in your favorite spot." She went over to the couch, nodding for Jen to take the small rocker, upholstered in gentle blue and brown floral. "I made Red Rose tea. Did you see the TV commercial? The Englishman enjoys Red Rose on a trip here, but then he's upset to learn he can't return home and buy Red Rose tea in England. I haven't seen the ad lately. Say, my cousin from Vancouver called to say he got the promotion he hoped for."

"Good! He sounded deserving. You mentioned that he found it difficult to promote himself."

"Yes, he does. But he's very capable, and after a time a person in charge recognizes that."

"Sometimes. With waitresses it doesn't always work. You can have a new waitress come along who advances herself. If the boss is a woman, she gossips to her about the others. If it's a man, she rolls her eyes, uses her body language to charm him, and then tells lies. A boss can get the impression that Miss Trouble-maker is the one keeping everything together."

"Did you have that happen?"

"Oh, yes. But it all comes out in the wash eventually." She gave a mirthless little laugh. "There is another expression, 'comes out in the wash'. That's one that is still understood. Speaking of wash, mine is piled up. But it's sure good to have a break."

Concerned, Sylvie asked, "Jenny, I wish you'd let me bring some of it over here and do it."

"No, no. I'll catch up. It's just lately."

"Well, don't be afraid to ask. We want to communicate! In the middle of summer I was puzzled when you turned down chances to go do things. I thought maybe you were tired of it."

"No. I wasn't."

"Figured you might be bored with our little town. That it was too unsophisticated to be of interest any more."

"No. I like it here."

"Well, I wasn't sure. The reasons you gave on the phone sounded... I don't know... inconsequential... and I thought you might be shy to come out and tell me the truth – that it was boring. I didn't want to push you. I've sure enjoyed getting together."

"My fault. Don't worry about it. It was my inadequate explanations. So you don't mind if I enjoy a cup of your good tea?" Jenny asked, changing the subject. She picked up her mug and held it out.

"Of course you'll enjoy tea...Right here with me!" Sylvie grinned at her attempt at drivel.

Jenny let a wisp of a smile cross her face. "You can laugh at yourself. That's nice."

They talked on about the latest news in the local weekly paper. Added to that was the talk on the street. People gave 'informed details' that might or might not be accurate. Who knew whether the 'particulars' they added were really true, or just their own views. Sylvie refilled the two tall porcelain forget-me-not mugs and handed Jen's back to her.

"Now..." Sylvia paused. *I must get to the bottom of this, even if I have to pull it out of her.* "Tell me how Michael is. What about the tests he had last week? I thought the doctor was going to have the results?"

Tests, Jenny thought, with frustration. "Yes, I thought he would, too. The tests were inconclusive. He wants to do them again. At least we have good bus service. I've learned my way around. Sometimes it's the office, sometimes it's the lab."

"I sure wish I could take you to appointments and the lab."

"No, Len won't have it. Nice that you're willing." Sylvie nodded. Jen thought, *I can't tell Sylvie that Len said he had it all figured out – that Larry will be the driver sometime, and will make advances. And that he couldn't trust me, either.* She wondered how you could persuade a person otherwise, when he was already convinced. She had tried to be careful never to flirt.

Sylvie was thinking how it upset her just to have Len's name come up.

Jen gave a sigh. *I must hold my feelings inside. I start feeling so helpless, wondering what is coming next. It's so up-in-the-air – like Michael and I are bits of debris, sucked up in a whirling tornado. Maybe Len feels that way too. Maybe that's why he has gone back to Seattle a lot. At least it's probably part of it. Who knows what he will plan from here on – I never know.*

Jen realized all of this was flying through her mind, and there had been silence. She returned to the medical questions. "The tests seem only to bring more questions, not answers. I don't know if it's serious. I don't want to blow his illness out of proportion. At first it seemed like the family doctor would get to the bottom of it right away. You know, growing pains, this type of thing. Then the doctor starts talking about serious stuff. You know how they can be – some medical people expect the worst. Now I am sort of telling myself, 'focus on today – we've got to go to the lab', or 'today we rest for the next appointment'. Like a check list."

Jenny settled back into the rocker and pulled up the blue and white afghan around herself. "I can only tell you this," she continued. "The doctor said that two of the blood tests will have to be done again this Friday. He'll see if there is a continuing trend. So now we wait on those results. Not much, is it? Here I thought by now we would get some definite answers." She paused. "I have tried not to complain to Len during these months. Just hold myself together. But I feel so shut off from him. It's almost a relief that he's been gone a lot lately. He has never been easy to get close to. But the last couple months he has talked less, shared less. He seems so disapproving." She sighed.

Sylvia could see that Jen had resolutely dammed her tears inside herself. "I'm so sorry." And she wondered what more she could say. She hoped Jen would keep talking.

"Len says things to Michael," Jenny continued, "like, 'Buck up. Keep yourself busy. Tomorrow you are to straighten your desk and dresser. I'll check it. Put some of your books into a box in the closet. You have too many out. You need something to do. You need a sense of accomplishment. Aim at a goal and then do it. You'd feel better about yourself if you'd get busy and do something.'" She turned and looked into Sylvie's eyes. "I wonder if he has any idea how Michael feels physically. Or how he feels in any way – like, emotionally. Michael believes he is a complete and total disappointment to his step-dad. Len doesn't see there is something wrong medically, or doesn't want to see it. I guess it's depressing for him, too." She was quiet.

Sylvia nodded, but kept quiet. *Oh, Jen, please, just let it out. All I can do is be here for you, and listen.*

"In Seattle Michael alternated between his normal energetic self, and days when he was bushed. Just before we moved here, he was playing basketball and he was really drained after practice. The coach said he wasn't trying, wasn't 'giving it his all'. Len was picking him up sometimes, and he would watch the last few minutes of practice. Then he and the coach would talk about Michael's progress. Rather they'd dwell on his lack of progress, sometimes right in front of him. In the car coming home..." she paused, disturbed, then finally collected herself. "Michael finally told me... I had to ask questions to get the picture. In the car Len would tell him how lucky he was to have this good coach for basketball, and lucky his school had an excellent sports program, lucky to have a step-dad to pick him up and show an interest in him. Then he said to Michael that he was unappreciative of all this. Michael felt awful, like a failure. Finally Len began saying those things at the dinner table, in front of me. 'Your coach is getting fed up with you. You are being *lazy*. You hear me? LAZY. Why don't you get in there and really play?'

"It was so hard to hear Michael berated, to watch his face. I tried to explain he didn't feel good. But I learned that it only prolonged the tirade when I entered in. I felt confused. I did feel I was making excuses for Michael. But by spring I finally decided to pay attention. I saw that Michael truly was worn out. Some days were good. I thought he just needed more rest, so I tried getting him to bed earlier. About that time we moved out here. He perked up for a while. But he started to run out of energy again, so I figured it was a virus. It lasted, though. That's when I took him to a doctor." Jenny shook her head. "This all started out like a bad dream, as I think back on it. But now it has become a nightmare that's still here. I can't wake up."

A long wet snuffing came from Jenny. Sylvia looked upward, trying not to roll her eyes, thinking, *I can not believe the insensitivity of that man. Yes, Jen, go ahead and cry.* Jen's tears began flowing.

"Oh Sylvia...Oh, God..." She softly sobbed. "What can I do? What's going to happen with Michael? What about Len? He's away so much. Where is he? What *do* I do about this marriage... I feel like my world has fallen apart."

Sylvia took a deep breath. "Oh, Jenny. You sound completely drained. I don't know Len well enough to know what he's thinking... or feeling. Maybe he's feeling guilty for condemning Michael, though he might not admit it, even to himself." She was grasping at straws, and she knew it. "That's what would hit me if I were him. Or maybe it's fear or anger – that life is out of control. Whatever – I don't know." She stopped to think. *I'm making excuses for him – how dishonest.*

"But Jenny," she continued, "my heart goes out to *you*. You have been keeping this all inside you – carrying it all *yourself.* You must feel so alone. I have read that it's a big strain on marriage, dealing with a serious illness. I know I like to share things with my husband, and you must long to, also." Immediately Sylvie felt less than honest. *Oh, I'm making it worse. Theirs just isn't that kind of marriage, so why pretend? Get real.* "Jen, I don't know the answers. You've been getting worn out from getting up at night. And... I wonder if you have been hoping...hoping you could hold everything together? Hoping that you could nurse Michael back to health by your own effort, if you tried hard enough? Hoping that you can get Len to understand Michael's problem if you explain it just right?"

Sylvie knew she needed to be totally honest. "Jenny, you must be exhausted physically and emotionally. Frankly, I don't understand Len's outlook. I hear his verbal abuse to you and Michael. It's so harsh. You are a wonderful mother. Please never doubt that. I see it over and over again. Michael knows it, in so many ways. You take time for him, listen and value him. Kids feel secure that way." Sylvia thought *I wish I could find some better way to help than just taking over a casserole, or picking up a few groceries for her.* Then, with sympathy in her voice, she said, "I don't know where you find the strength to do it."

"I can't do it." Jenny's lips twisted downward and her hand flew up to cover her face. *Oh, that's all I needed – uncontrollable grief. I'm losing it.* She began to sob.

Sylvie almost reached out and wrapped her arms around Jen in a big comforting hug, but thought; *I can't – she stiffens up with physical affection. And as for thinking of advice, what should her next step be? I don't know what to tell her. But I can express something. Please, God, help me say something she needs.*

"Well..." Sylvia started and paused, "maybe that's a realistic point to come to – to say, 'I can't do it'. I know I couldn't have carried on like you have, exhausted." Sylvia ran out of words. She looked at her mug, closed her eyes, and held onto the image of the dainty forget-me-nots. Simple flowers – if only life were simple. *Dear God, if only I can be of some help to her – show me.* Jenny continued to sob, and Sylvia prayed that the tears would bring some release from the tension that had her bound in a knot. Gradually Jen's sobs slowed to labored breaths, like an exhausted swimmer, gasping for air. Tears still slid silently down her cheeks.

Jenny lay back in the rocker, resting her head and keeping her eyes closed. "I'm sorry to bring all this misery to you."

"Oh, no! Please don't be. I want you to talk."

"I guess I have been holding that in for a long time." She dabbed her cheeks with a tissue, added it to the ones in her lap, and pulled two more out of the box. "I'm a mess." She laughed dolefully.

She looked at her soggy tissues, wadded in her hand and on her lap. "Let me go wash my face," she said, rising.

"There are washcloths in the cupboard, and hand towels beside them."

When Jen returned, Sylvia said, without looking at Jen's blotchy face, "Let's go look at something I have upstairs! A little serendipity." She led the way through a door and up a stairway. Old-fashioned wallpaper covered with roses was along the stairs to the second floor. Sylvia said. "Not much sunshine lately. Good to have this closed off bedroom. I'll show you why!" She opened a door into a spare room at the back. Sitting before them on a table near a window was a Christmas cactus with dozens of buds on it. "It will bloom too early for Christmas, but at least it will bloom this year. It's cool up here. That helped. That, and cutting back on water for a while, must have done it."

At first Jen let out a low 'ahh' of wonder, then came closer and said, "I can't believe how many buds there are. But why is it called a cactus? There are no spiky prickles on it."

"Just because it's in the succulent family, I think. Actually, it needs more water than real cactus. I don't really know why the name."

"Can I touch it?" Sylvie nodded.

Jen was in awe of the multitude of buds. A few showed pink at the tips. "It's going to be beautiful!"

Sylvia watched Jen's face. *At least for a few minutes she can give her attention to something beautiful. Even in the midst of her difficult life, it's nice to think there can be some sunshine. Too bad it will be so short-lived.* Sylvia knew nothing by which she could raise hope with Michael's situation. But just as bad was her lack of hope for any change in Lennard. Rather, a change by Lennard. She saw that there was little possibility of it at this point. One of several books Lisa had given her, was a guide for spouses in Al-anon; another was a counseling book on alcoholism that Lisa had lent her. It was thorough, and gave the signs and consequences of alcohol addiction. It had taught her to be realistic – to understand it was a long haul for someone attempting to live sober, and honest with himself. Though there was hope for anyone, it seemed only a sliver of hope for Len, presently. The chance of it happening was low, considering his belligerent attitude… maybe nil. The decision to change was in his hands alone. She had read that only after willingness began, would reality set in.

All this went through Sylvie's mind as Jen was walking around the room, looking at what was growing. A large tray held geranium slips that were rooting, and there was an ivy that needed re-potting.

Jen looked out the window and through the tops of the tall trees at the back of the property. "Nice view," she said without enthusiasm. They walked down the stairs, and Sylvia pointed out a houseplant on a stand.

"These like low light." Jen nodded.

They stood quietly for a moment, and suddenly Jen asked, "Any words of wisdom?" She had no real expectations – except another person's perspective was good.

In a flash, it came to mind. Sylvie said, "Actually, I *was* reading something heart-warming. Just yesterday an email was sent to me. It said they checked, and found the middle verse of the Bible. It's Psalm 118 verse 8, and guess what it says?" Jen shook her head. "It says,

'It is better to trust in the LORD
than to put confidence in man.'

"I thought that was neat. Interestingly, it has fourteen words, so the center of it is two words – 'the Lord'. It's like God is saying, "Hello there. I'm the One to trust!"

Jen had trouble understanding why she should be encouraged by this. She felt her hopes dulled. "I wonder who took the time to do that?"

"With computers I guess it wouldn't be difficult."

"Yeah. But heart-warming? I'm not sure I see it – what you're seeing."

"I take it to mean, 'people will let you down'. God is always there. Being reminded of it just yesterday, it's like, pointed out fresh, for you and me to share. Hearing what you've said, well... No human being can fill all our needs. Only God can. To look to a husband is a good feeling – at least when things are going well. But even my husband, great guy that he is, lets me down. I get hurt when he doesn't even listen to what I'm saying. There are times I feel like he doesn't care." Jen had a disturbed look on her face.

Sylvia wondered, but went on. "When I think how the Lord cares, how He has made me His child and is waiting to share thoughts with me and hear from me, then I am reminded of the faithful relationship He promises. Sometimes I feel bad that I haven't been open to Him. In my frustrated state, I haven't kept in touch. I've fretted, and let my mind wander when I pray. I've neglected reading His word. He wants to encourage me with the Bible. Best of all, he wants me to enjoy His presence, the way two friends do. He's that close."

Jen turned away and gave a slow, negative shake of her head, disagreeing. "I realize you believe that, but I can't. I just don't see it. I don't understand how people can talk about "the Lord this, and the Lord that", as though he's involved – like he's interested in people's lives. "

"Well, His encouragement has kept me going in dark times. I've found Him to "be there". And I want you to know I'm always here for you. Whenever you need to talk. I don't have answers like a professional who studied relationships, but I do care."

"I know that. Thank you. I feel your caring. It helps to have someone listen."

Jen had to go. In the kitchen Sylvia pulled an A.A. book out of a stack. "I have been reading this. I wondered if you'd like to go with me to a support group meeting where others will talk about coping?"

"What group? Coping with what?"

"An Al-anon meeting – it's for those who are married to an alcoholic."

Jen took one look at the book and got a startled expression. "Al anon?" She shook her head. "Oh, no. I don't have time now, with Michael sick. We can talk about it some other time." She went quickly out the door, calling her good-bye over her shoulder and thinking that Len might come back and find her in an A.A. group and then she'd get a beating.

CHAPTER THIRTY-ONE

Jenny's familiar rapping at the door startled Sylvia. She said, "Come in!"

As Jen's smile appeared, it spoke of happy thoughts.

"Say – this is a surprise! Come on in!"

"I hope it's not too early. I just had to show you this! Mary sent a note and a picture of John and herself. It's a nice close-up. Here!" She held it out. "I wish you could meet her."

"How nice to see her face; both of them. I need a visual, although I feel like I know Mary after hearing what a help she was. That was special, to find a place for Michael with someone who cares. Someday I may get to meet her." As she said it, she thought, *It isn't impossible, but it's unlikely. I wonder just how much effort I'd be willing to put out to meet her? I enjoy my routine life out here and get lazy.* She turned to Jen, "So, is Michael any better today?"

"Actually, he is. Aunt Peg is still here. Last day. You should come meet her."

"I'd like that. Maybe I'll come with, when you go back. But for now, how about a cup of tea? This is so nice to can sit down and relax."

"Sure, I'd love it!" Jen pulled out the chair, and Sylvia thought how good it was to see Jen feel at home.

"I like these flowers you have on the table. The bright orange and yellow blossoms are cheery. They look a little like a cross between daisies and sunflowers. What did you call them? Something like Rebecca?"

"Almost! Rudbekia. I like them, too. That's one of the perennials we'll divide this fall for your yard! They come back for several years. I like their bright colors, too."

They chatted over their tea for a half hour and Sylvie noticed that Jen's worried look had lightened. It was so nice that she needn't be in a hurry. Sylvia got up to heat more water.

Jen looked at that bothersome motto again, and silently read the words. "O Lord help us to become masters of ourselves, that we may be the servants of others." She decided to come out with it.

"That plaque – the words you said were from a monk. Might as well tell you. I went to a parochial boarding school. That's why I got angry about a monk trying to pass off his religion. If that's Christianity, I don't need it. *No thank you.*"

"Oh." Sylvia had never seen Jen this agitated. "Things were bad there, eh? I guess there are all kinds of teachers in every school. I remember outstanding ones." She chuckled. "Then there were some I'd rather forget."

"It wasn't just one teacher. It was the whole place – the condemnation. Even the boarding house. The old biddy that ran it hated me. She told me how wicked I was all the time. She made sure I felt guilty most of the time, whatever I'd done." Jen shook her head. "No, not about what I *did* – I felt guilty about *what I was*. She told me, 'You'll always be wicked. It's in your blood.' Said I was evil and reprobate. I had never heard the word reprobate, but I got the message – I was past hope. You know, even though I took it as fact, that I was hopeless, at the same time I rebelled against it. I couldn't sort it out. One thing for sure; she hated me. There were other things, too. I guess I focused on the matron because I had to be around her so much. All I knew was, since these people spoke for God, then God must hate me... and I figured I deserved it." Sylvia was speechless.

Jen paused a moment, then went on. "I wanted to run away from it all. But I couldn't find a way. I would whisper to myself, pretending I was talking to her, *"Fine. You can keep your stinking religion. I'm out of here."* Of course, I couldn't leave. So I acted up bad. So bad that my "new step-father", as he was called, finally had to come get me. When I got home they were in a new house. I was put back in public school.

When he had first come, it didn't take me long to realize he wanted to get rid of me. I didn't like him from day one. He knew it, so he just shipped me off, and said it was a privilege he would pay for. I don't know to this day if he really married Mom. She called him her husband, but I doubt it."

Jen hung her head, ashamed. When she looked up, sadness and a far away look filled her face. "I look back in time. Think of when he first visited Mom. He took her out for a few hours to shop, to buy her nice clothes, but he'd go back to a hotel room at night. He didn't seem our type. I wondered why he came. I didn't realize my mother was still young and pretty, lonely and too willing to please. Then he started to take Mom away overnight, and then for a couple days at a time. It was summer. I was there to babysit. She'd bring home hotel notepads and the napkins from places they'd gone to eat and drink. And presents, too, for each of us. I couldn't feel happy getting a present. He and I were at each other's throats, arguing, especially when she wasn't around. My mom quit being a person; did what he told her to do, what to think. Not me. I bucked everything he said. Didn't take long before he shipped me away to that school. Guess they hired a babysitter to take my place, to watch my brother and sister. When I returned from the boarding school it was to a totally different kind of home – he had control of everything. Mom was a robot, worse than before. I could see there was no one to stick up for me. Mom had been tough on me, the usual kid-raising stuff. But now I was causing her big trouble – with him not wanting me. I figured I'd lay low. Keep my radar on to pick up on his next move. I determined I would take care of myself." Jen took a deep breath.

Sylvie said, "That's terrible." She was in a dilemma, just absorbing all of it, and couldn't find the words she wanted to respond.

"As for church," Jen laughed cynically, "I still was made to go. It conveniently put me out of the house. I'd walk slowly, dragging along, until I made sure I was late. I'd slip in the back. They'd say prayers and I'd mutter along, but inside I was saying, "I hate you all. I don't need this." I decided that it all was a lie, the whole story. As the years passed, I thought maybe people made up religion for their own convenience, to suit themselves."

"What is it that would suit them?" Sylvia interrupted. "I don't understand."

"Oh, I figured there might be a variety of reasons. Some people might like to make rules that were easy for them to keep because they were 'good people'. Then they could feel pleased with themselves. You know – pride. Other types might want to use rules to keep everything lined out – the organized type. Some are controllers, so they want to keep the followers in line. They set up a structure and become the major general over a group who follows them blindly."

"Are these the *only* kinds of religious people you've seen?"

"I admit, I do see people who seem to have a genuine connection to God. It's real for them. But my own *"religious experiences"* were the end of my *"believing"*. I figured there wasn't a God. Or if there was, he was so uncaring that I didn't want to hear about him… So now you know why I don't have much use for religion." To Jen, the look on Sylvia's face could only be called 'stunned', and she felt bad. "Guess I never have spouted off like this before. Too bad for you to get the whole load. But I *know* by experience how *good* the people were who shoved God-stuff down my throat. Never felt I needed it after that." She stopped. "Sorry to get so intense." She was drumming her fingers on the table. Then she picked up her tea cup and drained it, thinking, *That ought to do it. I didn't realize I was so angry. At least I won't have to cover that topic again.*

Sylvia drew a deep breath and shuddered involuntarily. "How horrible – for you to go through all those experiences." She reached out with both her hands and enclosed Jen's hand. Her mind numb, she questioned, *How, dear God? How can this happen? Can a person recover from this kind of mistreatment?* Squeezing Jennifer's hand gently, she tried to convey her feelings – that she cared. Show her the love she so badly lacked in years past. But could that count for anything, in the face of so many years of bad experiences? People who didn't care. People who didn't try to protect her, or couldn't? What she was hearing caused Sylvia to ask herself, *What responsibility did the adults have? What steps could some of them have taken?* Certainly her mother had the responsibility for her daughter's protection. There probably were good men or women at the school who would have helped if they weren't afraid. However, they were under the authority of others. In their thinking, it would be 'rebellious' to stand up against those authority figures – in fact it was probably called 'ungodly'. It could happen in other denominations with religious schools, too.

As jumbled as her thoughts were, Sylvia recalled something hopeful that might help Jen. "I was a teenage volunteer, a candy-striper in a church hospital, and the staff were wonderful, caring individuals. I could tell many stories about the kindness I saw given by a number of the nuns." She saw a hard look on Jennifer's face. "I realize that doesn't take away your pain. You said you don't want religion, at least the organized type. Now I certainly understand why." She paused and shook her head. "What awful experiences. I am so very sorry you went through it... all."

Lord, help me think, Sylvia prayed. *This isn't what You are like. It's people. It's human nature. It's angry, controlling people who let their power go to their heads. They still are what they 'are'; they haven't let You change them. Being in a religious setting doesn't change them – they use any religion. They even use Your name. In a setting where people should be able to trust, to get help, these controllers feed their own egos and their unhealthy needs. So, help me, Lord.*

"I never went through anything like you have," Sylvia said, trusting God to give her words to speak. "I don't know why some children do, and some don't. I don't think I have an answer for that. As for church, I realize any church, any denomination, can have problems, because they are just made up of people, like any other group. I suppose that tight control over people might lead to a feeling that they shouldn't think for themselves. It's not right. God is big enough to handle our questions. You can ask questions. I've asked my share." Sylvia was speaking quietly, aware that what she was hearing from Jen was extremely deep pain. "The Bible stands on its own, though. Its truths have helped countless millions, including me. I guess I already told how I accepted Jesus as my Savior"

"Yes."

"I felt relieved as I realized I wasn't alone any longer, and I certainly felt like a weight was lifted from me."

"You were just a kid, though, and from the good side of town. You didn't have a lot of troubles or sins, as you call them. Wasn't that much 'weight' to be forgiven."

"I knew I had a need. When I heard the Bible explained, I knew I needed forgiving for *my* sins. It wasn't how big or how many sins. It was sin, period. I saw I couldn't *do* anything about it."

"So then did you get religious?"

"I don't think you'd call it that," Sylvia smiled. "After that week of Vacation Bible School meetings I mentioned had ended, I asked my parents if I could attend the church. Mother reluctantly agreed. Dad was for it. The neighbors picked me up and took me every Sunday. I went for a year. Then my mother said I had had enough religion, that it would give me a warped view of life and I should get more well-rounded. I had enjoyed the people; they were so kind. I felt at home there. I liked our children's class; I learned a lot. I even understood the sermons in the adult service. I asked my mother if I could be baptized as a believer. She said no – in fact, I think that's when she began saying I needed to stop going. She said something about how they just wanted to make me a member because they wanted people like me, who were easily convinced. She made fun of me because I had given my little donations. I wanted to. And I trusted the church folks. She didn't. I knew those people. Whatever I gave, they would never use it wrongly. They just weren't like that. I was confused, torn between my mother and the people at church. Then my mother explained something on her mind. Said that I wouldn't learn how to be 'classy' with 'those ordinary people' who believed in Jesus. She began to arrange for me to rub shoulders with the right people – people of her choosing. She made sure I was invited into their homes. I didn't socialize well. I was uncomfortable and lonely in those settings. So my 'getting classy' lessons fell through." Sylvie laughed. "I threw myself into my studies, instead. I made good grades. Church fell by the wayside. Getting good grades pleased both of my parents."

"Well your church experience was good. I'm glad," Jenny said.

"I have gone some to the church Lisa introduced me to. I liked it. Maybe we could go together sometime."

"No. That's not in the picture for me. You can check about the Sunday School time for Michael, if you want, but he seems pretty worn out. May not get up to go." She paused. "I was wondering if that church in your childhood was one-of-a-kind."

"Oh, I don't think so. Lisa has found a good church in Seattle. She's really happy there."

"Oh, I do remember Lisa saying that. Is she coming out again?"

"I hope so! She got busy at work. I'll give her another call."

They visited a while longer. Jen had to leave and Sylvie decided she had better wait to meet Aunt Peg. She had to get dinner ready on time, since Larry had a meeting.

Sylvia woke before dawn, feeling gloomy. The days were getting noticeably shorter. It was late enough to get up, so she crawled out and grabbed her thick robe. Going to the kitchen, she made coffee and sat down with her Bible. Thumbing across the whole of it, wondering where to read, she stopped at Psalm 119, and her eyes were drawn to verses she had underlined – verses 97, 105, and 132.

"Oh, how I love Your law. It is my meditation all the day.
Your word is a lamp to my feet and a light to my path.
Look upon me and be merciful to me,
as Your custom is toward those who love Your name."

There it is again – it is God's habit to look on His children, on me. And He is merciful. Since He is merciful to me... How does He feel about Lennard? I've read that He's not partial...if only Len would trust God; stop having all the answers himself. That man rubs me the wrong way every time I think of him. No. It's not just irritation; I have hated him for what he is doing to his family. But he needs love in his life. How badly he needs love. Her eyes fell to the page and she again read, *"Oh, how I love Your law! It is my meditation all the day. You, through your commandments, make me wiser than my enemies; for they are ever with me."* She prayed, *Oh, Lord, he is my enemy, not because he is pointing a gun, but because his actions are so against You.* She read verse 104. *'Through Your precepts I get understanding; therefore I hate every false way.'*

Lord, although Len's actions are contrary to Your nature, so are mine at times. I need mercy, too, and I thank You for it. Please be at work in Len's life. I pray he will let You show him Your mercy and love.

CHAPTER THIRTY-TWO

Poor Jen, Sylvia thought. *It's overwhelming just to think about her childhood. It seems to be lacking basic care and security, and real demonstrations of love that every child needs. But to live through it – I can't imagine. What memories to deal with. Oh, God, help her!*

There was so much to take in. Sylvia pondered different aspects; the controlling step-father, the religious angle, and Jen's mother... and father.

Sylvia hadn't seen the book for many, many years. She lifted it from the box and traced her fingertip over the lettering on the cover. "Nursery Rhymes and Poems". Memories flooded in as a door opening in her mind and carried her back in time. *I am very small – five years old. I can smell apple blossoms in the air and it's late spring. I'm alone in my bedroom, sitting on a rug. I turn the pages of this special book Mommy and Daddy have given me. Looking at the pictures, I pretend to read the rhymes and poems. I can hear Mommy reading as I turn the pages. I pretend she is holding and cuddling me. She's not here. Maybe she will read to me later. Suddenly Daddy comes to the doorway of my room. His face is twisted up, and I don't know what is wrong. He doesn't talk for a minute, and I am afraid. He says the neighbor will stay with me, but he must go to Mommy. He comes and kisses me quickly – too quickly. And then he's gone. He doesn't come home all afternoon. He doesn't come home for dinner or to tuck me in at bedtime. Why isn't*

Mommy coming home? Where is my daddy? I cry myself to sleep. When I get up in the morning, it's still just the neighbor lady. No daddy and mommy. I feel a dark dread. The lady doesn't talk. After lunch I am in bed for my nap, crying. I keep crying lots of tears that run hot down my face.

I hear the car. Usually I would be obedient and stay in bed, but I jump up and run to the window. Daddy is walking, alone, from the car, and he looks up at me. He looks sad and tired. He doesn't even wave, and I don't wave either. Something very bad is happening. Daddy comes up to my room and hugs me and says, "I love you my little Sylvia, my Silver Moonbeam." I don't know why he is crying. He wipes away his silent tears. Then he sits back a little so we are face to face, and he says, "Your mommy is sick. She will get better. She will be home in a few days." He doesn't tell me why she is staying away. He says, "Mommy will be sad for a while, but she will get better."

Empty hours and endless days pass, waiting for Mommy. She does come home. But she is different. She cries a lot. Even when she quits crying, it's different. She doesn't laugh. She doesn't even smile. One day she takes me up beside her on the big couch in the living room. She tells me, "You had a baby brother coming. But he won't come to us now – or ever. He is gone." When I ask why, she says, in a funny voice, "Who knows? He's just gone." She doesn't cry; she just sits there. Her arm is around me, but she doesn't cuddle like before. I slide off the couch and leave the room. It feels cold. Whenever I ask Mommy to read with me in the little poem book, she won't. She says she is too busy, or it's time for a bath. No matter how much I beg. I hold it But now it is a sad book. I put it on its shelf. I don't take it out again. I feel bad that it just sits there.

Years later we are packing to move. My father sees it in a box and, in one of his rare moods of talking, he tells me what they had planned when they bought me the book. They could picture me looking at it happily, while Mother rocked our baby nearby. She would read it sometimes. And after I learned to read, I would read it to my new brother or sister. Mother, he explained, struggled to get that picture out of her mind.

Things changed in other ways. My older sister quits playing

with me; she's too busy. And she gets mad at me a lot. She tells me, once, that our mom got hard. I don't know what 'hard' means. Years later, when my father talks, I remember her words. I tell him what my sister said. He says my mother did change after the baby died – she was overcome with sadness. I say I don't understand why she had to change. He doesn't answer.

Sylvia slowly turned the pages of the book that held a whole piece of her life, and thought, *This book means Mother... the good times, before she changed. Each picture and poem holds vivid memories. It had started so wonderfully.* She held the little book, closed her eyes, and felt the warm presence of a long-ago mother. *Where did she go? Why can't I connect on a feeling level with her? I wanted to, all those years. Oh, Mother, you hurt me. In your pain, you hurt me. Yes, I'm angry. I had you, only you, as my mother; I had only one childhood. Did you enjoy me at all after that? Did you enjoy my sister? Did you love Dad? Or did you just get bitter.*

Sylvia stopped her thoughts short, for the next question was whether her mother's quest for money had filled the empty place; one that she could have allowed a husband and daughters to fill. Sylvia put down the book. *All I know is, that it's past. Done. I can live now, in this moment and let it go.* She looked at the book. *Emalie will enjoy it. I can at least use the book to give pleasure again. I will read it to Emalie and tell how Grandma was once a little girl, long ago. I'll show her a page or picture that was special to me. Tell her how I liked the soft colors, the dreamy artwork. Emalie and I can pick out little details; she can find her own favorite pages. She won't be able to believe that Grandma could be as small as her. But she will sense that the book is important. It can be shared anew. It will again be special... and it will no longer bring pain.*

Sylvia put away the book. Her thoughts again turned to Jennifer's childhood. *When a mother doesn't help a child in such desperate need as Jen had, it must feel awful. I think of my mother, now. How she pays more attention to her business than her family, but I have to admit I was cared for as a child. I felt secure.*

Inside, Jen felt a longing. She wandered around the house. She turned over Sylvia's words about God, and the rude answers she had given her. She wondered, *What is it I am longing for? I don't know. A peaceful home might be a terrific start. Len seems, when he's here, to be building up more and more of a 'mad' over something. How or when could this man be happy? Never?*

Jen cleared the shuffle of papers that cluttered the back of the kitchen table. They had been shoved aside and the phone book had covered them. She thumbed through some old envelopes. *Here is that bank statement,* she thought, surprised to see it after so long. *I guess I never opened it. I saw Mary's postcard, got excited, and never went back to it.* She ripped open the envelope, pulled out the balance sheet and read it. Shocked, she read it again. *There must be some mistake. Less than thirty dollars? How can that be? It's gone – most of my savings from tips, gone. What has happened? The bank must have made a mistake. I didn't withdraw, only just a little.* She saw two large amounts in the withdrawal column. But it was her account. How could this happen… She looked at the top of the sheet and a chill went down her spine. The account name was Jennifer *and* Lennard Brown. How could that be? Then she remembered how busy the first week after moving was. She remembered Lennard handing her papers from the bank. He said they needed signatures for both accounts. She was in a hurry – must not have looked at what each sheet said. Now she knew. One paper had changed her account to both names. Strange – signature papers like that required verification. They were usually signed in front of a teller. How had he managed this? Could he have given another woman a piece of my I.D., and taken her in? Maybe he said his wife was bedridden, or in the hospital, or something, and even forge their Seattle doctor's name. She sat down, feeling weak. Sick. As she turned it over in her mind and recovered from the shock, she was seething inside. *Wonder when I'll get a chance to ask Len about this? I don't want to start it in front of Michael. It will be another "scene". I have to have money to carry me through several days in Seattle. Thank God the Deli Diner's medical insurance carried on for ninety days. It will pay the hospital. 'Thank God'… that's funny. I sound like Sylvia. What did God have to do with insurance?*

An hour later Jen sent Michael out to take Goldie to run in the back field. Then she gathered her nerve.

"Len?"

"Yea. What?"

"I have something to ask you. I checked my bank account. You took the money out of it. How could you do that?"

His voice grew loud. "To pay bills! You *knew* the bills were overdue when we moved."

"But you got work. You said you were paying them. *That* money was for emergencies."

"So what? What's the big problem. I *told* you – the bills were overdue. A power bill, other bills that *you* help make. You *say* it's important to pay them."

She looked away. *What can I answer to that? It's true. I do want them paid. He brings up things I'm responsible for. It's a no-win situation.*

The phone rang, interrupting Jen's reading. She set aside the book in which she had buried herself.

"Hello?"

"We have made an appointment at Children's Hospital in Seattle for Michael," the doctor's receptionist said. "There are some tests to be run, and an examination by a specialist will done." Jen was stunned. *At a hospital? Why? Have I missed something the doctor explained?*

After she hung up, she sorted out her thoughts. Three days from now. She and Michael could ride the bus to Everett, then catch the Greyhound to Seattle. She would have to get ready to stay in town. But where?

Jenny called Sylvia and asked if she could come over. She appeared at the door moments later, and said, "I'm just here for a minute. Can't stay long."

"That's fine. I already put the water on – coffee or tea?"

"Oh, I don't have time now, really. I'm sorry. I just wanted to catch you up. I found out that the doctor definitely made an appointment for us, but this time it's in Seattle."

"Seattle? How long will you have to be there?"

"I have no idea. It's sounding like a couple days to several days. You know tests; and an exam, too. This has been hard to zero in on and diagnose." She grimaced.

"Did they tell you about the special accommodation for parents?"

"No. Not yet anyhow."

"Well, they probably will. Just in case, I'll give you the address." Sylvia took out a piece of paper, flipped open a phone book, and wrote the number and address.

"Okay. Thanks," Jen said as she folded the paper. "I'll let you know what's happening whenever I find out. Come over tomorrow, after I pack, and we'll have a cup of coffee then."

* * *

"Len."

"What?"

"The doctor's office called today. Michael has to go to Seattle for tests three days from now."

"That's crazy. They can do the tests in Everett. Phone them up and tell them you want them done here."

"No. They have arranged an exam by a specialist, too. They have to be done in Seattle at Children's Hospital. I need money enough to stay for a few days."

"That kid is nothing but trouble."

Len threw four twenties down on the table. "There. That will have to be good enough. Don't waste it."

Len was angry again. Jennifer heard rocks hitting the house as Len spun out in the pickup and roared down the driveway, throwing dirt and gravel behind him. She had never liked having people's attention drawn to her. Lennard almost seemed to enjoy having people look at him. Their neighbors in the Seattle apartment had heard everything that went on. She would cringe and ask, 'can we talk quieter?', and he'd say, 'So what! Let 'em hear.' As for riding with him, she usually arranged another way. She was terrorized by his driving.

* * *

The boy and his grandfather had finished chopping the wood and splitting the kindling – enough for the next day's fire in the old kitchen stove. They carried the wood to the house. The boy reached down and petted their Border Collie, and asked, "Grandpa, can we take Danny for a run in the fields, and maybe even go down to the creek?"

"Sure." The boy looked up at his grandpa with appreciation in his eyes. They finished their work and started into the field.

During school there hadn't been time for long walks. Now they had free time to roam over the farm land. Once they had owned a herd of sheep. Two large fields had been reserved for hay. In another pasture a string of milk cows had grazed. Now there was one. Those farm days were over, but the old man, his daughter, and her son got along on a pension and money from her housecleaning and selling butter. Their greater pleasure was in each other. And it shone on the faces of the boy and the old gentleman.

Len came to an open stretch of road and floored the gas pedal. He had no idea how fast he was going when the black and white dog ran out. He lifted his foot from the gas as he heard the thud. A man and boy were running to the dog before Len could slow down and stop in a cloud of dust. He angrily jammed the gearshift into reverse, backed up, and stuck his head out of the window.

"You ought to keep your stupid mutt off the road," he yelled.

"I realize it's our fault he ran out." The man was kneeling, the dog's head was resting on the man's arm, its body stretched out, limp. With the other arm the man hugged the sobbing boy. "We had just taken off his leash for a run in our field when he saw a rabbit and chased it onto the road. My grandson was running after him pretty close. You were going awfully fast. I'm glad the boy didn't make it onto the road."

"What do you mean," Len yelled, "'going fast'. If your stupid mongrel hadn't been out there, he wouldn't have got hit." Len got out, menacing fists clenched, shoulders held stiff. He slammed the pickup door. The man rose to his feet, with one hand guiding the boy behind him.

"I'm simply saying that you were going far too fast." The old man's voice had an even, authoritative tone, and he looked steadily into Lennard's eyes. He then bent toward the still form of the purebred Border Collie. Len couldn't keep his eyes from following. He saw the dog. The man's next words hung in the quiet air. "That could be a child laying there, dead. Though we're upset to lose our dog, there's nothing to be done about that. We don't want money. We can't replace Danny. I just want you to think about your speeding. *That's all.*" The emphasis, like an order, hit Len.

"Oh, you do? Do you?" Stepping forward, Len sneered in the man's face. "You want to make a big deal out of it. I bet you *do* want money. Stupid mongrel, that's all it is. My driving is *just fine.*"

"Just take note of it. You were driving *too fast.*" The grandfather barely got the words out of his mouth. Len drove his fist into the man's face. He fell backwards at the feet of the boy, blood spurting from his nose.

The boy dropped down beside him, screaming, "No! No! Don't kill him." His terror-filled eyes turned upon Len, pleading.

The old man gathered himself, and unsteadily stood to his feet. "What's the idea?" he asked Len. Blood flowed down the man's chin. "All I said was 'You're driving too fast' and you can't admit it?" The next blow struck his jaw before he saw it coming. He went down. Pieces of broken teeth were mingled with blood in his mouth. He spit and looked up. *Thank God,* he thought, as the crazy driver went striding to his pickup. The boy was bawling, and he turned to reassure him.

Len hopped up, then turned and yelled at the boy, "Go get your ma." When he drove away, the spinning tires threw gravel at the three figures.

The Washington State Patrol car pulled up to the Sigurdsen house. Officer Larson got out and went to the door. When Sonja answered, he said, "I understand you have reported a case of 'extremely dangerous driving', to use your own words. Is that right?"

"Yes, Officer. Please come in. I wasn't there. You'll want to talk to my father."

The officer came into the kitchen and quietly took the chair offered him. Mr. Sigurdsen came in holding an ice pack to his face. He had changed from his bloody shirt. Introductions were made. "Mr. Sigurdsen, do I understand that you have something to report?"

"Yes, sir, I do. My grandson and I both witnessed it, but I'd rather be the one to tell it, and not put him through questioning, if that's all right. He's in his room, crying for his dog that was just killed."

"That will work. I only need your report. May I ask if his dog's death was a part of this incident?"

"Yes. Besides killing the dog, the man did a job on me, too."

"What do you mean, sir?" The officer gave him an intent look as he held his pen in mid-air.

"The man was speeding." Mr. Sigurdsen went on to describe how it took place. With the help of the questions the officer asked, Sven recounted in order what happened.

"This is dangerous driving, alright, but it's more than that. It's assault. Are you willing to press charges?"

"Yes. To save other people. That man's not normal."

"Good. But to arrest him, we have to find him first. Though we don't have a license plate number, the description of the pickup is a help. Would you recognize it?"

"Oh, yes. I certainly would."

"Well, then, thank you Mr. Sigurdsen. And thanks to your daughter, too. I'm sorry about the boy's dog. And sir, I think you should get in to see a doctor."

"Oh, I plan to. Probably a dentist, too." He said with a good-natured chuckle.

The patrolman shook his head. *Tough farmer*, he thought. *He's a solid old one. Now that I see his face I can't believe what a beating he took. No wonder he had an ice pack. I wouldn't have had him answer any questions till later if I'd seen. It's a wonder he hasn't passed out talking to me.*

Fifteen minutes after he'd come, Officer Larson left with concern knitting his brow. As he drove down the road he thought, *This isn't just a dangerous driving report. This jerk could do a lot more damage in the future. He will be big trouble. Maybe he was intoxicated or on drugs, maybe not. One thing is for sure; he could become violent again, with no provocation. Who knows what the consequence would be next time?* His grim expression deepened, and he made a promise to himself. *If I have anything to do with it, he won't stay incognito for long.*

* * *

When Jennifer came home she saw a note on the table that Michael had written:

Mom, Len phoned and said to tell you – He won't have the use of that pickup any more. It didn't work out to buy it. He is looking for a bargain vehicle to drive. Doesn't know when he'll be back. Might go to California to buy one, and get work.
Love, Michael

The answer had finally come to the one question that had been gnawing at Jen. *Len "doesn't know when he'll be back." He probably won't come back. He was clear how he feels about Michael.* He had been distant. Wouldn't explain much when he left. Just said it was another trip to Seattle. Said he was laid off work for a week. Fire-hazard restrictions were on again and crew sizes were reduced, so he might as well be in Seattle. When he said earlier he expected a complete mill shutdown, it didn't ring true. *So now I have no idea what will happen with his bills. They will probably be sent out here. All I can do is return them,* "Not at this address." *In the past, I've learned not to count on him, but I'm really in a lurch now.* She had wondered, when he left, if he planned to keep checking with the mill. Now she saw he hadn't even planned to return home. *Home –* that word again. So now she might need to swallow her pride and apply for government assistance. No. She wasn't desperate. If only she could get a job.

The next day she checked the help-want ads for anything, even jobs she wasn't qualified for. One caught her attention. It was a job cleaning a greenhouse and transplanting for the fall sales. "Heavy work" it said. *I can do it. After all, I carried heavy stacks of dishes for years.* When she phoned, the man hired her, sight unseen, and asked if she could start the following week. That would be perfect – after the hospital checkup.

* * *

Michael was looking worn out by the time they reached the hospital. At Registration they learned it was a long 'hike' to the lab where they were to check in, so a wheelchair was offered. It hit Jen hard to see Michael in it. After blood was drawn, they waited until a pleasant doctor called them in. He took a history from Jen, though he already had the records that were sent to him. After examining Michael, he wrote an order for more tests, and simply said he would need to see the results and would like to have Michael stay for two more days. She was discouraged. She'd learned nothing that the G.P. hadn't already said. Michael was admitted.

After seeing Michael settled in his new room, then going with a nurse who gave a quick tour, she said goodbye. Michael needed to nap before he had a scan.

Jen found a phone. The house for parents had an opening for one night only. She would run out of money at this rate. The bus hadn't been cheap. There was the ticket home to buy. At least one night, probably two, in a hotel. She took a Seattle Metro to a nearby area that had restaurants. One by one she entered and asked if they could use an experienced waitress for fill-in. Finally she found work to start the next morning at five a.m. They paid cash. She didn't ask why no paper signing for Workmen's Compensation, etc.

Jen took another bus to an area of hotels she could afford. Finding a decent one, she reserved a room for the next day. Then she got the bus back to the hospital area and the parents' house.

Jen laughed to herself. The parents' house was everything anyone could ask for. *Too bad I can't just volunteer here, and live in it permanently! Have Michael go to school in Seattle.* But she remembered how happy they had both been in the country.

The next day, after working at the restaurant, she was glad to say she would come in again the following morning. Jen left, and walked through a little business district, saw a florist, and went in.

"Hello," Jen greeted the pleasant looking lady. "I only need a few cut flowers, not an arrangement. I guess I actually need a grocery store. Is there one that sells cut flowers in the area?"

Jen got directions and started to leave when a Help Wanted sign caught her eye. She stepped back in and inquired.

"We are willing to train someone, but you should be able to commit to long-term employment. It's a permanent position." That settled that.

Finding a little bunch of daisies in a store, she also saw the perfect mini-card – a smiling frog. Just right for Michael.

At the hospital, as she came past the volunteer's desk, she saw a sign that read, "Do not bring fresh flowers due to allergies." She set the daisies on the desk and left, since the lady was talking to someone. *Ah, well. That fell through.*

She took the card to Michael, who was in good spirits.

"I had a scan," he said. "The people here are really nice. I got lots of good food." He admitted he didn't eat all of it. They took a walk, and played games. He tired out fast. The afternoon went quickly. He needed to rest. It was time to go. She felt numb when the nurse said that he should not have an evening visit.

As she left, Jen realized she was tired from her early morning. One thing cheered her, unexpectedly. As she went out, the same volunteer lady called to her, and handed her the forbidden daisies. Thanking the woman, she thought of Sylvie. *That's something she'd have done when she was a teenage Candy Striper.* It brought a smile to Jen's face.

The job gave her enough money to pay for the hotel. Fortunately both were on a bus line to the hospital. Too tired to think, she got to her room, and then wondered why she hadn't eaten a hamburger on the way. She knew of a chancy-looking cafe nearby. That would have to be the answer tonight.

"My name is Tyler." A voice behind her called as she left the hotel. "I'm heading out for a bite to eat. May I suggest a better café this direction, if that's what you're looking for?"

"Oh, well, I guess so. I'll be here for only a short time. I don't know the area." She felt clever, getting in the 'short time' part. If he was a flirt, he wouldn't bother.

"On the next block is one that does a home-cooked meal.

Cleaner, too."

"Oh. Good"

"Mind if I walk with you? We don't need to sit together, once we're there."

"Sure. I'm just here for a couple days. I have a ten-year old son in Children's Hospital," she began. *Get things on a motherly, domestic footing,* she thought. They chatted on the way. He said he came to the city on a regular cycle with his work. They sat together at the cafe, after all. There seemed to be no flirtation intended. At the hotel when they returned, they parted in the lobby. No question asked as to room location.

Jen's room was adequate. She slept soundly after taking a bath. She had to be up early to work.

The following morning she arrived at the hospital early to meet the doctor.

"I am releasing Michael. No definitive answer shows in tests so far. It's too soon to say. The scan results will be sent to your doctor when they have been analyzed thoroughly."

Fine, she thought. *Lots of good this is doing.*

* * *

Michael slept on the bus going home. She thought of the old 'useless' car Len left behind, and wondered if it would do the odd short trip just a little longer. Jen realized she needed to tell Sylvie the whole story – that Len was gone. It was already arranged for Michael to stay at Sylvie's when Jen was at work. But no mention had been made of Len. Once at home, she settled Michael for a nap and phoned Sylvie.

"How did it go? What did you find out?"

"Not much. Doctor said it was hard to narrow down. That they'd send any results they find. I don't know. Seems like an exercise in uselessness."

"Oh, I'm sorry Jen. Surely the tests will help, somehow. How did you make out for housing?"

"Quite well." Jen heard Sylvie's relieved, 'ah'. "I appreciate you giving me that info so much. The parents' facility was perfect. When that was full, I got a decent hotel for a good rate. Some kind of discount when it's for medical visits."

"That's great! I'm glad it worked out. Now, when do you go to work?"

"Tomorrow. So will it be okay for Michael to come over to your place at seven-thirty in the morning?"

"Definitely. Glad to help a little."

"It's a big help. I appreciate this so much. Len has left and I don't know when or if he's coming back"

The next morning Jen got up, got herself ready, and then bundled Michael over to Sylvie's house. She gave a house key to Sylvie in case she needed something for Michael. As the bus carried her along, she thought how Sylvie said she would not accept anything for keeping Michael. She wondered what she could do to thank her.

Once at the greenhouse, Jen didn't have time to think. She was focused on trying to absorb too much new information. She saw the layout of the potting sheds and where the supplies were kept. Then learned how she was to do the tasks. Their spring rush of annuals was tapering off. First of all was cleaning and disinfecting. Then re-potting young perennials into bigger pots so they'd grow and sell for a higher price. There were two other workers who didn't talk much. By the end of that first day, her back ached. But she wasn't surprised or sorry; just glad for the job.

CHAPTER THIRTY-THREE

J en saw the riddle book on the floor where Michael had dropped it when he fell asleep. As she picked it up, it brought a smile. *Michael – always using his brain. I'm so proud of him.* She shook her head. *I can imagine it made him feel good when he baffled his mom with that riddle. I'll have to tell Sylvie how happy he was, telling me that he tripped her up, too.*

Jen pulled up his covers, then went down to take a shower. She would perk up – could get some housework done before going to bed. The greenhouse work took it out of her. But after a week of work, she knew she could do it. She was glad she and Michael had the hours after work together. She'd have to stick to a tight schedule to keep up with the house, full-time work, and spending time with him each day. School would start soon. Sylvie said he could get his homework done in the afternoon at her place, and that she'd enjoy helping him. Hopefully he would stay on top of it.

* * *

Finally. A day off. Jeremy had arrived to visit Michael. They would be fine together, so Jen decided she'd take Sylvie up on the invitation for coffee. She walked into Sylvie's kitchen and gasped when she saw colors spread across the kitchen table.

"Oh! That is so beautiful! Like a quilt." Pieces of Christmas-motif fabric in the usual background colors of green, red or white covered the table. To one side were skeins of embroidery floss, spread in a colorful array, like a mini peacock. Narrow ribbons spilled from a paper bag. Sylvie picked them up and was spreading them across the fabric – blue, dark green, red with gold edges, and blue with silver-edges. They flowed like country roads over fields filled with tiny trees, candy canes, holly sprigs and stars.

"Oh! It's beautiful. So dainty!" Jen gazed, taking in details. Slowly, she shook her head. "Where did you get pieces of Christmas fabric? They aren't in the stores now, are they?"

"No. I've gathered them over the last few years. I grab remnants at Christmas-time, or better yet, just afterward, when the prices are marked 'way down. It's fun to rummage through clearance bins and get bargains. Nice to have them on hand. I have been thinking about the quilting we saw at the Fair. Thought we could try some. But I know real quilting can be frustrating and time-consuming. A few years ago, I tried. My first quilt blocks were okay, but I used them on a pillow top. I had sown such small seam allowances that it came apart in a few weeks. You can imagine how upset I was after putting hours into it."

Sylvia held up a multi-color ball, a Christmas ornament. "But take a look at this. I made it a couple years ago, after seeing a friend's. I thought you and I might make some now. The Craft Fair got me in the mood."

Jenny reached out and took the ball. It consisted of tiny, irregularly-shaped panels, like windows, but pooched out like pillows. "This is delightful!" Each window was a tiny motif, a candy cane on green background, a bunch of holly on white, or a little star, bright against a deep blue.

"I'm surprised it is so lightweight. What is it made of? And how?"

Sylvia uncovered a box of foam balls she used as the foundation. "I'll show you! Would you like to try it?"

"Oh, yes! Is it hard to do?"

"No." Sylvie picked up the scissors. "You just cut a tiny piece of fabric. Best to make them irregular. You press them into place, one window at a time." She held the piece on the foam ball. "Using a dull object, like the end of a teaspoon handle or a small dull knife, poke the edge of the cloth into the foam. It makes a trough, or channel, where the fabric stays. Work around it until all the edges are pressed into the foam ball. You have your first window. Make another irregular-shape window beside it as you press the next piece into the same channel, on one side of the first. Add one piece after another, cutting each the shape you want. Each time, start in one of the grooves already used. If edges come out, we can use some glue. It's not normally needed, though."

"I think I can do that!" Jen picked up a tiny piece with miniature green holly leaves and red berries on a white background. She pressed an edge into the foam ball, keeping one eye on Sylvie. "Why, it's not too hard. I wonder if Michael would like to try this. He needs some quiet projects." *No, I don't want to think about anything serious. Not for a little while, at least.* She hastened to ask about calligraphy symbols on a jade and raspberry piece.

"Yes. We can have Michael over here to try it, or you can show him at home."

"Maybe he'd like to do it when he is here, after school, if he has the pep."

"I'd enjoy that with him. He's sure good. Fun to have here. But take some stuff home, anyhow, in that empty box to show him. Pick out fabric pieces you think he'd like. I'll scare up some yardage pieces with kid motifs. When he comes, he can mix them in with Christmas. Speaking of that, I'm going to put on some Christmas music." She grinned sheepishly. "I know. It's kind of early for it!" She laughed. "I love Christmas music anytime, but I usually restrain myself until autumn. Isn't it okay today, though, while we work on these?"

Jen just smiled, and said, "Sure." *Christmas. I wonder what it will be like this year. I usually dread it* – and she pushed the memories away.

Engrossed in choosing and cutting out bits of cloth as the music played in the background, Jen was surprised at how quickly her first ornament went together. "I can't believe this!" She held it up.

"How pretty! I like your choices of fabrics – how you placed them. Light next to dark. Fussy with plain. Each one stands out, and yet it's not confusing to look at the whole." She took it, and held it up. "Isn't that nice!"

"I have to admit I like it. May I do another?"

"Oh, of course.

The music stopped as a CD finished. Another began that Jen noticed was not Christmas music. It had a familiar melody. Memories returned from when her Aunt Sally played records. It sounded Hawaiian or Maori. Words came to mind. "Now is the hour..." But the words being sung were, "Search me, O God, and know my heart today; Try me, O Savior, know my thoughts, I pray. See if there be some wicked way in me; Cleanse me from every sin, and set me free."

Jen wondered, *Why such frightening words? Who wants a God who can see right through you, looking for sin? As for wicked ways, I suppose I have had plenty of them. Know my thoughts? No, thank you, I'd rather You didn't. Just go away... that would be better.* The song finished, but a phrase lingered "...set me free."

Another song began. "Lord, you are more precious than silver." Sylvia began humming along. "Lord, you are more costly than gold. Lord, you are more beautiful than diamonds. And nothing in this world compares to you." She looked up at Jen, smiled, and said, "I love those words."

* * *

Jen stood in her upstairs closet, among things packed away. It put her in a mood to rummage, and she pulled out one box that caught her eye. Memories of Aunt Sally's 'mothering' came back, as she unwrapped tissue and saw the small plaster Christmas ornaments. Her own childish hand-painting was on them, sloppy and too bright. She remembered being proud she had made them. Dear Aunt Sally – times with her had been precious. She worked full-time. Busy as she was, and even after she had moved, she managed to have Jennifer come out once in a while. Sally's children sometimes popped in, but were often with their own friends.

Jen looked at the sloppy paint smeared outside the lines. She remembered how she had looked forward to hanging them on whatever tree her mother managed to get. But instead her mother ridiculed them. *I admit they weren't works of art. It was all I could do.* She felt the shame again. They were awful. She covered them with tissue paper. Why she kept them, she didn't know. So many memories – good ones, bad ones. *But this Christmas can be different. I can bring in greenery that I cut from lower tree branches in the woods. The Dollar Store will have cheap ribbon. I'll tie it on the greens and make a swag for the door. And smaller arrangements can sit around the house, maybe by a chair – a place of quietness. A place to sit and listen to music. I like to look through the colorful holiday ads. I can already smell the nice evergreen fragrance.*

* * *

Jen phoned over to say that she needed to borrow baking powder. Sylvia's Bible was on the table when she walked in.

"I've been reading. I want to show a neat verse to you. It's in Proverbs. I thought of all your responsibilities when I read it. It's "A merry heart does good like a medicine." I guess I worry about you – I want you to have some "merry heart" medicine! I wish we could take Michael on your day off and go down to Everett. We'd have some laughs together, some window shopping."

"I'm sorry. I don't think I can now. But it's nice of you to think of it."

"Okay. Oh, I meant to ask if you'd learned who Michael's teacher will be, before he goes in tomorrow?"

"Yes, we checked. It's Ian Logan."

"Ah, yes! He's a great teacher! I know him personally. He's just as nice as he seems. I think Michael will like him very much."

Jen and Sylvie went out, and she started down the steps, saying, "Thanks again for the baking powder. Right in the middle of a recipe; what a time to run out. You saved me!" Sylvie laughed. Jen took a deep breath. She went on. "You are light-hearted. Easy to... well, you make me feel at ease. But I'd better get back to baking. Bye."

"Talk to you on the phone." Sylvia watched her go, and thought, *Light-hearted. I'm certainly not always. And little does she know how it bothers me to see her more and more burdened, worrying. Michael's not well. Barely making ends meet. What a picture, "light-hearted" - compared to a heavy heart.*

As Jenny stepped onto her driveway, she was surprised to see a pickup she didn't recognize parked there, and Len coming out of the house. "Oh, I'm surprised to see you."

"Yeah, I needed a few things before I left for California." She looked at the suitcase he carried, and the laundry basket, stacked with bread, canned goods, boxes of crackers, and his jeans. She skipped commenting on the basket or the foodstuff in it.

"Will you be able to use that pickup for the trip?"

"No." He couldn't see over the armload of stuff. He tripped on Goldie. Cursing, he raised his boot and stomped her paw. Yelping in pain, she limped away on three legs.

"Why did you do that?" Jen asked angrily.

"I almost fell. Can't you see? I hate that mutt. Always in the way."

Jen knew, after raising her voice at him, that she was safe only because Len's arms were full. After he put the things in the passenger side he went the long way around the pickup to get in. Watching him, she saw the big picture of that move – that was his way of avoiding her, showing how separated from her he was. And she was glad. There had been no goodbye hugs for a long, long time. There never were hugs of the kind she saw other couples enjoy. She certainly didn't want a hug now. He started the engine and took off.

* * *

Marie clenched the phone tightly as she listened to her sister. "So Mother has been having these pains for weeks? And the doctor did nothing? Well, yes, I'm glad she was going to him, at least. But why aren't they getting answers? Good. Just a second; I'll get a pencil. What is the date again for a specialist appointment? All right, yes, I understand – I won't need to come back there now. So they think it is gall bladder or pancreas or what? Well, okay. Please phone as soon as you have any ideas. I guess it sounds worse at a distance. I can't see her face and talk with her. Lately I felt like she was being vague about how she was doing. Now I know why. Thanks so much for calling. Oh, of course I realize she can't come visit. Well, then, I'll wait to hear from you. I love you, too. Thanks again. Bye."

Marie set down the phone. What disappointing news. No wonder her mother had put off booking a plane ticket to come out for a fall visit. She was sick and in pain. Now, at least, she would get the tests and specialist visit she needed. Coming to visit just wasn't going to work out for quite a while. Marie looked at Emalie who was playing happily in her special corner where her playthings were kept, and sadness came over her. When would her mother get to see this little darling for herself? The most recent visit had been last Christmas. Phone calls and pictures were a poor substitute for real life cuddles and talks, and watching a child play in her own home.

After Marie phoned to tell her the news, Sylvie walked around her living room, sorting her thoughts. Marie felt it wasn't possible to go back now to see her mother, but when would it work out? If Mrs. Rodriguez didn't need surgery, or it was the non-invasive method, she might be able to come at Christmas. It was wait and see.

PART FOUR
PAIN

September – October

CHAPTER THRITY-FOUR

Jennifer Brown sat in her upstairs hideaway, holding her journal. She had begun anew in May, when she moved. She looked at it, disgusted with herself. *I haven't kept it up. At least I jotted notes about the garden. If I can afford to stay here, that will give me a better start on next year's garden. As for real journaling, it has just been too confusing lately. But I jotted some personal bits. They may be of interest in the future.*

She turned to the first page, where she had listed poems by page number. *I sure haven't written poetry for ages.* A small calendar picture of a flower garden was tucked in. She had cut it out with high hopes. But the flowers she had planted had struggled in the rocky soil. Some had been flattened when Goldie lay on them repeatedly. Forgetting to water them hadn't helped, and she had refused having Sylvie water for her. She'd become preoccupied with Len, and then Michael's issues. Too much.

Jen turned to lay the journaling notebook on the little table, scooting some papers to one side. That uncovered the booklet on co-dependency given her by Maggie at the Deli Diner. She had read some of it during the summer. *Hmm. At least understanding co-dependency helps me understand my situation a little. My own unhealthy needs are part of it. Feeling like tip-toeing around Len. At the same time, some of the ideas makes me laugh. What a ridiculous suggestion, to 'Confront unacceptable behavior'. Sure! Like I'm suppose to say, "We MUST pay these bills!" or "Len, get up off your butt and pay the bills." Yeah – right. I remember just using mild firmness. It got me a black eye. At least, in one way, things got better here. In Seattle he was careless about bruises – no neighbors noticing, being friendly, or asking questions. The booklet had suggestions to get better father-child relationships. Between him and Michael? I didn't even try to go there.* She put the journal and the booklet in a box. Seemed like it was over, anyhow.

Sylvia knocked on Jen's door Sunday afternoon, and stood, waiting. When the door opened, she was surprised how dragged out Jen looked.

"Oh, Jen, I hope I didn't get you up from a nap?"

"No. Come on in." She stepped back listlessly.

The house was dark, but she saw Michael on the couch. "Well, Hello, young man," she said.

"Hello, Sylvia." He didn't sit up.

"I'm sorry I disturbed your rest."

"That's okay." He looked exhausted.

"I guess you don't feel like asking me a riddle, eh?"

"No. I don't have one today. I'm sorry."

"Oh, Michael, don't be sorry. But when you're ready, I'll be ready for it! Bring your book to my house. I'll try really hard to think of the right answers."

Michael simply smiled. Maybe he had that awful flu going around. He acted too tired to talk.

Sylvie realized that Jen didn't look like she was up to having company, either. *But, it seems like she sure needs cheering up. I guess she'd say so if she wanted me here.* "Well... I didn't mean to disturb you. I guess you must have had a bad night, eh?" Jen nodded. "Come over to my place later, okay? Any time."

"Alright. Thanks." Jen answered with little interest. "Sorry to be a deadhead."

Now what? They both had looked much better Friday when she picked up Michael. If she is too tired to visit with me, what can I do? Nothing? Be content just making a place for Michael? Could be she is reacting to Len leaving. Sounds like he's gone for good. Mixed feelings, maybe. But what's the answer on Michael?

Jenny phoned a couple hours later, wanting to come for a quick cup of tea. To Sylvie her voice sounded closer to normal.

Jen settled herself; Sylvie poured. "I'm so glad you called back and came."

"I haven't much time, but I had to let you know – it's not lack of wanting to come. Just that it truly was a bad night. Friday wasn't good either. Right now I have to keep my eye on the clock, get back home. But maybe this week I can stay a little while when I come for Michael after work. Not tomorrow. I hope he's better in the morning; good enough to go to school. Third day of classes. What a start on the school year."

"So... since there's no word yet on Michael's tests, I guess it's the waiting game..."

"Mm-hmm. I expect a call soon. I hope. It's hard – seeing how Michael gets worn out more quickly as time passes."

"How did he do in school?"

"He loves Mr. Logan. You were right. I talked a bit with him. Explained that Michael had no strong father figure – except Larry Ford! He remembered you folks. Said Larry would be good for him. That he'd also encourage Michael as opportunity came."

"Oh, I knew he would!"

"I'm worried that he might not even have the energy to go to the classroom to do his work. But Mr. Logan said, if necessary, Michael is capable of keeping up from home. He could come to school for tests, or as often as he's able. I think it's a poor way to start a new year. I don't want him to get behind, or miss the socializing, either."

* * *

Michael looked down at the book. He saw that the other kids had finished their assigned reading, and were enjoying free time, talking quietly. *I can't concentrate... what did I just read? Why won't my brain work?* He looked up at Mr. Logan, who caught his eye and smiled.

* * *

Sylvia was in the middle of her lunch when the phone rang. She was glad when call display showed it was Marie. She had encouraged her to keep in touch when she had a free moment, knowing she was getting over the disappointment of her mom's canceled visit.

"Sylvie, I'm excited! I had to tell you. Mark has been going down to a refuge for women in downtown Seattle, the south end. New Beginnings it's called – a residence and drop-in center. There's another one for men. Mark was told about it by a guy at work. He went in and got the necessary police check, and he's been going there to do carpentry and odd jobs. He comes home and tells me about it. He's been touched. Most are single moms, some with kids. Some are trying to get a fresh start. They have lost custody of their kids for various reasons."

"That is really sad. I can't imagine."

"Mark said he had no idea that life was so rough for these women. Some are struggling to stay off drugs and alcohol. Many moms are working hard, learning personal and job skills, getting a diploma. They hope to get their kids back. I got interested. So, guess what! Last Friday I took Emalie to a friend's place and went with him. Wow, did I get my eyes opened. While he was in the back, unloading some donated goods, I talked with two of the women. I always thought, *"oh, they could get a job if they wanted."* I never really thought it through. So many of them have inadequate education. Touching personal stories. Some bad decisions were made. I woke up to the fact that it's not about checking up on how things *were*. It's not about me moralizing. It's "now" that's important. Help a woman. Give her a hand up to a new way of life. She's been through 'who knows what'. I saw such sincerity in these two... wanting with all their hearts to make the future better than the past. Especially wanting their children's lives to be better. The director talked with me, and the next day I sat in on an informal meeting for volunteers. One said, "If they choose to leave here too soon, it's a legitimate choice. As hard as it is, we have to "let them go, and let God", as the A.A. people say. We trust that a woman has gotten something good here to take with her. Maybe she'll return if she needs to. If she goes back to self-destructive living, we can at least hope and pray that a 'reality check' will come. That the woman will wake up and say, *"I can't do this anymore. I will go where I can get help."* Oh, Sylvie, I am looking forward to getting some training and helping out."

"Oh, Marie! This is interesting news. You're expanding your horizons. I knew you cared about people. Even though you're busy with Emalie, I bet it's a good feeling to help others."

"It is. I'm eager to go back. If you want to come, I'd sure welcome the help watching Emalie. My friend can only keep her sometimes. If you come we could take her with us. You could meet some of the ladies."

Sylvia thought, *I don't know about Emalie going. Could be a rough place for a toddler. We can talk about it. Marie says, "Ladies". It's so nice to call them ladies, when they probably don't feel like they have any dignity. It reminds me of the poor women in India that my uncle pointed out when I was there. He said they believed that they were way down the social ladder, below a good donkey. Some of the husbands were okay. Mostly the wives did the work, at home or out. If ever they had land, it had been lost through debt for seed and fertilizer. One had to admit it was hard for men to get regular jobs. It was mostly day-labor, and too many for too few jobs. Many women didn't even have husbands, and a woman widowed or rejected was nobody. What a place to be born. So Mark is here, at this New Beginnings, helping our struggling ones in America. I'm surprised he has the time, but it's good.*

She voiced her thoughts, "So Mark is involved. I'm glad he has fulfillment besides his work life. Work doesn't always do it!"

"Oh, he does feel that way – and it is fulfilling. He very much looks forward to going. He's changed. He seems more tender toward me because of what he has seen." Sylvia stiffened at the implication. Marie continued, "I guess it's just a new awareness."

"I suppose it is hard for a man to put himself in a woman's place," Sylvia said. *But Mark's always been tender-hearted, sympathetic. Maybe she hasn't appreciated how good he is to her.*

"Emalie has been getting acquainted with the neighbor's new dog. It's just a puppy, and at first she was afraid of it. It's so wiggly. Now she can't leave it alone. The puppy does seem to understand innocent poking or over-zealous patting – just moves away. Some day we'll have a yard. We're not ready for a dog. But I'm glad she can get acquainted with one. So, come see us! Whether it's to make a trip down to New Beginnings, or do something else, come visit soon!"

"I'll do that! Maybe just to visit with you and Emalie this time. Let's plan on that. Oh. I just thought of something. Could you pick up some printed info on abuse and battered women? Jennifer, my neighbor, had bruises that made me concerned. I don't know how to learn whether Len did it – how to get her to talk. She seems like she's covering up. Now Len, the guy she's married to, has left her high and dry. I hope she is out of danger now. I need to learn more about it."

"Will do."

* * *

That afternoon Sylvie noticed how dragged out Michael was when he came from school. He quickly accepted the idea of laying down in the living room for a rest. When Jen came for him, he had only done half of his homework.

As Michael went out on the porch, Jen got Sylvie aside and said, "I don't think he can go in tomorrow."

"I was thinking the same. I'm glad to have him here during the day. I've nothing planned that can't wait."

"Oh, thanks! Too bad that he'll miss class time with the other kids, but I think I'd better phone Mr. Logan and tell him. I'll ask him to drop off Michael's work after school. He offered to. Said he'd bring it to your house if I'm not home yet. "

Sylvie nodded. "I don't know how much of it he will get done. He was beat today. Maybe he'll be less tired when he's not walking around school and riding the bus."

"I hope so. Thanks so much, Sylvie. I'll bring his current book and his game, too. Got to go. He's waiting on the porch. Bye."

Sylvia stood motionless after Jennifer left. Now there were no light-hearted times between them. When she moved in and they first got together, it had automatically meant good times. They had been drawn together from the beginning, and their friendship showed signs that it would last over the years. It was hard to believe that they had only met in May. She remembered that day she heard their truck arriving, and went over to greet them. Sylvia smiled as she recalled how astonished Jen was, that a woman she'd just met would want to help. In a short time they were sharing their thoughts, getting Jen settled. But Len... she made an effort to accept the man. No doubt, she thought, there had been serious trouble all the time, not just what she saw. After a time there were serious conversations with Jen as she shared her worries, her childhood pain, her attitudes about religion.

Sylvia sat down. She felt nauseated to even think of what Jen had gone through. And it was a heartache to realize what it had done to her understanding of God. And maybe to her choice of a man. But then again, Jen's own father had been a kind man – a good model of a loving God. *I don't know how well I explained that God is different from what she experienced. Maybe she will let me know by questions she asks.*

Sylvia realized she had lost opportunities to visit with Jen recently. She got preoccupied with several things, like spending more time with Larry. That was important. Typing college papers that Nadine emailed, including suggested corrections, had taken time. Nadine had worked full-time, taken summer classes, and was now in the fall term. Yard work was heavy through summer and early fall. Too bad Jen wouldn't let her come help with her yard. Said it was her 'project'. She wanted to see if she could do it herself. And now Jen was working full time.

Getting out together, taking walks with Jen, laughing, and talking had been so good. It was mentally stimulating and physically refreshing. Now Jen was worn out from work and worry. Sylvie thought of how Michael had looked, lying on the couch. Though he'd been 'under the weather' before, he hadn't looked like this. Starting to miss school... Sylvie shook her head. *How difficult for Jenny to watch her son weaken and not know why. She must be sick at heart, worrying. I remember how I felt when my children just ran a fever a few days. This is going on and on.*

* * *

Jenny tore open the letter she had written to her sister, Patsy. It had been returned. When she wrote, she had been in the mood to communicate. Even though it was a slim chance the post office could deliver it to Patsy, it felt like a contact. Jen began reading. It was like a diary. "The homes here are far enough apart. I don't have to feel I must hide from neighbors' prying ears and eyes. I have nobody living on one side. On the other are good neighbors. I wish this place was our own. Why Len talks like he is losing his job, I don't know. Maybe I should go to town and listen for the latest gossip! Find out if the mill is laying off permanently. If they aren't, I guess I will still be in the dark, wondering if Len's gotten himself in trouble. And wondering what he's thinking of doing next. "

Jen folded the paper and shook her head with a rueful expression. *I don't need to try and figure that one out now. Funny how quickly things change – just since this made a round trip in the mail, Len is gone. California again, and, according to the last message, he'll stay... indefinitely.*

CHAPTER THIRTY-FIVE

After breakfast on Saturday, when Michael had showered, he lay down on the couch to rest in the basement room. Jen entered from the laundry area with an armful of clean clothes and spread them over Michael's blanket.

"Son, you are buried in a snowdrift!" she said, and sat down to fold them.

"Sure, Mom!" He humored her. He wadded a towel while she was looking down, then threw it, startling her. "Snowball!" Before she could return a wad, he said, "Mom, you know that movie of Lassie, when she found a lost lamb out in the hills. Do you think a dog could do that?"

"Yes, she could. She's a shepherd-type dog. When I first saw it, I doubted it, too. I had only seen ordinary dogs, figured it was make-believe. But later I heard some fantastic stories about sheep dogs. Their training is so good that they will obey a hand signal at a distance. They really take charge of the sheep. It's funny. They're bossy, like they understand that sheep are not very wise; that they know what is best for them."

"How did you hear about sheep dogs, Mom?"

"I had an uncle, well, an adopted uncle, who was a friend of my dad. He kept sheep on Vancouver Island, in Canada. He visited us when I was really little. He used to tell me about sheep dogs. How the winter storms blew off of the cold waters of the Strait of Juan de Fuca. Sometimes it was icy sleet, or it rained so heavy that the creeks flooded. He said his dogs would take the sheep to a sheltered spot even if he was not close enough to direct things. He would hurry to them as soon as he was able and they would all be fine when he arrived. Of course when I watched Lassie, I was impressed that she seemed so...so capable. It was almost uncanny how she was able to help with a problem."

"So you saw Lassie when you were young?" he shook his head, astonished.

"Yes, I watched Lassie."

"Wow! I thought the programs were really old. I figured you weren't even born."

"I guess it was re-runs of early programs." She laughed. "I wasn't born when they first filmed it. But, yes, I watched Lassie."

"When you watched it, you must have seen Timmy's family do lots of stuff together." He sat back. Dreamily he said, "Timmy must have loved to have Lassie for his very own dog, and be in that family. They seem really, really happy. I guess long ago families were like that. Like the way Sylvia must have had it as a kid. They didn't yell a lot and have bad fights, did they." He said it as a statement, not even needing an answer.

"I've got to put the towels away," Jenny said, and left the room, tears springing into her eyes. She blinked hard to make the tears fall, so she could see. *Oh, God. I mean it, God... if you're there, show me answers.* That was the extent of her prayer. *Anyway,* she thought, *is God there? Probably not.*

Oh, no! Goldie has dug another hole! Jen stepped off the porch to look closer. *Just when I get a few flowers to bloom – get one thing upgraded – two other problems come along. This place is hopeless; these rotten porch boards remind me every time I step outside.* The day before, when Jen had scrubbed at mold on the wood windowsill in Michael's room, her fingers sank down into the soft, spongy wood – rotten wood. On top of it all, there was the heating problem. A couple of nights were chilly, so the furnace came on. In summer Larry had mentioned to Len the name of an oil delivery service, but Len said it was all taken care of, he had a name from the landlord. Larry said, "Good, because if it runs very low on oil it will be down to the sludge in the tank bottom, and that might mess up the furnace, requiring a repairman. Jen didn't know how to check the level. Len was gone. She wouldn't be asking Larry – he was busy with longer hours and more trips away from home. *I should have the oil man come, get half a tank at least. There's some savings in the bank from the greenhouse job. Wonder how much it costs.*

Jen crossed the rotten porch and went in the house. The morning had dragged by. It was Sunday. Michael had read and then slept. She wondered if he'd feel like going to school tomorrow.

Yesterday, when Sylvia asked me to come for coffee this morning, I didn't want to make the effort. It's a good thing; I'm still in my robe. What a slob. I've gotten nothing accomplished all morning. A bigger reason to tell her no, it's my turn to have her over here. Maybe when I get on top of this living room mess, I can. Needs some deep cleaning. I can't believe the amount of dirt and mud that came in after the last rainstorm. And I want to think of myself as a particular person...

Jenny looked over at the sink, stacked with dirty dishes – another mess she should dig into. And the containers of old food in the back of the fridge... by now they were growing green or black 'hair'. Needed to be thrown out. Probably the containers, too. *I'm so far behind. I think I can work and support us and keep up at home? I can't even keep my fridge clean.* She remembered the restaurant on the highway where she had gotten a couple shifts. When the greenhouse laid her off for winter, she might get more work there. Maybe even banquets and Christmas parties. *But what makes me think I can work, plus deal with doctors' appointments,* and *be home with Michael on days Sylvie can't, because that will happen.* Jen reached down and picked up a piece of paper from the floor. On it, in Michael's writing, was a list of words: square, quail, qualms, qua, written under the heading, Good 'q' Scrabble Words. *Too bad to let that go like we have,* she thought. *He enjoyed it so.*

Jen shuffled down to the basement to do more laundry that had piled up. Ruefully she thought how that was something she usually enjoyed. The next two hours dragged by. She sorted laundry, washed, dried, and folded part of it. Some she spread out lightly wherever there was an empty surface in order to come back later to fold it when she had time. When she peeked in on Micheal, he was sleeping soundly. A puzzle book from Michael's school library caught her eye. It lay dropped onto the sleeping bag spread on the floor. That was where, when he felt better, he used to stretch out and read.

* * *

Sylvie picked up her phone to call Jen, and then set it down, thinking, *I don't need to call and invite her over. I'll go there instead.* She grabbed her sweater and went across to Jen's path, as she'd come to call it.

Sylvia knocked. Jen opened her door and a surprised, almost shocked expression filled her face. Sylvia smiled. Jen didn't.

"Oh," Jen said soberly. She stood stolidly, blocking the doorway.

"Hi! I dropped over to just say hello."

Jen moved uneasily and looked annoyed. "Oh. Well... the place is a mess. I, uhh... come on in..." She moved back. "If you want." Sylvie stepped in past Jen. Goldie was laying quietly on a blanket near the door, and she rolled her eyes toward Sylvie. There was an accumulation of dirt and mud scattered across the floor. Sylvia reached down and stroked Goldie's head, but she just groaned, and the tail-wag was missing.

"Is she feverish? Or just getting the royal treatment - becoming a house dog."

"She got an infection in that paw that was sore before. If I let her stay outside, she gets the bandage dirty in the mud. Then it needs changing."

"Oh, you sure don't want unnecessary veterinary charges."

"We didn't go. I just put peroxide on it and wrapped it myself. Have a seat."

The dog lifted her head as Sylvie passed, then laid it back down dolefully.

When Sylvie rounded the end of the couch, she saw that it was covered with newspapers, magazines and a heap of laundry to fold.

"Ah... can I fold the laundry for you?"

"Don't bother. I'll put on some coffee. Do you mind sitting at the kitchen table? Or I could move this stuff." The room was dark.

Used coffee mugs and papers cluttered the coffee table. Cast-aside garments were here and there in the room. She chanced a quick glance at Jen, who had an annoyed look on her face.

"The kitchen will be fine, Jen. You must like that kitchen, the way the sun comes in first thing in the morning, though now it's rising later. In the summer it was shining on my back porch from the northeast before I got up. Now the sun shines in the kitchen window a lot later and lower. Guess summer's over."

"Yeah, guess so."

Sylvie waited for Jen to say something. *This conversation is so tense. What is it? Is it Jen or something I've said? Or is it something about the dog? I wonder how Goldie got hurt in the first place? Why is it Jen kept saying accident, but never said what happened? Does Goldie need to go to a vet? Would I dare ask? I hope Jen's not keeping back something big, like moving away...*

Jen was occupied scooping coffee, tipping the can to get the last bit in the bottom. Sylvia started up out of her chair, saying, "I can go get some coffee at my place. I just shopped."

"No." Jen put out her hand, gesturing 'stop', and spoke in a definite tone. "There's enough here." She finished and put out two small mugs. "Sorry I don't have cookies."

"That's okay. With less work in the garden I don't need the calories. Not burning many now." Jen seemed so unresponsive; was she going to open up and talk? Sylvie knew she would have to lead the conversation. "I guess Michael must be taking a nap; it's so quiet."

"Yeah. Fell asleep reading. How is your family?"

"I'm not hearing much from Issa. Marie and Mark and Emalie are fine. Marie has been enjoying getting involved at a place called New Beginnings – kind of a women's shelter, though not a typical Safe House where men can't come around – guys help out there. Mark is helping. He enjoys it. I'm going in next week. I'd be happy, if you had the day off, and could come with me. Marie gets excited telling me about women who are making better lives. Some are learning life skills that were missing, or taking special training for a job, maybe getting free of unhealthy attachments to people who harmed them. They improve their lives in a safe, supportive setting.

Some attend classes for their GED."

"What's that?"

"Classes to get a high school diploma. And social times are important. Marie is planning and helping them put on a Christmas program. They have all expressed a desire to work on it. Some want to be backstage instead of in the 'public eye'. Marie said some experienced people have volunteered to come guide practices. One is a teacher who loves doing drama. Would you like to come with me and we'll have a coffee with the women there, with Marie?"

"That's nice for Marie. I don't think I'd be interested in going, though. No, it's too depressing to think of about what they've been through. How's Nadine?"

"She's back in school full time. Finding it a heavier load this year. More books to read, more reports to write."

"She's smart. She'll do okay."

Sylvia finally ran out of things to say. Jen didn't seem very interested. She was only giving short answers and asking 'appropriate' questions. Sylvia was beginning to feel like she wasn't wanted, and thought, *I just popped in – invaded, really. I caught Jen at a bad time.*

* * *

Jen picked up the coffee cups after Sylvia left. *Haven't gone for groceries. Not even to have a plain cookie to give with a cup of coffee...barely enough coffee.* She shook her head and laid the cups on the counter beside the mound of dirty dishes in the sink. Walking out into the living room she saw the pile of laundry to fold. She went over, sat down beside it, and laid her head back. Closing her eyes, she thought, *How humiliating. If only I had straightened up this place. It looks like a cyclone hit. No. It's not only cluttered, it's just plain dirty. Looks more like a slum. So what? Now Sylvia knows I am a slob.* Jen leaned over and settled onto the clean laundry. She pulled out a large towel to cover herself. She was cold. Soon she drifted off to sleep.

As Jen was standing in the kitchen trying to decide what to cook for dinner, a rapping at the door startled her. When she opened it, she faced a young man with sandy red-brown hair and a pleasant expression.

"Hello. I'm sorry to bother you. I'm Sam Brown. I talked to you on the phone in early summer." He paused, and she said nothing. "Explained that I was Lennard's son. I came by just hoping to catch my father at home. I have been away, working."

"Well, I can't be of much help. Len has left and..." *What do I say? Can I trust this guy? Probably – he seems okay. But I have too much on my plate with Michael, and I can't get him in touch with Len, anyhow. Poor guy. But I'd better tell him, straight out.*

"Len worked at the mill. When there was a temporary lay-off, he told them he'd be gone for a short while to Seattle. But then he phoned and told us he was going to get a job in California. He may not be coming back. I don't know."

She looked at him, waiting for a reaction. He looked puzzled. She added, "I think he's gone for good." If it sounded uncaring, or worse, disgusted with Len, she was sorry. But she was past trying to cover up for him.

Jen went on. "I can imagine you wanted very much to meet him after all these years. It's too bad." She softened her tone of voice. "I really am sorry. Let me think about it. I may have some things, like pictures, that you would want to see."

"Oh. That's so nice of you." He was young, eager, and open. So different in attitude from Len.

The phone rang. "Excuse me a moment."

Sam waited at the door, sorting out this news. His dad – well, biological dad – was gone. How long... until it might be possible to see him? Never, from the sound of it?

Jen returned. "Sorry about that. I'm thinking... if you could come back tomorrow in the evening, I'll have time to find some pictures for you to see, some for you to keep. I'm working at the greenhouse, so it has to be evening."

"I would appreciate that so much. I'll come after dinner. About what time?

"Seven is good. Is that possible? Are you staying in the area?"

"Twenty minutes away. I'll be here! Thank you very much."

He left, and Jen turned back to the kitchen with a strange feeling about all this. Funny that Sam came into their lives now. Oh, well. So much for perfect timing. Sam's face stayed with her as she fixed dinner. He had his dad's coloring, even to the eyes. But his eyes were gentle – the antithesis of Len's. The comparison gave her a chill.

As Sam drove away, he began to get a clearer picture – and it was broader than his own viewpoint. The first phone calls he made, Lennard had not answered, even with being reminded. *My computer business took me away, and I thought that I was the one holding things up. Now I see this isn't likely to happen. Doesn't look like he's coming back any time soon. Nor does it seem like he's sending money. So – Len was physically abusive to Mother. She was able to get away from him... I wonder if he has kept that up...*

* * *

Gloomy light had crept into the room when Sylvia struggled out of a disoriented dream that had Len, Larry and Jen in it; but she couldn't remember what had been happening. Laying there wondering, thoughts of Lennard loomed up, and she couldn't shake them. She quietly slid out of bed, took her robe and left the room, shutting the door without a sound. In the kitchen she put a filter in the Melitta cone for the mini-pot and measured out coffee for two cups, strong. For herself. *Might as well get good and wide awake.* She put on the water to boil and looked out the window.

Drizzling rain fell from a heavily overcast sky. She turned to the living room and wandered aimlessly. Her eyes fell on her dad's desk. *How sweet of him to give it to me.* She got a lump in her throat. *Dad – what a brick. Steady as could be – always there with eyes full of love for me, at least in these later years. He has time to enjoy life now, fully retired. Mother? Well... who knows what heights of success she will climb?* Sylvia got postcards from far-away destinations. After all, business trips have to be taken, her mother would declare, with a sparkle in her eyes and mock duty in her voice Though priority time wasn't invested in it, she firmly proclaimed that her marriage was happy. Whatever. Always there was another business meeting for her to attend, or a seminar that ran from Friday to Sunday; then a week here, or a week there. She was actively connecting with 'people in the know', or learning about leveraging time and savings, or making profits while 'servicing' people, but her mother's servicing sounded less like service and more like self-serving. Her words came to mind – "I'm not satisfied to just sit back." To Sylvie's ear, this all had the ring of 'I'm not satisfied'. Sylvia couldn't remember when that life of hectic activity had begun. And now, in her late seventies, she would say, 'tongue in cheek', "Oh, yes – I'm retired! Ha-ha – not really!" Sylvia realized, as she thought back, that her mother had been driven, even before entering the business world. *Well, Mom, it's a good thing that Dad is content to keep the home fires burning in your new California home. He can rest his weary bones. After years of work he has the sense to know he needs to be retired, and has the wisdom to actually do it.* She shook her head, wondering if, as the years continued to take their toll on her dad, her mother would regret not spending time with him. They didn't need the money.

Sylvia went up the stairs to the room where she kept her sewing supplies stashed. Opening a small drawer in a narrow chest she looked over the variety of white and cream laces and ribbons of many colors. She picked up a hank of wide ribbons, deep raspberry red. With the other hand she held up cream-colored lace. Laying them together, on top of the chest, she opened a larger, lower drawer and removed velvet material in matching raspberry. In her mind's eye she could see a darling winter dress for Emalie, with puffy sleeves; some cream-colored cotton lace material gathered over them, and a gathered band of it on the skirt. *Oh, I'll show this to Jenny; she'll like it. Or will she? I guess it would 'fall flat', now that she has so much on her mind. Poor Jen.* Discouragement settled over Sylvia.

CHAPTER THIRTY-SIX

Sylvia put the potatoes on to boil for dinner. She felt weighed down. Though it did no good, she had been fretting. Larry's moodiness lately had not helped her frame of mind. It was enough just to have Jenny to worry about. *Jenny has very real problems and that is enough to have on my mind. Larry... the matter of his work problems... I wonder when he'll get on top of this restlessness and make the decisions that he needs to make. He hasn't wanted to listen, to have any added pressure, when I need to share my concern about Jenny. I understand that. But he doesn't have to take his worry out on me by being cranky, either. Thank the Lord that Lisa is coming out soon. It's been so long since we really sat and talked. I need some time with her, and Jen does, too. Might cheer her up. I sure hope she comes over when Lisa is here.*

Sylvia wished the darkness would turn to the gray light of dawn. Hoping she wouldn't disturb Larry, she raised up carefully to see the clock which now read four-thirty. *Maybe,* she thought, *a lack of oxygen will work to make me drowsy.* She pulled the covers over her head and slowly breathed in the well-used warm air. She became aware of the tightness in her neck and tried to release the tension in her muscles and consciously let go. *Sleep will come if I'll just be patient,* she thought. She closed her eyes, but her troubled mind worked up imagined scenes and kept replaying them. She finally slid into a half-sleep. Nightmarish images appeared... Michael cringing as Lennard's hand put a vise-grip hold on his arm and twisted it backwards. Michael cowering, then ducking as Lennard raised his hand as to strike, then sneered at Michael's fear, gloating in his own power. Goldie was limping, holding up an injured paw like she was requesting help, and Jen was evading Sylvia's questioning look. A sullen expression dulled Michael's eyes. The resentment on his face spoke volumes without a word uttered.

Sylvia roused out of sleep; the weight of night terror pressing on her. She felt exhausted. Her energies had been expended battling the unnamed evil. She turned over again. She didn't mean to disturb Larry, but he grumpily asked, "You can't sleep?"

"No. I'll get up soon if I can't get back to sleep."

"Don't bother for my sake," he said in an irritable tone of voice that plainly meant the opposite. Sylvia had to put up with his recent moodiness, since his security at work was being undermined. A younger man who had a lot of enthusiasm was impressing the boss. The conflict in Larry's mind was that he didn't want the longer trips away from home, and this guy knew how to make himself look good to the boss. Larry knew he might lose out to this fellow. Big time. Was this man good for the company? Larry didn't think so. He was out for number one. He had told these things to Sylvia. Larry plainly felt threatened. He wouldn't make trouble. And he didn't want to appear to pit himself against the man and look like an insecure has-been. Most of all, he certainly didn't want to start looking for work at this age. He would be practically unemployable.

Sylvia turned over in her mind what Larry faced. The more she thought, the more she grew impatient with him. He wasn't standing up for himself. Why couldn't he see that he needed to deal with it? The unknown was the most frightening enemy of all. She slipped into a dream-filled sleep again.

Waking with a start, and knowing she wouldn't go back to sleep, Sylvia's irritation flared. *Forget trying to sleep. It's pointless.* She slid out of bed. In the kitchen she put on the kettle to boil, and went in by the the bookcase to browse and wait. Her eyes were drawn to the shabby, paper-covered booklet, some thirty years old. She reached down and took out her 'Diary of an Autumn in India'. *There is an escape!* Her mind suddenly came alive with memories. *What an opportunity I had – to go to that mysterious place where I would hear the strange music of a wedding procession, and see sari-clad ladies I longed to talk with. How fortunate, at nineteen, that my uncle and aunt invited me to come. Those months were so enriching. A year of formal education could not have given me the "feel" that I have for northern India. Though an inadequate perception, what I do have is vivid.*

Carrying the journal into the kitchen, Sylvie picked up the kettle and poured boiling water through the coffee. Stopping between pours to inhale the rich aroma, she thought how she'd like to share so much more with Jen about that time. She took her coffee mug, sat down, and propped up the diary. Though unimportant-looking, it held feelings and impressions that were priceless. *What thoughts are here? I was so inexperienced about other's lives. My uncle's letters about medical work among the people helped. But to actually see their poverty and seeming hopelessness changed me. I appreciated my life back home, my opportunities.*

On a happier note, she thought of telling Jen about the shopping. That first time out, she had gone to the bazaar with Sharanjeet, the kitchen maid. There were merchants for every imaginable product. She could see vegetables arrayed before her eyes, and across the lane the beautiful colors of spices were heaping out of their burlap or plastic bags. Another day she went to help buy yardage for curtains from the cloth merchant. Stunning fabrics were displayed. She lost interest in curtains, and instead handled the delicate yardage for saris. Nearby tailors worked old treadle sewing machines with amazing skill. She would ask her aunt about the practicality of her owning a sari.

Just then Larry wandered into the kitchen. He started fresh coffee in the automatic maker, and went back to the bedroom without speaking. Sylvia tore herself away from the diary, and resolutely took it back to the living room and placed it on the coffee table. She could escape again another time. It was surprising how clearly the visual memories came back.

* * *

Jen's phone rang insistently. She picked it up and listened to Sylvia's invitation. "No," she said. "I don't think I'll be coming over to visit when Lisa comes. She's welcome to drop in for a minute. It's better to be at home since Michael needs his rest and I need to catch up. Plus we have appointments with the family doctor and a specialist in Everett."

"Oh, can I take you to see them?"

"No. I have gotten so used to the bus, it's no problem. That leaves you free. You have spent so much time helping me out, taking care of Michael – you've done quite enough."

"He is such a pleasant young man. That was no trouble. I'm sorry you're not getting as many days at the greenhouse now."

"Oh, I'm glad it has dwindled down. The pay really helped, but it's so important to be home with Michael, plus do the appointments. Anyway, I won't be able to come; it's just too much. Thanks, though."

"Alright. Another time. That reminds me – I've wanted to ask if Michael has been able to keep up with the homework?"

"Yes. Some days are better, and we take advantage of those. I think Mr. Logan is only sending a limited amount of work. There was an introduction to a new math principle. I'm sure he didn't send all the assignments. Michael likes to read socials. English and Science were never hard for him. So it's going okay."

"Good! I'm glad. Remember, you are welcome to come over and see me any time you can. Or I can come over there, so Michael can rest when he wants to. But give me a call so I know when. I don't want to interrupt naps."

"Sure. Well, I'll let you go. Good-bye."

* * *

Marie picked up the phone, thinking, "I've got to let Sylvia in on this!" At the 'hello' she excitedly said, "Sylvia! Marie here. We just had a meeting of people interested in helping with the Christmas program for the kids at New Beginnings. I wanted to tell you about that and also how things are going for the women."

"Good. Sorry I haven't gotten back to you about the Friday night thing. Larry and I have been spending that time together and I kinda hated to be away. Tell me what's up."

"Oh I can understand you wanting time with Larry since he's

away so much. I'll tell you the kids' part in a minute. I have really gotten to know some of the ladies. I can't use names. I have to be careful what I say, but I'll change any facts that might reveal identity. I'll just make up a lady I call 'A' and give you a composite story of several. I'm amazed at what these women have been through. I mean, it's unreal. I'm so glad to get to know them and be a little bit of encouragement. So our fictitious lady, 'A', was twelve when she tried drugs that were given to her free. She was raped and forced into prostitution. Her pimp gave her drugs, and pretty things to wear. He kept the money she made. At the beginning she was "his special girl; his woman". Translate that "Slave." After he got bored, he had another girl to replace her. Then she became merchandise for customers – just one of the ordinary sex-trade workers. She wanted to get away but she never had the courage or money to do it. Years passed. She had two children during that time, managing to escape an unwanted abortion, but they were taken away from her by child protection and placed in a foster home. She could see them on supervised visits. Then on a visit she lost her temper. She yelled at them, and appeared to be on the verge of hitting them. The foster parent was there and reported it. Visits were limited and supervised at a neutral facility. She tried to get clean, quit drugs. She couldn't. She went to their foster home, knocked on the door, and screamed at the foster mother. She totally lost visiting rights. Finally she got older, and undesirable as a prostitute, and depressed."

Marie paused as she again considered. "I can't imagine such a thing happening." She went on. "As the kids got older, she was allowed back into their lives to a limited extent. She was trying to sort out this parenting thing. She would be angry and argumentative with the children, and then she'd wonder why she did it. She admitted she picked the fights, being bossy about what they should be doing in school, how they were failing in their everyday life-skills, and were not being responsible, not "growing up". She was trying to look like the smart one, but she was miserable inside, knowing that she was being unreasonable. She couldn't sort out all the anger welling up inside her. She kept feeling that she 'had to straighten things out'."

Marie paused, and Sylvia let out a long breath, "Wooah. What an eye-opening picture for you to see. I guess I don't know much about that kind of work. Just what I read in an article in the paper."

"Right. That's it. And I'm seeing my mis-interpretations. Thought I knew what the problems were, and how to fix them. Wasn't in the "learner" mode. I've found out how wrong I was. Sorry. Now I sound like a know it all!"

"Don't be sorry for being excited, and taking the opportunity to tell what you've learned – sharing what these women's lives have been like. How is this woman doing now?"

"She came to New Beginnings on the chance they could help. At first she hated her situation and she even hated the people who wanted to help her. But she stuck with it. Now she says she's come to realize that she really hated herself."

"How sad. What about being able to mother her children?"

"She hasn't been clean long enough to qualify for that. And the professionals who come to New Beginnings advise her to do a thorough job on the anger management course she is doing. She is studying the Bible, especially the book of Proverbs on relationships and wisdom for everyday living. But she has hope that she'll get them back, and be ready to be a better mother."

"Is it always that severe a situation?"

"No. For instance, others are left to raise little kids. Maybe the husband decides he can't take being out of work, gets depressed. He starts hanging around with a rough crowd or he might leave town to get a job. She doesn't hear from him any more after a while. Missing persons reports aren't much help if there's no indication of foul play. She's destitute, living in a cheap place, but can't even pay that rent. Ready to be evicted, she swallows her pride and comes to New Beginnings. She talks with a counselor and one of the women, a mother who has a chance for a good job but needs child care. We have access to living quarters in a rooming house we help run. She moves and the two women work out their schedule for paying jobs and watching each other's kids. Even at low pay, a woman feels good to have work and still have care for her kids. She gets counseling for training in a new type of work. One is being trained for a day care job."

"Wow. The women watching each other's kids could get

complicated."

"Yes, I guess it sounds that way. It's a ripe situation for misunderstanding between the mothers. It happens. Thank God there are two volunteers who come in to New Beginnings who have training in mediation. So the women even learn communication skills as they work out their misunderstandings. The women get help at the Food Bank if their hours at paying jobs are cut. What I think is best of all, they take classes and get their high school diplomas or go for further training. Another class is life skills. Someone in the situation I described as 'A', can get discouraged about how much she had missed in "basic living". They do shopping, plan budgets, handle money, and cook and serve evening meals at New Beginnings. Besides learning, they are not just receiving but are being a blessing to others."

"I can imagine that helps their moral, learning to give."

"Yes, and the folks who run it are so giving. They are great role models of that." Marie paused and drew a long breath. "Here I go again. Sorry! I'll let you talk."

"It is quite an amazing program. So what was this about a Christmas program for the kids there?"

"Oh, yes!" Marie laughed. "I took the long way around to get to that, didn't I? We are working with various volunteers. There are people from three churches and a school drama teacher who come. They want to try a low-key theater program for the women and their kids. They hope it can be held publicly, with free-will donations going to New Beginnings. I'm helping them – I have loved theater since high school. We'll do two short plays. One is scenes from "A Charlie Brown Christmas", and the other will be the Nativity. I am so excited about it."

"Sounds like lots of fun! Do you need me to watch Emalie?"

"No. Well, I may, part of the time. I'm not sure if it'll work, but I think I'll bring her in and she can be a little shepherd. I've taken her with me a couple times. The women love her. The kids, too."

"Oh…" Sylvia paused. "Do you think that's a good idea? There is so much sickness among those poor people. She could catch something."

"I guess she could. I'll watch her; see that she gets her rest so she won't get run down. She's dropped her morning nap entirely, so she takes a long afternoon one. Oh. Telling you what she's doing reminds me. I need a sitter for an appointment with the gynecologist. Are you interested in coming in and spending some one-on-one time with Emalie?"

"You can bet I am!"

Marie gave her the date. "I hope you can come to the Christmas program at New Beginnings when it's given!"

"Oh, for sure, we'll be there for the program! I'd love to see all the kids enjoying it – the adults, too. We'll get the dates from you later. See if Larry can be in town, too."

Well, Sylvie thought after hanging up, *what a great chance Marie has to help. Must be satisfying. I'm eager to see those kids do the plays at Christmas. But I still wonder about Emalie being there. She's so small.*

* * *

Jennifer was glad Michael had a nap and a good dinner. Sam was due any time. It would be nice to have them meet. When Sam did arrive, there was an element of disappointment.

"I appreciate you inviting me to come," Sam said, stepping in.

Jen introduced him to Michael. "Hello, young man. I'm glad to meet you!" He held out his hand. Michael shook, but with a preoccupied stare at this person who had the appearance of Len. Sam saw the look, and smiled.

"You're right, Michael. I look like Len, don't I!" He seemed completely at ease about it.

"Why, yes, you do. A lot!" Michael turned red, embarrassed at being caught staring.

Jen blushed. "Have a seat and I'll bring some refreshment. You may want to look at the pictures spread here on the coffee table. Michael can tell you when or where they were taken."

Michael sat down beside Sam, and looked at him sideways. He wanted to ask Sam, *How long has it been since you saw your dad? Mom didn't tell me much.* But he restrained himself.

Sam called after Jen. "I'd better tell you right away. I'm sorry that I have only a short time. I've just gotten a new client back east. The company called today with a job, and they want a rush. So, I'm sorry, I can't stay long."

"Oh." Jen turned back from her trip to the kitchen. "That's too bad. Do you have time for coffee? I have some freshly made."

"Sure." Sam picked up a picture and went quiet. Michael sensed that he wanted to look, and not talk. Setting it down, Sam leaned forward and looked at others, spread out, and began to ask questions.

Jen returned with the coffee and cookies, and said, "I thought we might as well get copies made. Then you can have whichever ones you want."

"Great idea. I have my digital camera in the car." He smiled. "The thought crossed my mind to bring it. I figured you had only one copy of most."

"There are more pictures in albums that I didn't take out. These are the loose ones. I don't know if you have time to shoot many tonight. You can come back when you have time to do it."

"That would be great. I am sorry, after you were so hospitable, not to have more time." He got his camera from the car and began to shoot pictures on the low table.

Michael held down the corners on the ones that curled. "This was taken at Lake Goodwin," he volunteered. "And that's Golden Gardens. That's salt water."

Sam enjoyed listening to his enthusiastic informant. The boy wanted to please, and took pride in being helpful.

"Oh, I'd better stop and enjoy this good coffee before it gets cold." Sam put his camera back in the case. "Could I ask you something? If it's not uncomfortable, that is."

"Well. You can ask. I may not be able to answer." Jen smiled. She hoped there wouldn't be any probing questions. Sam seemed like a considerate person – *unlike his dad*, her unasked subconscious wanted to add. She pushed the thought aside.

"Have you known Len long?"

"We've been married four years. I met him just before that. We've lived in Tacoma and Seattle most of that time."

Sam nodded. "We lived in California when I was born. Then we moved several times. I'm not sure where. I was too little. I go back to southern Cal a lot to visit with my mother. Bob, her husband, is good to her, for which I'm very thankful. And he's been a very good step-dad to me."

They chatted a bit more, then Sam said he had to leave. "I'll phone and come again, after I get this contract lined out. It might be a week."

Michael felt disappointed, and thought, *It might not happen at all. Sam will get too busy.*

Sam got in his car, and waved to Michael in the window. He thought, as he pulled out of the driveway, *Though Len has been gone only a short time, it looks like they have been abandoned for good. I feel sorry for them. Nice little boy. And a serious-minded mother. Things are up in the air for her, what with Michael being checked out by doctors...*Sam shook his head. *Ah, Len.* More lives thrown into limbo. *God, provide for them both.*

CHAPTER THIRTY-SEVEN

Jen buttoned her sweater higher, glanced at the Franklin wood heater, and shivered. Sam had brought it by two nights before. It would be so good when he came back to put it in working order. Larry had seen it arrive, and mentioned it to a friend who dropped off scrap wood from the mill. It was in a heap behind the house with an old tarp over it.

The phone rang. Before Jen knew it, Sylvia said, "I'm coming over with a thermos of coffee and a coffee cake I made. How about it? Is that okay?"

"How can I resist that?" she said, thinking, *I guess we're going to have a visit, whether I plan it or not. Well, with more appointments coming up to deal with, it will make a memory of better times.*

"Good. I'll be right over."

Jen opened the door for the bearer of treats.

Sylvie thought, as Jen opened the door, *I will be able to sit down with her, and help her get her mind off her troubles.*

"Boy, it's muddy." Sylvia said, handing over the brown paper bag as Jenny nodded. Setting the thermos on the floor, she pulled off her boots. "Right where the path dips down in that low spot, it's a lake. It's been raining hard, and it's so chilly." She thought, *It's so good to be here, in Jen's house; maybe I can brighten her day a little.*

Sylvie looked around. "A Franklin stove! Wow, you lucky! I like those, but we don't have the right spot with a chimney for one. Guess their days are numbered, with pollution controls coming. This

354

little valley used to have a cloud hanging over it when everyone had wood-burning heat. But it's sure nice and cozy."

"It is nice, isn't it. I guess Larry forgot to tell you about it. Sam, Len's son that I told you had come, brought it out. He's coming back to make it functional."

"Hey, I'll bring over my white enamel kettle to put on top! It's an original, chipped up a bit. We can make tea and cocoa right here."

"Yeah. That would fit."

"Now – I'll pour the coffee, if you don't mind, and play hostess, and you sit and relax! Does that sound good?"

"Sure." Jen nodded.

* * *

As Sylvie drove the car up her driveway, Goldie crossed her mind. *I haven't seen her. I wonder if she's been wandering again. She used to stay home. Guess she's lonely. Too bad there's no fence.* Sylvie knew Jen and Michael had doctor appointments. She parked and got out of the car, calling as she walked over to the empty house. Then she saw the notice on the door. It was an official form from the dog catcher and gave the description of the dog just picked up, stating 'If this is your dog, you can come to the animal shelter and pay the fine.'

"*Oh, no,* Sylvie thought. *If Michael loses that dog now, when he's sick…I can't let that happen.* She went back home, grabbed an old blanket from the porch, and quickly drove to the animal shelter.

Sylvie paid the fine and took Goldie to the car. She put an old blanket on the seat and had Goldie lay there. She drove to the hardware store to look at collars and found a harness that came behind the front legs. *Now we've got you, Goldie! You can't slip out of this! Larry can fix a clothesline so Goldie can run. At least she can feel free. Hope it works.*

* * *

The volunteer driver that had been arranged brought Jen and Michael back home, and left.

"Now, how nice is that? We got a ride!" Jen asked.

"It's great! The lady was friendly to us, like she wanted to help. Not like she had to do it. Sure quicker than going to the doctor's on the bus."

Jen was thinking of how the doctor had told her Michael would probably need to go in to Seattle Children's Hospital again. She could expect a call. She peeked out her kitchen window when she saw movement. A pickup and a faded blue car had pulled in. She dried her hands and went out on the front porch.

"Hello? Oh... Len? I thought you were in California." *How often will this happen? Him showing up here?*

He approached, carrying a backpack that seemed to be empty, and walked past her without a glance. "I'm going soon. I just came to get some paperwork and other items upstairs in my drawer." She couldn't understand why he had made the other man drive a second car and come here. Then she remembered the stove Sam brought. *What if Len sees that and finds out...what will he do? Maybe nothing. Who knows his reactions?*

Len came back out the door, and held out several papers to her. "Sign this. I'm leaving this car. Something you can drive – but don't ask a lot from it. The clutch is going, so ease it into gear. You know how to drive a standard. Remember it won't last if you drive it hard."

"Why do I have to sign this? You're giving it to *me*?"

"Yeah. Don't look a gift horse in the mouth. When you drive it, you have to prove ownership if you're stopped. It's not in my name. That name on there is the guy who had it – I just got it and didn't transfer it. We'll say you got it for two hundred dollars. It's written there. Just sign here."

It's happening too fast, Jen thought. *But what could be wrong? This way I'll have a car to drive Michael to Seattle. Maybe it's one of those "God-things" Sylvie talks about. I don't like the money part. Why does it matter to say I paid that?* She signed the paper, holding it against the 'new' car. Len grunted, and went to the passenger side of the pickup. The other guy had gotten behind the wheel. Len pulled a cap low over his face, and slumped down like he wanted to take a nap.

Jen went in the house. *Funny. Oh well.* She looked at the heater.

How in the world did Len fail to see the Franklin stove? Guess he had a lot on his mind. Strange about bringing that car all the way out here.

The phone rang. Sylvie asked if she could come over.

At the door she handed Jen a large lasagna. "There was a great sale on these. I'm putting a couple in my freezer. Enjoy!"

"Oh, you shouldn't have! Thank you very much. We have been at the doctor and I hadn't really planned for dinner."

"Say, what's the car in the driveway?"

"Ah, well, it's mine. Now I'll have a way to take Michael when he has to go in to Seattle again. I found out it will be another trip, for sure. Probably longer this time."

"Oh, no. Well. I shouldn't say oh, no, if they get answers."

"Yeah, don't hold your breath."

"So you went car shopping in town and found this?"

"No, it just showed up in my driveway – from a donor."

Sylvie wrinkled her brow and just stared at Jen.

"Actually Len just dropped it off. Then he's heading for southern Cal."

"He did?" Sylvia wondered why… she didn't know what to say. *He's here again?* Jen didn't add any more information and Sylvie didn't feel she could ask.

* * *

Sam came that evening. He asked about the car, but she was standing behind Michael, and gave a short answer about a donor who needed to stay anonymous, rolling her eyes downward toward Michael. Sam took the hint. He immediately began checking the old brick chimney inside and out. He put together the stove pipe, double-check the joints, and then went out back to chop wood. He carried in an armload, set it on an old rug, and, with a note of triumph, said, "Now we can test drive the heater! We want to be certain this old chimney is safe. I'm not leaving until I'm sure." He looked at Michael, who nodded solemnly.

Michael watched Sam to see how a fire was laid. After the match was struck and he saw that it would go, he lost interest, and busied himself getting out a Chinese checker board and marbles. Jen took the moment to quietly explain to Sam that she had told Michael about a donor, but went on to tell how the car got there. He was shocked to think he'd almost crossed paths with his bio-father, as he referred to him, except in front of Michael. Jen took note of how quiet he got.

Sam then walked into the kitchen and said to Michael, "We'll make sure this fire is giving off some heat without overheating the chimney. *Then* we can play a game. Actually, Michael, I'd like to play Twenty Questions first, all three of us. After that, either you and I, or all three of us can play Chinese checkers."

So Twenty Questions it was. Jen brought in some cocoa and cookies that Sylvie had baked. Michael had the first turn, and said "It's animal; twenty questions to guess it!"

When Sam and Jen failed to narrow it down before using up their questions, Michael said, "It's a sheep! Kyle's farm had sheep once." He turned to Sam. "I wish you could meet them. Sigurdsens are real nice. If you come out in the daytime, we can take you."

"Okay. I'd like to meet your friends."

Jen was thoughtful, and then added, "Yes. I'd like to get to know Sonja. We were introduced downtown, and talked on the phone a couple times – that's it. Can you come soon, Sam, to meet them? Maybe on Saturday? Or any day you're not working. I'll give Sonja a call to ask about dropping over."

"Sounds good. My work schedule is mine to set. That eastern contract is under control now. Actually, I'm looking into a work contract in the Everett area. Tell you more about it when it materializes. I'll phone after you have time to find out about Kyle's farm."

* * *

Emalie traipsed across the floor as the ballet music played. Sylvia, delighted, watched her prancing. They had done this together. Now it was more fun to simply watch. She remembered how it felt to be the little princess herself, see the delight in her parents' eyes. Later there was the excitement of imagining she was on stage in a tutu, pirouetting before an admiring audience. Now it was Emalie who was in ruffles, a big bow bouncing on her behind. The new dress Sylvie brought with her had fit. Emalie was tickled with it. Her eyes sparkled as she danced for her grandma. *She is the center of our family's loving attention. And she knows it. But I guess feeling secure and loved is a good thing.*

Driving in to Marie and Mark's to baby-sit was an excursion Sylvia *always* had time for. It was her chance to click a few new pictures on her camera, read stories, and play pretend with Emalie. Sylvia let herself be impressed with this child's precocious comments and unique way of looking at life. Sylvie answered her questions with openness, remembering how a child absorbs not only info, but attitudes. It was a precious trust to be in her life. *Lord,* she prayed, *help me to be the example she needs. What a tender, vulnerable time of life.*

* * *

Sam exited off I-5, and went the longer route to Granite, by way of Snohomish. *I want to look over this area. There's no reason for me to rent a more expensive place in Seattle when I can live anywhere and do my work. Life is lived at a more restful pace out here. I like the people I'm meeting. And I'd sure like to be around, to be a male roll model for Michael, 'as much as in me is'! I realize I don't know the half of what Jen and Michael have experienced.*

He shook off the dark feeling at that thought by looking around, paying attention to what was available in this area. Surprisingly, he saw a physiotherapy office ahead. It reminded him of his sore elbow. Maybe that was computer related. The pain went down from the elbow into his wrist. It could use help, regardless of the cause. He decided to check out the place. See if they had that electrical impulse machine to increase circulation.

Sam pulled into the parking lot, hopped out, and went in.

The receptionist looked up, a pleasant expression in her friendly eyes. She was young. Her name pin said Marissa. She had soft brown hair curling around her face, and friendly eyes.

Sam explained his pain, and asked if he could come in for his elbow. After settling the practical questions of the need and getting an appointment, Sam said, "That's a nice name – Marissa. I don't think I've ever met a Marissa before."

"It is an unusual name, but I like that."

"It didn't bother you in school – like when kids find a way to twist a name around and tease?"

"No. I learned quickly that getting hurt feelings just makes it worse. So I'd change the subject, or say something to show I didn't care. It worked."

Sam smiled and she smiled back. She was pretty, and smart, too. "Do you want to be a physiotherapist, or do you enjoy reception work?"

"I do enjoy working here, but actually, I'm a registered massage therapist. Not only is it shorter training than physio, but I know that I can help people with it. When I applied for a job, they needed someone for both reception and massage therapy."

"Oh, that worked out. How did you happen to look here? There are lots more places in Everett and Seattle. It's kind of off the beaten track."

"My grandmother lived near Granite Falls for many years; stayed on even after she was widowed. I often visited her, so I knew I liked the area. As for being remote, we have all the patients we can handle. When I applied for this job, I was also able to rent half of the house my Grandma had lived in. It's been converted to a duplex, but it still has lots of memories. After Grandma lost Gramps, it was hard for her to keep up with a house and yard. She's living in Everett now."

"Oh, I just heard about another grandma. Grandma Jones lives out here. I get to meet her this trip. I can guess she will be facing that same challenge."

"Oh, yes! I know her! She was an acquaintance of Grandma's."

"Were they neighbors? I'm getting to know that area."

"No. But they were part of a quilting group and became friends. That's special – you meeting Grandma Jones. Nice lady." The young woman began to turn away. "I need to finish this billing now. I'm sorry. I have to get it done. I have an appointment to give a massage soon, or I wouldn't be rude."

"Oh, of course. That's not being rude. I'm sorry to have taken your time, and kept you from your work." But he wasn't, really.

CHAPTER THIRTY-EIGHT

J en came out of the brushy path and, as she walked across Sylvia's driveway, looked up at the sky thoughtfully. *Am I coming here merely to pass the time? Really...I'd like to find out if Sam's ideas and Sylvia's are the same. That old "God question" keeps coming up.*

Sylvia poured their tea and sat down. After only a few sentences, there was a pause. Jen looked her in the eye, and said, "Explain what you mean when you say, 'faith in God'. I try hard to believe in Him, like you do, because it's helped you. It just won't come."

Sylvia simply said, "Jenny, I'd like to show you a few verses in the Bible. What *I* say is a human being's word. The *Bible* is God's word on life's big questions. Then you'll have the information you need. You can choose to do 'whatever' with it. In fact, you not only can choose, but it must be your decision. You have a will. God respects us and doesn't force himself on us. But He does love us, and he showed it, practically. I'd like to share it. Is that what you'd like?"

"Yes. I'll listen. I asked to hear it," Jen said.

Sylvia opened to First John, turned the Bible to her, and Jen read the words in chapter 5, verse 13 '...that you may know that you have eternal life.' Sylvia said, "God wants us to *know* we have eternal life. Not wish and wonder."

I don't know if it's possible for me to know, Jen thought. *But it must work for Sam. And Sylvia seems very sure.*

Sylvia held the Bible between them so Jen could see, and they turned back to Romans chapter 3. "Let's read this, about sin. Try to see it as information, rather than someone insulting you. Why don't you read verse 23.

Silently, Jen read, then said it aloud, "All have sinned." Sylvie flipped the page, and pointed. Jen read, "The wages of sin is death, but the gift of God is eternal life through Jesus Christ our Lord."

"Why death?" Jen asked.

"That's spiritual death – being cut off from God. He can't be part of anything sinful. We are sinners, separated from Him. He *wants* us in His family. He sent Jesus, the perfect God-man so He could ethically connect with us."

"Ethically?"

"Yes. God can't quit being God, that is, holy. Can't just settle for putting up with sin, and have it in heaven. He knows the damage sin does to every human being. We need to see our need – that a total change is required that *we* can't bring about. *He* changes us when we yield to Him. He gives us new life, the life of Jesus, inside."

"Damage to *every* human being? I thought some people were good enough.

"None of us are. The rules, or laws, were to teach us what sin is – no one keeps the Ten Commandments. They are our tutor to teach us, and bring us to Christ. In the same chapter in Galatians it says that righteousness couldn't come by keeping the law. The tutor brings us to Christ Jesus "that we might be justified by faith."

"That faith thing. I still don't understand."

"Faith comes by reading or hearing the Word of God. That's the way to have faith; not trying hard to believe."

"Oh." Jen kept quiet for a minute. "I remember how, *all* the time, I felt guilty. I don't want to feel that way."

"We want to get around feeling guilty. But that is the very thing that opens the door – seeing, admitting, our deep need. We're alienated from God, by our very nature. God is perfect. We're not. He *knows* we can't measure up and he never intended for us to gain heaven by measuring up. The commandments help us live well with each other."

"I wish. Too bad more people don't practice them."

Oh, oh, Sylvia thought. *Let's just stay on the issue of us.* "I remember feeling guilty and hiding from what I heard – that I was

362

a sinner. I said to myself 'I'm good. I don't do anything really bad." But I couldn't get away from that nagging feeling. I knew I needed to take care of admitting to him, "God, you are right about me." God knows we need to come to Jesus, but he waits patiently."

"From what I heard as a kid, He didn't seem very patient."

"That was people telling you what He was thinking. Reading or hearing God's word is how faith comes. Hearing it for itself, like we were just saying. I'm guessing you were hearing it interpreted, but weren't reading it for yourself much."

"Nope."

"So, we hear or read what God really asks, and we have time to take in His plan. We find out He asks one thing of us – faith. Faith in what He did. One day we listen to the nagging in our mind. We say, "Yes, God, it's true. I am a sinner. Your grace is a gift. I don't have one thing to offer You. I just come as I am. I'm in need. I accept the truth – that Jesus Christ died in my place. He's my Substitute. I can come through no other Door – nothing and no one else."

Jen listened intently, then she said, "You once referred to Jesus as the Good Shepherd. You told a story of a human shepherd who fought off wild animals to save his sheep, and then died of his wounds. I cried. Michael read that same story at Mary's. That day with you, it touched me." *But do Sam and Sylvia actually see God being like that? These people's God is a different kind than I have ever heard of before.*

"Jesus *is* the Good Shepherd, giving his life for his sheep. But our acceptance isn't based on how emotional and tearful we are when we're talking to God. It's simply a matter of saying, aloud, or in your heart, 'Forgive me, God, for my sin. I'm sorry. Take over my life. I trust You.' That's "accepting" Jesus Christ as Savior and Lord. Realizing, 'It's my own sin that's at issue. Nothing else, not my emotions or how much wrong or right I've done. The Lord forgives your sin, or my sin, no matter what you've done."

A thought occurred to Jen - *Your sin? Whatever that was. My sin...*Her gaze went to the tabletop. She felt a blur take over her mind as she began to rationalize; *Of course I've done wrong, but who hasn't? I'm not sure how much I feel bad about it. I do, and I don't.* Jen looked up defiantly at Sylvie. "But others have done a lot of wrong; others have hurt me deeply. Why should I take the blame? I'm the one who suffered their wrongs."

"Oh, Jen, that is so very true. You have suffered. And it is possible to address all that pain, deal with all the hurt you've been through. It *needs* to be dealt with – and it can be! It takes time. We can't undo what others have done. We will live with an effect from it, regardless. Lisa would be a better person to talk to for help, how to begin to deal with it. She understands about recovering from abusive treatment. But I can show you how you can have a relationship with God, personally. And after you trust Him, dealing with the abuse will be easier to do."

I don't want – ever – to talk about everything that has happened. Deal with it.

"Trusting Him is the key. Forgiveness and peace are waiting for each person who will come – you, too! Bring that feeling of condemnation to Jesus. Realize you are unable to fix it yourself, and simply *ask*. 'God, I ask for your forgiveness. I am a sinner. I trust Your word that Jesus has fully paid for my sin. I believe He took my place!"

Jen heard Sylvia's soft voice, full of firm belief, and sensed in Sylvia's quietness that she was at peace with herself. Jen herself felt all in a knot. *It's confusing. I can't. It's not that simple. It's okay for people like Sylvia who have lived a good life, maybe done a little sin, but nothing like me. We are just in different categories, and Sylvia doesn't realize that.*

"Well..." Jen paused, nervously, "It's something to think about." She went silent. *It's too much to think about. I can't think.* She hoped Sylvia wouldn't keep hounding her.

Sylvia spoke. "Thank you very much, Jen, for the chance to read the Bible with you. It's a special book. I believe that God can make it clear to you. Just ask Him." She stood to fill their coffee mugs, but Jenny got up.

"No more for me, thanks. I need to get home. When I left, Michael was on the phone with Jeremy. Of course, if he needed me, he knows your number. But it's about that time, anyhow."

"Sure. Say, I have some outdoor flowers for you. Ones that do well in the fall, and can stay in the pot if you want. Also, we really need to transplant some perennials into your garden beds. If you don't have time to tell me where, I think they may show up anyhow, and surprise you when you come home from a doctor visit!"

"Well, that's a nice thought. But you shouldn't bother doing that. And my gardening is on hold for now, with this new appointment being made at Children's in Seattle."

"Of course. Well, let's go take a look at the mums. I put them in a large pot a while back.

As they left the kitchen, Sylvia pointed to a folder on the counter. "I had some ideas come together for a chapter in the pre-teen book."

"Good for you," Jen said, and they grabbed their jackets and went outside. She turned a surprising thought over in her mind. Earlier she had wanted to leave when she felt the pressure to decide about God. Now she was feeling that the visit was over too soon. It was a paradox. And another one was Sylvie, saying that reading the Bible was a comfort, when she found it just plain hard to understand. It did help when Sylvie explained it.

They entered the garage and Sylvie brought out the wheelbarrow. Jen came alongside her and they walked to the far side of the house.

When Jen rounded the corner of the house, she saw a magnificent display of bronze-gold blossoms, just opening. She just stared. "Why...it's beautiful! It's so striking! I didn't know any flowers began blooming this time of year! Wow."

"They are chrysanthemums. They bloom in response to the gradually shorter days in the fall. I've enjoyed watching them develop buds and begin to open. Hope you enjoy them. It was fun waiting to surprise you!"

"Thank-you! Thank you so much!"

"Sure. Let's load the pot into the wheelbarrow and take it over to your place." They lifted the heavy pot together. Sylvie trundled it over the driveway. Jen reached out and touched the mass of buds and blossoms covering the top of the plants.

"So many flowers – this is *something*! Thank-you. I will enjoy them. I wonder about a place to put it so I can see it from inside." They were crossing the driveway, and Jen pointed. "Over there. Let's put it in the front and when I look out the front room window, I'll see it. It bothered me that flowers won't grow there because of the gravel." She turned to Sylvia. "This is the perfect answer."

"Yes, I think you've picked a great spot. Now, not to worry about the cold – chrysanthemums keep blooming, even during the night frosts of autumn."

"Okay! That's great."

They placed the pot and stood back. Sylvie said, "Perfect spot. Anyone going in and out of the door will see it."

"Yes. I love the cheerful color. What a beautiful warm bronze – or is it orangey rust?"

"You say!" She gave Jen a quick hug. "I have to get home. Enjoy!"

"You bet I will. Thanks again, so much."

After walking into the house, Jen felt warm again. Heat from the Franklin stove filled the room, but more than that, Jen felt the warmth of a reconnection with Sylvia. *I know I have been touchy. I don't understand – what do I do to receive such kindness? I don't deserve it.*

* * *

Sylvia got herself showered, then dressed with enthusiasm. *I'm off to Seattle and a visit with Marie and Emalie! And Woodland Park Zoo to top it off!* She recalled the phone visits – Emalie saying she "wanted to go to the 'do', like in her book." Today was also high time to do something just for fun. 'Semi-retired' felt better all the time. Her wages weren't necessary now, with the place paid off. Though the medical office job had been okay, Granite Falls Hardware had been great. She had a good boss to work for. And serving local clientèle meant that, as she stood at the till or helped them on the floor, she could chat with people who mattered to her and to the community at large. But this new phase of life was also good. Volunteering a few times at the adult day care had shown a place of need to her where she could really help. She enjoyed it. She'd do it more. *But now it's Time with my Granddaughter!*

After the three of them walked through just part of the zoo, Emalie was totally worn out. She'd been out of her stroller most of the time, and was literally dragging her feet, barely staying upright. Sylvie watched the contest of wills. She now resisted Marie helping her into the stroller – too tired to know what she wanted.

"Why don't we go to my place instead of to a restaurant for lunch?" Marie asked. She glanced down at the cranky toddler with a knowing look that said, 'she's had it – she's going to be a pill, eating out'.

"Good idea," Sylvia answered. "I can take you out to lunch another time. Maybe just the two of us!" She laughed. "I've sure enjoyed this. Poor Emalie hasn't our endurance yet. Wait till we teach her to shop!"

"You bet we will! I got some good pictures today of Emalie and Grandma. I'll email them. She was so funny with the lion."

"Yeah. 'Kitty, kitty.' Delighted, until it roared. Poor little sweetie." Sylvie shook her head. "Her sensitive ears must have hurt. I about jumped out of *my* skin. The petting zoo – that's the best. For Emalie, I think the young amimoes are her favorite. I could take a couple of them home with me!"

Marie said, "Emalie now says yanimoes. Though they are cute, I know I'm too short of patience for a pet now."

Sylvia nodded. "Yes, too much. The timing will be right one day. It's hard to keep one in the city, anyhow – for its own sake."

They chatted on as Sylvie drove to Marie and Mark's apartment. Emalie, in her car seat, started munching on the snacks her mother had put in her 'keep cool' lunch bag. Minutes later Marie pointed to the back seat and dropped her head, pantomiming that Emalie was sleeping.

After they parked, Marie carried Emalie inside, and said, "I'm sure glad she can finish off her nap. She'll wake up happier." They stood together, looking down at the peacefully sleeping child in her crib.

After lunch Marie got out the pictures her mother had sent of a recent two-day trip to the Atlantic shore. "Aw," Sylvie said, "Mrs. Rodriguez looks healthy there. These recent attacks of pain must be awful. I'm glad you can at least keep in touch by phone and emailing your sister. And all of us can be informed, to pray for her. I wish I knew your family better."

"Well, not much chance of that, with them living on the east coast and us in the west.

Sylvia asked questions as they looked at other pictures of Marie's extended family. It was hard for Sylvia to remember details of the lives of people that she had never seen face to face.

After lunch, Sylvia asked Marie, "Tell me how New Beginnings is doing."

"There are many challenges. But lots of help, too. Professionals give their time, holding workshops for the volunteers, spending time with the Russells, one on one. That's the couple who supervise. They are so dedicated. Though they barely make enough income to get by, they won't take a raise. Then more of the budget can be for clients' needs. They love what they are doing, and are so appreciative of us volunteers. Most important, effective support for the women is being carried on. Funding is private; some from churches. That way they are free to use the Bible as they counsel, and they have regular meetings, like a little church. It's a real combination – a residence, a drop-in for spiritual counseling, and education and practical information about organizing your life. Even help making out resumes and learning how to present yourself at a job interview." Marie's face glowed.

"Well, it's obvious you are enjoying it to the "n"-th degree! I hope you get many moments of personal joy as you see things improve in the women's lives."

Marie dropped her head. "Yes, there are those times. There are also failures – ones that don't make it." She was silent, obviously struggling to deal with the memory of a specific woman. She looked up.

"Well, Sylvie-Mom! Tell me about that dress you are planning to make for Emalie for Christmas."

* * *

Sylvia left Marie's late, and ended up in north King County's rush hour traffic, but the visit with Marie and Emalie had been so worth it. She pulled her car around a slow truck and got into the flow of traffic, if it could be called 'flow'. Afternoon rush hour was "all lanes filled" between Seattle and Everett. She gave it her full attention, knowing she'd soon leave it behind and be on her own country road again.

As Sylvia neared home, driving was easy, and she thought about the problems in Jennifer and Michael's lives. She felt bad for them – being left completely on their own. But having Len around was worse, and no one could change a situation involving him. He could have.

* * *

Finally, Jen thought. *A day when I have a few minutes to come over to see Sylvie.* She went up the rain-soaked steps and right on in, as Sylvia held the door open.

"Come, sit down in the living room. I have the coffee made."

"That sounds good."

"I need to catch up on your news. I didn't realize there was so much trotting to doctors."

"There is."

"Tell me how it's going. Did you say two or three specialists?"

"I guess it's three, counting the pediatrician. I feel like I've lost track." Jen smiled a pale version of her eye-sparkling expressions of the past.

"Aren't they coming up with any answers yet?"

"Not really. They are mostly just eliminating things. It's not an infectious disease with a name that specifically shows up in any blood tests they've done so far. He has an elevated white count, but that's not specific. They even tested for malaria because of the night sweats, but he hasn't traveled. I don't know why they bothered. They are hoping it's not multiple sclerosis, confused by simultaneous flu. It progresses differently and has different symptoms, so it's not likely. He's pretty young for that. It usually shows up in the twenty's or thirty's."

Sylvia couldn't take it in, the way Jen was rattling off information like an auctioneer. She was stunned into silence for a moment. "I'm sorry. I missed seeing how very serious this is."

"I couldn't absorb it, either. But what could you do? It's not something you can fix, or me either. We are going to a new specialist in Everett. He's just getting started. He seems to think it will take numerous tests and lots of time to get answers."

"Michael must get worn out."

"Yes, it is tiring. Of course we use a wheelchair to get around anytime we can." Sylvia was shocked to picture Michael in a wheelchair. The last time she saw him walking he wasn't moving very fast... but a *wheelchair*? However, he *had* looked listless and weak.

Sylvia nodded slowly. "What do you think of this new specialist? Sometimes they are so serious and highly educated that they are hard to understand. Is he easy to talk to?"

"Oh, he's fine." Jen paused, and considered as her voice trailed off. "Although specialists are brainy, he's okay. He explains what he can to me. Maybe they seem uninvolved, emotionally, because they know they will only have a patient for a visit or two. After they get the answers, they send a report back to the G.P.

Sylvia wondered, *This is a bit of a side-track. Is she not wanting to say what they are considering now? Well, I have to try.* "So... has he said what they are possibly looking at?"

"He wants to check Michael for cystic fibrosis, because Michael seems to have poor lung capacity. He's sending Michael to a respiratory specialist. Then our family doctor wondered about a form of TB. I think they did another test and got a 'No' answer on that for certain. Guess it's a settled issue. I get mixed up on what answers are for sure 'no', and which ones are still maybes. There will be more blood tests. That should eliminate or confirm leukemia once for all." She sighed. "Who knows?"

"Oh, Jenny. Leukemia? It seems unreal that they are thinking it is this serious." Sylvia shook her head. "You've had a such burden on your mind. Last time we talked I was just beginning to understand. Now it hits home for me. I guess because of hearing the names of these diseases. I'm so sorry that I haven't 'been there' for you. How much sleep are you getting?"

"Not sure – I do get tired, being up and down at night. I hear Michael tossing, and calling out in bad dreams. He has pain in his muscles, or even his joints. I rub his legs and his back and it helps a little. He gets a sore throat and the lymph nodes swell."

"Poor little guy. Poor you. Please let me come over and stay, while you get a good nap."

"No. I can manage. He sleeps in the daytime, so then I can, too."

"At night, after you've been up with him, and then get back in bed, you must find you can't sleep for worry. I had no idea."

"I admit I do lay awake worrying."

Sylvie shook her head. "Well... it's part of being a mother to worry, so I know I can't fix that. Wish I could eliminate it!" She smiled, but Jen didn't see. She had her head laid back and was looking at the ceiling.

"Yes. There's worry, but I also get detached. Maybe it's a protection. When I'm told the names of those awful diseases... it's like – no emotion. I tell myself that it will turn out to be the usual scare, like I've heard from others about their doctors. They tell them, 'If it's this, or this, you have six months to live'. The person goes home shaking and depressed. But after tests, and scans, and the latest techniques, they find out it was something inconsequential."

Sylvie said, "Yes, when you talked about Michael, you often made it sound – that's the word, in fact, – inconsequential. Like it was a lingering flu. What you told me was so believable. I got the idea that, even though he looked pale, it wasn't terribly serious – that the doctors were just worry-warts. I didn't think it was such a big problem – like he could really have a major disease." Sylvia thought, *You made it sound like you wanted to be left alone.*

Jenny said nothing. She thought, *Oh? It's pretty believable to me that it's a big problem – I think I was clear. You just weren't listening.* Irritation rose.

As they continued visiting, Sylvia sensed the distance that had come between them. Jen's topics of conversation became shallow. Sylvia, thinking that Jen was depressed, brought up pleasant events around the community. Though by comparison they were unimportant, she hoped that by hearing about other people's lives, Jen could be distracted, and get a little lift. It wasn't working.

Jen stood to go. "Don't worry about not being in touch. I've been too busy to even return answer machine messages. It's my fault we haven't talked." In her own thoughts, Jen added, *I'm too busy, but more than that – too tired or discouraged to want to talk. And anyway, you think that I just make things* sound *believable. That I don't tell the truth.*

"I wish I had known. Please keep me informed what's happening."

"Hmm, I'll try." She paused, and decided to say it. "I'll be honest with you. I'm guessing there are a lot of tests yet to go. Looks like a long haul. So I may not call about each step, since there's nothing to tell." And to herself she thought, *Really, I just don't feel like picking up the phone."*

* * *

Jen tossed on her bed and, in a half-sleep, tried to sort out images. Michael playing with Goldie, and in perfect health. Lennard appeared and a dark cloud came over the scene. She woke up enough to tell herself, *Lennard is gone; he's not coming back.* She couldn't shake the darkness from her mind. *I will think of things I like – see good word pictures and remember what Sylvie has told me.* She drifted along, half awake, seeing the scene of Jesus preaching on a large hill. His voice carried to her, even though she was at the back of the crowd – and it was full of tenderness. He was blessing with his words, and with his eyes, which, even at this distance, she felt looking on her. They were eyes full of love. He was saying 'Blessed are you when men persecute you.' *What is persecution? Am I persecuted? If I am, then am I blessed? Not likely. Is God there when Len hits me?* Resentment filled her heart. *The Bible says, forgive, but how can I forgive Lennard for being so cruel, so unfeeling, especially to Michael? I can't. And I* won't.

In her half-awake state, her thoughts got scrambled again, and she heard Sylvia saying, 'A woman who is living with abuse, needs first of all, to get safe. It is so crucial that she is safe.' *But the Bible tells me, 'forgive'. Sylvia tells me, 'If a woman gets safe, then she can think of moving on, forgiving and letting go of the past.' I don't know what to do.* She saw Jesus, standing there again. He was speaking words of comfort to her. *But God hates sin and wants to punish it. My sin. Confusing. So confusing.* She sensed the figure of Jesus, standing, waiting. She was afraid. Then someone came up beside her. She turned, and felt darkness – Lennard – he had a cruel look twisting his face. She was held by his gaze. Suddenly she woke with a start, and felt a suffocating presence in the room. Not Lennard. But what? Who? The accumulated fear of months, years, came over her like a great weight. Len oppressed her – Lennard was a man. But Jesus was a man. Was Jesus *that* different from other men? Did he see life from a man's point of view? Then again, Larry was a man, a good man. He would never beat Sylvia. It was all so confusing. Her thoughts whirled together until she couldn't sort them out, and she fell into a troubled sleep.

* * *

The house was chilly. Jen made cocoa, and she and Michael cupped their mugs and settled on the couch under a blanket. Wearing sweaters kept them warm. They could keep the furnace on low. They had been out for a short walk with Goldie. On the days Michael had less pain, Jen encouraged activity for the sake of muscle tone.

Michael soon took his cocoa and went to lay down with a book. Jenny got a dust rag to keep busy, but was still left with her thoughts. It rankled her that Sylvia had acted like it was hard to believe her. The comments were ringing in her memory... She could hear Sylvie saying, 'you made it sound so believable...that it wasn't a big problem.' She remembered thinking, *I don't have to try to make it sound believable. I don't have to make it sound either ordinary or extraordinary. It isn't anyone else's big problem anyhow. The Fords have been good neighbors. But why bother them? It's not Sylvia's problem. Not Larry's. It's mine and Michael's to deal with.*

She wiped the dust rag along the windowsill distractedly, then went to the front door to shake the dust cloth. The sky was gray. Going back to the kitchen to hang up the cloth, she saw the kitchen sink, the black chips mocking her. *That kitchen sink... enamel chipped off, there's no pride in this situation. But that's the least of it. These are just the ordinary problems of life. My reputation for telling the truth? Well, now – that's a different matter. Dear Sylvia, Life has been very believable. If you will listen carefully, that is, then you can hear. So, I made it sound believable, but it wasn't?*

Then that's the message to you – I am not believable. I just deceive people. Deceive them on a whim. Sure. Right – deceive people for no reason. That, dear Sylvia, was a roundabout way you had of saying I am a liar. You know what? In reality, I don't lie. I only wanted to save you from worrying. Well, I am glad to know how you feel about me. I won't lose sleep over it. I can save you from concern. I won't tell you anything at all. Your words show what you really think. But I can take care of myself. Have been for a long time.

* * *

Sylvia thought of the phone message Jen had left – that she might not be calling back, since her doctor's office warned her to be ready at a moment's notice. The call from Children's Hospital would be anytime, and she would need to leave immediately. Sylvia considered. *Several times I've tried calling. She isn't answering her phone. Probably lying down for a nap, or went outside or to the store. I'm glad her car is still working. Then again, she may have left already.*

PART FIVE
CHANGE

October – November

CHAPTER THIRTY-NINE

Jen clutched the covers to her face to stifle a scream of terror, and forced her eyes open. Her heart pounded. *Someone is trying to smother me.* The room was dark. The terror wouldn't go away, though she was telling herself, *there is no one here...but I am still being smothered. I'm seeing a confused picture – a small dark bedroom, a quilt over my face, I can't breathe. Nothing more.*

The picture had come, she knew, from the past – from reading her teenage journal last night. *I wonder what I was trying to accomplish? Why, as a teenager, I revisited memories of being seven? Even awake, last night, I couldn't make sense of it. My memories were spotty. We had moved to the tiny house. I remember that back bedroom. But I never remembered being smothered. Did that really happen? That house is where I was suppose to start a new school, but I never got enrolled. Dad was gone. Other men were there, not the so-called stepdad. It's all muddled when I try to picture what happened there, and how long till we moved out.* Feeling tired and 'low' last night, she had given up reading the mixed-up journal entries. Just got confused and went to bed. *Then this dream wakes me up. Are my past and the dream connected?*

Jen dragged out of bed. She knew she wasn't going to sleep

anymore. There was plenty to do to keep her busy till the sun came up. All the laundry needed to be caught up in preparation for that phone call to admit Michael to Children's.

* * *

Sylvia knocked on Jen's door when she returned from shopping, but got no answer. The car was gone. Discouraged, she wondered, *Why hasn't Jen even been answering her door when she's home? I suppose she's gone by now.*

Sylvia came into her own kitchen and went straight to the phone. After dialing Lisa, she drummed her fingers on the counter impatiently.

Sylvie began as soon as Lisa said hello. "I don't know what I did, Lisa. Jennifer has been off and on touchy. Now I don't know if she's here, or gone without even saying goodbye. It's been windy, though, and there may have been a note that got blown off. What bothers me most is she's been a different person lately. I'm worried about her. About our relationship. And I hope she's safe. Larry thinks she'll do okay in Seattle – I guess she will. But this distancing that's come between us – I don't want to lose her, Lisa. She has become a real friend and..." Sylvie couldn't go on.

"I'm so sorry, Sylvia. Can you remember something specific – why she'd be touchy?"

"Well, I can't say that I do. I think it's been coming on for the last couple visits. She would seem huffy. Get an odd look on her face, like I'd done or said something wrong. I don't know what. The strain wasn't there consistently. But more lately. I'm sad it's happening now. She needs a friend. Bad enough dealing with Michael's health needs. She's also dealing with Len leaving, then suddenly showing up, and leaving again. She has a limited amount of savings to carry her. He told her he's not coming back. She seems vague about it, but I guess it's because she never knows what he will do. And I think she's vague partly because she doesn't want to admit to herself that she doesn't want him back. Of course, she's worried about Michael. It's serious. I didn't know how serious until she named off a bunch of diseases being considered."

"I can certainly see how she'd be stressed."

"She might have been able to stay at Marie and Mark's, but it's quite a way from the hospital. They don't really have room, but they'd have her in a moment, if they knew. I started to tell her about them, but she refused immediately. She has so much on her mind; I feel sorry for her. But back to this puzzling question – I sense I've done something to offend her, and I don't know what. I'm beginning to feel like I don't really know her as well as I thought."

"It may or may not be anything you did. Probably it was because you have gotten close."

Sylvia puzzled over that a moment. "How do you mean?"

"Do you remember reading about walls, boundaries, and relationships in that book?"

"Yes. How does that figure with this?"

"Well, you said that you two have had good talks together – about the past, her past. Also about Len – that he is emotionally cruel to her and Michael."

"Yes. Wasn't that good – that she did talk? I was hoping that she'd come right out and admit that he was battering her."

"It's good that she let down her defenses and trusted you. But for a person who has never been able to trust other people, it feels unnatural. To trust women, especially, would be difficult. You said her mother pushed her children away, emotionally. Later, when Jen was pregnant with Michael, her mother wouldn't speak to her. Try and transfer her feelings then, in that relationship, to her present life. Can you picture how she feels trying to trust women? It seems to her it isn't worth taking a chance. Mary in Seattle was an exception. In fact, Mary is probably the reason why Jennifer trusted you. She had a good experience."

"But why would she get cold and distant toward me now? I'm still here for her."

"She isn't *able* to believe that. It's not *normal* to her. A woman will let her down, based on her past experience."

Sylvie turned that over in her mind – *not normal*. "Lisa, that's awful. How very sad. I can't imagine fearing that I'll be hurt by every woman who comes along. That I'd expect every new situation to go sour, and not want to get close. Certainly there are disappointments

– that's life. But to never be able to desire to get close… Sorry, I rambled. What else were you saying about walls and boundaries?"

"Boundaries are healthy. I need to "know where I stop and where you begin". Not get my emotions enmeshed with another person. If I lack boundaries, I'm always needy. I go to friends for their opinions, and then get muddled over what I would want. I would become a bag of nerves every time I have to make decisions. If I do make them, I can't find the will to act on them. Or I hesitate, time runs out, and I decide hastily. That's some peoples' method. Actually, that doesn't sound like Jennifer. She has been coping quite well, getting a job, taking Michael to appointments. Another unhealthy way of dealing with lack of boundaries is to throw up walls. This sounds like Jen. Challenge is painful. She won't consider other's opinions. She has convinced herself, out of fear, that only her answers are trustworthy, because she's been steered wrong. Co-dependence and isolation can keep a person from having growing, healthy relationships. Dealing with life in these ways is unhealthy."

"Okay. I'm beginning to see. I do remember reading about boundaries, but I didn't realize it applied here. So you think Jen opened up, then she felt threatened. One of her rules was 'you can't trust women', and another was 'you can't trust God or religion'. So she retreated – is that it?

"Basically, yes."

"Almost everyone has hurt her? I can't believe that."

"No. Everyone hasn't hurt her, but she 'learned', sadly, to keep people at arm's length. Partly, she didn't develop the social skills of a child in school, what with moving, feeling different, taking an adult roll with younger siblings."

"Tell me more; how a healthy boundary is different from a wall."

"A healthy boundary will allow us to hear another person's opinion without fear. I can say, 'Go ahead. Please tell me what you think.' Knowing I have the choice to make up my own mind.'"

"Oh. I can see that."

"She feared getting hurt." Lisa chuckled. "You are dangerous to her."

"*What*? How could I be dangerous to her? What could happen – in her thinking?"

"I don't think a person thinks about it consciously. It's more of a *feeling*. She may feel like you would get to know her and then, somehow, you would cause her pain. You might turn on her, hold her up for ridicule in front of others. Make jokes and be sarcastic. It's a small community."

"Oh, I *wouldn't* do that. Why would she think that?"

"Because it fits her experience. And notice I used the word 'feeling', not think. She didn't actually picture you turning on her, or ridiculing her, but the *feeling* is there, deep inside, that she might be betrayed. It's based on what she has felt when it was 'dished out' to her in the past. She might fear you would talk about her behind her back, just when she is getting to know people in the community. After all, you know a lot of people, and you know a lot about her. I would guess that right now she regrets sharing her thoughts, her past, with you. Her protective wall is gone."

"Okay. I won't say, 'but I wouldn't do that'. I see your point."

"Of course you wouldn't. Another part of it is, she began to like you and opened up her heart; let herself feel warm, good emotions. Normal friendship emotions began for *her*. It might have been scary. She's been disappointed. Her Aunt Sally was kind. That was an exception. But even there, she felt hurt. Didn't you say that her aunt moved away to be near her children?"

"Yes."

"Well, she ended up let down. Abandoned."

Sylvia pictured Aunt Sally, and thought of the great help and encouragement this woman had been. It was a loss, indeed, when she moved far away.

"Jennifer is probably mixing up her own negative opinions of herself with her perception of your opinions. She may remember any little thing you said, a suggestion even, but recall it as a put-down. Things that wouldn't bother most people. She has hit a bad time. She's depressed. She's turning over in her mind what's been said. She might magnify some comment until she 'sees' or *thinks she sees,* disapproval. Even a passing comment feels like heavy condemnation."

"Oh, no. Would she take it that hard? I did say a few things, like how she might respond in a healthier way to Len. How she could have better self-esteem, or could take better care of herself, eat more. I said it because I cared about her." Sylvie got thoughtful. "Oh. Another thing – I really encouraged her to go to Al Anon. Get a support group for herself; one made up of people who understand marriage to a user. She got a panicky look; seemed afraid to go, even once."

"A group could be scary. She might imagine problems. Though it's general knowledge that a support group can help, she may have been afraid of any group thing, like church. Even though in Al Anon, personal information is not to be taken outside of the meetings, She'd worry that it could happen. Len could have found out she attended. Fear is an awful taskmaster. She faces many fearful possibilities." Lisa paused, then said, sadly, "Too bad she chooses to face them alone."

"I wonder if she knows that I care."

"I know you've not only told her, but shown her. I guess it's difficult for her to believe. She can't absorb the "feeling side" of being cared about. She also may be choosing to face trouble alone, closing herself off from you, rather than take risks. She sees that your background is different, your upbringing, your family's values. You were beginning to understand where she's been in life. She knows her mother didn't value the things your family did. It's a sharp contrast. She's torn. She identifies with her mother, even though she disagrees with her values. But she hasn't gotten out of the unhealthy side of attachment to a mother – needing approval, yet fighting the desire for it. She might think you can't handle what you've learned, now that you really know her."

"It is true – I do really know her, and I care for her very much. Actually, we have important things in common. My mother, though moving in much different economic circles, valued, and still values, things I don't. Like money for its own sake. Jen would reject that thinking too." Sylvia got a rueful smile, and simply shook her head. "She could use some money. As a tool. But back to things in common – her mother and mine apparently wanted to work their way into the upper class. I wish my mom had known that a truly high-class person is altruistic, not self-serving. They use their abilities, their wealth and power, to at least create jobs, and often they also benefit or serve others in notable ways. I told Jen how difficult the phoniness was for me. It was upsetting. Doesn't Jen remember that we talked about that?"

"Maybe. But she may focus on the differences. She saw 'successful'. That intimidates her. Your family was "doing things right". She feels shame about her family. I imagine she doesn't see her own strengths."

"You're right. Jen doesn't. It's strange to think that she didn't look at what she had going for her. She wrote powerful poetry. Lots of creativity there. She had kept it inside. We were just starting to share our ideas and our past work. She is such a special person. I wish she could see that."

"Quite a few women say to me, 'If you really knew me, you wouldn't like me.' I'm thinking Jennifer didn't feel a bit special. You can't just talk them out of low self-esteem – can't make them believe that they have unique abilities. It may help some to be in a program on self-worth and faulty perceptions. But I think that, without finding God's deep, unconditional forgiveness and acceptance, it is not going to be fully effective. Self worth won't come until the woman feels the worth God places on her – special enough for Jesus to die for her! It's sad. Some are openly hostile and angry. They can be almost hateful, but they don't see it in themselves. In their blindness, they focus on the other guy as being to blame. It's one more distraction that keeps people from relationships with people, and from finding a trusting relationship with God."

"Are there success stories?"

"Oh, yes. But remember, many people need someone to talk to who has training, so be easy on yourself. Some women ask questions and learn their way around the Bible. But even though they come to trust the Lord and find His forgiveness, they still need a lot of time for building relationship skills. Feelings based on facts of acceptance with God come slowly. It helps to do a Bible study about God's love. A woman can read examples of real people who trusted God and obeyed him, in the Bible and the centuries since. They learn what happens – that people have big problems but God is there. Seems like a study of His nature and character is best. Get to know God and his nature. He's a promise-keeper to His own. I have seen them develop healthier thinking then, after taking in accounts of God's faithfulness.

"Aw, that makes me think of the talks Jen and I had once about Ruth in the Bible – how she learned to trust God. What you say is encouraging, even though it sounds like it's not overnight." She pictured Jen, as her whole being was weighed down by the distresses of many years. "No, I guess she won't get rid of deeply-ingrained condemnation just by trying to think 'positive'."

After Sylvia hung up the phone, she wandered to the front window. The evergreen trees were tossing in the wind. It was gray. *Lord, I don't feel like I have anything I can put into words to say to you. But I know You have us in mind all the time. I feel so tired. I think I just need a rest. Lisa is right. I'm not a professional. God, draw Jennifer to want help. Guide her to get the help she needs.* Sylvia paused in her thoughts, then continued with self-talk. *I guess I'm a worry wart. Maybe Larry is right. Jennifer will go to the city. She is a survivor and has some savings from the greenhouse job. She said she can get work at the same place where she got two shifts the first Seattle trip. It will be a good time for me to get away. I may go see Doug and Colleen in Vancouver, Canada.* Sylvia let her mind wander to that beautiful area. A city like Seattle, with salt-water air, and just as beautiful. Or, she thought, possibly a notch above! It was a matter of debate!

When I get home from shopping, I'll ring up Doug and Coleen to say I can take them up on their invitation to "beautiful British Columbia". See when it's convenient for them to have me. It will be a change of scene. Though I like their city, I especially like that stretch along the border, going east. Maybe, instead of driving straight to their home, I'll do a jaunt for an hour into a restful country scene. It might soothe my soul. She chuckled at all the maybes and mights in her thoughts. Then she nodded agreement to her plan. *Going now, in the fall, will whet my appetite for that B.C. holiday next year with Larry. We can repeat the trip we took years ago, to Hope and beyond, into the mountains! 'Foot loose, and fancy free'. Oh, my, I'm dating myself with that expression!*

* * *

Jennifer hurried over to Sylvia's, holding a note in her hand. There was no answer to her knocking. *Oh, well, I'll leave it tucked in the crack of the screen door.* Returning home, she wrote another note to Sylvie, in case the first blew away. She confirmed that Sonia said on the phone that they'd love to have Goldie stay with them. Jen held the note, thinking how Sylvie would come in and find it, using the key she'd used to check things during the last Seattle trip. Jen felt sad, thinking of leaving the country again. She started to put the note on the coffee table, but stopped to re-read it. *Sylvia and Larry, I have to go now. I'm glad Goldie is taken care of – Sonia said it's fine for her to come there as soon as you want. That halter and line Larry put up has worked well for her, and at Kyle's she can even run around loose part of the time. But now I have to get going on packing. So good-bye for now. Jen*

Back to work. Today was the day she drove Michael to Seattle and admitted him to Children's Hospital.

* * *

Len threw the cell phone down on the bed. He'd called repeatedly, and there was no answer. If Jen *had* picked it up, he would have hung up – he was just checking on her. This was not normal. She usually left the answer machine on.

* * *

Sylvia went over to Jen's house, knocked, and then used the key. Finding the note, she got tears in her eyes, wishing she could have been home, said goodbye. *I wish I could give you a big hug, Jen. I'm going to miss you, and worry about you. But I'll try to pray instead of worry. Pray that God keeps drawing you until you yield to Him, to his love, and come willingly to him. The Lord knows where you are, in more ways than one.*

CHAPTER FORTY

J en tried to use her most 'positive thinking'. She had made it to Seattle. Michael had been admitted. She had a waitress job. She was thankful for that.

This morning her mind was on the car as she changed gears. She knew the transmission was going to go. Or was it the clutch? Suddenly she heard a noise. *Clunk.* That was it. Stuck. *Now what do I do?*

A helpful man had heard and seen what happened. He came over to her window, and said, "May I help you push your car over to the side, to that parking place? It sounds like you may need a tow truck to get any farther than that."

"Yes. Thank you." Jen paused. "I guess that is all I can do for now. Thanks."

Once it was parked and the man had left, Jen tried to collect her thoughts. She was five blocks from the hotel. She plugged the meter with coins, knowing they wouldn't last the day. All she could do was catch a bus to work. Maybe she could keep money in the meter as often as possible. *What to do?* The waitress job was part time now, and slowing down. Repairs were out of the question. Maybe she'd find another restaurant job. She didn't know how long she'd be in a hotel. Money would run out, fixing cars. The wind blew off the water, cold, as she walked to the bus stop.

* * *

Sylvia put away the clean dishes as she fretted. *I don't know what has happened with Jen and Michael, or what the tests are showing. Jen's life is a total mystery. Where is she living? How is she going to manage when she runs out of money? Can she get a job? Can she get back in the residence for parents' of sick children?* Sylvia walked into the living room where Larry was reading. Usually she would have sat down beside him and enjoyed reading a magazine or listening as he talked about work. Tonight she stood.

"Larry, I don't know what's happening with Jennifer. I tried phoning the parents' residence and she isn't there. They're full. She hasn't registered, according to the receptionist. She could have phoned me – collect. But she hasn't. She knows I would want her to. I haven't heard a word from her."

"I imagine she's busy running to the hospital to be with Michael. Maybe she's picked up a few hours waitressing work."

"Exactly – that's what worries me! *Did* she get work? Is she running out of money? I don't know how much she had. Maybe she is depressed over what they've found wrong with Michael. She needs some moral support."

"Sylvie, you're trying to fix things again. Things you are imagining and don't know are even happening." He shook his head, sounding disgusted. "Will you stop worrying."

He had made a statement – not asked a question. She huffed, angry. He was irritated at *her*. He was accusing *her* of faulty mental work, and yet he couldn't be bothered to concern himself with Jen.

Larry continued. "She said before that she knew a good hotel she could afford. She's a survivor." *Yeah, right,* Sylvia thought. *Never mind. I can be concerned enough for both of us.* She went into the bathroom and drew a tub with her favorite scented Epsom salts.

* * *

Before leaving home, Sylvia wrote a note reminding Larry to take Goldie and the food over to Sigurdsens. Also to please be in touch with Jeremy. He might be needed to take care of the dog in case Sigurdsens had an emergency. Then she phoned Jen's one last time. *How foolish of me to try. I hoped she might have come back for something, or turned it on remotely. I would leave a message, and she would get it. Oh, Sylvia, stop kidding yourself. She's gone for a while. Just do what Larry says – enjoy your trip and try to relax. For sure, you need it. Jen is not here. She's in Seattle, but it won't be forever.* Sylvia turned things over in her mind... What had happened in Brown's house in the last few months had been a frightening question mark. Who could know? Now, hopefully, Michael's illness would be diagnosed. *Jen might even get help.* Sylvia considered a new thought, *Wouldn't it be wonderful if Jen connected with a program like New Beginnings, starting the classes as a drop-in!*

On a sentimental whim, one last time before she left, Sylvia walked over to Jen's yard. She stepped out from the path. Into the cold air flamed a bronze fire of chrysanthemums. A flame of love, like God's love. *Oh, Jenny, yield to Him. Just come!* She turned away, overwhelmed.

* * *

Jen's car sat there beside an expired parking meter. The officer stood, shaking his head. He had been keeping an eye out. Coins had been put in twice – with big gaps between. Pity. Someone was trying. It probably wasn't even running. He looked at the notice on the windshield that he had placed there. He had no choice. It had to go. From the looks of it, the owner likely could not afford the towing and storage fee. But it had to go. Within the hour, the car was hooked up and taken to a locked yard.

* * *

Sylvia had told her cousin, Doug, and Colleen, that, although she could arrive by one o'clock, she more likely would tour the area on the way. There would be a key in the flower pot, in any case.

Once out of the shady woods of Granite Falls, she enjoyed the direct sunlight. At the crossroad, she turned north onto Highway 9 where trees would block the view, but traffic was slower paced than I-5. Later she'd relent, and cut over to the interstate before reaching Mt. Vernon. But next summer she and Larry would take 9 all the way to the Canadian border. On the way they would wind through several tiny villages of a few houses. The odd one would have a gas pump and store, decades old, and a mossy cemetery. At one point they would pull off and take another picture of that beautiful mountain, Three Sisters, she thought.

Settling on a coffee in Mt. Vernon as her goal, she relaxed and let the peace of the surrounding country affect her. Cows grazed. A gentle wind ruffled the roadside grass. Sylvia took a deep breath. Peace and quiet. Farming must teach a person a number of things, like 'you don't rush the seasons.' 'Relax when you can.' With her hands on the wheel, she rotated her shoulders. She was determined to let go of controlling tension, and felt some release in her neck and back muscles. Breathing deeply and slowly, she arched her back, moved her hips, then did an all-over wiggle. Wiggle? Wiggles were something little kids did!

Laughing softly, Sylvia felt the apprehension she felt about Jennifer begin to ease. Chuckling again about wiggles, she pictured her three kids and their childish needs. They had been wigglers, on trips or sitting in long adult meetings. Ironic, how she had scolded them. Now she tried doing it, and it helped!

She drove over to I-5, and merged smoothly with traffic. Her thoughts returned to contemplating the summer's mental tension. She remembered a woman talking at the beauty shop, referring to "getting centered". But she meant something different than Sylvia. *God himself is the Center. I realize I am learning all over again to trust You, Lord. Lately I have not been spending time with You. No wonder I have been in a knot. I've enjoyed the time off work, but I haven't returned to the habit of picking up Your Word daily and reading it.* She remembered what an influence Lisa had been when they were neighbors. Maybe she could be the same kind of influence in Jen's life. She thought back to when she established new reading habits. *I spent a little time every morning reading a Psalm or some Proverbs, and then a portion in the New Testament. I was surprised how that reading brought everyday life into focus. I got the "big picture". My problems shrank; they were manageable. Here I am, I have shared with Jen what a help the Bible is, and I'm not consistently reading it for my own benefit.*

Sylvia's mind wandered to something Lisa had explained about Jenny. When mentioning that she had prodded Jen to eat more, Lisa noted that lack of interest in food probably was one indicator of clinical depression. Sylvia admitted she could be guilty of playing amateur psychologist as she urged and gave advice. It was kind of satisfying. But Lisa's explanation showed how serious problems might be. Casual analyzing was 'out'. As for the urging to eat more, Sylvia remembered Jen's angry response. It was a bad scene. She felt guilty picturing Jen's tense face and angry voice. "What! What do you mean by *'I should have more appetite, instead of robbing myself of pleasure*? You mean that I am so messed-up I don't want happiness?' Sylvia remembered shaking her head, saying, *"No, Jen. It's just that I can see that you might enjoy life if you could approach it with more enthusiasm."* At the time she didn't think the statement was a problem. Talking with Lisa, she realized she should have kept quiet.

Sylvia felt warm affection as she thought of Jen. *I am still troubled, but I'm getting a break, like Larry suggested. That's good, but Jen certainly is "worth worrying about".*

A good expression came to mind, *'Use things, love people.' It was not 'Love things, use people.' So true.* Another expression came to mind. "Why worry? Does it help?". She thought, *Love can, though. But how do you go about loving someone who doesn't know how to receive it? Poor Jen.* Suddenly Lennard came to mind. *Is he gone? Or will he return and hurt Jen and Michael again? Even if he didn't harm them physically, he would destroy their emotional well-being.*

Sylvia thought how she had seen increasing signs of abuse when he was around. To her untrained ear and eye, it looked serious, but nothing was clear-cut enough for her to "make a federal case" of it. Len would lie to cover it up, and maybe hurt Jen for revealing stuff. *What was going on when outsiders weren't looking? Apprehension used to fill the air when Lennard was around. I know he picked up on my dislike of him when I visited. That created more problems – he sensed it. So what? Let him. Jen wouldn't acknowledge abuse, but he gave it away. I doubt a display of my anger would change things. I did have a hard time keeping control of myself. The way he talked to Jen and Michael, he ought to have been rebuked. But Larry wasn't there, and Len wouldn't listen to a woman, especially me. Well, now Len is gone. Jenny is safe. I can let go of the worry.*

Larry's words came to mind. "You can't live another person's life for them. Let go of Jenny, and let her act on her own. She can think through some of the good advice you and Lisa have given her. She shouldn't be made to feel helpless. Let her take charge of her own life, and pray she seeks what help she needs." So Sylvia had given it an honest try. It was hard. Now Jen was in Seattle, preoccupied with Michael's health concerns. Maybe, after his diagnosis and the start of treatment, Jen would come out of the doldrums. Michael could come home and there'd be a hopeful future.

But there was more than just being in the doldrums with Jen. Her words came back to Sylvia. Voice tense, she had said, "So! I'm messed up – the 'needy' one, am I?" *Was that what was bothering Jenny? The feeling that others were seeing her as needy and inadequate? Oh, dear. I could have explained to her that I didn't think she was messed up. I could have reassured her, to give her a greater sense of support. We are all needy; it just shows up at different times in each life. Her need showed up now. But maybe I was insensitive. What have I done? Oh, there I go again.* Sylvia took a deep breath. *My mind going a mile a minute in the wrong direction – negative – I pick the whole thing apart until I analyze it to death.*

Sylvia looked out across the rich flat land she was covering. Hills were rising on her right. *I'll do better to think about where I'm at right now, on this road. Yes, live in the present. Mount Vernon is the next town. That neat bakery and coffee shop is where I'll stop.*

Revitalization projects had made small towns come alive. It was fun to stop and stroll, or browse the shops. She wouldn't go there today, but La Conner, just a few miles to the west of Mount Vernon, was a special spot. Over many years it had become run-down, a "has-been" on a side road. Lively trade in the early days, travel on the tidal waters and the Skagit River, had diminished. What a change now! La Conner fields were famous in spring for brilliant blooming daffodils and tulips. The main street was charming. Larry and she had strolled in and out of little shops, snuggled one onto another. Then they walked behind a shop and onto a wooden deck perched above the water. The Skagit River rolled by, strong and deep, full of snow-melt cascading from countless streams in the well-named Cascade Mountains. That fresh water had mixed before their eyes with the salt water of Puget Sound.

Maybe, instead of taking Highway 9 on the way back from B.C., I will go west. Have a little side trip to La Conner, and then go south into Stanwood. That is another 'used-to-be little' town. Now there are jobs and it has become a bedroom community for Marysville-Everett. Hah. I remember passing through Marysville as a child. It was only a wide spot on old Highway 99.

But right now what I want is a strong cup of coffee and a special goody in The Calico Cupboard in Mount Vernon. That's "a plan". I'll leave worry behind. This is a get-away. Sylvia started singing the Kenny Rogers favorite, "On the Road Again".

The border crossing was done. Now to enjoy B.C.! Sylvie drove through this wide farm land of blueberry bushes and milk cows, grazing or feeding in their barns. It looked good, but she was also eager to see Doug and Coleen, and catch up. She headed for a main road into the city. *I'll beat them home and get unpacked. Can't wait to see the view from their place.*

* * *

In the impound yard, the manager's alert eyes caught sight of a tell-tale weld. Bending down and making a closer examination, he knew he had a live one – a drug dealer using well-concealed compartments. He smiled. One phone call.

The police officer came. He did his examination, and, nodding slowly, said, "Good work. Interesting. I checked the papers when you phoned it in. This is registered to a woman who has no record. There's more to the story. We'll just keep an eye on things. She may phone you. We are going to move the car to another yard, so go ahead and tell her that the police had an interest in it. We'll be keeping an eye on her, maybe even interview her. But at least we will be watching who visits her, who she talks to."

* * *

Jennifer hurriedly left the interview with the hospital doctor, then slowed as she headed down the corridor. "We believe we are getting closer," he had told her. *Is that all? Closer? And he has no idea how long it will take. I can't believe it.* Tears filled her eyes. She saw a restroom ahead and quickly ducked into it. Two women were at the sinks so she entered a cubicle. She hung her purse on the door, grabbed a wad of paper and held it to her eyes. After a minute she blew her nose. *Okay God, where are you now? Why can't you help us? As if you cared.* The women left. Jen went out to the sink, and splashed water on her face. Dabbing it dry, she saw that her eyes were going to look awful, regardless of what she did. She turned and hurried off toward the too-familiar coffee shop. It was rest time for patients. She had an hour to kill before visiting Michael again.

Jen sat on the side of the hotel bed, shivering, too tired to get up and rummage around for a sweater. *It's been a long day. I'm so alone. No one cares. Why doesn't God, that loving God of Sylvia's, care?*

"*He does care, Jennifer. Give Him a chance – be open to Him. He'll show you.*" It was a strange feeling, like Sylvia was in the room, reaffirming what she'd said. Jen sat there, mulling over conversations with Sylvia. It got late. She was so tired. Feeling like a lump of clay, she simply slid under the covers and went to sleep with the light on.

In the morning, Jen was stiff. It seemed like she could get one good night's sleep, alternating with one bad one. Last night was a fitful one. She got herself ready for work. *Another day, another dollar. That's what I remember Dad saying. I'll see Michael after work. At least I'm able to visit earlier today. Then home by six or so. Maybe spend the evening reading in the bathtub.* It would help her not be lonely and sad for Michael, cooped up in the hospital.

* * *

Sylvia had been glad for the time away. But, as she drove home, past the La Conner turnoff, she had to admit her mind had been on Jennifer and the fact that she had no way to contact her. As she pulled into her own driveway, so near Jen's house, it suddenly struck her. *I can't write to her directly, but I can write to the hospital! Surely, if I send a card to Michael, she will see it! Of course! Why didn't I think of that before!* She could grab a kid card in town. She began on notepaper, wishing Michael good health, asking if he could see much out his window, and what the play-social area was like. Then she asked if he could write back, or have his mom write a note in the stamped envelope enclosed. She found her Seattle phone book and got the address. *I'll drive to the post office now. It will go out today.*

She walked into the post office and stood in line, but her mind was busy with possibilities. *I'd like to word the question so I get the most cooperation. Hmm. All I can do is try.*

She stepped up to the counter. "Could you please tell me – I need to find out if my friend, and neighbor, Jennifer Brown, is having her mail forwarded to Seattle."

"Oh, I cannot divulge information of a personal sort. That is against privacy laws."

Sylvia turned away, disappointed, but at least she had hope of the possible contact through Michael's card. *Why didn't I think of this before?* She smiled.

The next day Sylvie had something to take care of before anything else. She drove to the little church she had visited in the spring. Parking, she took the key out of the ignition, and sat, looked at the house next door – the parsonage. Would there be help here? Mustering courage, she went to the door and knocked.

"Hello!" The young woman answering the door had a welcoming smile.

"Hello. I've come to your church a few times. My name is Sylvia Ford."

"Oh, yes, I remember you! Come in. My name is Karen Lundgren. Have a seat.

May I get you something; a cup of coffee, maybe? Or tea?"

"Well, if you have coffee made; sure."

After they were settled, Sylvia plunged right in. "There is a woman I am concerned about. I'm quite certain she's being physically abused. I've seen the emotional abuse, the intimidation. She won't admit, when I've seen bruises on her, that it's abuse. I've been frustrated with my own lack of knowledge about these things. For now, she is away in Seattle. Her sick son is at Children's Hospital. I don't know how to go from here when she returns. A couple of times I've made a point of mentioning help for abuse, but that hasn't worked at all. She gets irritated. Changes the subject. I thought you might have a book I could read to help me. And maybe one that I could give her to read."

Karen looked thoughtful. "I am really glad that you are concerned about her. Sounds like she needs help. I do know that a third party intervening is important, but you must be careful, too. I don't have special training in counseling, myself. My husband does, so you should talk with him. But I do have books you can borrow. I can imagine your concern. Sounds like you've given her the message that you care. That's a big one – for her not to feel alone. It seems that an abused woman hides the problem, and has a feeling of shame. Even though she is the victim, she may feel she is the guilty party, somehow causing trouble or deserving pain. Sometimes it's just plain fear of what will happen to her if she reveals the abuse – she's being threatened."

"Yes, I think she's ashamed, at least. She just shuts down the conversation. I don't know about threats to keep quiet... could be."

They talked more in detail, and then Karen brought out some books for Sylvia to borrow.

Looking at information on the covers, Sylvia said, "This is good. I realize that I need to learn more. Maybe I've needed moral support, too. I suppose I should make an appointment with your husband." Sylvia shook her head. "Most of all I wish she would come to talk to your husband herself, when she gets back. But, it's not likely." Sylvia got quiet. Gathering the books, she said, "I'll read these for now."

"Let's have prayer for this lady, that she will be willing, and have the courage, to reveal her problems." Karen almost added, *before it's too late.*

Karen prayed, asking for relief from the stress for Sylvia, and for the unnamed lady to be willing to get help.

"Thank you so much." Sylvia rose to go. "Just talking to someone about it is a relief. I wish I had come sooner."

As Sylvia drove onto the road, Karen looked out the window. *What a dilemma. Oh, God, you make us with a will. I'm glad for that. But it's frightening, how far we humans go. We attempt to solve our own problems, pushing You away. Preserve the woman's life, Lord. She is in such danger.*

CHAPTER FORTY-ONE

Jennifer felt dull; her fingers fumbled as she buttoned up her blouse. It was the lack of sleep from an over-heated room. She had tossed in bed till midnight, and then shivered the rest of the night. *I'll grab a coffee and toast before I catch a bus to the hospital. Today I will be early and I can talk directly to the doctor. Too bad I only get a half shift, but I will see more of Michael.*

Coming back to the present, Jenny's eyes rested on a pamphlet laying with other papers on the bedside table. "Signs of a Mate Who Could Beat You." She had read it. She remembered how Sylvia had opened it and said, "Pleeeease read this. Oh, Jen, just do it now, for me." She had. After reading it, she said, convincingly, to Sylvia, "You're imagining things." But the pamphlet had bothered her. It did sound like it was talking about Len's attitudes. She remembered telling Sylvie that things were fine, saying, *Lennard's not going to do that awful stuff. Anyway, he's in California, getting 'whatever' out of his system. I don't think he'll be back. So I'm not going to be in some melodramatic front-page newspaper story, stabbed all bloody, or shot full of holes. Mainly because he doesn't own a gun, or use a knife.* Finally Sylvie gave up, but Jen remembered her final words. "Be careful. I think you need to talk to a counselor." She had scoffed, waving her hand in the air to dismiss it.

Jen laid the pamphlet down, remembering how she'd taken it home and hidden it, on Sylvie's insistence. She had worried about getting caught. Funny. Lennard had only been around two more days. Then he was gone, only returning briefly. She remembered his last words.

"*I'm never coming back to that wimpy kid and you. You're useless. It's sickening the way you fawn all over him. And he just eats it up. Yeah, you make a pair.*" He went on and on with it. "*As I leave, I wish you God's blessings. Blessings on the two of you – you know, like Sylvia said on that card she gave you. 'The Lord bless you.'*" The scorn in his voice had chilled her, and the memory of his contemptuous look lingered. *I suppose I really do baby Michael. Well, I never said I was a perfect mother. Now I'll be a parent alone, I guess. Lennard said he's gone for good, but he's done this before. Leave, disappear, re-appear. Gone for days or weeks at a time.* She only had feelings of a dull apathy at his absence. *Our home... that is, our hate zone, or war zone – is not a real home. I've been in a real home. Mary and John have a home. Sylvia and Larry have a home. Together. Oh, God, is there no way I could have what these people have? What a mistake I made. As for calling out, 'Oh, God', I take that back. I doubt you're real. Sylvie just has positive thoughts. Anyway, it's my problem; why would I ask for help? I'm to blame for my trouble. I picked him, or let myself get picked. It has taken a while to see how stupid I was. What a dad poor Michael got. Maybe this is what women like me get, but Michael didn't deserve it.*

Jen grabbed her purse. As she reached for her watch, she saw the gospel tract from Sylvia, and picked it up. Sylvie's words came to mind. "*Gospel is the word for 'good news'. Read this! It is good news! It's how to trust Christ as your Savior! We need Him totally – we all have a deep need. God is so holy, and we are sinful. He died to freely give His holiness to us. There's no other way. It can't be earned. It's by trusting Him!*"

So easy, Jen thought. *Too easy. It can't be that simple. This one little piece of paper with its few words.* Yet Sylvia said, "*It tells about the greatest gift ever. It's the most important thing to come into your life – what God has done for me, for you, Jennifer, on the cross. Imagine being forgiven and belonging to Someone who cares that much!*"

Well, if it's so, then it would be true that it's the greatest news. If. She remembered the times with Sylvie. It was good to be together. She remembered how sincere Sylvie had been about Jesus – calling him *"Lord and Savior"*, or *"my Friend"*. *Sylvie truly believes in Him. Her pleas to me to trust Him were heartfelt. She cared. But that camaraderie we had is gone. I get tiresome to people. Though it's nice to recall the good times, it became tense, strained. Those good times are over. And I can't figure out this stuff. Not now.* She stuffed the tract in her open purse and checked for the room key.

Jenny left, ran down the stairs, and walked to the café. This morning it would be a quickie. She only wanted a little something to go with coffee. She'd overslept, or she would have made a cheese sandwich and eaten that. Inside, she glanced around, and then saw Tyler who lived at the same hotel she did. They had talked yesterday in the lobby. He had befriended her the first time she had brought Michael. He beckoned to her to come over. He held a cup of coffee, and she thought how good it would be to just sit and talk with someone. Not always be alone. She slid in the booth. A tasty-looking Danish was on a plate in front of him. The waitress caught her eye across the room, raised a mug, and Jenny nodded, and mouthed "to go".

"So you are on your way to the hospital, are you?" He paused. "Tired?" She knew she had deep circles under her eyes. Tyler looked concerned. She had briefly mentioned Michael's illness. Though she had said next to nothing about Lennard, Tyler must wonder why he never came. She had explained that his work took him out of town. His work – *what was his work, anyhow?* She wasn't sure. She wondered for a moment how Lennard saw himself. But then, why be concerned? He was gone. He didn't care about her. He'd be here if he did.

"Oh, yes," she realized she hadn't answered. "I am going to the hospital. Sorry, I was thinking." She made eye contact with Tyler as the waitress set down the coffee. "And I am tired – but that's life." She smiled at the waitress, "I'll take one of those, please." She pointed to the Danish.

"My boy is twenty-one now," Tyler sighed. "Hard to believe. He's working on the east coast. How old is Michael?"

"Ten," she replied, noticing that he remembered Michael's name. "He's ten and too old for his years." She looked down. *Better leave all that alone.* "Sickness takes an emotional toll." Tyler nodded. He picked up the magazine he had been reading and pointed to an article about the Space Needle. The issue was celebrating the anniversary of the Seattle World's Fair, and gave a glimpse back in time. She hadn't even been born in 1962.

"I went to the World's Fair as a little boy. Excitement, I'll tell you! Michael would have enjoyed it!"

She smiled back at him and nodded. "I'm glad I wasn't there – all those rides... My stomach would flipflop. Michael would have liked the pavilions where the countries show films and give you that "being there" feeling."

"Oh, he is a serious-minded type, is he?

"He is. Always learning."

"The African and Asian countries' pavilions were excellent."

She nodded as she washed down the Danish. "He reads all about the people and animals of other countries. Learns about environment issues. But he likes puzzles and riddles, too. Not all serious!"

"That's good. Environment wasn't big then. Natural beauty was what enticed people to visit abroad. The Fair did educate about the interesting people groups of each country. The fine handcrafts were impressive – my folks bought mementos. Mother explained about the baskets being beautifully made afterward, and admired the jewelry she'd bought. I was too little to buy nice items."

Tyler talked about the Fair, but Jenny's mind wandered to Michael, sitting in a hospital bed. And she realized she needed to wrap up the rest of her Danish, and get out to the bus stop.

"Well, I had better get going. Thanks for talking to me. Nice to have..." *Oops. Watch it – not too friendly. You're all alone.* "Nice to find a person who can say 'Hello'. I find the city unfriendly. And to think I spent years here." She put the money on the table as she got up.

"Here, let me get it." Tyler picked up the money and handing it back to her.

"No." She laid it back down. "Thanks, anyhow."

"I insist." He picked it up and handed it back to her. "Have a coffee with it at the hospital instead." She felt like saying she had enough money. Then she realized he was just giving a small kindness.

"Well, thanks. I'll treat next time."

"Sure."

Jenny left the café and hurried to the bus stop. After dumping her empty coffee in the trash, she climbed the bus steps, found a seat by a window, and let herself be rocked along. Her mind wandered to the past. *Where has my life been going? Seems, now, like a nightmare. Michael hurting in the middle of the night; me not knowing what to do. After he settled in to sleep, I'd crawl back in bed, hoping for some warmth and rest. Yeah, right – Hoping to get back to sleep. Waking Lennard and trying to justify myself. Why should I have to justify myself for taking care of my son? To think, he could have put his arm around me, cuddled up to get me warm, and sympathized.* Tears came to her eyes. *When I've remembered falling in love with Len, I almost missed him. Now I hope I never see that man again. Confusing.*

The bus jostled Jen as it came to a stop, and school children got on. They looked well-cared for. She started thinking about mothers.

When I talked to Sylvie about the bad time I had in school, I remember brooding afterward. Mom didn't seem to care that I was put in boarding school, kept away from her. When I became a mother, I cared for Michael. It seemed so wrong that Mom hadn't stuck up for me. She could have brought me home, and kept me with her. Could have gotten rid of that two-faced man that sent me away. I guess she didn't have the strength to make her own decisions. I hated her for it. I still get angry. She patted a tissue onto the silent tears sliding down her cheeks. Feelings flooded over her. *Abandonment. Where were you, Mother? I was all alone. I couldn't please you when I was at home. I never did enough, no matter what – I did laundry, cleaning, cooking. You complained about me. You complained that my father had brought all this unhappiness into our lives. Somehow that didn't ring true. I couldn't understand how, being dead, he could still be to blame. But then, he had left us. He left you alone, Mother.*

A shudder came over Jenny, involuntarily. She remembered the feeling of loneliness when she heard that her dad wasn't coming back home. *He left me. I remember the hard time we had. I tried to help you – but I still couldn't get to school on time, we couldn't pay the rent, my homework was half done, in a hurry. I only got good grades on tests, because I listened in class. When I showed signs of developing into a woman, you pushed me farther away from you. What had I done? At school they told me I wasn't trying; that I had more potential and could do better. Never good enough.*

Jennifer's throat ached from the strain of suppressed crying. *I'm not trying any more.* She shook her head. *I'm not going to try to measure up to other people's criticism, or to an impossible standard that they thrust on me. It is impossible. Who do I think I am – that I can accomplish that miracle?* She laughed to herself. *Jesus? Yes, that's what it would take to meet the impossible standard – as Sylvia said, the perfect human, Jesus.* She laughed again. *Am I seeing the light side, or am I being silly? Ridiculous requirements. Why did I not give up long ago? Trying to please a man who hated me? Trying to make things 'work' as a child, at home, even though I was little, and should have been the one cared for, not doing the caring. Now I know it was the adults' problems that needed to be solved – by the adults. I couldn't. But all I knew then was 'try hard'.*

Jen took another tissue out of her purse. She saw the tract again.

* * *

Sam revved his car up the driveway to Sylvia and Larry's place. When he hopped out, Sylvia was standing by a garden bed of freshly turned dirt. She had mud on her hands. A tray of bulbs lay on the ground.

"Hello Mrs. Ford!"

"Well, hello to you, Sam!"

"I was just going to ask if you remembered me, since our meeting at Jennifer's was brief. Guess you do."

"Oh, of course – how could I forget, after you fixed up Michael and Jen with that nice Franklin stove! I sure do! Sorry to be a mess. I'm planting bulbs. I won't shake hands. But what can I do for you? Do you want to come it?"

"Oh, no. That's okay. I've lot's I need to do. I just wondered if you'd heard anything from Jennifer?"

"No. She left a note, but it was more about the dog than her. I wish she'd phone where she's staying. I'd like to call her."

Sam nodded slowly.

"So… I'll share any news I hear. You're moving out here, aren't you?"

"Yes. I'll be renting a room with Sigurdsens. Be completely moved in by the end of the month."

"Good. I'll phone Sonia or her dad if I hear anything. You can call us, likewise. We're in the phone book, Larry Ford."

"Sure. It's more likely she'd contact you. Be nice to hear something soon."

Sylvia looked Sam in the eye, and gave up the effort at faked nonchalance. "Jennifer is completely out of touch. Has no friends in that part of the city. I'm concerned."

Sam nodded. "Me too."

After she had finished the bulbs, Sylvia went in, cleaned up, and sat down with a book on abuse that Karen Lundgren had lent her. Reading it made her think of possible ways to support Jennifer. *Maybe, when she comes home, she will go with me to talk with the pastor or his wife. After that she would probably open up to getting help from a trained support person, a professional counselor …if she is willing.* Sylvia shook her head. *If.*

* * *

At seven o'clock in the morning, an unmarked police car cruised by Jennifer's hotel, and pulled up behind a parked car. Brent Sullivan, a young officer in his first year with the force, held paperwork in his hand. Halliday, the senior officer, drove.

Inside, Jen was ready to leave her room when she noticed the envelope on her bedside table, addressed to Sylvia. She would finish her note tonight – add a few lines about getting more work hours. Give Sylvia the address of the hotel so she could send a card for Michael if she wanted. Now she needed to get going.

Sullivan and Halliday didn't have long to wait. The woman named Jennifer Brown came out of the hotel. Brent carefully assessed her as to age, general appearance, and the mood she indicated by her business-like walk. It was a 'just get it done' walk.

"What do we know about her?"

"Not much." Officer Halliday shook his head, aggravated. "The car is registered to her only. The address on the registration is Granite Falls. No criminal record. We are looking into why she is here. May be a courier for the operation. They like to use the innocent-looking ones. We'll find out. Too bad for you – you are stuck here with office duty this afternoon. I'm going out to Granite and look around. Talk to the neighbors. May even have a watch put on that property."

Brent saw the woman go in the door of the cafe. Five minutes later the woman reappeared with a to-go cup of coffee and a napkin-wrapped item. She walked to the bus shelter, sat down and ate. The bus came and she left, eastbound. Brent considered their big question – *was the woman a knowing part of the operation?*

Officer Halliday, in plain clothes, knocked again on the door of the Ford home. When there was no answer, he walked through the path to Brown's and stopped. Glancing up to the second-floor window, he wondered if he had seen a movement. He dismissed it.

What Halliday couldn't see was the man eying him from the shadows behind a filmy curtain. The officer again noted that no car had been in here since the last rain. No sign of recent activity in the garden. Cobwebs were across the front door, though it was likely a person would use the back door, which revealed nothing. Lack of activity. Would certainly be helpful to talk to the Fords, the absent neighbors next door. Bad that they were gone. The local gas station had revealed that the husband, Lennard, worked at the mill. That was the next stop. Halliday went to the road, started the car, and drove away.

Upstairs, Jen's Quiet Room was anything but peaceful. Len, standing tight-muscled, waited until the unmarked car went down the driveway. He could smell a cop a mile away. Then he strode back to the bedroom. Clothes were gone out of Jen's drawers. *Where is that woman? Why are the police here anyhow? Yeah, so...there was the bar fight. So what. It may have got their interest. That's all. Then again, there's that stupid old man with the dead dog. He probably gave quite a spiel to the police out here. But this didn't look like local police. It doesn't figure.* Len checked the drawers and closet again to find out what Jenny had taken. Enough was with her to stay for a while. *Probably the kid was in the hospital again – the puny wimp.*

Len went down stairs and out the back door. He glanced over toward the Ford's house, expecting to pick up some noise. Still no life there. And he hadn't seen the dog – or any new holes it had dug. He picked his way carefully along the driveway on the short grass. No footprints in mud. Lucky break that Fords weren't home. They couldn't see through the trees. *But I'll still be careful when my ride comes along on the road. Just make it look like a hitch-hiker being picked up.*

* * *

Questioning the mill boss had revealed more information than anything else. He hadn't heard a word from Lennard Brown in weeks. Brown shaped up to be very interesting. The boss had nothing but detrimental comments to make about him – he had been a royal pain for the men to work with. Picked arguments, and had tried to bait two different men into fist fights. All in all he could be intense and unpleasant, but not consistently so. Halliday would keep Brown at the top of his mental list. *We will be looking into that fellow. Warrants for arrest will show up. He's suppose to be in California, is he? Maybe. If he has an operation here, he'll be back.*

Later that day Brent stood reading the report Halliday sent from his laptop. There were no discoveries on the property in Granite. But a chatty neighbor boy at the store heard Brown's name mentioned by the officer and had told that Michael, Jennifer Brown's son, had gone to Children's Hospital in Seattle. He even gave the boy's whole name – Michael Hanson, not Brown. That would bear checking, asking the staff about a possible appearance by this Lennard Brown. Brent considered all the information. He'd like to hope they were making progress. He again picked up the report on the car. Definite traces of drugs, but very little – well wrapped. The next item that he read was an arrest warrant for Lennard Brown in Snohomish County. He was wanted in connection with reckless driving and assault on an old man. Brent read the full report and shook his head. This was a mean character.

* * *

Len Brown entered Children's Hospital. He had only a few minutes. Then his ride would come back to pick him up. He saw that two people were at the patient information desk. It had better move fast.

Jen left Michael's room, as the nurse had requested, and sat down in the waiting room nearby. Michael could visit only a little longer; then it was time to get ready for bed. She settled onto the couch, weary. *I'm glad for the shift at the restaurant this morning, but another split, starting early, finishing late. I guess I'm feeling the effects of not eating. Oh, well. Good to have a little money. At least I can grab a to-go* dinner. Her mind wandered. *Should really save money and heat up canned soup in the electric pot. Eat some fruit. Cheese in the ice chest. Good thing to have on hand.* She was too tired to think. Numb, she settled back and rested her head. She'd get a breather from standing all day – until she could go back and say good night to Michael.

Down in the lobby, Lennard Brown strode over to the woman at the information desk. He wanted to make sure the kitten was in the bag.

"My friend's son is here. I have a card for him. Could you tell me the room number of Michael Hanson?"

"Yes, of course, sir. But you realize visiting hours are over for tonight. You can visit again tomorrow." He nodded. She began to check her computer. She reached for a pad. *Sure enough, Michael is here. All I have to do is watch for Stupid. Not now – later. That silly woman will come to see her precious little boy. When I come back and follow her to where she's staying, then she will get smartened up real fast. I'll work a few things out of her – she'll talk. I'll see to it. Maybe she's been chummy with the police. She can't go messing with me. Squealing. And I can imagine who else she's been chummy with. She's not going to cause me any more trouble – no more than she already has.*

Len took the paper with the room number that the woman gave him. He happened to glance toward the elevator across the room. Out stepped Jen. She was preoccupied. *Wouldn't you know,* he thought, and smiled. He turned his face back toward the clerk. *Don't see me now, Stupid. Later. Yes, later, I'll have a surprise for you, you whore.*

Len kept his face averted and walked to the restroom where he could keep out of sight. He stepped in and ditched the unsigned card for 'his friend's son'. Watching through the crack of the door, he saw Jen go to the snack machines. Then she walked slowly to the main entrance. He pulled his cap over his face and walked out into the lobby. He held back at the entrance area until he saw her standing at the bus stop. *How could he work this out?* Then he saw a taxi stand.

Jen caught her bus. Len went to a taxi. "Follow that bus." The driver looked at him funny. "Don't look at me. Just do it." Len placed a twenty dollar bill in the man's hand. "My friend's wife is cheating on him, if you must know." The driver shrugged.

When Jen's bus slowed down and she got out, Len had the taxi driver pull to the side. She walked a short distance, then entered a hotel lobby. Len snickered, and thought to himself, *I wonder what kind of trouble she gets herself into there? We'll see what goes on. I'll be back. Tomorrow I'll be waiting for her.*

* * *

Brent Sullivan was restless, sitting in the car. "We know Len Brown is probably around. California police had a warrant out on him. He won't stay there." The young officer couldn't shake the uneasiness, knowing this man liked to use his fists. "We should let this Jennifer Brown in on what we're doing – that we're watching for a 'person of interest', who happens to be her husband. It bothers me that, when he was home, mill gossip said that he talked about 'straightening out' his wife. He made it plain, without using the words, that he hits her. I wish we could have her on our side, have her help."

"Nope. And it's time to go. We'll come back."

Lennard watched the unmarked police car drive away, and then stepped onto the sidewalk. With a hat pulled down over his eyes, he entered the hotel. At the desk a disinterested clerk said, "May I help you?"

"Yes. I want to drop this off in Jennifer Brown's box for her son." He held out an envelope with Michael's name printed on it. "It's from Big Brothers." Inside Len had taken the time to print a message as if to a child. It offered 'get well', and willingness to visit or help, signed Big Brothers.

The clerk took it, picked up a pen, and wrote a room number on it before tossing it aside. *What a piece of luck,* Len thought. *Figured I'd watch while he put it in a mailbox, but he even wrote it down in plain sight.* If Jen did pick it up, she would think nothing of it. Just take it to Michael. Len thanked him and walked out. He waited outside, as if for a bus, until he saw the clerk walk into the back room.

Lennard Brown slipped in and went up the stairs. He waited in the fourth floor stairwell with the door slightly ajar, watching the room with Jenny's number. He saw the piece of paper tucked in the crack of `the door. The hall was quiet. Len slipped across to her room. It was too early for her to be there. He removed the piece of paper.

Opening it, his eyes went to the bottom, where it was signed Tyler. Len's hand shook. "Come down to 102 for some take-out lasagna for your dinner. It will cheer you up. I hope Michael is better today. Tyler." He poked it back in the crack. *So you have been running around on me, out with every Tom, Dick, and Harry. Well, I'll see to you! I'll be here tonight. And you, figuring this dinner out is like any other night. You only wish. This is a night you'll never forget.* Lennard stepped back into the stairwell and climbed to the landing above. He looked out a window onto streets, with buses, coming and going. It was the top floor. Everyone used the elevator. He was safe. He could stay put, here. He rolled his jacket for a pad, sat down on the floor, pulled his hat low and clenched his teeth.

CHAPTER FORTY-TWO

Officer Sullivan tried his arguments on Halliday again as they pulled into position across from the hotel. "When she comes home, we can talk to her. When she phoned the guy at the impound yard about the car, she told him she may not be able to redeem it. That he might as well sell it for what he can get. That she'd come down and sign the papers. Doesn't sound like a pusher. Too cooperative."

"So? She will sign papers – What's that tell us? Nothing. You went to her door with the manager supposedly to check about cooking smells and potential fires. You looked around the place. Nothing suspicious. That tells us nothing. Seeing nothing does not prove innocence."

Brent sat back and took a deep breath. *I'm concerned that we don't know what's going on in there. Our "person of interest" might have slipped past us and be waiting in Jennifer Brown's room.*

* * *

Walking home from the bus stop, Jen was thinking of Tyler. Silly to be suspicious of him. He wasn't trying to be romantic. She had never gotten that feeling from him one time. She did feel vulnerable. He was concerned. She was alone. *I don't want to send the wrong signals. But I don't think I am. And he's not. He is just a nice person.* Jenny rode the elevator up to the fourth floor and walked over to her door.

As she got out the key, a piece of paper in the crack fell to the threshold. She picked it up and read, "Come down to 102 for some take-out lasagna for your dinner. It will cheer you up. I hope Michael is better today. Tyler." She had planned to walk to the cafe and eat something. But this sounded better. At the same time, she felt uneasy. It seemed old-fashioned, but the old adage that a girl never went to a guy's room came to mind. She shouldn't. But Tyler was okay. He wasn't going to bug her, harass her. She threw her jacket on the chair, went back out the door, locked it, and headed for the elevator and 102.

* * *

Jenny entered her room and flipped on the light. The clock read 10:30. Later than she had planned. She shouldn't have talked so long with Tyler, but he had been a gentleman. Now she needed a good sleep. A TV was blaring down the hall. *Wouldn't you know. Sounds like it's in here, full volume. If I get ready for bed and read, I'll get sleepy, or it might get quiet.*

The room was overheated tonight. It was freeze or fry. After she put on a short, thin nightgown, she threw back the covers on the bed. A knock came at the door. Strange. She went over and opened the door a little, holding it secure with her foot.

"Hello?" she asked. Someone pushed hard, forced the door, and suddenly Lennard's angry face thrust in. *Impossible; he's gone.*

"Hello..." she repeated weakly, her heart pounding. He pushed completely into the room and locked the door. She saw his face, twisted with fury, and she couldn't take her eyes off his. They were – *dead.* He had been angry with her – hit her – but never had she seen this depth of hatred controlling him.

"So!" His voice demanded her attention. Jenny was afraid to look at him, but she couldn't stop. *Oh, no,* she thought. *...I'll be beaten and twisted. Like his mouth is twisting. It will be the worst ever. He is crazy with jealousy. I am going to die...*

"So," he demanded, "where have you been?" Jenny was afraid to look at him. "While Michael has been in the hospital I see you got lonely." He pointed to the bed. "You didn't *want* to be lonely. You found a way not to be lonely, didn't you?"

Jen tried to understand.

He raised his finger into her face until it was pointed right in her eye. "You have things ready for the guy in 102 to pay you a little visit, *don't you?*" He twisted the words; the accusation was filled with evil.

"What?" He was talking in riddles. *How long has he been waiting, angry?* Feeling stupid, it dawned on her. *He saw Tyler's note. I am amazed at how incriminating this looks.* The slap jerked her head sideways, but she took it, standing. He strode away to the window and looked down at the cement sidewalk four stories below. Jaw muscles tight, he moved back toward her menacingly, with fists clenched. His detached stare terrified her most.

"Slut! I should make dog meat out of you and that guy, too."

He hit her hard in the jaw. Stunned, she fell against the wall, her head swimming. As she struggled for balance, she wondered, *How much can I take? That pamphlet. What did it say – act strong? But I can't aggravate and feed his frenzy. Act helpless? If I fall down, will he leave? No. A victim, I'll be only an object. ...I have no escape... I'll be beaten... to death.*

She was fixed on his eyes, like a deer, helpless in car headlights. She couldn't take her eyes off of his – dead staring eyes – detached from reality.

He is crazy... those dead eyes... Michael, my son, what will...

Lennard's fist came at her face. Blackness was closing in. She fell backwards over a chair and onto the floor, a knife-like pain shooting through her ribs. Blood and broken teeth filled her mouth. Yanked up, a blow to her ribs doubled her over. Light and dark swirled. Her arm was twisted behind, tighter, until her shoulder couldn't... A blow in her belly – pain turned into a dark gulf. She was sinking. The voice full of hatred grew dim.

* * *

"Sir, I'd like permission to go up to the fourth floor and have a look around the hall." Brent Sullivan couldn't shake the strange feeling.

"Permission granted," Halliday grunted. "You might as well get some exercise."

After asking the clerk if there had been any unusual activity, and getting a 'no', Sullivan took the elevator to the fourth floor. He thought he saw a quick movement at the stair doorway as it closed. But he heard a long, agonized groan – Jennifer Brown's door was ajar. He rushed into the room to see blood all over the woman's battered face and across the carpet. But her twisted arm and shoulder were worse – unreal. He knelt beside her. The skin was white. Breathing was shallow. Pulling her eyelids up, he saw her eyes were unevenly dilated. Then he saw the leg. It was unbelievable.

What can a doctor do with that? But this whiteness of skin – there's internal bleeding. Life-threatening. Head injury, who knows how serious. Maybe bleeding inside the skull. He slipped out his phone and called 911 for an ambulance.

Calling Halliday next, he said, "Come up quick. She's been beaten. Ambulance on the way. Tell the clerk to head the paramedics up here."

Halliday burst into the room, and swore. More experienced, he dropped down to do a medical check. He took her pulse which Brent felt he had neglected. But he told himself, *I know she's alive, that her heart is beating. But alive for how long?* He shook his head. *I'm going to nail this scum.*

He stood. "I'm going to get tissue for DNA quick – they'll come to take her soon." He went about his work with the slim hope that there was enough of the man's skin in the abrasions from his fists to identify him.

Halliday had thrown a blanket over her for warmth. She was in shock. He slid up the gown at her waist.

"What do you suspect?" Brent asked.

No answer. Then her distended belly gave the answer.

"Probably a ruptured spleen. That's why her color's so bad. She could bleed to death fast."

Officer Brent Sullivan felt nauseous, and thought, *I can't let this happen to me. I need to keep busy.* He visually checked the room for evidence, and took fingerprints, probably hers. *Halliday and I haven't touched the door handle. It was ajar. But on an outside chance, Brown might have. I'll do what I can. She opened the door;*

410

it hasn't been forced. I hope he touched it. Brent finished as the ambulance crew came from the elevator. They eased her body onto a stretcher, asking few questions, as Halliday gave his comments. They did their work and were gone.

Brent felt irritated with himself and with Halliday. *We could have done a better job. We could have warned her that Brown probably was not in California, but was right here in Seattle. Especially, we could have hidden out in view of her door, and watched.*

He walked over to the bedside table, discouraged. He had gathered the evidence. Done what he could. He again saw the open letter he had read. He would put it in an evidence bag. The handwritten sheet lay there, unfinished. It was addressed to Sylvia Ford. He dropped it in the bag. Just chatty news. It did mention Michael at Children's Hospital.

Oh-oh. He immediately radioed the station, and asked for a watch around the clock on Jennifer Brown's son, Michael Hanson, at Children's; that they should give a directive that no information be given to any callers. He hung up, thankful that the last name had been given by the friendly boy in Granite Falls.

He jotted Sylvia Ford's address in his notebook, and walked over to Halliday. "Sir, is this the name and address of Jennifer Brown's next door neighbor in Granite?"

"It sure is. I've got it. We'll follow this up. Talk to them.

Brent wondered what the situation had been like, there in the country. Was Jennifer's life, or her son's life, just a fearful existence? What had it been like at home? It did seem, by the letter, like the Ford woman was a friend. But maybe not close. Would a woman being abused get close to anyone? Unlikely. He knew he shouldn't consider the emotional side. *Get too 'involved'. But that's life. It's ugly for me as a cop, what I see and hear. And guessing from the note, this Sylvia Ford cares, will wonder where Jennifer Brown has gone. Good thing that we already need to talk to Ford for the investigation, so it's not a "privacy" issue. The story will hit the paper and be public, anyhow; but there sure won't be any details given.* He nodded to himself. *Yes, a little shared information would be acceptable.*

* * *

Sylvia entered the hospital, sick at heart with what the police had said, but glad she knew to come. She found Jennifer's room, and, as she came in, Jen met her gaze with blackened eyes and unbelievable bruising on her face and arms. "Oh. Jennifer." She spread her arms open to Jenny, then stopped. "Oh – I can't hug you. I'll hurt you. Where doesn't it hurt?"

"A little touch on the right side is okay, but not my ribs, please." Sylvia reached out and patted Jen's right arm. The ugliest bruising she had ever seen covered Jennifer's face – swollen purple. She stroked Jen's hair gently, avoiding the shaved area with stitches. Her eyes met Jennifer's, and she tried not to see the swollen face, just focus on her eyes.

Sylvia couldn't keep control, knowing Jennifer could have died. Tears slid down her cheeks, and then Jennifer teared-up.

Sylvia quietly said, "I am *so* glad to see you. So glad." She allowed herself to try to take in the injuries. The whole left side of Jen's face was purple, just beginning to go into yellow-green. The jaw was stitched and pinned. Must be a fractured jawbone. She was nauseated as she imagined the pain. She swallowed hard, and asked again, "What hurts most, and what can I do?"

"I think the doctors have done it all." She talked with difficulty. "Why don't you sit down. It's really good to see you."

As Sylvia sat down she saw that Jen's exposed right leg was in a cast, elevated on pillows. It started at the knee and went down around the heel and foot. *What kind of a break could that be?*

She asked, "This cast – are both of the lower leg bones broken?"

Jenny looked down at her toes. "Yes, and ankle bones, too," she said simply. "The doctor says it will take a lot of rehab to get movement in the ankle – a lot of damage where the leg bones join the smaller bones. I don't remember anything. That must have happened after I passed out. The doctor thought it had been stomped on with lots of force."

Sylvia felt sick. She had to say something to not picture this, so she became clinical. "What is the extent of upper-body injuries?"

"Several ribs broken. Got a concussion and passed out. That was good." Her smile twisted between humor and sadness. It exposed two broken teeth. Sylvia thought, *Dental work to do besides all the rest.* She looked down at Jen's bruised left hand and wrist, and Jen followed. A sling covered the arm and shoulder.

"I remember that arm being twisted. It was dislocated."

Sylvia realized that Jen hadn't mentioned Lennard's name once. *Everything is passive, happening* to *her, but done by* whom? *Maybe that keeps Len from being real. He has simply disappeared into thin air.*

"The doctor discussed some internal injuries, but I don't remember much of it. Told me they did abdominal surgery. I can see the incision." She smiled. "I was out for a while, then came to gradually. When I started to wake up, I tried to ask to use the phone. Still foggy, so I couldn't. Thought maybe I'd call you. Then a policeman came, and he asked for names of people he could talk to. I told him you or Mary Henderson. I hoped someone would go see Michael, so he wouldn't wonder where I was. I suppose they would send a social worker to talk to him. The policeman was so nice. He said he'd get the message to you and Mary to phone here. Sure be nice for Michael to see a familiar face."

"I would love to go see Michael. Will they let me? I called and they wouldn't reveal anything."

"Oh. I think they will. The police came and questioned me. They wanted to know all about Lennard. You don't think he would come back and hurt Michael, do you?"

"I don't know, Jen. I've been worried about you two for a long time."

"I know. Guess I played the fool. When the police asked, I didn't feel up to telling them much."

"Oh... can you try to tell them? I will come and be with you if it would help. And don't say fool about yourself. Too trusting, maybe. Jen, you will take care of yourself from now on, won't you – please? Get protection."

"There probably won't be a next time. Wonder when and where they'll find him? He will be in the mode of "I'm sorry I did it" by that time. So there isn't really much to tell the police."

That doesn't sound healthy, Sylvia thought. *But they will pursue it. They're doing a good job of asking questions. They'll work until they find that brute and make him pay.* Then she reflected... *how could he pay? How could Lennard ever pay anything back to Jenny for what she has gone through – all the pain she feels every moment, all the on-going fear she's had for months, years. She must have been wary, looking over her shoulder constantly, wondering what she's "done wrong". Even in her own home – I can't imagine not feeling safe in my own home.*

Sylvia came back to the present. "Will the police do... something to help you be safe after you're out of the hospital?"

"I don't know. Haven't gotten that far. The doctor says I'll be going to a rehab place after hospital rehab. I don't know when. They can work on other things, my shoulder and wrist, until the ankle is coming along. Not sure of the details. I am also scheduled to go to counseling right away. Guess they'll get me down there in a wheelchair. It's a "healthy thinking" kind of class. Maybe they'll put me in a halfway house for stupid women and teach "How to choose a man who only hits you a little bit." Or a class called, "Learn karate and level your mate!" Her wry half-smile returned. There was a movement by the door and a nurse spoke.

"Five more minutes. Then the patient needs to rest." She disappeared.

Sylvia glanced at her watch. "Guess I'll have to go. But I'll be back tomorrow."

"Rest. That's what they want for me. Rest, rehab, and food. Food looks good. I'm limited of course." Jenny's ability to talk had been affected. Sylvia could only imagine how hard it was to eat.

"Are you eating very much?"

"It might surprise you. No more I.V. I'm eating soft stuff. I've had broth, custard, and juices. They want me to eat all I can. I had lost weight while I was back and forth visiting Michael and working, too. Eating at the restaurant or out of an ice chest gets old. And an empty hotel room is dull." She stopped and thought of the last night when she had talked with Tyler. It almost was the last night of her life.

Sylvia shook her head sadly. "An empty hotel room – to think of you, alone in the city."

"Well, now you are here. And maybe Mary can come. Speaking

of Michael, the doctors are still tracking down what's going on with him."

Sylvia felt bad that she hadn't asked more about Michael. "I'm so glad to hear that, but it's taking a while, eh? I'll get right over and see him."

A voice said, "Time for a nap." This time it was a different nurse. She stood at the doorway, waiting. "You have to go."

Sylvia gently squeezed Jen's right hand, the good one, and bent down and kissed her forehead. Tears came into Jen's eyes. *How can I be loved? It feels strange.*

* * *

The next day Jen got a phone call from one of the doctors who were seeing Michael. "We believe that we have narrowed down the cause of the problem Michael is having."

Jen's heart gave a lurch. He sounded so serious. "Yes, what is it?"

"It is rare for children to have this condition... "

Just get on with it, Jen thought.

"Normally adults in their thirties, forties, and older, with worn out, stressed immune systems, get chronic fatigue syndrome. That is what we believe we are seeing in Michael. Rare in children. There is no conclusive test that tells us this diagnosis. It has been a process of elimination. It will take time, many months, for him to build up his health and regain a modicum of his former energy."

Jen didn't know if he was done talking, but she spoke. "What a relief. I've heard of it. It's not cancer or some other terminal illness. Thank you so much, Doctor. Thank you."

He then said that Michael would be released soon, explaining that first he would receive instruction in diet, gradual increase of activity, and generally how to live well with CFS. Someone would visit her with the same information. He answered Jen's questions, and then hung up.

The relief Jen felt was like a weight lifted gently off her whole body. *This is beyond wonderful! The nightmare is over and Michael is going to live!*

415

CHAPTER FORTY-THREE

Mary Henderson was suddenly there in her room.
Jen blinked and came awake. "Oh, Mary! Thanks so much for coming. How did you know I need a cheering section?"

"I talked to Sylvia Ford on the phone. The police called, too, and asked a few questions. I didn't know Lennard, so they didn't visit me."

"It is *so good* to see you!"

"You, too! I phoned Michael yesterday. So good to talk with him!"

Jen motioned Mary to sit. "I bet he was happy to hear your voice!"

"Yes. We had a good chat. And I had a message from John for him. He's to come out and work in the shop as soon as the doctor says it's okay. That got him going!"

"I can imagine!" Jen got a serious expression. "It's been hard not to see him. They've been good here about letting us use the phone a lot. It will be so good to have him with me when I get out of rehab."

"I can imagine!"

"Oh! You don't know yet – Michael has chronic fatigue syndrome they think! Not something fatal! Mary, I can't tell you what good news that is! I don't have a dying son, just one who needs to recover gradually!"

"Oh, Jennifer, what a relief!" Mary hugged her gently. "What wonderful news!" She had tears in her eyes and then Jen got teary. Each of them reached for tissues, and gave a happy laugh as they blew their noses.

"The Victim's Assistance people have talked with me. I've started counseling. It will be on-going for a while. I talked to the social worker yesterday. I think she was from the police department. There had been a question of custody because of what happened to me. I have been asked in detail whether Michael is in danger of being abused by Len – abused more, I should say."

"You mean they were concerned enough that they might have kept Michael from you?"

"Yes. If a child is in danger, they have to check it out and make sure he is safe."

"Well, of course. But I never thought about Michael – that you might lose custody."

"They thought I might go back to Lennard. They asked 'if you do...' Well I'm not! So the child protection people are willing to let Michael live with me as soon as I find a place. They know I'm firm now, especially with counseling help. That I won't tolerate contact by Lennard – with me or Michael. And I mean it. They are still hoping to arrest him and bring him to trial up here. But I doubt that will happen. The California police are pretty sure he is staying across the border in Mexico. He's never beaten me like this before and I just have this instinctive feeling that he might have been 'slightly horrified' when he saw what he'd done to me."

Mary couldn't handle that picture of Jennifer. "Sounds like you are realizing how serious the situation is."

"Funny how slowly the reality comes. When I started seeing through others' eyes that Lennard's behavior was unacceptable, I only admitted a little bit that it was true." Jen raised her eyebrows and sucked in her breath slowly, as if to emphasize how much work it was taking to admit it.

Mary, listening, let herself consider what a prisoner mentality Jen must have had, and as she did so, she felt sick. "It's so sad to think that women are going through emotional intimidation, verbal and physical abuse, day after day. I wonder how many?" Her voice trailed off.

"I have no idea. I'm also starting counseling sessions in a group setting. I don't know how much I am up to – hearing everyone's problems gets very heavy. I'll wait and see what it's like, I guess. At least I find it easier to say Len's name now. I talked with the counselor about the frozen feelings I had. Then finally I was able to speak aloud of that horrible black night of the beating. That was tough. At the time I didn't think I wanted to, but afterward it seemed to shrink it down to an event in the past instead of a nightmare that was hanging over me. Some of my feelings of helplessness have been there a long time. Now, part of the time at least, they are being replaced with a feeling of having some power over my own life, having the privilege of making decisions. Not just *thinking* of a good decision, but acting on it. I realize that a cruel, bullying person is attracted to someone who feels she is helpless. I think a controller desires to squelch a person perceived as weaker."

Mary encouraged Jennifer to explain what the counselor had been saying, knowing it would help her retain her new understanding. But within herself, Mary was trying to cope with her own emotions as she pictured what had been happening behind closed doors.

Jennifer began to get sleepy, so Mary said goodbye and slipped out.

Jennifer dozed off and on. Everyone was in her dreams, all mixed up. Mary and John, Larry Ford and Len, Michael and Sylvia talking about riddles and sheepdogs and shepherds. Gradually she came out of the drowsiness, and felt a bit rested. Painkillers were being reduced, so the pain made itself known, especially in her broken ankle. But the sleep was becoming more natural. She shoved up with her good right arm to straighten herself.

The table that hovered at meals was handy, and she pulled it over and opened the small drawer. She found a pick and straightened her hair. When she slid it in the drawer, it lifted a sheet of paper. *That tract Sylvia gave me.* Taking it out, she realized it was tucked in the New Testament from Sylvie. She pulled that out, too. Taking the tract first, she read again how Jesus had taken her place on the cross. Somehow, it seemed more real to her now. A gift. "The wages of sin is death, but the gift of God is eternal life through Jesus Christ our Lord."

A gift. Sylvia said that a gift, when it was given, could only be received, not purchased. Jen shook her head slightly. *Could it be that simple?* She picked up the Testament and Psalms. *Psalms. Sylvia also said that the psalms expressed every emotion a human can go through.* Jen turned the pages and browsed. The first verse of Psalm 57 read "Be merciful to me, O God... until these calamities have passed by". *Until these calamities have passed...* It brought a sense of something bigger at work than herself. She read the whole thought – "and in the shadow of Your wings I will make my refuge, until these calamities have passed by."

Jennifer reread the first verse. "Be merciful to me, O God... for my soul trusts in You." Tears sprang to her eyes. *Oh, God, I haven't trusted in You. I've rejected You. I've been totally wrong. I am so sorry. Suddenly You overwhelm me – I realize my sin and my rejection. I see You judged all sin – Jesus came under Your judgment. He took all my sin on Himself. I am free of condemnation! I trust You! Oh, Father...*

Peace, complete release, came over Jen.

Jen awoke. She had dozed off feeling so peaceful. Then it came to her. *God cares. And I'm forgiven! It's so good! Funny. Of all people I would like to tell about this peace with God, it would be Sylvia or Mary. And they're not here. Oh, well. God, I can talk to You, can't I! It's so – strange. Wanting to talk to You. The fear is gone.* She shook her head in wonder, and picked up the little Book of books.

* * *

Jennifer looked around the room at the other women in counseling. *So we all get to listen to each other's problems. And then what?* She didn't know.

Doreen, the facilitator, welcomed them. Then she handed out two stacks of papers, one to each end of the semi-circle. "What I have handed out are two companion poems. The woman who wrote them wants to be anonymous, but was willing for them to be used as we consider abuse issues.

The first one, 'Angry', she wrote, as it were, from the heart of her five-year old daughter who had been through a very traumatizing situation. Please read along as I read aloud.

Angry

I want to kick, I want to scream, I want to break
almost anything
You don't know, don't understand
You only think that I demand
I feel alone, out of control
My heart is hurting, my very soul
I wish that I had words to say
but maybe couldn't, anyway
My wounds are deep
more than you know
I only wanted just to grow
Why can't I be that child of three
Running, dancing, playing free?
I am angry don't you see?
But please just love me
Love me for ME.

Anonymous

Doreen said, "I'd like to continue with the second poem without comment yet. The mother is answering her daughter."

My Precious Child

My precious child I wish you knew
just how much I DO love you
I understand more than you know
I only want to help you grow
You are so brave, so strong for five
for all that you've gone through, survived.
Some say the wounds could be much worse,

I say "you're right, but it still hurts."
My child, when you strike out at me
I try not to take it personally
Sometimes your anger makes you wild
I don't know what to do, my child
At times I end up yelling too
but mostly just shed tears for you.
I want to do my very best
Lay your tear-stained face
upon my chest
The storm is over now until
the pressure builds and starts to spill
over into a raging storm
and then has to be calmed again.
The words you say I know you don't mean
There's so much sadness, so much pain
My precious child I love you so
No matter what, I will not go
I'll always be right here for you
Until this angry storm is through.

Anonymous

Jennifer felt her hand shaking the paper, and her eyes went blurry with tears. A child who needed protection had slipped through the cracks.

* * *

Jennifer hung up the phone. It had been a good chat with Mary. She wheeled back to her room. She thought of her counselor's words. They had talked about anger and how it was used for a defense against controlling people, or to avoid getting close. Jennifer contemplated her new knowledge that feeling of fear and of anger were closer than she'd thought. Both showed that there was a need not being met. They were warning signals to be checked out, but not acted on to anyone's hurt. *Funny,* she thought. *I felt I had to either stay angry with a person, especially a woman, or submit to her. Neither one was an answer to my problems. Too bad anger got transferred to the wrong people, like Sylvia. I'll have to give her that book I'm reading when I'm done. It explains so much.*

Jen found a note from the nurse. It was a short phone message from Sylvia that she wouldn't make it to the hospital as planned. It seemed their son, Mark, had a medical problem at work. He was being checked out at the hospital.

* * *

Several hours dragged by with Marie, Sylvia and Larry taking turns beside Mark's hospital bed. Tests were being done for a possible heart attack. They wearily walked about the waiting area when they took turns out of the room.

Sylvia stood beside Mark, with her hand on his, and asked, "Are you having pain now?"

"No, it's not bad now. Guess they're taking good care of me." He sounded dopey, but he smiled, and she saw that color was returning to his face. Just then a doctor came in.

"We believe there may be a little damage to a small area of the heart. We are keeping you overnight to run some more tests tomorrow. You are in fairly good physical shape, but I believe you will be wanting to make some changes for your own good. Things like diet and exercise."

"Yes, sir. I am in a mood to listen. Been hearing from my wife that I need to get out and walk more. Watch my diet." The doctor smiled and just nodded.

A nurse walked in with Marie and Larry. The doctor repeated their findings, and left. After hugs all around, Larry and Sylvia decided to say goodbye and go retrieve Emalie from the neighbor's and take her to her own home. They'd stay with her. Marie could feel free to spend as much time with Mark as she wanted.

Leaving the hospital lobby, Sylvia saw that it was dark. She realized she was dragging. "I'm really wiped."

"We'll soon be with Emalie, and as good as at home." Larry smiled. "I hope that her nap was a short one so she'll sleep tonight.

You really do look worn out."

As Sylvia dropped into the car seat beside Larry, she felt like she'd rather sink into bed. She laid her head back to rest as Larry drove to the apartment.

They stopped down the hall for Emalie first, and Larry scooped her up in his arms. The poor little toddler was tired, and hugged him tight, asking where Mommy and Daddy were.

Once they got inside and settled in with cocoa and more hugs, she began to relax. Normalcy was returning for all of them.

CHAPTER FORTY-FOUR

Jen heard a familiar voice and opened her eyes to see Mary, Cora, and another lady, older than Cora.

"Oh! What a lovely surprise!"

Cora spoke. "I haven't seen you for so long, Jennifer. Only at Mary's one time after we first met on the bus. We mustn't wait so long! Here's a card to give you a chuckle and help you get to feeling better. And this is my friend, Mrs. Munro. We were together today. I didn't think you'd mind if I brought her along."

"I'm glad to meet you."

"Hello, Jennifer." The new lady held out her hand, then pulled it back. "Oh, I'm sorry. I bet you aren't shaking hands much at the moment. Well, nice to meet you, anyhow." She gave Jen a big smile.

It reminded Jen of how she had met Cora, and been put at ease by her kindly smile. "Well! You all take my breath away – in a good way! It's great to have company. And yes, I can shake." She reached out with her good right arm to Mrs. Munro.

"I smuggled three pears in my big purse." Mary opened it. "But I did ask the nurse about what you're allowed, and she said anything soft. So I showed her the pears. She laughed, and said yes, you'd get by with thin slices. Enjoy!"

"Oh, thanks so much. You know how anything given as a kindness always tastes better. But I must say that I'm enjoying the food here, now that I'm getting some. I suppose it will get old after a while, especially if it keeps being mashed. But I'm glad to be off the bottle – the drip bottle that is! Rather, a bag – liquid steak, they call it."

The ladies all chatted about the plans for rehab, which unit Jen would move to, and assured her they'd visit, since it could get boring.

Mrs. Munro spoke up. "Actually, my coming has a bit of a plan to it, Jennifer. I wanted to meet you, and let you meet me. When Cora told me this morning about you being here in Seattle, we got to talking. I'm glad to hear more about rehab and your plans. Our lives have crossed, and I think it could be for a reason. I lost my husband in the spring. I went to California this summer, visiting family here and there. But staying away from my house any longer would have been unrealistic. I had to face facts, even if I didn't want to. The hardest fact was my empty, lonely house. I told Cora two weeks ago that I wanted a roomer. I need a roomer about the place."

"This morning as Cora spoke of you, I felt that you might be the one. Just say no at any time, if you sense that's your answer. I would like you and your son, Michael, to think about coming to live with me when you start the outpatient phase of your rehab. I like children, and I hear from Cora that you have a very nice son. I drive, so I can take you to therapy. If it's okay with you, I would like to go with Cora and Mary to visit Michael at Children's. Let him meet me. Now, please take your time, and think about this. I don't want to be forward. There's no rush. But I realize, as a widow, that I don't like living alone. I have more than enough financial security. I don't want or need to charge you. My home is open to you until you get completely mobile and able to be on your own." She paused and gave Jen a gentle smile, with a little tilt of her head to one side. "You would be doing me a favor, to have someone in my home, someone to cook for. Know that it's a two way street – for my benefit as much as for yours and Michael's."

Jennifer was speechless. "I don't know what to say. I have wondered how things would work out. I talked with Michael just last night. I... I was wondering – when he said the doctors were happy he wouldn't have to be in the hospital much longer. I was... wondering where we'd live. If I needed to stay in therapy here in Seattle, I didn't know how... I just don't know what to say."

"Of course not. Take your time." Mrs. Munro smiled, came over to Jen's side and held her good hand for a moment. "I should mention that I am a Christian. The Lord has been good to me. I just want to pass it on."

A warm look filled Jen's face, yet a look of amazement. "Mary!" Jen looked over at her. "Sylvia has been talking to me, telling me verses from the Bible. Explaining how she believes – like you... I argued with her." She paused, and Mary waited, sensing Jen was struggling to express something important. "No matter how I argued, she never gave up. She..." Jen got tears in her eyes, paused, looked away, and tried again. "She also tried to warn me that I was in danger, and I wouldn't even listen to that – wouldn't listen to anything she said. God is good. He showed me – it came clear to me, when I again read the tract she gave me. I understood. I – I believed what God said. I trusted Jesus." Her eyes filled with tears, but she was smiling.

* * *

Jen's nurse came in, and Jen roused from her nap. "You've got a phone call from Sam Brown."

"Oh, good! Let's go."

The nurse got her up in the wheelchair and took her to the patient phone.

"How are you anyhow?" He asked. "Are you keeping warm, so far away from the Franklin stove?"

"Oh, Sam! It's good to hear from you! I'm warm, but I miss that comforting heater! You are due to join us again for hot cocoa. Guess what! We got word that Michael has chronic fatigue syndrome – not something life-threatening! He'll recover slowly, but he'll recover!"

"Oh, that's wonderful! When do you think you will be 'back on the farm'?"

"Don't know where I'll be. But it's not for a long time. I need lots of rehab, Sam. Lots."

"So I can come see you, and especially Michael." Sam took down the room numbers and the addresses of the two hospitals. Jen was cheered, knowing another person visiting with Michael was as good as done.

"We would both enjoy that! I should free up this phone, Sam.

Someone is waiting to use it. Thanks so much for calling."

Sam hung up the phone and put his thoughts together. He could visit Michael, and maybe Jennifer, too, on the weekend. Two more days. He'd phone the Children's Hospital and ask to talk to Michael, now that he had the room number. Ask what he could bring him that he'd really like. Even if he couldn't talk with him, he had a pretty good idea. He tried not to picture Jennifer's condition the way Sylvia had described it. He felt choked when he thought, *My own bio-father did this. Oh, God.*

* * *

Larry held the steering wheel tight and stayed in his lane. The morning traffic was bad. When he went back to thinking of the situation at work, his stomach churned. Sylvia was right and he knew it. He was too stressed. He remembered hearing a fellow who went to the gym say, *Jog a mile; walk three. But don't make your body go through the punishment of constant worry.* It was true. He was asking for it – a reminder that his body wasn't meant to take punishment like this. He thought of Mark. And he knew that this was the morning he would talk to the boss; as soon as he got to the office. *The office – more time in the office would be just fine. Maybe the new guy should do all that travel that an expanded territory required.* Whatever happened, he was going to clear the air. He was sick and tired of being sick and tired.

* * *

Sylvia hung up the phone, trying to internalize the answers. The social worker seemed to know the type of self-questioning that she had been going through. It was helpful hearing it out loud. She was not responsible for Jennifer Brown's injuries. She probably could not have stopped what happened. Lennard was out of control.

Sylvia made herself a cup of tea and sat down to think. All well and good. But one thing was for sure. She had learned a lot about abuse. Learned that it is hidden by the abused woman. Even when someone wants to help, it is hidden. She realized that she didn't have enough clout – as a woman she couldn't have required accountability from Lennard. Maybe a man with authority, like a policeman, could. Maybe not. Self-deception was strong. She knew now that she would get help if something like this happened again. She'd be pro-active.

She wondered what Jennifer was thinking. They hadn't talked about Lennard.

Sylvia heard the fire engine coming nearer, and went outside on the deck. Horrified, she saw smoke billowing over the trees from Jen's direction. She ran along the path and got to Jen's driveway just as the fire truck pulled up.

"Stay back, lady," the man waved and pointed.

The smoke seemed to come from the opposite front corner. At least it seemed small, but black. Two firemen broke out a small window in the basement and were shoving something into it. Others entered the house. In only a few minutes it was over. Retardant was dumped where the furnace and oil tank were located. Water had been pumped in at the basement window.

Sylvia asked questions about the furnace, but was told that they didn't know, and that an investigation would take place. Yellow 'restricted area' tape was put up.

Walking back home, Sylvia considered the effect of telling Jen that her house had caught fire. She promptly decided to wait. Nothing could be done. After the investigation she could use her key to get the clothing, so she could wash it. The she could tell how much smoke damage and stink there was. Later would be soon enough to inform Jen.

Two days later Sylvia had the opportunity to do some creative eavesdropping. She was working in the yard and over heard voices. Someone was really steamed. The anger rose, and she heard, "How could any landlord expect someone to survive in a place like this? The structure is sound. But there are so many code violations I don't have enough paper to write them. The wiring is bad..."

The voice trailed off, but Sylvia had heard enough. *Hey, that louse isn't going to get away with being a slum landlord any more!* As soon as she thought it, she regretted the words. Poor Jen didn't deserve to have the hardship of that house's condition, but the word slum would never do. Thankfully, it looked like there would be some answering.

* * *

The next week flew by for everyone. Mark had been thoroughly assessed. His cholesterol was high, especially for such a young man. He was put on medications, given a strict diet, and scheduled for more tests. The time off work was welcome at first. He played with Emalie and the three of them took walks and went for drives and generally acted like it was a vacation. Sylvia had been able to get to the hospital to see Jennifer and hear her surprise news of trusting Christ as her savior. Sylvia was speechless. "What a doubting Thomas I was becoming! I let myself get discouraged about the time it happened!" She laughed with Jen. They talked excitedly about how good, how different their visits would be. There was so much to talk about. They could pray together, and read the Bible together. She could again see Jennifer's smile.

On Sylvia's next visit, Jen knew the plan for rehab. She'd be at an inpatient unit for a while. After that, as a rehab outpatient, she would move to Mrs. Munro's house. Michael was soon done with his hospitalization, but was not able to re-enter regular school yet. Jen had shared that with Mary when she visited. The next day, John and Mary asked if Michael could come live with them while he recuperated! He was going to love that! It would be perfect until they'd were under the same roof again.

Sylvia decided that there was no better time to tell Jen of the house fire. "I have some bad news for you. There was a small fire at your house. It started in the front corner of the basement, but was confined there. Inspectors think it was wiring. Oil-soaked wood helped it along. The furnace is way too ancient to be up to code. I heard through the grapevine that the landlord is in deep trouble. He was threatened with fines."

"Oh – a small fire? Did much of my stuff get burned?"

"No, I don't think anything. I went in and checked it out. The fire was in the front of the basement. Didn't go through the living room floor. You hadn't stored anything there. It was where those old clotheslines hung around the furnace. That's also where the water damage was. The smoke smell was throughout."

"I guess my things will stink."

"I brought your clothes over to my house and washed them. I hope you don't mind me going ahead with it."

"Oh, thank you. I appreciate it. Have you seen the landlord there?"

"No, but I've been gone a lot. One person said that if he brings the electricity up to code and puts other things in order, they may lower or cancel the fines. He will be inspected, and that means he will have to make it right. This morning I saw a restoration company's truck there. I think they can take out smoke smells. The inspection means he will not only fix wiring, but put in a new furnace, repair bad flooring, and repaint. What a good deal."

"Wow." Jennifer paused. "It's hard to think about that place. I have so much going on here in the city. I don't even want to think of leaving until I'm sure these rehab pro's have worked me over. Rather, make me work. It's sure painful. I'm getting some use of my left wrist and shoulder. And, with help, I'm learning to walk between parallel bars with my one good leg. The cast is so heavy. But they want the thigh muscles to be worked. I get the cast changed to a lighter one soon." She stopped. "I just can't think beyond these things right now."

"I'm glad you're getting all the help you need. It sure would be good to have you back out here as a neighbor!"

"The landlord won't hold the house for me. I owe rent. I haven't even been in touch with him since I've come to Seattle. Never expected to be this long."

"I wouldn't worry about a single thing with him. That landlord is dealing with a lot more than a month's rent. If I see him, I'll tell him that you were laid up. He is probably afraid that you will sue him for renting an unfit house!"

Jen smiled to herself, picturing the rotten porch boards. "I wonder what the timetable would be. Too bad. I do like the school out there for Michael. Say! Doesn't Sam know a young lady who is a therapist?"

"I think she is a massage therapist. But she works for a physical therapist. I'll pick up their business cards. You could ask at the rehab. They might transfer you. As for how long he would hold the house, he'll be busy hiring work to be done on it. A lot of work."

Jen felt a little better. She had absorbed the news about the fire. Realized it hadn't burned up her personal things, or harmed the furniture. But it was all sitting out there in someone else's house. Just getting moved to Mrs. Munro's with Michael, adjusting to being there, and doing rehab, would take her full attention. *But one never knows. We could be moving out to the country again.* That was something to consider. It made her think that God was showing how He was at work in her behalf. *How amazing – this relationship with Him!*

* * *

The sun was setting when Larry arrived home from work. Coming boldly into the kitchen, he grabbed Sylvia around the waist. The serving spoon she was using waved in the air.

"Hey! What's this all about?"

"It's about you! You got your wish! The boss called me in today – after a talk I had with him last week – I'm out of work."

"What? Oh, no, Larry. I never wished that. I'm so sorry – you must be... why in the world are you smiling?" She pulled her head back to scrutinize his face.

"Oh, it's just temporary! Not my smile – the boss gave me holiday time. Plus, it's with double pay to show appreciation for my work. I'm getting my Christmas bonus, early and extra fat. I've already checked the air fare and car rental. We are going to California, like you've wanted. Can you be ready in three weeks? We'll be gone for two weeks."

"Two weeks... *I* feel weak. Is this for real?"

"Yup. I had a heart to heart talk with the boss last week. He thought over my desire not to traveling so much. He is giving me more office time – likes what I do there. He's hiring another man to expand sales. And, to answer your next question, No. 'Mister smart Alec' doesn't have the boss fooled. He's skating on thin ice, instead. The boss knows." Larry paused. "So – you're speechless! How about it? Does sunny California sound good, what with our days getting shorter?"

"It sounds wonderful!"

* * *

Jen picked up a folder that was among the things brought to her room from the hotel. It was her journal thoughts and some other writing. Her heart skipped a beat when she saw "Sometimes". *I recopied that poem, and here it is, popping up now.* It was an emotional read.

Sometimes

Sometimes, I wish I could fly away
on the wings of a bird
Or snuggle into a burrow with a field mouse.

Sometimes, I wish I could transport myself instantly
to some other place, some other time.

Sometimes this world with all its struggles, this life with
all its burdens just seems too much to bear and I wish,
just for a little while, to see, to feel, to think no more.

But this is only sometimes...

Other times, I see my child's face and could get lost in
his eyes forever, or feel his arms around me and think
"There's nothing that's better than this!"

Sometimes I could sit and talk and laugh with a girlfriend,
until there were no more words, or moments to share!

Then there are times when I feel so confused, about what to think,
or how I feel....

Sometimes the tears come and I don't always know whether they are tears of happiness or sorrow, memories of joy or grief or maybe, a little of both...
Sometimes the despair is all there is.

How sad. Jennifer grabbed a pencil and thought, as she started to write, *there is an ending and I know it now!*

Sometimes
(The Rest of It)

It is in these times when only He Who knows me best is able
To reach down deep into my soul
And lift me up again – to bring me peace.
He wraps His loving arms around me and whispers,
"It's okay, I love you
I will take care of you and all whom you love.
I will give you strength in the tough times.
I AM, and I will be with you always, not just "sometimes"."

EPILOGUE

Jennifer wonders if her leg will be functional after rehab in Seattle. She longs for Michael's return to Mr. Logan's classroom and country life. Will she keep her new-found joy and assurance of God's love? Will she sort out her own abuse issues? Mary and John Henderson are back in the picture. Marie takes Sylvia to New Beginnings, and they bring their abilities alongside other volunteers in helping hurting women find healing. But Mark resents Marie's intense focus away from home and little Emalie. As Lennard slips through the western states, past the police, he will find pain and truth. Mexico will be his desert. But will he and Sam ever be reunited?

These people continue to "Journey" in the next book, "Saving Stubborn Sven" (from himself), which also tells of beloved seniors, Sven Sigurdsen and Grandma Jones. Seniors resist the doctors' advice, but living at home is becoming impossible. Friends and family members who love them are caught in a confusing conflict of sympathetic love, guilt trips, resentment, and painful accidents. Can they be allies, and also do what is right? And who makes the decisions?

"The Journey" series now takes us on these two paths: Jennifer's path, and the second path, trod by the elderly and those helping their elders cope with aging and its challenging decisions, while still dealing with the needs in their own lives.

LaVergne, TN USA
06 May 2010
181812LV00002BA/2/P